HEARTLAND HEROES

ANDREA BOESHAAR

BARBOUR
PUBLISHING

Published by Barbour Publishing, Inc., P.O. Box 719, Uhrichsville, Ohio 44683, www.barbourbooks.com

Our mission is to publish and distribute inspirational products offering exceptional value and biblical encouragement to the masses.

 Member of the
Evangelical Christian
Publishers Association

Printed in the United States of America.

Dear Readers,

My career in the healthcare field taught me so much. I worked in the ER (emergency room) as a registrar which gave me a unique perspective of the goings on around me. I had patient contact and worked closely with doctors and nurses, too. Pretty soon the idea for *Prescription for Love* took form. When I'd have questions, I'd wait until there was a little downtime, and then I'd ask my co-workers. They all knew I wrote Christian romance, and they were actually excited and, perhaps, even amused to contribute to the story.

Then when my son Rick got his job as a paramedic, I was inspired to write *Courting Disaster*. He's also a flight medic with the Army National Guard, and after hearing about his heroic efforts to save lives, I knew I had to write about someone in that occupation. Special thanks to my friend Holly, a nurse in a busy trauma room, who often took time to answer specific medical questions.

The Superheroes Next Door doesn't have a medical setting, but I think readers will find Luke and his kids are heartland heroes too—just in a different way. I want to thank my mother for all her support and encouragement as I wrote this story. And my "sis," Pat Malone, who spurred me on when the going got tough.

As always, I love to hear from my readers. Feel free to contact me at andrea@andreaboeshaar.com.

And log onto my Web site where I write a blog called Everything Writerly. There you'll find behind-the-scenes stories about the books I've written and what the journey to see them into print has entailed. Whether you're a writer or a reader, I think you'll enjoy the blog: www.andreaboeshaar.com.

May God Richly Bless You,
Andrea Boeshaar

PRESCRIPTION
FOR LOVE

Chapter 1

The late April sunshine sparkled off the blue-green water in the swimming pool and bounced off the blacktop on the tennis courts. Up in her third-floor condominium, Ravyn Woods stepped away from the window and breathed in a sigh of contentment. "What a view!"

"Yep. You've got a nice place here, sis."

"Thanks." She glanced over her shoulder at her younger sister, Teala, who had stayed overnight to help her unpack. "I've saved for a long time to buy this condo."

"I think it was worth it, although Mom and Dad are of the opinion you paid too much for your unit."

The remark didn't surprise Ravyn. She knew her parents couldn't understand her need to move out and into a home of her own. "Oh, they'll just miss my cooking and cleaning and paying rent each month."

"Yeah. Now Violet and I have to pick up the slack."

Teala laughed and Ravyn smiled. The truth was Ravyn never minded helping with housework and paying her folks the small rental fee they charged. In fact, she often purchased groceries and stocked the kitchen cupboards. She cooked supper, too, on the nights she was home, although that wasn't often. Nevertheless, she saw to it that there was food in the house. Ravyn only hoped her family didn't starve to death now that she'd moved out of their modest home on Pennsylvania Avenue.

Grinning at her facetious thought, she peered outside once more. She stretched like a feline and appreciated the scenery below. Life couldn't get any better. But the best part would begin Monday night. That's when Ravyn would officially begin her new job as a registered nurse in the emergency room at the prestigious Victory Medical Center. It was the job she'd been striving toward for years and the stepping-stone she needed to attain the rest of her goals.

"It's all coming together," she muttered. "Just like I planned."

"Did you say something, Rav?"

"Oh, just muttering to myself." She turned from the window just as Teala reentered the room.

"I took something into the kitchen and missed what you said."

"I was just thinking aloud, that's all."

Teala continued to empty one of the many boxes strewn around the living room. "I hope you'll let me come and stay with you sometimes."

"Of course I will." Ravyn watched her sister blow a strand of tawny hair out of her aquamarine-colored eyes. "You can stay with me anytime. Violet can, too, although if you two come at the same time you'll still have to share a room."

"Oh, I plan to visit, all right," Teala said, her eyes sparkling with enthusiasm, "but are you ever going to be home? Being a nurse seems awfully demanding."

"If I know you're coming for a visit, I'll adjust my schedule."

Teala paused and regarded her askance. "Don't you think you work a little bit too much? Mom thinks so, and she worries that since you've got this condo now you'll be working more than ever."

Ravyn shrugged out an initial reply, then added, "I do what I have to do. I'm single. I don't have kids. Why shouldn't I work hard?"

"That makes sense, but—well, you might stop and smell the coffee sometimes." Teala grinned at her.

"Oh, I smell the coffee. It's the sustenance that gets me through those double shifts. In fact, I bought a new latte machine. It's around here someplace." Ravyn eyed each box, trying to recall where she'd packed her new "toy."

"What about church?" Teala removed bathroom paraphernalia from the box she continued to empty. "I'm not taking attendance or anything, but Mom and Dad are concerned because you never go to church anymore."

"I will. As soon as I get my life on track."

"When will that be?"

"Soon. I'm almost there. I mean, a few years' experience in Victory's ER and then I can apply for that research position I've been coveting at the University of Wisconsin Hospital in Madison."

"You're such a brain, Ravyn." Her sister laughed. "And you're a hard worker. I admire that."

"I just don't want to end up a charity case like Mom and Dad were all those years. A real job means money in the bank. Don't let anyone try to convince you that ministry alone will support you financially. It doesn't. We know that firsthand."

"Some ministries do."

"Maybe, but I'm just emphasizing what I believe. God expects us to be responsible." She narrowed her gaze. "Don't you remember how many times we went to bed hungry because Mom and Dad were waiting for God to provide our next meal?"

"That wasn't God's fault. He provided. It's just that instead of going to the grocery store, Mom and Dad spent their last dollars on paint and canvases for Dad's next production."

"Yeah, well, that won't happen to this girl." Ravyn pointed her thumb at her chest. "I never want to emulate our parents' lifestyle. They were—irresponsible."

"I agree." Teala wiped her dusty palms on the back of her blue jeans. "But, you've got to admit, people have to enjoy what they do. At least Mom and Dad have been happy all these years."

"I can't argue with that. They're like big kids." Ravyn gave her head a few wags in exasperation. She'd had to grow up fast and help take care of her family—including her parents. But her childhood hadn't been all responsibility and no play. Most of the time her fond memories overshadowed the difficulties. Her family was, in fact, very close-knit, and Ravyn felt especially grateful for her younger sister's companionship. Although Teala was six years younger than she, Ravyn thought of her as a special friend.

"Hey, Rav, I forgot to tell you; I'm changing my major again."

"Again!" She shook her head in wonder. This was the third time Teala had changed her college major. "So what is it now?"

"Communications. I found out the hard way that a degree in business isn't for me."

"Well, I'm sure you can do a lot with a communications degree. It's general enough."

"That's what I thought, too." A mischievous gleam entered her eyes. "On the other hand, I suppose I could marry a millionaire and buy a house as big as this entire condominium complex."

"Sure, and you could capture a rainbow, too." Ravyn arched a brow. "You'll marry Greg. He'll continue to be a hardworking Christian day-school teacher and you'll be a professional student the rest of your life."

"Oh, you just hush. What do you know, anyway?"

"I know *you*, that's what I know." Ravyn couldn't contain a little chuckle.

Teala feigned an indignant look.

"You're smitten and that's the end of it."

Acquiescence poured over her features. "You're right. I am." A faraway look suddenly entered her eyes.

"Good grief." Ravyn sent her sister a pathetic glance. However, as Teala's big sister, she heartily approved of Greg Charney, the tall, blond, handsome young man who could easily be a modern-day John Wayne. "Teala, you're a dreamer. Just like our folks. I knew it all along."

"Hey, I have a mother who is, by her own words, a 'paintress' and a father who heads up a Christian theater group. I was doomed from birth."

"Yeah, maybe I was, too," Ravyn conceded. "But every time I think about how Mom or Dad would handle a situation, I do the opposite."

"Ooh, yeah. That's a good idea." Teala smiled and sat cross-legged on the plush carpeting. She tipped her head and strands of her golden-brown hair fell over one shoulder. "But you know what? Whether we want to admit it or not, we all have our dreams—including you."

"I have goals, not dreams. And they're all very practical." Ravyn lowered her slender form onto an adjacent cardboard box. "But what's really important to me is that I have a meaningful career and enough money to live on. I want new clothes—not raggedy ol' things that even resale shops won't sell—and I can see myself driving a hot red sports car."

"With lots of speeding tickets," Teala added with a snort of laughter.

"Oh, stop it." Ravyn shot her a look of annoyance. "I just want the conveniences a woman in this day and age require for a comfortable lifestyle. In other words, I want my needs met for once in my life." She glanced around her new home. "And it all begins with this place."

"Um, aren't you missing something very important in all your *goals*?"

Ravyn regarded her sister askance. "Like what?"

"Like love!"

❧

Her younger sister's reply haunted Ravyn for the next twenty-four hours. But, as she drove to Victory Medical Center where she'd soon begin working the night shift in the ER, she pushed aside the notion that her goals in life didn't include love. Of course they did. Every twenty-seven-year-old woman Ravyn knew wanted to get married and raise a family—including her! At the present, however, she didn't have time to cultivate a romantic relationship.

Ravyn clutched the steering wheel of her two-door compact car. The vehicle was far from the hot red sports car that she had mentioned to Teala, but its dependability suited her needs for the time being. But someday that shiny new auto would be as real as her condo. As for love. . . Well, the sports car seemed more attainable.

Ravyn stopped at a red light. Up ahead she glimpsed the hospital's impressive brick structure, illuminated by numerous street lamps. She recalled her announcement to her family years ago that she would become a nurse. Her parents were disappointed at first. They would have preferred that she pursue something in the arts. But Ravyn knew firsthand that the term *starving artist* wasn't just a mere cliché, and she wanted more in life than to wear secondhand clothing and depend on public transportation.

Now she was in the process of attaining those goals.

Ravyn drove into the concrete parking structure connected to the hospital and pulled into a slot. She couldn't help feeling a bit nervous, even though she was confident about her abilities. She'd spent the last few years working on the surgical floor in preparation for this job as an ER nurse. Now tonight, after a week of hospital orientation, two weeks in the urgent care department, and another ten days training in the triage area, she was officially beginning the job she'd longed to do for years: work in the ER.

Entering the hospital through its employee entrance, Ravyn headed for the locker room that she shared with several other female nurses. Once she had changed into her light blue scrub pants and a colorful printed smock top, she strode toward the ER. The soles of her white athletic shoes squeaked against an unfamiliar gleam of fresh wax that shone from the light-colored floor tiles. Sounds of a vacuum cleaner off in the distance added to Ravyn's odd feeling; she was accustomed to being here during the daytime when this hospital bustled with patients and visitors. Now it seemed—deserted.

Her perspective soon changed, however, as she walked through the emergency room's automatic doors. A kind of controlled chaos buzzed all around her, and in that moment, Ravyn felt like a lost little girl at a crowded shopping mall.

Moments later, a tap on her shoulder caused Ravyn to turn. She immediately came face-to-face with Liz Hutchinson, a veteran trauma nurse. Ravyn had become acquainted with Liz during her training in the triage area, and Liz was assigned to be Ravyn's preceptor for the next eight weeks. The middle-aged woman had a bawdy edge to her personality, an edge that ran contrary to Ravyn's private, no-nonsense qualities. Nevertheless, Liz's nursing skills had impressed Ravyn from day one.

"Bus accident," Liz said as she snapped shut the chart she held.

"Are you kidding?" Ravyn couldn't hide her disbelief.

"Honey, I'm as serious as a blood clot." Weariness shone in Liz's blue eyes. "A tour bus was on its way back from a Wisconsin casino when the driver went off the road. Busy night—and I just happen to be working a double shift. I was hoping things would be quiet, but. . ." She glanced around. "The dice didn't roll in my favor."

Ravyn grinned at the pun, then gazed around at the numerous patients on gurneys. Some of the portable beds lined the outer wall of the ER's main area called the arena.

"No life-threatening injuries," Liz continued. "Just your typical lacerations and a few broken bones."

Ravyn nodded for lack of a better response and followed Liz's stocky form to one of the counters that ran parallel to a row of exam rooms.

"Are you punched in?"

"Yep."

"Good. I could use some help."

"Sure."

Liz sent her a grateful smile, then bobbed her head, causing the top of her short, light brown hair to bounce. "Get *George* over there to sign these orders so we can discharge the patients in rooms 6 and 7." She slid the paperwork over to Ravyn.

"Who's George?"

"The resident over there." Liz inclined her head once more, and this time Ravyn followed her co-worker's gaze to where three men stood near the health unit coordinator's desk. "See the guy who looks like that actor from that hit TV show—"

"Oh, right. I see him." Ravyn had never watched the TV series, which, in her opinion, was nothing more than a nighttime soap opera, but she'd heard enough about it and read plenty of reviews. "That show is totally unrealistic. Who should know that better than you, an ER nurse?"

"What can I say? I love the drama."

Ravyn couldn't keep the grin off her lips as she regarded George. He stood not even twenty feet away from her—the man in the white MD jacket worn over light green scrubs. He was average in height and weight, with dark brown hair, graying just slightly at his temples. It was true; he did resemble the actor.

She froze as recognition set in. She narrowed her gaze. *No, it can't be.* She blinked. *It's him!*

"His name is really Mark but we tease him—mercilessly, I might add."

Ravyn knew exactly who he was: Mark Monroe. He'd grown up in northern New Hampshire and when Ravyn knew him, he'd loved the Lord and the theater—or so it had appeared. One summer, almost eleven years ago, he'd stayed with his great-aunt and great-uncle here in Dubuque and performed in one of her father's productions. Mark had played the lead opposite Ravyn's best friend, Shelley Jenkins. Ravyn knew her friend had fallen hard for the guy and entertained thoughts of spending the rest of her life with him. But then, after Shelley got sick with some sort of stomach flu, Dad had insisted Ravyn step into Shelley's role. She'd rehearsed enough with Shelley, and had even agreed to be her understudy, but that had merely been an excuse to hang out at the auditorium.

They'd had a lot of fun that summer, she and Shelley and Mark, along with the rest of the cast members. They'd occasionally go out for pizza after rehearsals and, on a rare day off, they had attended a couple of Dubuque's riverside festivals. Ravyn had fond memories of those days, even with her little sisters, Teala and Violet, tagging along. The cast and crew never objected. Ravyn had thought of Mark as a good friend, and Shelley was her very best friend.

Then things had changed.

Shelley became ill and Ravyn had been forced to step into the lead role. Unfortunately for her, she'd dreaded being in front of an audience. Mark had spent hours coaching her, but it hadn't seemed to help. And if stage fright and flubbing her lines hadn't been bad enough, Ravyn felt she betrayed her best friend each time she acted out the last scene in which she and Mark kissed. Every time he took her into his arms and her lips met his, Ravyn's guilt had mounted. It hadn't mattered how much she'd told herself that it was a play. Acting. Pretend. She'd enjoyed it.

Worse, she'd been able to tell that he had, too.

And then the worst that could happen happened—Mark broke Shelley's heart and dashed her hopes and dreams for the future. Weeks later, Shelley disappeared. Rumors circulated that she'd gone to live with some relative in Florida, but although she'd tried, Ravyn could never confirm it. Shelley's parents had refused to talk about it. Months later, they were gone, too. Obviously the situation had devastated more people than just Shelley.

And Mark Monroe was to blame.

"He hates it when we call him George." Liz's deep voice brought the present back into focus. "But that only makes razzing him all the more fun."

Ravyn gathered her wits along with the paperwork. "Which form does he sign?"

"This one—oh, and, I should warn you. George is spoken for. See Carla over there? The x-ray tech?"

Glancing across the ER, she spotted the curvy blond and nodded.

"I guess she and George are dating—at least that's what Carla told us last week when a bunch of us went out for breakfast."

"I couldn't care less," Ravyn said, "because I'm totally not interested in *George*."

Liz snorted with laughter. "Famous last words."

Ravyn scooped up the documents, walked over to the three men, and tapped George on the upper arm.

"Excuse me. Will you sign these discharge orders?"

He turned and within moments Ravyn saw recognition spark in his brown eyes. She, on the other hand, said nothing. The swell of unresolved sadness over losing Shelley's friendship wouldn't allow any words to form.

He tipped his head. "Ravyn Woods—is that you?"

She managed a nod and hid behind her professionalism. "Hi, Mark. I need these papers signed."

"I didn't know you worked here at Victory." He took the proffered chart. "I thought you lived in Wisconsin and worked at the University Hospital."

"That's where I'm headed—eventually." Surprise loosened her tongue. How did he know that?

"Oh. Well. . ." He continued to smile at her, and she resisted the urge to squirm under his intense scrutiny. "Have you been at Victory long?"

"A few weeks."

"That explains why I haven't seen you before now."

Ravyn longed to wipe the silly grin off his face.

"It's really nice to see you again."

"Thanks."

"Ironic how we both ended up in the medical field."

"Yeah." She tapped her finger on the chart. "We're waiting on your autograph here, *Doctor*."

"Oh. Right." He glanced down at the paperwork. "Who's being discharged?"

"Ian Jeffers and Wanda Smith. The patients in rooms 6 and 7."

Mark glanced at the white board behind him on which every patient's first name had been written. "Great. I'm sure they'll be happy to go home." He pulled his ink pen from his white jacket's breast pocket and scratched his signature across each page.

"You know, it's crossed my mind to give you a call," he said. "Aunt Edy's done her best to keep me up-to-date on you and your family. She said you lived at home—"

"Not anymore."

"Oh." He shook his head, looking embarrassed. "I haven't heard an update in a while. Med school and my residency have absorbed most of my adult life." He smiled. "And keeping up with you and your family was a lot easier when they belonged to the same church as Aunt Edy and Uncle Chet."

Ravyn figured that was probably true. At one time her family attended the same church as the Dariens. But when it grew too large, the pastor felt it became too impersonal and he developed an idea for a spin-off church on the other side of town. Ravyn's folks were always up for an adventure and volunteered to be some of those members who left to help start the new church.

"Last I heard you'd graduated from college. I even saw your picture in the newspaper."

"That was five years ago."

Mark nodded. "Like I said, I'm out of touch. But maybe if things slow down later we can talk and catch up." He handed her the sheets of paper.

She pushed out a tight little smile.

"Or, better yet, give me your phone number and I call you sometime soon."

When pigs fly!

At that instant, Carla walked by and sent Ravyn a scathing look. Ravyn's opinion of Mark slipped a notch lower. Not only was he a hypocrite and a heartbreaker, he put Casanova to shame.

Without another word, Ravyn strode back to where the patients' charts lay on the counter. She slipped the multicolored forms into the appropriate chart. When she looked up, she caught Mark's dark-eyed stare. He smiled and Ravyn quickly lowered her gaze.

"Hey, quit making eyes at George, will you?" Liz came to stand alongside her. "I need help with Mrs. Johnson in room 8."

"I'm not making eyes at anyone. That's the last thing I'd do—especially with *him*."

"Oh?" Liz's expression said she was interested in knowing why.

But Ravyn wasn't about to divulge her personal reasons. This was her job. Her livelihood. Unfortunately, her nerves felt jangled as she carried the charts to the unit clerk's desk. The night wasn't off to the start she had hoped for. Her new position was suddenly overshadowed by a real-life drama—one she wanted no part of. A wandering-eyed resident, a loudmouth co-worker, and a jealous x-ray tech.

Ravyn began to dread the next eleven and a half hours.

Chapter 2

D r. Mark Monroe glanced at his wristwatch. The time he'd been waiting for was now just minutes away—time to go home. He was going on twenty-four hours without a decent night's sleep and he felt exhausted. His body craved a soft mattress covered by clean, fresh-smelling sheets, a far cry from the lumpy bed in the residents' room outside of the intensive care unit. But when Ravyn showed up in the ER, Mark suddenly felt a surge of energy. It was great to see her again; he felt like he'd run into a long-lost friend. But did he detect a hint of animosity? Maybe he'd been too forward in asking for her phone number. Under other circumstances, he wouldn't have been so bold, but he was acquainted with Ravyn and her family. Of course, Ravyn might be dating someone. Maybe she'd even gotten married.

No, Aunt Edy would have heard that news and told him.

"Hey, Monroe."

Mark gave himself a mental shake and turned to see Dr. Len Tadish, the house MD, marching toward him, wearing his ever-stoic expression. The man looked like a drill sergeant in physicians' garb.

"Baker's got pharyngitis. I need you to stay until tomorrow morning."

Mark knew better than to argue. "Okay." One more shift and then he'd be off for eight hours. Maybe it wouldn't be so bad.

The veteran physician gave Mark a friendly slap on the back. "You're covering the ER. Looks like there are four patients who need consults, and you've got two traumas coming in."

"Won–der–ful." Mark didn't even attempt to conceal his sarcasm.

"Have a good one." Tadish gave him a grin and exited the ER.

Mark blew out a weary breath and reminded himself that it wouldn't be long now; he would complete his residency at the end of June. Even though he had *MD* behind his name, since graduating from med school, he couldn't have his own practice until he finished his residency. But even after he finished here at Victory, he wouldn't settle into a clinic or further his education here at the hospital. Instead he planned to travel around the country, going from church to church, gaining support for his move to a tiny country off the coast of Indonesia where he planned to work as a medical missionary. He'd join up with a team of volunteers already there making great strides in providing basic education and health services to the nationals.

Serving the Lord in a full-time capacity was one of the things he'd taken away from his time with Al and Zann Woods that summer so long ago, and he hadn't forgotten those lessons learned, even though he had long since ditched his dreams of becoming a famous actor. Pursuing his next best interest, a career as a medical doctor, had seemed more reasonable and God-honoring for him. However, there were days Mark had to seriously wonder at his decision. When all was said and done, he'd have put in thirteen-plus years of school, which included the time it had taken him to earn his bachelors degree in premed.

Nonetheless, this was the Lord's will for his life. Mark felt sure of it. He wanted to help people, not only physically and mentally, but spiritually, too. He couldn't imagine having gotten this far without his great-aunt and great-uncle, Edy and Chet Dorien. They'd opened their home on the outskirts of Dubuque after Mark was accepted to med school here at Victory Medical College, an affiliate of Victory Medical Center. Then the Doriens had funded much of his education. They said it was their way of supporting God's work.

But in spite of the financial and emotional encouragement, med school and his residency hadn't exactly been a walk in the park. It had consumed all his time and required dedication. However, the end was near. He had a month to go. . . .

His pager bleeped, announcing the first of the two traumas.

Mark drew in a breath and slowly exhaled. Looked like it was going to be one long night.

🙙🙖

Ravyn yawned as she made her way to her car the next morning. She had concluded hours ago that working the night shift was going to take some physical adjustment. While she had worked odd shifts before, she'd never been a third-shifter on a regular basis.

As she walked down the long hallway, now filled with employees coming in to work for the day, she opened her small black purse and began searching it for her car keys. She slowed her steps while she hunted.

"Hey, Ravyn, wait up."

She grimaced at hearing Mark's voice behind her. She had managed to avoid him for the past eleven hours, even eating her lunch in the women's locker room instead of dining with the others in the twenty-four-hour coffee shop and café located on the lower level. Just her bad luck to run into him now as she was leaving.

Keys in hand, she decided to pretend she hadn't heard him and quickened her pace. But Mark caught up to her in no time. He cupped her elbow and gently pulled her to a halt.

"Whoa, Ravyn. Hang on."

Having no choice, she turned to face him.

"I just wanted to apologize if I was out of line when I asked for your number.

I realize a lot probably changed over the years." He let go of her arm and shifted his stance. "For all I know you're married now with a couple kids."

She did her best to give him a polite smile and momentarily debated whether to divulge her marital status. The truth won out at last.

"I'm not married. No kids."

"Yeah, I rather thought Aunt Edy would have known about something like that." A pleased-looking smile spread across his face. "I'm still single, too."

Ravyn couldn't have cared less and turned to walk away.

Mark took hold of her elbow again. "Want to go out for breakfast?"

She glimpsed his hopeful expression but couldn't believe his nerve. "Won't Carla mind?"

"Carla who?" A confused frown furrowed his dark brows.

Some of the decade-old resentment she still carried in her heart spilled out into her laugh. "Very good, Mark." She applauded. "It's Oscar time for you."

"Huh?" His frown deepened. "What are you talking about?"

Ravyn had wheeled around and was now making purposeful strides toward her car.

"Ravyn."

She unlocked her vehicle, yanked the door open, then slid behind the steering wheel. Before Mark could say another word, she pulled the door closed with a slam.

❧

Mark lay in bed, staring at the ceiling. Despite pulling the shades and drawing the draperies, the sunshine still managed to seep into the room. The sounds of children playing outside combined with a neighbor's lawnmower did little to lull him to sleep. Worse, now that he was so overtired he felt high-strung and tense.

He closed his eyes and tried deep breathing exercises. He worked to conjure up pleasant thoughts, but all he saw in his mind's eye pertained to the fast-paced hospital setting that he knew so well.

Then he envisioned Ravyn. He could picture the way her sky blue eye shadow matched the color of her scrubs, both accentuating her pale features and contrasting with her black hair and eyes. She'd been a pretty girl when she was "sweet sixteen," and she'd matured into a beautiful woman.

Memories resurfaced and he couldn't stifle the grin that tugged at his mouth. He'd been attracted to her from the time he met her and, at first, he'd thought she was older. She'd behaved older—hardly a giggling teenager. He was twenty and when he learned she was four years younger than he, Mark didn't dare pursue a romantic relationship. But they became friends, and Mark would forever think back on that summer as one of the most memorable in his lifetime. He'd looked forward to waking up each day and, except for acting out his role, he couldn't recall not having a smile on his face—from mid-June to Labor Day.

Then, when Ravyn stepped into the lead role and he was actually *required* to kiss her, it had made his whole summer complete.

Mark continued to grin as he remembered Ravyn and her sisters. Each had been named after a color since their mother loved to paint. Ravyn got her name because of her dark features, Teala because of her blue-green eyes. And Violet—

Mark pursed his mouth in thought, unable to bring the reason for her name to mind. Had he ever known it?

He pondered the question a few moments before his musings came back around to Ravyn. Why did she seem angry with him? What had he done to offend her? Surely it couldn't have been the mere phone number question.

He thought awhile longer.

Bigger question yet, why had the Lord brought Ravyn back into his life?

Mark mulled over the latter. Ravyn and her family lived in the College Grandview District of Dubuque, not far from the university. Comparatively, Victory Medical Center was located west of the city and so was the newer subdivision in which Aunt Edy and Uncle Chet had built their home. Mark had always hoped to run into the Woodses. He'd even thought of dropping by for a visit since the distance between them wasn't all that far. But it just never worked out. He had practically lived at the hospital these past four years. It wasn't called a residency for nothing. Prior to that, he was in med school and that hadn't exactly been a picnic by the river, either.

He expelled a long sigh and reminded himself that his hard work would soon pay off. By the first of the year he hoped to be on the mission field.

He was so close to attaining his goals now. So close. . .

🍂

"Mark! Mark! Come quick! Hurry!"

He awoke with a start, unaware he'd even been sleeping. The sound of Aunt Edy's panicked voice penetrated his foggy mind and he bolted out of bed. Wearing a pair of gray gym shorts and a navy blue T-shirt, he left the bedroom and followed the sound of Edy's calls.

"Mark, hurry!"

"I'm coming!" He ran down the carpeted steps. "What's going on?" He fought to clear his fuzzy brain.

"It's Chet," she said, meeting him at the foot of the stairs and wringing her hands. She sounded winded and her perfectly combed and styled honey-colored hair looked almost as frantic as the light in her hazel eyes. "He was tilling the flower bed and collapsed. He's breathing, but—"

"Did you call 911?" Mark rushed past her and headed for the backyard.

"Not yet. I'll do that right now."

Mark dashed outside and across the wide, well-groomed lawn. The grass felt soft and cool beneath his bare feet. In seconds, he reached Uncle Chet, who lay on his side, his back to Mark.

He knelt over the older man who'd been a bulwark of encouragement to him the last several years. "Uncle Chet, what's going on? Can you talk to me?"

The older man groaned in reply.

Mark assessed him—pale, clammy, and his pulse beat in irregular rhythms. Uncle Chet clutched his chest and seemed short of breath. Mark guessed he was suffering a heart attack and took action at once to keep him stable until the emergency personnel arrived. Then, once the paramedics showed up, Mark stepped back to allow the two men to perform their jobs. Minutes later, they loaded Chet into the ambulance.

"Which hospital?" one of the medics asked. Tall and blond, his blue eyes sparked with intelligence and capability. Mark instinctively knew his uncle was in good hands. "Do you have a preference?"

"Take him to Victory Medical Center." Mark helped Aunt Edy into the vehicle. She had decided to ride in back where she could be with Chet. "I'll get dressed and meet you there."

She nodded and then the paramedic climbed in. The ambulance doors were closed and moments later, lights flashing and siren screaming, it took off down the street.

Neighbors stood on their front lawns and gawked, but Mark paid them little attention. He had to get to the hospital and, as much as he loved Chet, this certainly wasn't how he imagined spending his day off.

Chapter 3

H i, I'm Ravyn. I'll be your nurse now because the shift changed and..."
She stopped short. After casting a smile, at first her patient and then at the older woman seated beside him, Ravyn caught a glimpse of Mark Monroe, wearing an apricot polo shirt and blue jeans, perched on a hard plastic chair in the corner of the ER's exam room.

She felt her body tense. Ever since their meeting last night, she had known she would run into him sooner or later. Ravyn had only wished it'd been later.

"Hi, Mark." She kept her tone polite and professional.

He sat up a little straighter. "Hi, Ravyn. Nice to see you again."

She caught his smile and decided he looked tired. "Are you on call?" She hadn't heard Mark was around, and from what she'd gathered, the buzz that *George* was in the ER usually preceded him—not that it mattered to her, of course.

Ravyn just wished she could shake him from her thoughts. She had tried to sleep today, but she'd kept reliving that summer when she'd first met Mark. She felt indignant for Shelley all over again, and the guilt that she'd been the cause of Shelley's breakup with Mark had gnawed at her for hours.

"No, I'm not on call." He nodded at the older couple. "Do you remember my aunt and uncle?"

"Of course, but I—" She opened the chart and peered at her patient's name. She suddenly felt foolish for not recognizing it at once. "I guess I didn't put two and two together."

The older woman smiled from her bedside seat. "Mark told us that you're working here at Victory now."

"Yes. Just recently started." Ravyn decided Edy Darien had a timeless appearance, right down to her khaki slacks and hunter green cotton sweater.

"How nice to see you again."

"You, too." The reply seemed a tad automatic, although Ravyn had always thought the Dariens were warmhearted people.

"Now and then I run into your mother at a women's retreat or seminar," Mrs. Darien said. "Are your parents doing another play this summer? I look forward to them every Labor Day weekend."

"Um, yeah, I think Dad's holding auditions pretty soon. It's about that time." Ravyn began to feel uncomfortable with the topic. She knew what was coming even before it came out of Mark's mouth.

"I had a blast that summer I worked with your folks," he said. "I'd call it a life-changing experience for me."

Life-changing is right. Ravyn decided to snip the personal thread. She glanced at her patient and strode to his bedside. Out of habit, she checked his wristband to be sure the name correlated with the one stamped on the paperwork in the chart. "And what's going on with you, Mr. Darien? You're not feeling so good, huh?"

He managed a groggy smile, having just returned from the cardiac cath lab.

Ravyn sensed three sets of gazes on her and felt oddly conspicuous. She concentrated on taking Mr. Darien's vital signs, a routine done at the beginning of every shift, and noted they appeared to be normal.

"So how much longer until I get outta here?" her patient groused.

Ravyn pulled her stethoscope from her ears. "As soon as a bed is available, you're being admitted for observation." She peered at Mrs. Darien. "Didn't anyone tell you that?"

"Yes, but Chet must have forgotten." Mrs. Darien patted her husband's arm.

"I don't think it registered with Uncle Chet because of the cath and the meds," Mark added.

"Very understandable." Ravyn avoided looking at Mark.

"Do you think it'll be much longer before a room opens up?" his aunt asked.

"No. I'm guessing it'll happen in the next hour." Ravyn glanced at her wristwatch. "Dr. Loomis, the cardiologist, is just finishing the orders. Then once the admitting department assigns Mr. Darien a bed, a transporter will come and take him up to the floor."

Her patient drifted off to sleep before Ravyn finished her explanation. But at least he seemed stable now.

"It's a blessing to see you again, Ravyn. I feel better knowing you're Chet's nurse," Mrs. Darien said.

"Thank you." Ravyn pushed out a smile. "Well, it's back to work for me. Before I go, can I get anything for you, Mrs. Darien? Would you like a cup of coffee? We have regular and decaf. How about a glass of ice water?"

"Oh, no, dear, I'm fine."

"And I know where every coffeepot in this hospital is." Mark chuckled.

"I'm sure you do—I mean, working crazy shifts at a hospital." Ravyn shoved her hands into her smock's pockets and reminded herself she couldn't afford to appear rude. She was new to the hospital, while Mark had been a resident here for years. "Um, Dr. Loomis should be coming in any minute now."

"Thank you, dear."

"Yeah, thanks, Ravyn."

She gave both Mrs. Darien and Mark a polite nod. Then, without another word, she exited the exam room. When she reached the unit clerk's desk she let out a long sigh of relief.

🐾

The pinks of dawn streaked across the horizon as Mark stared out Uncle Chet's hospital room window. The medical center's landscape below looked almost serene at this time of morning, but in a few more hours it would be bustling with patients, visitors, physicians, medical students, and other staff.

He yawned and stretched. After his uncle had been moved to the cardiac wing late last night, Mark had driven Aunt Edy home and then returned. Now that he felt confident his uncle would make a total recovery, he was preparing to leave, too, and catch a few hours' sleep.

There was just one thing he wanted to do first: talk to Ravyn. She'd been noticeably cool and standoffish. Even Aunt Edy had mentioned it, although to her and Uncle Chet, Ravyn behaved as "polite as raspberry punch," as his aunt would say. Mark had even seen Ravyn laughing at something another nurse said. It wasn't her personality or his imagination. It was just *him*. Mark probably wouldn't care if he and Ravyn hadn't been friends and if her parents hadn't made such a profound impact on his life. But for those reasons, he felt concerned and he wanted to do what he could to make things right between them.

He checked on his uncle, who slept soundly in spite of the various ticks and hums from the surrounding machines. He gave Uncle Chet's forearm a soft squeeze and then left the room and headed for the ER.

He glanced at his watch. Seven o'clock. Ravyn was probably just finishing her shift.

🐾

Ravyn hung up her smock in the tan metal locker. She pulled off her scrubs and stuffed them into the hospital's hamper. Next she donned the blue jeans and pink long-sleeved T-shirt she'd worn to work last night. Several feet away three other female nurses sat on backless benches and traded information about their significant others while they dressed. As Ravyn listened, a feeling of envy began to sprout somewhere deep within her being. She squelched it before it took root; she didn't have time for a love life, although she had to admit the thought of going home to someone who adored her seemed much more appealing than returning to her lonely condominium.

I'll get a goldfish, she thought with a cynical note.

Ravyn shut her locker's door a bit harder than intended. The other nurses stopped talking for several long seconds. She smiled an apology and the ladies resumed their chatter. Folding her jacket over one forearm, she slung her purse strap across the opposite shoulder and headed for the door.

As she made her way down the hallway, she passed employees who were on

23

their way in to work. Suddenly Ravyn's whole world seemed topsy-turvy, from working the night shift job to the nonexistent romance in her life—and it was all Teala's fault. Her sister's favorite topics of late were her boyfriend, love, and weddings. What's more, Teala's final project for a sociology class was to interview singles and couples and to draw conclusions as to why some men and women preferred their marital status—or why they didn't prefer it.

"You sound materialistic, Ravyn," her sister had said during a phone interview yesterday afternoon. She'd called to ask questions for her project, but she didn't stay objective for long. "It's like you're putting monetary things above relationships, people."

"That's ridiculous."

"Oh? Well, when's the last time you chose to go out with friends over working? When did you choose church over a double shift?"

The inquisition stung, especially since Ravyn had been thinking about Mark and Shelley all day. With regard to her faith, she knew the Lord understood, and Ravyn even felt His love for her and His support of her hard work. But yesterday afternoon didn't seem like the appropriate time to argue with her sister, let alone tell her that she'd met up with Mark in the ER. So Ravyn kept the news to herself.

She quickened her steps down the hallway as her aggravation mounted.

"Hi, Ravyn."

Mark stood from the bench near the entrance doors, and she nearly tripped over him.

"I need to talk to you."

"Um. . ." Ravyn felt taken aback by the near collision.

"It won't take long, but if you've got some time, I'd like to buy you breakfast."

Her initial reaction was to refuse the offer. Not only did Ravyn automatically dislike Mark Monroe for what had happened the summer when she was sixteen, she didn't want to get mixed up with all the drama he caused in the ER.

In the next second, however, Teala's remarks came to mind. Having breakfast with Mark would prove them—and her sister—wrong. Ravyn had always enjoyed blowing up misconceptions. As for her co-workers, she figured she could explain it away easily enough if they ever found out. After all, she and Mark knew each other long before they'd entered the medical field.

Besides, she had a few choice words to say to him, too.

"Um. Sure. Breakfast it is."

Mark looked a bit surprised that she'd accepted the invitation, and Ravyn almost laughed.

"Good." He rubbed his palms together and sent her a grin. "How about if we go over to Oscar's Family Restaurant? It's right up the block and they serve a terrific omelet."

"Okay, I'll meet you there."

While Mark took the parking structure's elevator to reach his car, Ravyn walked out to the main floor, found her vehicle, and climbed in. She decided that one benefit to starting her shift at six thirty in the evening was that parking slots were plentiful. Clinics were closed when she began working, and except for a few departments, staff, patients, and visitors had gone home.

As she drove to the restaurant, Ravyn mentally rehearsed what she'd say to Mark. Maybe she'd wait until after they'd eaten—or would it be better to tell him what a jerk he was right away and get it over with?

She found the small eatery without any trouble and drove into its crowded asphalt lot. After circling twice, she finally saw a vacant slot and parked.

Her fingers curled around the gray steering wheel as she, once again, went over her list of grievances. Then a soft tap on her window gave her a start, and Mark Monroe's grinning face peered through the glass.

Ravyn sucked in a breath and gathered her resolve. There was no turning back now.

Chapter 4

Ravyn sipped her coffee and decided it was the best brew she'd tasted in a long time.

"This place makes dynamite coffee," Mark stated, as if divining her very thoughts. "But don't plan on sleeping anytime soon after drinking it."

"I don't work for the next two nights, so I'll be okay."

"Work the weekend?"

Ravyn nodded and eyed the menu.

"I don't think I've had a weekend off in five years." Mark chuckled. "Med school was four years. My residency another three—"

Okay, it's time. She slapped the menu closed and stared across the table at him. "What do you need to speak to me about?" She suddenly saw no purpose in the polite small talk they'd engaged in since entering the restaurant.

Mark pursed his lips and sent her a glance. Then he, too, closed his menu. "I just wondered if you're all right."

"Me?" She raised her eyebrows.

He nodded.

Before Ravyn could answer, the waitress appeared.

Mark ordered for the both of them. "Two of your Greek omelets with the works."

The chubby brunette in her brown polyester uniform nodded and collected the laminated menus before hurrying from the table.

Ravyn couldn't contain her annoyance a moment more. "You've got a lot of nerve. How do you know I'll eat a Greek omelet with the works? For all you know I could be allergic to eggs."

Mark tipped his head. "Are you?"

"No, but—"

"Then it's all good. And you've got to try these omelets."

Ravyn bristled.

"Hey, why are you so angry? You look furious." Mark leaned forward, placing his forearms on the table. He still wore the apricot polo shirt from yesterday, and the bright color defined his swarthy features all the more. "Are you mad at me—or the whole world?"

"I'm not angry. But you're an egomaniac."

"Ah." He bobbed his head. "So it is me. I rather thought so."

"See what I mean? It's all about you. You're arrogant."

Mark actually grinned. "I'd like to think I'm just confident, Ravyn. How else could I have made it through med school? Those who doubt their abilities drop out before they even get to their clinicals."

"You say confidence. I say arrogance. Let's call the whole thing off."

Mark obviously recognized her parody of the 1937 Gershwin song and laughed. Could it be that he actually recalled how her father liked to play Gershwin's music during rehearsal breaks? The quip had rolled off her tongue without a single thought, but now Ravyn felt somewhat taken aback by Mark's reaction.

"I always appreciated your sarcastic wit."

"Whatever."

Ravyn worked at regaining her momentum while Mark took another long drink from the cream-colored stoneware mug.

"So are you dating anyone? If you are, he's one lucky dude."

"Mark, false flattery will get you to zero with me. In other words, I'm not impressed."

He held up his hands in surrender. "Okay, okay. I'll try to remember that in the future. Except, I meant every word. He *is* lucky."

Ravyn didn't bother correcting him. Talk about *zero*! He probably sweet-talked his way through med school, too.

"As I recall, you're a lot of fun. You used to get me laughing so hard I couldn't stop. Remember that Sunday morning in church? I thought your dad was going to have a conniption because the two of us laughed so hard we shook the entire pew."

"The three of us."

"I beg your pardon?" Mark's brows drew together in a puzzled frown.

The moment she'd been waiting for was at hand. "There were three of us sitting together that morning. It was you, me, *and Shelley*."

Mark turned momentarily pensive. "Shelley? Shelley who?"

Ravyn clenched her jaw. He claimed not to know Carla at work and now he doesn't remember Shelley? What a rat!

"Shelley Jenkins. She was my best friend and *your* leading lady in the play."

"Oh—okay. I kind of remember her now." Mark wore a pensive expression as he probed his recollections. "But I couldn't say for sure if Shelley was there in church with us or not."

"She was." How could his memory be so hazy? "And she was at the carnival, too. Don't you remember how all of us, cast and crew, persuaded my dad to let us out of rehearsal early one Saturday so we could go to the summer carnival? I'll never forget it. My father has never been easily swayed—but he was that day."

"Oh, yeah, the carnival. That was a lot of fun." He smiled. "We were good friends, Ravyn. That's why I don't understand—"

"For your information, I spent that entire summer before my senior year in high school, listening to my best friend talk about how in love with you she was."

"Oh?"

"Yeah." She sent him an appalled glance. "And don't look so pleased. Your ego is showing again."

"I'm not wallowing in pleasure at the news. I'm surprised." Mark lowered his voice. "I had no idea. Give me a break, will you? I didn't know Shelley, other than she was my leading lady until you stepped into the role."

Ravyn thought it over, summoning up the countless stories she'd heard about Mark from her former best friend. He'd held her hand, kissed her—said he loved her. How could he not remember Shelley?

"You're lying—there is no point in continuing this conversation." She slid out of the padded vinyl booth and took a step toward the restaurant's door.

Mark caught her wrist. "On my honor as a Christian, I swear I'm telling the truth." He inclined his head toward the place where she'd been sitting. "Why don't you sit back down? Please. Let's get this straightened out once and for all."

Ravyn pulled out of his grasp, then glanced around the restaurant. She noticed curious stares from people she thought she recognized. Did they work at Victory, too? The last thing she wanted to do was add another link to the gossip chain. She sat back down and tried to muster a bit of dignity.

"I've always been fond of you, Ravyn," Mark said in a whispered voice, "and your parents had a huge impact on my walk with Christ. It really hurts to find out that you've harbored such resentment against me all these years."

She didn't reply but smoothed the paper napkin back over her lap.

"Please believe me when I say there was nothing between Shelley and me."

"And I suppose that means nothing's going on between you and Carla, either?"

"Carla?" A look of puzzlement spread across his face. "Who in the world is that?"

Ravyn tossed a glance at the ceiling. "The x-ray tech in the ER? Are you going to tell me you don't know her, either?"

"No, I don't, and that's the honest truth."

He seemed so sincere, but was it an act?

Mark stared into his coffee cup. "My rotation in the ER hasn't been easy. It really irks me when the nurses call me George. I want my life to emulate the Lord Jesus Christ's, not some doctor on a TV drama." He looked up. "When I saw you a few days ago, Ravyn, I felt like God brought me an ally. I'm sorry to see that I was wrong."

Ravyn folded her arms and pressed her lips together, refusing to be swayed by guilt.

"But maybe we could start over." He took a sip of coffee. "Look, if I broke

Shelley's heart it was unintentional, I assure you."

Their food arrived before Ravyn could answer. After the waitress walked away, Mark asked the blessing on their meal. His simple prayer somehow reached through her animosity and touched her soul. *He can't be a fake.*

"Amen."

Ravyn looked up to see Mark lift his fork and dig into his omelet. Bite after bite, he ate with a mix of haste and gusto, like a man accustomed to living his life on the run.

Meanwhile, Ravyn began to concede. She supposed it was her Christian duty to forgive and forget. Shelley was long gone; Ravyn hadn't seen or heard from her in more than ten years.

"So what do you think?" he asked. "Can we leave the past behind us and move on?"

"I guess so." Ravyn took a bite of her omelet, enjoying the rich flavor. She chewed and swallowed. "I sense that what you're saying is true, but—it's just hard for me to believe Shelley lied. She was my best friend. She told me about the two of you." Ravyn cleared her throat. "Up in the balcony. Does that ring a bell?"

Mark's jaw dropped, and judging from his expression of disbelief, Ravyn deduced the episode never occurred.

Shelley lied to me. The stark reality numbed Ravyn from head to toe. *She lied to me!*

Mark leaned forward, his gaze sharp and narrow. "Are you accusing me of some sort of misconduct?"

"No." She rescinded. After all, she had no proof. How could she, in all fairness, hurl such profound allegations at him based on what she recalled hearing at age sixteen? "No, and I'm sorry. I shouldn't have said what I did. I get the distinct feeling Shelley fabricated the romance between herself and you."

"That's some heavy-duty fabrication." Mark sat back. "Maybe I should have a talk with her."

"Good idea. If you can find her. I haven't seen her since she left Dubuque almost eleven years ago."

"What?" He looked both perplexed and amused. "And you've been mad at me all this time? For nothing?"

Humiliation, confusion, and remorse converged inside her heart. "Well, it's not as if I thought about it night and day. I didn't."

"It was over ten years ago!"

Ravyn lifted her chin. "If what Shelley had told me was true, which I now realize wasn't, then I had good reason to dislike you."

Mark held up his hand, palm-side out. "All right. You've made your point."

Ravyn mentally groped to make sense of it all. Then she ended up spilling out the story to Mark.

"So I always felt responsible," she stated at last.

"Because Shelley got sick and you stepped into her role?" He shook his head. "You had no control over that."

"But I thought she blamed me for the failed romance between you two—the one that never existed." Ravyn massaged her temples. She felt a headache coming on.

"Hey, look, you and Shelley were both kids back then. Let's just forget it, okay?"

She nodded but sensed it wouldn't be quite that simple. What Mark didn't understand was that she and Shelley had been so close for so long it had felt like losing a limb when Ravyn lost her friendship. Shelley had left Dubuque without even a good-bye.

Mark glanced at his wristwatch. "I need to get moving. I promised my aunt I'd pick her up and take her back to the hospital."

His comment reminded Ravyn of Chet Darien's heart attack. "Is your uncle feeling better?"

"Not sure. He was sleeping when I left this morning. But I think he'll pull through just fine."

They slid from the booth and stood. Mark paid the bill at the front cash register, and Ravyn felt as though she owed him an apology. She'd said some awful things and he hadn't been obligated to explain himself, but he did. A lesser man might have lost his temper.

They walked into the parking lot, and she zipped her jacket as the cool April wind felt more like winter than spring this morning. They'd had some warm weather, but now the air had a decided nip to it.

"Hey, Mark, I'm sorry for—"

"Forget it." He pulled on his navy blue sweatshirt.

"Thanks for breakfast."

"My pleasure." He gave her a smile. "Let's be friends, all right? Life's too short for Christians to hold grudges. Agreed?"

"Agreed." She looked into his brown eyes and saw only earnestness there.

"I'll see you back at work in a couple of days. We'll talk some more then."

"Okay." Ravyn fished the keys from out of her purse, unlocked her car, and climbed in. She started her car, replaying her conversation with Mark in her mind. She believed him, although she couldn't seem to come to grips with Shelley's decade-old lies.

"Mark said he loved me, Ravyn, and right after I finish high school we'll get married. Will you be my maid of honor? I've never been so happy in all my life!"

Shelley couldn't have possibly feigned that starry-eyed gaze.

But Mark looked equally as genuine today.

Suddenly Ravyn sensed something was very, very wrong.

❧

"Hey, the place is really coming together."

"Thanks."

Ravyn bid her sister entry into the condo and closed the door. She glanced around the living room, pleased with what she saw. Her new cranberry-colored sofa with its six loose pillows had arrived yesterday, and the carpet she'd recently purchased—a woven wool blend in shades of beige, crimson, and gold—added just the right contrast. In the far corner, a beautiful oak entertainment center housed a large flat-screen TV, along with a state-of-the-art video and DVD player.

"Nice, Rav." Teala ran her hand over the beveled-glass top of the coffee table.

She felt her smile broaden. "Looks better than in the catalog, doesn't it?"

"Sure does."

Ravyn headed for the kitchen. "Would you like some coffee? I just made a fresh pot."

"No, thanks."

After plucking a large mug from the cupboard, Ravyn filled it with the rich-smelling, steaming brew.

"Hey, I'm sorry about what I said the other afternoon," Teala said, walking up behind her. "I know you care about people. That's why you're a nurse. It's just that—well, Greg and I are so happy and. . ." Her cheeks pinked in a way that made Ravyn grin. "I just want everyone to experience the same *euphoria*."

"Euphoria?" Ravyn rolled her eyes. "Good grief."

"Okay, okay. Maybe I'm exaggerating just a tad. But will you forgive me?" Teala looked at Ravyn with those wide, blue-green eyes and did a great imitation of the adorable puppy-in-the-window look.

"Of course I forgive you, but I think Greg has his hands full." Ravyn grinned before sipping her coffee. "Oh, and speaking of men, guess who I had breakfast with a couple of days ago?"

"A *man*?" Teala feigned an expression of sheer mortification.

"Knock it off, you drama queen." There was little wonder in Ravyn's mind as to why Dad cast Teala in so many of his productions. Unlike her big sister, Teala had no problem performing in front of a large audience. In fact, the more spectators, the better.

"So, do tell, Rav. Who did you have breakfast with?"

"Do you remember Mark Monroe? You may not because you were only ten when—"

"I remember Mark. In fact, I've run into him a bunch of times over the years, but I've either been with Mom or Dad, so I just kind of stood by while he talked to them. Is that who you had breakfast with?"

Ravyn nodded. "He's finishing up his residency at Victory."

"He's a nice-looking guy—and a doctor, too?"

"Uh-huh."

"Single?"

"Yep."

Teala's eyes sparkled with possibilities. "He sounds perfect for you. A guy who's going to make tons of money."

"There you go again. You make me sound totally materialistic." Ravyn turned and strode toward the living room.

"I didn't mean it that way." Teala was right on her heels. "I just meant, well, you know. You've got, well, certain standards you've set for yourself."

Ravyn halted and Teala smacked right into her. The coffee sloshed over the mug and splattered onto the tan and off-white ceramic floor tiles.

"Oops. Sorry, Rav. I'll wipe it up." Teala traipsed to the stainless steel sink and ripped off a piece of paper towel from the wooden holder mounted beneath the oak cabinets. "So are you interested in him?"

"No. We're friends. That's all." Her conscience pricked. If she wasn't interested in Mark, then why couldn't she shake him from her thoughts?

"Being friends is a good place to start."

"And a good place to end."

"Oh, Ravyn. Give the guy a chance."

"Maybe he doesn't want a chance. And you're a hopeless romantic."

"That'd be me."

With the spill wiped up, Ravyn led her sister into the living room where they sat on the sofa.

"The thing is," Ravyn said, sipping her coffee, "in talking with Mark, I discovered that Shelley lied to me about something that's been haunting me for years, except the incident—make that incidents—never even occurred."

"She was mean. I didn't like Shelley."

"You used to say I was mean, too."

Teala relented. "Well, yeah, but that's because you always had to babysit for Violet and me."

"The bossy big sister and her equally bossy best friend?"

"Something like that."

They shared a laugh.

Ravyn folded her legs beneath her. "I just can't believe Shelley would lie." She shook her head, thinking back on those summer days so long ago. "She'd talked about Mark all the time and she was devastated when he broke things off. But he says there was never anything between them, so there was never any breakup. I sense he's telling the truth, but that means—"

"Maybe Shelley didn't really mean to lie. Could be she was just so infatuated that she lost touch with the reality of the situation."

Ravyn had never considered it quite like that before. "Think so?"

"Well, sure. I mean, people believe all sorts of stuff that isn't true. Think about it."

"Well, yeah. It makes sense. We were both very naive at age sixteen."

"Way back in the day."

"It wasn't *that* long ago." Ravyn sent her younger sister a quelling look.

"Long enough. Who cares anymore?" Teala made herself comfy by kicking off her shoes and setting her feet on the coffee table. "I want to hear more about you and Mark. What did you two talk about at breakfast? What kind of doctor is he? What was he wearing?"

Ravyn rolled her eyes. She had a feeling it would take some effort to convince Teala there was nothing between her and Mark.

Absolutely nothing.

Chapter 5

Mark sat in the ER at a vacant workstation located between the phlebotomist's area and the unit secretary's desk. There was an incessant buzz of male and female voices all around him while telephones rang, monitors bleeped, printers and copiers hummed. He tried to ignore the commotion as he scanned the computer for lab results. A positive test meant calling and informing the patient.

A nurse leaned over him and snatched a chart off the countertop. She apologized before scurrying away. Mark barely noticed. He'd learned to tune out everything but the task at hand. However, the sudden *tap, tap, tap* on his left shoulder blade commanded his immediate attention.

He swiveled in his chair and found Ravyn smiling down at him.

"You must be really concentrating," she said. "I called your name twice."

"Sorry." He sent her an apologetic grin.

"How's your uncle?"

"He's doing well—probably go home tomorrow. Doesn't look like he'll need bypass surgery. The angioplasty seems to have been effective."

"That's good news."

"Sure is." In two quick glances, Mark took in Ravyn's appearance. The sky blue scrubs accentuated her petite form and complemented her black hair, eyes, and thick lashes. His gaze moved over her face and he found her dark features a striking contrast to the paleness of her skin. He had to admit he liked what he saw.

"Mark?"

"Huh?" At the sound of her strong but smooth voice, he shook himself. He felt chagrined for staring. "Oh, sorry. Guess I zoned out. I'm tired." He hoped it sounded like a viable cover.

"No problem."

It worked. He expelled a breath of relief, although his reply hadn't been too far from the truth. The word *tired* could just as well replace the *MD* after his name.

Ravyn folded her arms. "When are you done with your residency?"

"End of June." He leaned back in the chair.

"Quite an accomplishment."

Mark arched a brow and couldn't help teasing her. "You sound surprised."

"No." She lifted her small shoulders in a noncommittal way, but seconds later two pink spots spread across her cheekbones. "I didn't mean it that way."

He chuckled, finding a peculiar delight in causing her to blush.

"Hey, George!"

Mark's good humor vanished and his patience threatened to follow. He glanced to his left and peered at the middle-aged nurse who'd hailed him. He abhorred the nickname but supposed he should feel flattered. After all, there were worse names RNs could call residents.

He took the proffered chart and read it while the nurse voiced her request. After scribing the order, Mark turned back to Ravyn, but to his disappointment, she'd disappeared.

❧

When her lunch break arrived, Ravyn walked out onto what was referred to as the smoking deck. The large cement slab had been constructed adjacent to the ambulance bay, and it served as a patio and smoking area for the ER staff.

Sitting down at one of the picnic tables, Ravyn unzipped her thermal lunch bag. Next she removed the curry chicken and rice mixture that Mom created the other night. Teala had brought over a good-sized portion of the spicy concoction yesterday, and all Ravyn had had to do was heat it up in the break room's microwave tonight.

She began eating and glanced around the darkened deck. Only two halogen lamps on either side of the building provided light, but Ravyn felt safe enough. Several feet away, one male nurse whom she recognized from the ER chatted with two females while they took long drags on their cigarettes.

Ravyn regarded them as they conversed and laughed at something the other had said. A sudden pang of loneliness caused her to set down her plastic fork. She realized it was hard to be new at any job, and she welcomed the challenges this position at Victory brought her way. At the same time, however, she missed the people who had become her friends at her former place of employment. There she never used to have to eat alone.

"Mind if I sit here?"

Before she could answer, Mark plunked himself down on the bench across from her, shaking the entire table unit with his weight.

Ravyn gave him a sassy grin. "Sure, this is public property. Make yourself comfortable."

He already had. "Just for your information, I'm not stalking you or anything," he sassed right back. "I do get an occasional break, and since I saw you sitting out here, I thought I'd keep you company."

"I'm glad you did." She smiled. "Seriously. Your timing couldn't have been more perfect."

"Good."

An awkward pause settled between them.

Then Mark leaned forward. "What are you eating? Smells good."

"It's something my mom made. Want a bite? I think I have an extra fork in my lunch bag."

"Well, maybe just a little."

Ravyn fished the disposable utensil from her gold and black-trimmed lunch bag. After handing it to Mark, she pushed the plastic container of meat, vegetables, and rice across the table.

He took a forkful. "Hey, this is pretty good." He took another bite. "Has kind of a kick to it."

Ravyn nodded and watched Mark eat some more. Deciding to let him polish off the curry chicken, she extracted a yogurt and spoon from her bag.

"Are you as good a cook as your mom?" The question came in between mouthfuls.

"I'm actually a better cook than Mom—and I don't mean that in a gloating way. But my culinary skills are well known in my family because I did all the cooking until I went to college. After that, I didn't always have time, so my sisters took turns. Mom only recently developed an interest in cooking."

"No kidding? You did most of the cooking growing up?"

"Yep. I did all the laundry and housework, too."

"Hmm."

"Mom and Dad were always gone."

"Your parents are remarkable people. They really impacted my life, particularly your dad."

Ravyn didn't reply, wondering what Mark would think if she told him how truly "remarkable" her folks had been. Al and Zann Woods had traipsed from one public housing complex to another with their daughters in tow. Ravyn remembered those years well—too well. While her parents had viewed their bleak surroundings as mission fields, Ravyn saw them as misfortunes.

"My great-aunt and uncle have influenced my life in a positive way, too. I'm the third kid out of six and I guess I always felt neglected. That's why acting appealed to me. It was an acceptable way to get attention."

Ravyn smiled.

"But your parents and my aunt and uncle helped me see outside myself and put my focus onto the needs of others."

"I'll share that with my father. He'll be very encouraged."

"Good."

Mark took another bite of Ravyn's dinner, and several moments of clumsy silence passed.

"So. Are you seeing anyone?"

She blinked. "What?"

"Any special guy in your life?"

His question made her laugh. "Mark, you're about as subtle as an atomic bomb."

"What can I say? I'm a busy guy." The chagrin was evident in the tone of his voice. "I mean, for all I know you could be in the throes of planning your wedding."

"Hardly. In fact, Teala will probably get married before I do. She's dating a teacher at Our Savior Christian School. We joke about it. Teala, the professional college student, dating a teacher."

Beneath the dim lights, Ravyn saw Mark smile. He'd left his MD coat inside the hospital and only wore his light green scrubs. After an unseasonably warm day, the nighttime temperatures felt brisk. The ER, in comparison, was hot and stuffy. No doubt Mark came out here to cool off.

"So how come you're not married?" She figured one good inquiry deserved another. She grinned. "I should think you'd make a fine catch for any girl."

"Well, thanks. But, um, the right one just hasn't come along yet."

"Hmm." Ravyn decided he got out of answering that question rather easily.

"Actually, I dated someone on and off for a couple of years, but it became clear to both of us that marriage wasn't God's will. We broke things off and it was a mutual decision."

An image of Carla's pretty face flitted through Ravyn's mind. "Does she still work here?" She caught herself. "No, wait. You don't have to answer that. It's none of my business and I shouldn't have asked."

Ravyn finished the yogurt and reached for the red licorice she'd packed in her lunch bag. She tore open the bag.

"It's okay, Ravyn, I don't mind answering your question." Mark polished off the rice and chicken entrée and reached for a couple braids of licorice. "No, she doesn't work here. Never did."

Ravyn paused in mid chew.

"Never assume," Mark said, waving a long piece of candy at her. Then he chuckled.

"You're right. It's just that most of my friends are usually co-workers—because I spend so much time at work."

"Natural deductive reasoning on your part." Mark continued to smile as he bit off a piece of licorice. "I met Hannah at church."

"Hannah who?" Ravyn wondered if she knew the woman since she'd grown up in the same congregation. She'd only left when her folks did in order to begin the sister church.

"Remington. Hannah Remington."

"Oh, sure. I graduated from high school with Shawn Remington. Hannah was a year or two older."

"That'd be her."

Ravyn summoned up memories of Hannah. She had always won home ec awards in school, and she had typically been voted Nursery Worker of the Month at church.

"You must like the domestic type."

Mark pursed his lips and raised his broad shoulders in a casual shrug. "Never really thought of it like that. I guess when the right one comes along, the Lord will let me know."

"Hmm." Ravyn made a mental note to ask Teala for the scoop on the situation. Her younger sister, it seemed, was in the know when it came to the who's who in the dating scene. Ravyn, on the other hand, was hopelessly out of touch.

She finished her piece of licorice, and while Mark helped himself to a few more strands, she reached for her apple.

"What about you? Any close calls, romantically speaking?"

"No." She mentally went over the list of guys she'd dated in the past. "No one's managed to sweep me off my feet." *Except when I was sixteen,* she added silently, giving Mark a little smile. He'd certainly accomplished the job. Of course, back then she had never purposely encouraged him in any way. She knew Shelley had her heart set on him in spite of their age difference.

Sudden memories like flood waters seeped into the crevices of her consciousness. She heard Shelley's voice in its dreamy state drone on and on about Mark. *"He said he loves me. He wants us to be together forever—"*

"Ravyn?"

She snapped to attention and glanced across the picnic table at Mark. Could this seemingly upstanding man in the light green scrubs be the same creep who'd devastated Shelley so long ago?

The pieces didn't fit together, but maybe Teala had been right about Shelley losing touch with reality. Perhaps that's why Shelley disappeared from Dubuque without a word—she had some kind of breakdown.

Ravyn shook off her speculation, then glanced at her gold bracelet-watch with its large round face. "I need to get back to work."

"Me, too."

They stood, and Ravyn covered and repacked the now empty container. As a courtesy to her, Mark tossed her yogurt carton into the nearby trash bin. When he returned to the table, he set his hand on Ravyn's shoulder.

"Are you okay? You sort of spaced out for a moment and now you're awfully quiet."

"I'm fine. I just remembered something I have to do," she fibbed. She didn't want to bring up the subject of Shelley again, even though the situation continued to puzzle her.

As they made their way back to the ER, they passed Carla and another woman whom Ravyn didn't recognize. They're expressions brightened when they saw Mark, and Carla actually giggled.

"Hi, George," they stated in unison.

Ravyn glanced at Mark in time to see him incline his head, a gracious reply since he despised the nickname.

Her heart went out to him, and she nudged him with her elbow. She meant the gesture to say, *Don't let them get to you*, but whether Mark understood it or not, he gave her a playful nudge right back. But his sent Ravyn halfway across the hall.

Mark caught her by her upper arm before she could trip and fall, and they both laughed.

"You're such a little thing—it wouldn't be hard for a guy to sweep you off your feet."

"You mean *knock* me off my feet."

They laughed again and continued their trek to the ER.

"By the way, that was Carla. The blond who just passed us."

"Carla?" Mark took at quick look over his shoulder. "I've seen her around."

"She's the one who apparently claims the two of you are dating."

He chuckled. "It's news to me."

Ravyn believed him. "I hate all this petty stuff."

"I do, too, but this particular third shift is notorious for it." He gave Ravyn a smile. "Who knows? Maybe you'll be the one to change things. God obviously put you here in the ER and on this shift for a reason."

Ravyn hadn't thought of her career at Victory in that light before. She'd only seen it as fitting into her plans, not God's.

Mark pressed on the silver automatic wall plate, and the frosted glass doors to the emergency room opened.

"Speaking of the Lord, what are you doing tomorrow?" Mark paused just before they reached the U-shaped counter that encompassed the unit clerk's desk and the other computer work areas.

"Um, sleeping, I guess. I work tomorrow night."

"Can you catch a few Z's in the morning and come to the late service at church? It starts at ten forty-five." Mark grinned. "My aunt's playing the piano for a special music piece, and it wouldn't be any big deal, really, other than she just started taking piano lessons about six months ago."

"Really? Piano lessons?" Ravyn felt a smile spread across her face. She was impressed that Mrs. Darien would take on such a feat at her age. "Good for her."

"Yeah, too bad my uncle has to miss her great debut."

"Aw, yes, that is a shame."

"Well, listen, plan on coming to lunch with my aunt and me after the service. Uncle Chet won't be discharged until later tomorrow."

Ravyn felt herself stiffen. "Whoa, Mark, wait a second."

He obviously didn't hear her as the staff physician called him over. "Catch you later," he called with a backward glance at her.

Watching him go, Ravyn elected not to pursue the matter, but she'd have to tell him she couldn't accept the invitation. She had to sleep sometime and she'd hate for it to be during Mrs. Darien's solo. On the other hand, she wouldn't mind spending more time with Mark. She sensed his interest in her, but would it result in anything more than a friendship? Did she want it to be anything more than a friendship?

A vision of her condo on its lavish grounds flashed through her mind. The rest of her goals mentally surfaced, too. Her older model sedan wasn't going to last forever, and somewhere there was a shiny new sports car with her name on it.

She told herself she wasn't materialistic. Rather, she was ensuring she wouldn't end up having to live with nothing, like her folks had done. The only reason they owned their own home now was because Grandpa Woods had left it to them in his will. Without Grandpa's generous gift, Ravyn sometimes wondered if her family would still be destitute.

The thought motivated her to work even harder. She picked up a patient's chart and tried to ignore the rueful weight that settled in her heart. The fact of the matter was, she didn't have time for a relationship, be it with Mark—or God.

Chapter 6

For the next two weeks, Ravyn managed to sidestep Mark each time their paths crossed. She tried to avoid talking to him unless it involved work, and she ate her lunch in places where he wouldn't think to find her. His obvious interest caused her a measurable amount of unease.

But then after Teala came back with glowing reports, having done a bit of research on her own, Ravyn felt less wary. Hannah Remington had only good things to say about Mark, although, as Ravyn pointed out, Hannah would never say a word against anyone. In addition, everyone in the ER seemed to regard him as an all-around nice guy who was honest to a fault and extremely serious about his medical career—too serious, according to some female staff members.

On a particularly slow shift in the ER, Liz and a few other RNs took delight in teasing Mark to the point where Ravyn sensed his indignation. He never uttered a single retort, even though Ravyn knew he could hold his own if he chose to do so. Nevertheless, when her break time rolled around, she decided to seek him out in a small show of moral support.

She found him in one of the back offices where residents often studied, and knocked on the door, which stood partway open. "Anybody home?"

Mark glanced up from the thick textbook in front of him. "Hi, Ravyn, what can I do for you?"

The curt greeting caused her to feel a tad bit guilty. He had first thought of her as an ally, but she hadn't been much of a friend the last ten days.

"Want to get a cup of coffee with me?"

He actually had to think about the offer and Ravyn's regret mounted.

"Mark, I'm sorry I've been so standoffish. I. . . Well. . ."

He held up a hand. "You're learning a new job. I'm sure it's been stressful."

She didn't answer, deciding his deductive reasoning wasn't so far from the truth.

"A cup of coffee sounds good." He stood and stretched. "I could use a bit of a reprieve."

Ravyn's opinion of him went up another notch. He wasn't about to play games, and that said a lot about his character.

Turning from the doorway, she stepped toward the hallway when Mark grabbed hold of her elbow.

"Let's go down the back stairwell."

"No, let's take the elevator." She'd heard taking the stairs was the long way to the coffee shop on the lower level.

"Nah, I don't want people to talk."

"I'm not afraid to leave the ER in your company, Mark, if that's what you mean."

"That's precisely what I mean." He put his hands on his hips, pushing back his white physician's coat and revealing his light green scrubs. "Look, in a month, I'm out of here but you'll still have to work with these people."

Ravyn weighed her options and decided he had a good point. Without another word, she followed him to the exit at the end of the hall.

"I'm beginning to see why some of my co-workers have worked third shift for years." Her voice echoed in the empty stairwell. "They'd never get away with all their goofiness on first shift."

"Very true. There seems to be more of a corporate feel around here during the daytime."

Ravyn agreed and quite frequently she found herself wishing for dayshift again instead of having to work the graveyard shift. Nonetheless, this job was the stepping-stone she needed in her career, so she'd put in her time and then make the switch once her probationary period ended.

They strode across the wide landing and down a second flight of steps.

"Just for the record, those women like you, Mark." Ravyn sent him a grin. "That's why they pick on you."

"I'm flattered," he quipped.

She laughed.

"Seriously, though, I don't want to encourage anybody the wrong way, so it's best I keep my mouth shut. Someone's liable to get her feelings hurt, and I could imagine an entire fiasco resulting."

"I suppose you're right; take the Carla thing." Ravyn opened the door and Mark followed. They left the stairway for the long corridor that led to the cafeteria. "I wonder how the rumor got started about the two of you seeing each other."

"Funny you mention that particular person. I discovered there's a group of people who go out after work a couple times a week and it sounds like they drink too many Bloody Marys. Carla's part of what's been referred to as the Breakfast Brigade."

"Hmm, well, boozing at breakfast would explain it." Ravyn gave him a side-long glance. "Do you know I've never tasted a single alcoholic beverage? I saw enough drunks at the low-income housing units we lived in when I was a kid to never want to touch the stuff."

"Yeah, I don't think we're missing anything."

They made their way to the self-serve coffee carafes at the side counter, and Ravyn chose a flavored brew and mixed it with half a cup of decaf so she'd be able to fall asleep later today. Mark selected a roasted blend.

They stepped up to the cash register, and a couple of fellow residents called hellos to him and asked if he was ready for their next final exam. Ravyn felt glad she'd finished school; however, the learning process never stopped. As a RN she was required to take periodic exams in order to maintain her license. She also attended various workshops and seminars in order to keep up with the ever-changing medical field.

Ravyn slipped into a chair at a small table near some vending machines. She checked her pager. Nothing—and that meant all was still quiet in the ER.

Mark sat down across from her.

"How's your uncle?"

"He's feeling great. He's lost some weight and walks every day."

"And your aunt's piano lessons? Is she still playing?"

Mark nodded. "Uncle Chet bought her a beautiful piano. Had it delivered the other day." He raised one dark brown brow. "Too bad you missed her solo a couple of weeks ago."

"Sorry." Ravyn sipped her coffee.

"Stood me up and everything."

She laughed. "Well, if you would have allowed me to reply to your invitation, you would have known I wasn't available and saved yourself from being stood up."

"Okay, you win."

She glimpsed his wry grin before he took a drink from his tall Styrofoam cup.

Then his brows knitted together, forming a heavy frown. "You mentioned living in low-income units. I didn't know that."

"Yep. We lived in various rental units, all in rather seedy parts of the city, until I was about fifteen. Then my parents inherited the house they still live in today."

Mark pursed his lips in a thoughtful manner. "I always imagined your family living in a huge mansion—like movie stars."

"Hardly. We were dirt poor. But then my grandpa died and left my parents money. That eased our financial plight."

"I would have never guessed. Your folks are such classy and creative believers."

"Yes, they are, but class and creativity don't pay the bills and put food on the table. I believe there's a fine line between waiting on God and being plain ol' irresponsible."

A curious light sparked his dark brown eyes. "How so—if you don't mind me asking?"

"Well, either one of my parents could have gotten a paying job in between productions when times got tough. But they contended they were in full-time ministry and 'trusting the Lord.' They'd tell everyone who would listen about our needs, always insisting that 'God would provide.' Then the neighbors and church members donated stuff to us. It was like my parents were"—Ravyn waved a hand in the air, searching for the right analogy—"socially acceptable beggars."

Mark didn't reply but, instead, studied the rim of his coffee cup.

"I guess that's why I work so hard. I don't want to ever send my children to bed hungry."

He perked up. "Maybe you should work on getting the husband before worrying about any future kids."

Ravyn crumpled a paper napkin and flung it at him. "You know what I mean."

He chuckled and shot the wad back at her.

She successfully dodged the hit.

He leaned back in his chair, and all traces of humor vanished. "Doesn't sound like you have a very positive opinion about people in full-time ministry."

She shrugged. "I rather think some people use the term full-time ministry as an excuse not to work a regular job. I mean, isn't it true that we're all called to *full-time* ministry if we're Christians? I guess that's how I look at it."

"I can't argue," Mark said, sitting forward again. "When Jesus gave us the Great Commission, He didn't discriminate. He's an equal opportunity employer."

Ravyn grinned and sipped her coffee. She had to admit, if only to herself, that if Jesus were her earthly employer she'd probably get fired very soon.

Lord, just as soon as I save a little more money, I'll be able to think about You and attending church again. Promise. . .

Mark flicked a glance at his wristwatch. "I think my break is over."

"Mine, too." Ravyn stood.

They walked back to the ER, exchanging amicable banter and sharing a chuckle or two.

❧

Mark stopped in the small, unused office in which he'd been working, gathered the textbooks he used in preparation for his board exams, and sauntered out to the arena area where things were beginning to pick up. A man who'd been in a bar brawl needed his hand x-rayed, and a woman with an ankle injury was just being admitted.

Sitting down at a vacant workstation, Mark logged on to the computer. He flipped open one of the thick publications, but studying seemed impossible. He couldn't help watching Ravyn out of the corner of his eye. He wondered about her and would have never guessed she'd had a less than idyllic childhood. The Woodses always seemed like the perfect family to Mark. It pained him to hear Ravyn's parents put their ministry before their daughters' needs. But, he reasoned, perhaps that was why Ravyn made a good nurse; she'd had a lot of experience taking care of people.

She emerged from an exam room with a baby in her arms and Mark stared, half amused, half amazed. The child looked almost as big as she did. By the time he could think of forming the question, Liz, that little bulldog of a nurse, asked it for him.

"What are you doing with that kid?"

"Mrs. Rolland, in room 7, is going to x-ray, so I'm holding little Jessica." Ravyn bounced the baby on her hip. "She's almost six months old. Isn't she adorable?"

"What do you think this is, a day care?"

"No, it's night care." Ravyn laughed. "I mean, we are the *night shift*."

"Very funny." Liz stood with her hands on her hips.

Mark grinned at Ravyn's retort and returned his attention to his book, but he surreptitiously kept an ear on the conversation. He concluded Liz was Ravyn's preceptor, and while he respected the older woman and her nursing skills, he had a hunch that she was the instigator of much of the teasing and, possibly, the rumors around here. Regardless, Ravyn didn't seem intimidated.

Then, much to his surprise, Liz was soon *gaga*-ing and *goo-goo*-ing at the baby, making little Jessica smile.

Finally, the patient was returned to her exam room, and Ravyn took the child back to her mother. Mark figured he'd witnessed another example of Ravyn's care with people—babies, in this case.

He attempted, once again, to focus on his studying, but Mark's gaze kept wandering everywhere Ravyn did. He watched, fascinated, as she flitted around the ER. He noticed she did her best to exude a no-nonsense presence around co-workers, but Liz, it appeared, worked just as hard to act like a clown and make her laugh. Each time Liz succeeded, Mark had to smile, deciding, and not for the first time, that he enjoyed the sound of Ravyn's laughter.

Little by little, her personality emerged. She seemed dedicated to her job, sensitive toward the patients, and possessed a good, although guarded, sense of humor. She put up with her preceptor, after all, and Liz was a woman who thinned Mark's patience each time she called him George. But tonight he weathered the razzing so he could hang out in the arena area and continue his observation of Ravyn. In a word, he felt enchanted.

At long last, she plunked herself down in the chair beside him. "Need some help?"

"Nope."

"I don't mean to be nosy, but I don't think you've turned a single page of that textbook in the last hour."

Mark chuckled. "You're right. I haven't. I keep getting distracted." He sent her a meaningful look and she blushed to her hairline.

Conversation lagged as he regarded Ravyn and she him.

Finally, Mark scooted his chair closer to hers. He glanced around to make certain any curious nurses were out of earshot. "Hey, Ravyn," he said, his voice barely above a whisper, "how about the two of us going out to dinner sometime?"

She took several long seconds to consider his offer, but soon bobbed out a reply. "That would be nice. I'd enjoy it."

She smiled, causing Mark to grin.

Reaching into the pocket of his white overcoat, he pulled out his leather-bound calendar, containing his schedule. He opened it to the month of May. To his dismay, almost every square representing the days in that month had something scribbled on it.

Ravyn produced her schedule, too. Its cover was brightly colored and plastic-coated, and it was slightly larger than the size of a checkbook. She, also, opened to May. Doodles and appointment times filled the month. Coordinating an evening when they were both free wasn't going to be easy.

"This is going to take some doing." Mark glanced from her calendar to his.

Ravyn laughed and sat back in her chair. "I can't believe I've finally met a man whose hectic schedule resembles my own."

"Must be destiny."

"We'll see," she quipped.

Mark chuckled, but in his heart the word *destiny* rang out loud and clear.

❧❧

Mark sat at the desk in the family room, tapping the end of his pencil against his textbook. Next thing he knew, the writing utensil was snatched from his grasp.

"Will you knock it off, already? You're driving me crazy."

"Sorry, Uncle Chet." Mark stared up into the older man's age-lined face. "I'm just deep in thought."

"I know, but that tapping is as nerve-racking as a leaky faucet."

Mark chuckled.

Chet tossed the pencil on the desk. "What are you thinking so hard about? Your state boards?"

"No, but I should be." He slapped the book shut. His brain had absorbed all it could for one night. Sitting back in the wooden desk chair, Mark allowed his gaze to wander around the familiar, oak-paneled room. "I'm thinking about Ravyn."

"What, we got a bird around here?"

Mark looked up at the ceiling and groaned at the wisecrack.

His uncle snorted with laughter as he collapsed onto the black leather sofa. "I've heard you mention that girl's name quite a few times in the last week or so. Pretty gal."

"I agree."

"And she had the warmest fingers out of all the nurses who took care of me in the hospital."

"That's encouraging to hear." Mark lifted his stocking feet onto the corner of the mammoth oak desk.

"Being a nurse, she'd be a help to you on the mission field." Uncle Chet paused. "Of course, I'm being awfully presumptuous here."

Mark shrugged. "It's crossed my mind."

"Just don't let yourself get waylaid this late in the game."

"Don't worry. I won't."

Mark's conscience pricked. He wondered if he'd been waylaid already. Unfortunately, he hadn't told Ravyn about his plans to move overseas. He had a feeling she'd want nothing to do with him if she knew. She didn't seem to have much regard for people who made serving the Lord their life's ambition, and Mark guessed that her spiritual walk wasn't what it ought to be. Apart from being a registered nurse, she truly was the most unlikely candidate for a medical missionary's helpmeet.

Nevertheless, Mark felt compelled to pursue her.

Compelled—or did he just feel challenged?

He looked over at his uncle, who stared back at him.

"Am I detecting a slight problem regarding a certain pretty nurse?"

"Maybe." Mark put his hands behind his head. "But I'm not ready to discuss it yet."

"Okay." Uncle Chet looked away and picked up the remote off the sturdy coffee table. He pointed it at the wide-screen TV. "In that case, I'm turning on the basketball game."

Chapter 7

Another quiet night in the ER. Ravyn stifled a yawn and flipped through the pages of the Pottery Barn's most recent catalog. Her shift seemed to drag on forever when nights were slow like this. She noticed that Mark, on the other hand, relished the extra time he could spend studying. He had less than three weeks to go until he finished his residency program.

Ravyn paused to scrutinize the wood table and four matching chairs in the thick, glossy advertisement. She tried to envision Mark sitting there in her kitchen, drinking his morning coffee.

She gave herself a mental shake, realizing the direction in which her thoughts had strayed. She'd had too much time for pondering lately—and more often than not the topic of her musing was Mark.

Must be spring fever.

She stood, then strode across the nursing station and handed off her catalog to a nurse named Betsy who had asked to see it next. Ravyn stifled another yawn and decided that, with the ER still quiet, she'd head for the lower level cafeteria and buy some flavored coffee.

She made her way through the silent hallways. Reaching the coffee bar, she selected the mocha caramel blend before heading to the cash register. She was just checking out when her pager's high-pitched, consecutive bleeps gave her a start. Several hospital staff members in line behind her chuckled when she jumped.

Finishing the exchange with the cashier, Ravyn glanced at the pager. It read: TRAUMA. 16 YOM. GSW ABD. ETA 7 MIN.

Adrenalin rushed through her body and filled her limbs. A teenager with a gunshot wound to his abdomen was on his way into the trauma center. Ravyn dropped the pager back into her pocket and, steaming java in hand, ran for the ER.

She took the steps, two by two, and when she arrived in the arena, she set down her coffee in the back of an unused work area. Next, she dashed for the trauma room—the four-bed unit, separate from the main part of the ER. A flurry of activity ensued. Residents, nurses, the staff MD, lab, and x-ray personnel were suiting up, pulling the protective clothing over their hospital scrubs.

Ravyn quickly slipped the leaded vest over her scrubs top. The weighty garment would protect her from the x-ray machines' harmful radiation. Next she pulled on a disposable gown and cap, a mask with its clear plastic eye shield, and, lastly, the latex-free gloves. She took her place at a sterile, linen-covered gurney.

This was her first trauma without her preceptor's help, and she wanted to do her best. What's more, Mark would take the helm under the direction of the ER's staff physician. Ravyn hoped to prove herself to him and the rest of the team.

The ambulance arrived and the patient was transported from the vehicle into the trauma room. The paramedics updated the medical team while the patient was loaded onto the gurney.

Everyone raced into action. Medical personnel pressed in around the patient, examining his wound and checking his vital signs.

Mark stood at the head of the bed, calling out orders and talking to the patient. "What's your name?"

"Jace." The name sounded muffled from under the oxygen mask covering his nose and mouth.

After the initial assessment, Mark called for the radiology staff. Everyone shifted, making room for the portable x-ray machine.

As Ravyn threaded the IV needle into the teen's arm, he moaned. Mark continued asking him questions. Where was the pain? Did he have trouble breathing? The young man answered and Ravyn happened to look up just in time to glimpse the fear in his blue eyes.

"Don't let me die," Jace eked out, staring directly at her. "Please. Don't let me die."

"We're all doing our best. Just relax." A haunting feeling descended over Ravyn's being, but she pushed it aside and concentrated on her job.

More staff pressed in around the bed as the flurry of activity continued. But moments later, the teen's blood pressure dropped. His heartbeat raced.

"We're losing him!" another nurse called out.

The patient lost consciousness.

Mark listed off the medications he wanted administered and Ravyn set to task. To assist with Jace's breathing, the staff intubated him and, finally, his vital signs were stable again. Several members of the trauma team whisked him off to the radiology department for a CAT scan, and the trauma surgeon was called.

Ravyn stayed behind and helped the other nurses with their portion of the cleanup before the housekeeping personnel came in. She prayed the gunshot wound patient would recover, and his plea not to let him die played over and over inside her head. So young—just sixteen years old. Ravyn's heart broke, not only for him but for his family. Jace was somebody's son, somebody's brother.

Oh, God, she breathed in prayer, *let him be okay.*

🐝🦋

Back to an all too quiet ER. By now the nursing staff had learned the trauma patient's full name: Jace Lichton. Ravyn had overheard the social worker say that the young man had been involved in a fight over a girl when his opponent pulled out a gun and shot him.

As Ravyn busied herself with miscellaneous paperwork, she thought about the senselessness of the tragedy. Still, she continued to hope and pray that Jace would survive. She kept watching the clock, but no news came from the surgery team.

The hours ticked by at an agonizingly slow rate. Finally, she couldn't stand the waiting anymore and persuaded Liz to tap her resources. But even the veteran nurse couldn't find out Jace's fate, other than that he was still in surgery.

At last, the scuttlebutt that George was on his way to the ER reached Ravyn's ears. She felt herself tense, praying she'd hear something positive from Mark.

He reentered the emergency room with two other residents. Ravyn watched from the far side of the nurse's station as he shook his head—a somber reply to Liz's query.

Jace didn't make it. Tears blurred Ravyn's vision but she blinked them back. She felt almost alarmed at her show of emotion. It wasn't like her and it wasn't professional.

Drawing in a calming breath, she continued opening plastic-sealed forms and filing them on the appropriate shelves. Busywork. Something to do. But, perhaps, this sort of work was all she was cut out for. The caustic thought ate away at her confidence, and soon she wondered if she'd really make an effective emergency room nurse. The surgical wing at the other hospital had been so different. More controlled and less—*traumatic.* Now she felt unskilled and ill prepared.

Mark approached Ravyn with the bad news. "Our trauma patient died in the ICU."

"I gathered as much." She cleared her throat to keep her emotions at bay, not daring to envision the sad scene with Jace's family around his bedside in the intensive care unit. "That's really a shame."

"I'll say. Only sixteen years old." Mark sat down on the edge of the desk. "Bullet nicked his aorta and—"

"Mark, please." Ravyn felt her throat tightening and held up a hand. "I don't want to know the details. We did what we could. That's all that matters."

She turned and walked away, leaving the forms spread across the work area. She had a half hour until her shift ended, and since she hadn't taken an official break, Ravyn decided to wait out her time in the women's locker room.

Once she got home she'd have a good, hard cry.

❧

Mark yawned as he braked for a red light at a busy intersection. He'd been thinking about Ravyn as he drove home, and he sensed something wasn't right between them. Had he offended her? She'd morphed back into an ice princess and he'd thought they'd long since gotten past those cold shoulder reactions. He'd found out from other nurses that she'd been asking about the trauma patient. Was she upset about his death?

"You're home early." Aunt Edy met him at the back door.

"I start first shift tomorrow, so I've got the rest of the day off." Mark strode to the refrigerator and opened the door, looking for something to munch on.

"I made rhubarb pie."

The statement captured Mark's attention. He closed the fridge, turned, and watched Aunt Edy take a plate from the cupboard. Next she sliced a large piece of the tart treat, set it on the plate, and handed it to him. Mark pulled a fork from the silverware drawer and took a big bite of pie.

"Mmm, good stuff."

She smiled, looking pleased. "Did you get any sleep last night?"

"A little."

"What's on the agenda for today?"

"Well. . ." Mark gulped down another forkful of pie. "Uncle Chet asked me to mow the lawn, so I'll do that."

"Good. I've been worried he'd try to do it himself."

Mark acknowledged the remark with a nod. "But first I want to see if I can get a hold of Ravyn. We had a trauma last night and the patient didn't make it. I think it upset her. Could be my imagination, though, or maybe Ravyn just had a bad day, but I'd feel better if I could talk to her and make sure. Problem is I don't have her phone number, although. . ." He paused to form his plan. "I suppose I could call her folks."

"You care about this girl, don't you?"

Mark attempted a reply but his aunt kept talking.

"I've always liked Ravyn. She's a sweet little thing."

Mark just grinned.

"Sort of seems natural, doesn't it? You're a doctor. She's a nurse."

"We'll see, Aunt Edy." He laughed, partly to hide his sudden embarrassment.

"Tell you what," she continued, "if you'll mow the lawn now before Chet gets any big ideas, I'll call Zann Woods and get Ravyn's phone number for you."

"Okay, but please be discreet. I don't want to alarm the Woodses, nor do I want them to think there's more going on between Ravyn and me than there really is."

"I'll be as discreet as a church whisper."

"Oh, brother! Now I'm worried."

Aunt Edy waved off the teasing with a flick of her small wrist. "Go mow the lawn, would you?"

"Yes, ma'am."

He moved away from the counter, but not before he saw the determined gleam enter his great-aunt's eyes. Mark guessed that she was suddenly a woman on a mission.

Chapter 8

Ravyn stared out the kitchen window, over the lush green golf course. Several golf carts with white canopies puttered along the fairway. As she sipped her latte, she could hardly believe she was enjoying breakfast at four o'clock in the afternoon. But after she'd arrived home this morning and indulged in a private sob session, she'd taken a shower, then fallen into bed and slept for the next six hours. Sleeping did wonders for her mind and body, and her perspective seemed brighter, although a niggling doubt about her nursing abilities remained. Never before had she doubted herself and her future. But she kept recalling the teen's pleas to save his life, and the memory beleaguered her until she began to seriously question whether she had what it took to be an ER nurse. Maybe she didn't. She couldn't help save Jace's life, and the pain caused by that fact didn't seem worth any sort of financial gain.

Suddenly Ravyn found her goals slipping from her grasp.

The doorbell buzzed, startling her from her personal pity party. She traipsed to the door, half expecting her visitor to be Teala, so she was surprised to hear a man's deep voice resound through the intercom.

"Ravyn? Ravyn, it's Mark."

Her shock mounted. *Mark?* How did he get her address?

She buzzed him up from the secured lower lobby, only to realize she looked like a veritable slob in her oversized sweatshirt, blue jeans, and fuzzy pink slippers.

She dashed into the bathroom and gave her ebony tresses a good brushing. As she did so, she stared at her reflection. Her dark eyes looked sad and the skin below them was so transparent it almost appeared bruised. Her cheeks seemed paler than usual and, overall, she decided she resembled a drowned kitten.

Great. Just great.

The condo's doorbell chimed and reluctance weighted Ravyn's every step as she went to answer it. She opened the four-paneled door with the chain still secured and peered through the narrow opening to be sure the visitor was, indeed, Mark. Then in three succinct moves she closed the door, unlocked it, and opened it again.

"What are you doing here?"

He gave her a disarming smile. "Can I come in?"

"Sure." Ravyn opened the door wider and bid him entry. "Sit down. Make yourself comfortable."

He walked in and she shut the door behind him. She watched as he glanced around the living room area.

"Nice place."

"Thanks. I just moved in last month and I'm still getting settled."

Mark lowered himself onto the sofa and Ravyn saw his gaze stop at her pink slippers.

"Cute." An amused grin curved his lips.

She shrugged in hopes of covering her embarrassment. "Look, you can't expect much when you come over unannounced, okay?"

"I'll keep that in mind."

Ravyn ignored his laughing expression. "Want some coffee? I have a latte machine."

He held up a hand. "No thanks. I have to sleep tonight. I start first shift tomorrow and then I'm on call for the next twenty-four hours."

Ravyn sent him a sympathetic grin and sat down beside him. It was either that or take a seat on the floor; she hadn't gotten around to purchasing coordinating furniture yet.

The smell of his musky spice-scented cologne wafted to her nose, and she noticed he looked quite appealing in his blue jeans and aquamarine crewneck sweater with its sleeves pushed up on his forearms.

She corralled her wayward thoughts. "So, um, what did you want to talk to me about? And how did you find me?"

"In answer to your last question first," he replied, still looking amused, "my aunt called your parents' house." He lazed back against the throw pillows. "Initially, I just wanted your phone number, but once I had your address, too, I figured I'd stop by rather than call."

Tucking one leg beneath her, Ravyn shifted her weight sideways, facing him. "Must be important."

"I thought so. I was worried about you. You seemed upset this morning when you left work, and I wondered if it had to do with our trauma patient."

Ravyn suddenly felt as though she might burst into tears all over again. However, she hesitated to admit the fact to Mark. She didn't want him to doubt her nursing skills even though she herself was doing that very thing.

"Listen, if it's any consolation, feeling bad after a patient dies only makes you as human as the rest of us," Mark said. "We care about people. That's why we chose the health-care profession."

She gaped at him. "Are you a mind reader, or what?"

Mark chuckled. "You're easy to read."

She glanced down at her blue jeans and picked at a fray in the seam. "I care about people, but I also wanted a good-paying job. A job in the medical field seemed to fit the bill."

"Ditto."

Ravyn looked back up at Mark. Maybe they had more in common than she ever realized.

And maybe he'd be the one who would understand.

"I just don't feel like much of a nurse right now."

Mark stretched his arm across the back of the couch. "You're really beating yourself up, aren't you?"

"That kid begged me not to let him die," Ravyn said, tears clouding her vision. "I felt so helpless."

"Join the club. I was the guy calling the shots. I couldn't save him, either. Nor could the trauma surgeon. But we all did the best we could." He paused before adding, "The truth is, our powers are limited."

"I know that on an intellectual and spiritual level." She expelled a weary breath. "But somehow I let my emotions get all tangled up in the incident, and there is no room for emotions in the medical field."

"True. But we're not exactly robots, either."

His expression said he related to her feelings, and Ravyn felt grateful. If she had tried to talk to Teala about this, her sister would have never been able to understand.

"You're an excellent nurse. I've seen you in action."

"Thanks." She lowered her gaze, wishing his compliment would sink in so she'd believe it herself.

"You're kind to the patients, and you endure your co-workers without complaint. The latter's quite admirable."

Catching the facetiousness in his voice, she looked up and saw him grin. She smiled at his comment, but moments later a sincere light entered Mark's dark gaze that made her breath catch.

His hand moved from its resting place along the top of the sofa, and with his forefinger, he caressed her cheek.

Time stood still. Ravyn couldn't think straight. Then Mark leaned forward and touched his lips to hers. The tender kiss made her feel heady, and it was sweeter than she remembered from a decade ago.

And on that thought her senses returned.

Ravyn placed her hands on his shoulders and pushed him away.

A little frown marred his forehead.

"Mark, is this for real or—" She narrowed her gaze at him. "Or are you just a smooth operator?"

He pulled his chin back, as if insulted, and Ravyn almost apologized. Almost. Lately she doubted everyone's motives.

She tossed the pillow aside and stood. "For your information, I'm not that kind of a girl."

As she strode to the kitchen, she hoped Mark would be offended enough to leave. Instead, he followed her, caught her wrist, and spun her around to face him. His grip was strong yet gentle, determined but hardly rough.

"For your information," he countered, "I'm not that kind of a guy."

She stared up at him, unsure of what to say.

"The truth is, I care about you, Ravyn." With that, Mark released her wrist and gathered her into his arms. His voice was but a whisper. "Can't you tell?"

"Well, yes, but—" She felt almost dazed.

"But what?"

Within the warm circumference of his arms, all words escaped her. He kissed her again and this time Ravyn didn't push him away. But just as her knees grew weak and his hold around her waist tightened, the sharp buzzer from downstairs sounded.

Ravyn jumped.

"Whoa, a little edgy, huh?" Mark laughed and released her. "No more lattes for you."

It took a good moment for her wits to return, and she fought the disappointment that enveloped her. She had enjoyed that brief romantic interlude.

She trudged to the door. "This is probably my sister Teala."

Mark shrugged and sat back down on the sofa. "I'll consider myself fairly warned."

She grinned, but when her mother's worried voice echoed through the intercom, Ravyn felt anything but amused.

"Honey, buzz me in. I want to make sure you're okay. A doctor was looking for you this afternoon. Are you sick? What's the matter? Let me in."

"It's my mother." Ravyn glanced at Mark. "You can escape out the patio door."

He regarded her askance. "Are you telling or suggesting?"

"Suggesting."

He smiled. "Then I'll stay. I always liked your mom."

"O–ka–ay."

She pressed the button that unlocked the lower-level entrance. Within a few moments, Zann Woods appeared at the doorway, a springtime vision in a flowing patchwork-printed skirt, white blouse, and tan, wide-brimmed hat. Ravyn thought her mom looked like she'd stepped out of a pastoral painting. The only missing element was a bouquet of wildflowers in one hand.

"What's wrong?" Zann's frown furrowed her deep brown eyebrows. "You do look peaked. Are you okay?"

"I'm fine." Ravyn waved her in and after her mother's strappy-sandaled feet stepped into the tiny foyer, she closed the door. "You remember Mark Monroe. He's *Doctor* Monroe now."

"Of course. Hello, Mark." Ravyn watched as her mother crossed the room and headed for him with an outstretched hand. "How nice to see you again." She glanced at Ravyn, then looked back at Mark. "When Violet said a doctor needed Ravyn's address and phone number, I thought. . ." Her gaze returned to Ravyn. "Well, naturally, I assumed it wasn't for a social call. I was thinking more along the lines of pneumonia or a car accident."

"No, Mom, I'm really fine."

The buzzer sounded again.

"That would be your father."

"Dad's here?" Ravyn couldn't contain her shock.

Her mother removed her hat and shook out her brown-black hair with its streaks of silver. "He was worried about you, too."

One glance at Mark's composure and polite smile told Ravyn he wasn't the least bit concerned. But as she buzzed her dad upstairs, she almost felt sorry for Mark. If the interrogation matched the one that Teala's boyfriend Greg underwent, the word *drama* wouldn't come close to describing it.

Her heart sank. After this evening, Mark might not care about her as much as he thought.

🐝

"And just what are your intentions concerning my daughter?"

"Dad!"

He laughed and gave Ravyn a juicy-sounding kiss on the cheek.

"I'm glad you're all right, sweetheart."

"I'm fine."

"And now for you, young man—"

"Oh, Dad—please. Mark is my guest."

"So I see." He grinned and stuck out his right hand.

While shaking Alfred Woods's thin hand, Mark smiled at Ravyn's obvious embarrassment. He knew the older man was just giving him a hard time. Mark could tell by the way he purposely dipped one grayish blond eyebrow.

Al chuckled. "How long has it been, Mark?"

"A long time."

"A lifetime ago."

Mark nodded. "Just about."

"Ravyn, where did you get this sofa?" Zann asked, changing the subject. She sat down, running her hand over the armrest. "I hope you didn't pay full price for it. I recently saw one exactly like this at the secondhand shop downtown. I know the manager. She probably would have given it to you for free."

Mark caught Ravyn's exasperated expression before she walked toward the kitchen.

Al stood, arms akimbo. "I think you need some more chairs in here, honey."

The last word had just parted his lips when Ravyn returned, carrying a wooden kitchen chair under each arm. Mark guessed they weighed more than she did, and he rushed to take them from her.

He set down a chair for Al, who lowered his tall, lanky frame onto the hard seat. Mark then claimed the second chair for himself. Ravyn sat down beside her mother.

"I appreciate your concern," Ravyn said, "but if you both would have called I could have saved you a trip across town."

"Guess we wanted to see for ourselves," Zann said.

"So, Mark." Al cleared his throat. "What made you decide to give up a career in theater and go into medicine?"

"The paycheck for one," Ravyn said.

Mark chuckled.

"Well, I really thought you had potential on the stage," Al continued. "And as I recall, you had a serious desire for the ministry."

"Still do. That part hasn't changed." Mark stopped short of sharing his plans to travel overseas and work as a medical missionary. But why? Was it because he feared Ravyn's possible rejection of the idea—and of him?

He regarded her as she sat curled up at one end of the sofa. She appeared so small and helpless that Mark had to fight the urge to sit beside her and slip a protective arm around her shoulders. However, he had the strong impression the word *helpless* didn't accurately describe Ravyn Woods. In spite of her petite frame, she was a capable woman.

But was she a derailment or the woman God wanted him to pursue? Mark did, indeed, care about Ravyn—more than he understood—and he sensed he was helping her over some emotional hurdles. But where was their relationship headed?

He decided that perhaps Al Woods had started off by asking the appropriate question after all: Just what were his intentions, anyway?

Chapter 9

For the days that followed, Ravyn couldn't shake off the dark cloud of gloom that seemed to follow her everywhere she went. Her conversation with Mark had been an encouragement, and his kiss was like sweet salve on her wounded spirit. Her parents' visit had turned quite amusing as they, along with Mark and Ravyn, reminisced about that summer a decade ago in which Mark had the lead role in Dad's play. They laughed about things that Ravyn had long since forgotten, and they mentioned people she'd never forget—such as her former friend Shelley. Then, after ordering pizza, Mark suggested he and Ravyn look her up and give her a call. Make peace with the past, so to speak. Ravyn supposed it was worth a try, although she couldn't imagine when she'd have time to plan a visit, assuming Shelley agreed to it. As it was, Ravyn and Mark were still trying to free up one Saturday night from their schedules so they could go out to dinner.

But even with those issues occupying a corner of her mind, a more recent matter weighed on her conscience: Jace, last week's shooting victim. The tragedy had affected her more than she cared to admit. In fact, she felt so troubled about it that on Mother's Day she didn't need to be begged or coerced into attending the church service with her family. She came of her own free will. Mom was thrilled.

There, in the gleaming wooden pew, Ravyn sat sandwiched between her two sisters. Their parents occupied the two places on one side of them and Teala's boyfriend, Greg, sat on the other.

Ravyn glanced at her parents. Her mother had dressed in a colorful outfit while Dad wore an outdated brown suit that looked almost fashionable again. They turned her way and Ravyn gave them a smile. For all their mistakes when she was growing up, Ravyn never doubted that her folks loved her.

She never doubted that God loved her, either. She just figured He would wait patiently for her, perfect Hero that He was, until she got her life's plan set in motion and came back to Him.

It won't be long now, Lord, she promised. *I'm well on my way to achieving my goals.*

A group of children made their way to the front of the small church and took their places on the three long steps of the altar's platform. They wiggled and grinned, and a few waved to their parents. However, they quickly donned serious expressions as the choir director commanded their attention.

The pianist began to play and the children sang.

> When we walk with the Lord
> In the light of His Word,
> What a glory He sheds on our way!
> While we do His good will
> He abides with us still,
> And with all who will trust and obey.

Ravyn smiled. She knew the old hymn well—as well as she knew her own name.

> Trust and obey—
> For there's no other way
> To be happy in Jesus,
> But to trust and obey.

The familiar and fundamental message burned within her heart. Trust and obey—no other way—happy in Jesus.

She suddenly longed for simpler days. She wished she had her younger sisters' vibrant outlooks on life. Ravyn could only recall how depressed she'd been feeling. The stress of her new job in the ER combined with the tragedy of experiencing a patient's death had depleted her courage and motivation and put a large chink in her sensibilities.

Lord, I just want to be happy again.

"Then 'trust and obey,'" she seemed to hear God say. "*Don't be troubled about anything.*"

Ravyn recalled the biblical command and felt led to read the rest of the passage. She lifted her small Bible and as the children began singing the third stanza, she flipped through the pages of the New Testament until she found the verses in Philippians 4.

> But in everything, by prayer and petition, with thanksgiving, present your requests to God. And the peace of God, which transcends all understanding, will guard your hearts and your minds in Christ Jesus.

Ravyn closed her Bible and settled back into the pew. She relaxed her mind and made the decision to trust and obey. God was here in this sanctuary. She felt His presence. Like the scriptures taught, His arm was not so short that it could not save. God was able to steer her life back on course. She believed what the Bible said was true.

A languid peace flowed through her veins and, yes, she even felt a swell of happiness. Trust and obey.

It had been years since she'd heard God's still small voice—

And it had been even longer since she had listened.

🙢

"Hey, Monroe!"

Mark turned and waited in the hallway as Geoff Ling, a fellow resident, approached him.

"Got something for you." He handed Mark a square, white envelope. "Is it your birthday?"

"Nope." Mark inspected the handwriting but didn't recognize it.

The Asian American doctor peered through his glasses at Mark. "One of the ER nurses gave it to me on her way out—said she was hoping to run into you last night."

Mark immediately thought of Ravyn. "I got tied up with consults."

"Too bad. She's pretty. Black hair, dark eyes—"

"I know who you mean."

"Figured you did." The guy gave Mark a friendly sock in the arm. "They don't call you George down there for nothing."

"Oh, cut it out. You know I hate that."

Geoff snickered in a good-natured manner and went on his way.

Mark tore into the envelope and pulled out the yellow greeting card. The words *THANK YOU* were embossed on its front. Curious, he opened it and read the words Ravyn had scribed.

> *Thanks for your listening ear. You were a big help in encouraging me. In church on Sunday, the Lord really spoke to my heart and that uplifted me more than anything. This morning I read from the book of Philippians. Funny how I'd forgotten all about God's command to "be anxious for nothing." I decided I'd better obey.*

Mark grinned at the smiley face Ravyn drew. He felt encouraged. Highly encouraged.

Smiling, he tucked the card into his white jacket pocket and returned to the nursing station to tie up any loose ends before going home. All night long, new patients arrived in the ER, nurses had questions, and every so often one of his cronies spotted him, walked over, and started up a conversation. Most of his fellow residents, Mark had learned, were either pursuing a specialty here at Victory and/or had careers lined up at clinics or at other hospitals. Several of them were engaged and planned to get married this summer.

He squelched the pangs of envy. A family of his own appealed to Mark, although he knew it couldn't take precedence over the plans he already had in place. They began with a long overdue visit to New Hampshire where he'd spend some time with his family. After that, he'd start the candidating process, visiting two churches a week and gathering support for the mission field. By January of next year, Mark planned to join the team of medical personnel with whom he'd been corresponding via the Internet and occasional phone calls.

He sat down and drew in a deep breath. He needed to share his vision for his future with Ravyn soon, before she heard about it from someone else.

He patted the card in his pocket. Maybe now she was ready to hear about it.

Ravyn gave her reflection one last look and decided the kiwi green tank top and coordinating cardigan matched nicely with her navy capris. The dark blue slip-ons completed the outfit and gave her some height. Ravyn felt satisfied that she'd dressed appropriately for a casual dinner with Mark tonight. If she felt too warm, she could take off the lightweight sweater, and if the air conditioning in the riverfront restaurant had been cranked up, she wouldn't freeze.

We actually coordinated our schedules. She still couldn't believe it. Ravyn hadn't made time for a date in years; she usually opted to work an extra shift and make money. But, lately, she made time for the people in her life. She talked to Teala, her parents, and Violet nearly every day, relying less on her answering machine. Three times this week Mark had called, and Ravyn stopped whatever she'd been doing to converse with him. They'd turned out to be lengthy chats, too, but Ravyn enjoyed each minute.

And now their first official date.

She strode through the hallway of her posh condominium and paused at the kitchen table where she gathered her cell phone, sunglasses, and car keys. After slinging her small handbag's leather strap over her wrist, she continued out the door and into the underground parking area.

Today had been unseasonably hot in northeast Iowa for this last weekend in May. Temperatures soared well into the nineties, but the air felt cool and dry in the basement area. Ravyn climbed into her car and started its engine, then drove out into the blinding sunshine. Before long, she began to perspire, so she closed the windows and turned on her vehicle's air conditioning.

As she drove through the hilly streets of Dubuque, Ravyn wished she had allowed Mark to pick her up like he'd offered. However, being the ever-independent woman, she chose to drive herself to the restaurant, but she'd forgotten it meant going through a rather seedy part of town. Seeing people on the sidewalks and street corners, laughing and carousing, Ravyn thought of how busy the ER would likely be tonight. The warm weather seemed to draw revelers from their homes and into the bars. Already she heard sirens in the distance.

Her cell phone rang and Ravyn worked the hands-free earpiece into place before answering the call.

"Hi, Rav," said Teala. "A few of us girls are going out for a pizza tonight. And guess who's coming? Carolyn Baker. You two haven't seen each other in eons. Want to come out with us?"

Ravyn couldn't help the smile. "Nope. I have a date."

Silence at the other end.

"Teala, I have never known you to be rendered speechless."

"Wow, we must have a really bad connection. I thought you just said you had a date."

Ravyn laughed, knowing her sister's facetious streak. "Oh, hush up. I'm going to dinner with Mark tonight. I guess it is an official date, but we're still just friends. I think."

"Your first date with Mark, huh?" Teala sighed. "I remember when Greg and I first started seeing each other—officially."

Ravyn had heard this story a hundred times, but she listened to it again. In fact, her younger sister talked for the rest of the drive to the steak house where Ravyn had agreed to meet Mark.

"Hey, Teala, I've got to disconnect. I'm at the restaurant now."

"Okay, *ciao*."

Ravyn found a rare parking spot near the entrance and pulled alongside the curb. She unplugged her earpiece, then stuffed her cell phone into her leather handbag.

For a moment she sat behind the steering wheel and watched the many passersby. This was a bustling part of the city because of its close proximity to the Mississippi River and its subsequent recreational areas. The restaurant would probably be noisy and crowded, but oddly, Ravyn felt hardly intimidated. She was more looking forward to dining with Mark than worrying about getting shuffled about by pushy patrons.

An odd mix of anxious flutters and anticipation multiplied inside her. She bowed her head in a silent, quick prayer.

Lord, this thing with Mark—I think I'm a little scared. Losing my friend Shelley was tough; I can't imagine losing my heart. Will You please show me if this is a relationship worth pursuing?

Ravyn finished the petition to her heavenly Father before opening her eyes and glancing up—just in time to see Mark enter the restaurant with a tall, full-figured blond. Ravyn recognized the woman at once.

It was Carla, the x-ray tech from work!

Chapter 10

Ravyn wrapped her palms around the steering wheel, wondering if she should take flight or fight. Mark wouldn't have been stupid enough to ask her out on the same night he asked Carla for a date—would he? But, perhaps, in all the busyness of finishing his residency, his schedule got mixed up.

No, it couldn't be.

Or could it?

Curiosity won over indignation as Ravyn climbed out of the car and stepped into the shadows of the historical red-brick building. She yanked open the rough-hewn door, using more force than necessary, and stomped inside the dimly lit establishment. She almost collided with Mark as her eyes adjusted from the sunlight.

Before even uttering a greeting, he cupped her upper arm and led her toward the restrooms. "Ravyn, I need your help." She felt his lips near her ear, drowning out the loud music. "On my way in, I met up with Carla. I don't know where she came from, but she's got a head laceration. I told her to wash up and then I'd look at it." Mark steered Ravyn toward the ladies' room. "Can you go in and check on her?"

She pulled out of his grasp. "Give me a break. Carla's an x-ray tech. She's more than capable of washing a gash on her head."

"ETOH."

That's all Mark had to say. Ravyn was well acquainted with the acronym. She arched her brows. "Carla's drunk?"

"Extremely."

Ravyn winced with embarrassment for overreacting. "All right. I'll check on her."

She entered the restroom, unable to ignore the relief zinging its way through her limbs, but stopped short when she saw the shapely x-ray tech sprawled out on the brown and beige tiled floor. Her back was up against the wall and her legs stretched out in front of her. Blood stained her long blond hair and the front of her two-sizes-too-small white T-shirt.

After setting down her purse near one of the three porcelain sinks, Ravyn knelt beside her co-worker. "Hey, Carla? It's me. Ravyn. Looks like you hurt yourself. What happened?" Ravyn carefully picked at strands of Carla's blond hair in order to get a look at the wound.

"I fell."

A knock sounded on the restroom door. Ravyn stood, crossed to the door, and opened it to find Mark standing there. He held out a pair of protective gloves.

"The bartender said he keeps a box of these handy. I s'pose that's not a bad idea in his line of work."

"Thanks." Ravyn sent Mark a grateful smile, took the proffered gloves, and let the door close. She pulled the protective coverings over her hands and returned to inspecting Carla's wound. Sorting through crusty strands of blond hair, she still couldn't see the woman's scalp. She stood and wetted some paper towels and tried again.

On her knees next to her co-worker, Ravyn did her best to clean the area. All the while she felt the other woman's stare.

Finally, she met Carla's gaze and momentarily scrutinized her features. Ravyn hadn't ever seen her up close before and never paid her much attention. She assumed they were peers, but now Ravyn realized that Carla couldn't be any older than twenty-one. Not any older than Teala.

"You hate me, don't you?" Carla muttered.

"I don't hate anyone."

Locating the laceration, Ravyn realized it required stitches. She straightened and crossed the room. She used another piece of paper towel to pull on the door handle. Mark stood several feet away and she motioned to him.

"She's going to need some sutures and, considering her condition, maybe we ought to call an ambulance."

"Good as done." Mark pulled his cell phone from out of the pocket of khaki pants.

Once again, Ravyn let the door close and turned back to Carla, who continued her ramblings about how everyone from her boyfriend to her mother "hated her." After soaking more paper towels in cold water, Ravyn hunkered down and held the wad against her co-worker's head. She watched as a tear slipped from the younger woman's left eye and drizzled down her sunburned cheek.

"Don't cry. It's okay."

A strange sense of pity engulfed Ravyn. She found it odd when usually she felt almost hard-hearted toward intoxicated individuals. She had observed a number of drunken souls at the low-income housing units in which her family had lived. But this instance seemed different—perhaps because Carla was a co-worker.

Ravyn recalled what she knew of Carla. She was never boisterous at work, like Liz, but kept mostly to herself. Her only fault, as far as Ravyn knew, was hanging out with a bunch of staff who enjoyed boozing at breakfast.

That, and lying about Mark, of course.

Carla began to sob, and while Ravyn suspected the show of emotion was alcohol-induced, she couldn't help feeling sorry for her.

"It's okay," Ravyn repeated. Her own sob session last week came to mind—one that couldn't even be blamed on alcohol consumption—and her empathy for Carla mounted. She, like so many people, needed help—needed to know God. Was this Carla's cry for help?

As if in reply, more tears cascaded down Carla's pink cheeks.

"Shh." Ravyn looped one arm around the younger woman's shoulders. "Everything's going to be all right."

"Maybe for you," Carla eked out. "You're dating a doctor who's not only great-looking and single, he's really nice, too." She choked back another sob. "My boyfriend can't seem to hold a job for more than two weeks. When he runs out of money it's suddenly *my* fault."

"Find another boyfriend." The answer seemed easy enough to Ravyn.

Carla tipped her head, giving Ravyn a curious stare. "In case you hadn't noticed, there aren't that many guys around to choose from these days. Half of them are married. The other half are divorced and come complete with court-ordered alimony payments. Either that or they have issues—like felony convictions."

"Where do you go to meet these guys? They sound like losers with a capital *L*." Ravyn shook her head. "Seriously, Carla, I think you're in need of a new hangout."

"Yeah? Like where? I suppose I could play Bingo on Friday nights at church with all the boring religious people."

Ravyn grinned. "Mark's religious. So am I. We're both born-again Christians."

Carla didn't look surprised, although she didn't have a comeback, either, but Ravyn let it go. She suspected her intoxicated co-worker wouldn't remember much of what went on in here tonight; however, by God's grace, a seed could have been planted.

A seed. . . As the thought took shape, Ravyn felt suddenly privileged that God would use her to plant a seed of faith in another person's life. She didn't deserve to be an instrument of God's love; she could count on one hand all the times she'd attended church in the past year. Yet here she sat, on a cold, tiled floor with a hurting soul in her arms. Ravyn knew this event was no coincidence.

A hard knock sounded at the door, jarring Ravyn from her thoughts. She looked up to see Mark peer into the restroom. His dark gaze found Ravyn's. "Paramedics are here."

"Great. We're ready for them."

❧

"Admit it," Mark said, grinning and pointing his fork at her. "When you walked into the restaurant, you were ready to chew me up and spit me out. I saw that gleam in your eyes."

"Gleam?" Ravyn batted her lashes in feigned innocence. "I have no idea what you're talking about." She sipped her diet cola.

"Whatever."

Ravyn tried not to laugh at Mark's skeptical expression.

After the ambulance arrived and transported Carla to the hospital, Ravyn had needed to change clothes. Since she had to return to her condo anyway, she'd suggested that she and Mark eat at the restaurant on the complex's lavish grounds. The temperature had cooled and it seemed a perfect evening to dine on the restaurant's patio, which overlooked the eighteenth hole.

"Do you play golf?" Mark asked, cutting his veal.

"I've played in the past, but that's not why I bought a condo here at The Pines, if that's what you're wondering." Ravyn watched the wind tousle his dark brown hair. "I think it's pretty out here. It's a gated community and each section of condos has a locked lobby, so I feel safe."

"That's important—to feel safe."

Ravyn agreed.

"I've often heard the safest place to be is in God's will, no matter where you're at here on earth, even if you live in the toughest of neighborhoods."

"Hmm." Ravyn gave it a moment's thought. "Yeah, I suppose that's true enough."

She thought back on her growing-up years in the rundown public housing units. Her parents had left Ravyn and her sisters so vulnerable and unprotected around the riffraff they called neighbors. Anything could have happened to them. But, as Ravyn's father was fond of pointing out, God had, indeed, protected them.

"I forgot. I have something for you." Mark stood and pulled what appeared to be a small envelope from the back pocket of his trousers. He reseated himself, then slid the paper item across the white wrought-iron table. "It's an invitation. My aunt feels compelled to have a party for me, although I've told her it isn't necessary." A look of embarrassment heightened the ruddy hue of his cheeks. It was a nice contrast, Ravyn thought, with the deep green polo shirt he wore.

"I don't blame your aunt for making a fuss. It's not every day that a person completes his residency."

"I know, but all the extra attention is embarrassing."

"You love it. Don't lie." Ravyn laughed at his hooded glance. Then, with the tip of her fingernail, she slit open the envelope and pulled out a three-dimensional, handmade card, inviting her to Mark's party.

"I wish I had Aunt Edy's time," he said. "She created about fifty of those cards."

"Impressive." Ravyn looked over the colorful invite before carefully placing it near her small purse. "And your great-aunt plays the piano, too?"

"Yep. And she bakes the best rhubarb pie you ever tasted."

"She sounds like quite the talented lady."

"She is."

Ravyn noted the grateful expression on Mark's face as he forked some salad into his mouth. He chewed and swallowed. "Without my aunt and uncle's support, I would have never made it through my residency program. I owe them a lot."

As Ravyn listened, she picked at her grilled salmon.

"They believe in me and the goals I've set—goals that go beyond my medical training."

He sat forward in the candy-striped padded chair and set down his fork. "I never did tell you my plans for the future once I'm done with my residency."

"No, you never did. I'd love to hear about them."

As Mark began to divulge his passion for the souls in a tiny country off the Indonesian coast, Ravyn had a sinking feeling inside. She forced herself not to react negatively when she heard the words *medical missionary*, but it took so much effort she could barely concentrate on anything else he said.

"I'll spend my summer candidating at various churches," he added, reclaiming her attention. "Once I've accumulated enough support, I'll head overseas. The director of the missions team drew up a five-year contract, but he promised me furlough every eighteen months."

Was that supposed to make her feel better? It didn't. "So, in essence, all your time in medical school has been—a waste."

"A waste?" Mark sat back hard in his chair. "How can you say that? I'll soon be a board-certified MD."

"Board certified in America." She shook her head, feeling disappointed in him. "And why would you ask churches to support you when you could earn a good living here in the U.S.? You could pay for your own missions trips overseas. I mean, think about it. You could make enough money here in the next couple of years to support yourself in a third world country for a very long time."

Mark didn't reply and Ravyn suspected she had said too much. She stared down at her half-eaten dinner.

"There's accountability in enlisting churches' support for a group of missionaries," Mark stated at long last. "Not only will I have to answer to the Lord for my decisions and actions, but I'll report to a board of godly pastors."

Ravyn could see his point, but she still believed he was about to throw away all his years in med school if he followed through with this ludicrous plan. "Mark, in the five years that you'll be gone the health-care industry will have changed so much here in the United States that you might find yourself behind the times and unable to practice. Then what?"

"Then I—"

"Wait. Let me guess." Ravyn held up a hand. "You don't have a plan now, but you're going to *trust the Lord*."

"Right. Minus the sarcasm, of course." He sent her a wry grin.

"Look, I believe that we, as Christians, must trust and obey God's Word and His leading, but I also think there's a fine line between blind trust and irresponsibility." She tipped her head, regarding him. "Your plan sounds like it teeters on the latter."

"Irresponsible?" Mark shook his head. "I disagree. What I've learned in med school is going to help me care for souls in a remote country who'd never receive health care if it weren't for me."

"And you have to do that full-time for five years?"

"Well, yeah," he said, as if it were obvious. "It takes time to build a good testimony on a foreign mission field. The locals have to see that I'm genuinely concerned about them. Once they realize I can help them healthwise, they'll listen when I talk to them about their souls' eternal resting place."

He's a dreamer, Ravyn realized. She looked away and focused on a distant golf cart. Regret flooded her being. She had hoped to get to know Mark better. In fact, she had hoped to fall in love with him and live happily ever after.

And now who's the dreamer? Ravyn silently berated herself for her girlish fantasy.

"Many parts of the country are built up for tourism," Mark said on a persuasive note. "The capital city, for instance, has an urban feel to it. It's really a beautiful place."

"Where is this place again?"

Mark hailed the waiter and asked for an ink pen. Then he drew a rough map.

Ravyn felt her heart plummet to the depths of remorse. The small country was on the other side of the world.

"I visited there only once, but I immediately developed a burden for the island people."

"That's important." Ravyn forced herself to say something upbeat and encouraging. "They'll be lucky to have you there."

"I appreciate your saying so." Mark sent her a curious glance.

Ravyn didn't say any more. She already felt the pinch of guilt for her negative responses, but she battled her own emotions. Disappointment weighted her heart like lead. Next to Teala, Mark had become a confidant. She looked forward to seeing him at work. His sense of humor lifted her spirits. His easygoing outlook on life alleviated her day-to-day stress. His faith in Christ strengthened hers.

And now Ravyn found herself missing Mark already.

Chapter 11

I t's still early," Mark said, glancing at his wristwatch. "I'm sure we can find something fun to do."

"No." Under the moonlight, he watched as Ravyn shook her head. Several strands of her black hair fell against her face, and the humidity in the air kept them adhered to her pale cheek until she brushed them away. "I should go in."

Mark leaned against the white stucco archway that led to the complex's surface parking lot. He folded his arms across his chest. "Hmm, was it something I said—like I'm going to the mission field?" He couldn't keep the facetiousness out of his voice. He felt more than a little hurt at Ravyn's obvious rejection. Then, again, he had anticipated it.

She lifted her chin and squared her shoulders, and Mark fought off a grin. She might be petite, but her feisty spirit more than made up for her small stature.

"I'm very fond of you, Mark," she began, "maybe more than I should be, and I don't want either of us to get hurt." She raised a hand before he could refute her comment. "I can't just be your friend, either. The night you kissed me changed our relationship for me."

Mark lost his surefootedness as he bore responsibility for his actions. She was right: He had been the one to kiss her, and if it had impaired their friendship, there wasn't much he could do about it now.

"Our future goals are very different. Too different."

He hated where all this was leading, but supposed he should let her have her say.

"I hope to end up working in Madison at the University of Wisconsin Hospital. Overseas missions. . ." She shook her head. "Not for me. Besides, if that's what God wants, I can be a missionary on the job right here at home." A rueful grin tugged at her pink lips. "Maybe I'm more like my parents than I ever imagined."

Mark shifted his stance. "How so?"

"Mom and Dad chose the theater to try to reach people here in Dubuque. Just recently I've been able to see a mission field in my own backyard, too. I think of Jace, our GSW patient in the trauma room. Today's teens need to know there's Someone they can turn to with their anger and frustration. They need Christ.

As weird as my upbringing was, I at least knew I had Jesus in my heart. Looking back, I can see how He was my source of strength and protection."

It did his heart good to hear her talk about the Lord. "I don't doubt there's a mission field here at home."

"And think of Carla, drunk and vulnerable in a public restroom," she pressed on. "I hate to even speculate about what might have happened to her if she hadn't stumbled into you—*literally*. There's an obvious need in her life, too."

"You're probably right."

As her words sank in, Mark actually felt hopeful. What he heard Ravyn say was that she was *willing* to heed the Lord's voice when it came to serving others. Who could ask for more than that?

She glanced away. "The way things stand, Mark, there's really no point in us seeing each other."

"Hmm. Interesting. But what do you think God has to say about it?"

She swung her gaze back to his face and grinned. "You're very stubborn, aren't you?"

He pursed his lips in thought. "I like to think that I am determined."

"You say determined. I say stubborn—"

He laughed. The repartee wasn't lost on him. "But I'm not ready to call the whole thing off."

Still smiling, he leaned toward her, placing a kiss on her cheek. "G'night, Ravyn." He paused and stared into her dark eyes. She looked lovely under the glow of the moon. On impulse, he touched his lips to hers, stealing another quick kiss. "See you later," he whispered against her soft cheek.

Stepping back, he glimpsed her stunned expression and tried not to chuckle. But he grinned all the way through the parking lot and to his car.

❧

With a long sigh, Ravyn entered her condo and dropped her belongings on the kitchen counter. *Determined, my foot. Mark Monroe is one of the most mule-headed men I've ever met.*

The phone rang and Ravyn searched for the cordless handset. She found it in the pillows on the sofa and pushed the TALK button. She half expected it to be Mark, so she felt surprised when her mother's voice wafted from the earpiece.

"You're not supposed to be home."

"Yeah, well, here I am."

"Teala said you were out with Mark tonight."

Ravyn swallowed the last of her annoyance. "I did go out with Mark, but I'm home early."

"Home?" Her mom paused. "Does your place feel like home? It's so odd not having you around here. I miss you."

Her mother's rare admission touched Ravyn's heart. On the other hand, independence is what Ravyn had wanted for years. "It's getting to feel like home. It'll take a while to get the rooms furnished and decorated to my liking."

"I suppose that's true enough."

"Besides, I've always worked so much over the past years that I was never at home. You didn't miss me then."

"That's because I knew your bedroom was just upstairs, not on the other side of Dubuque."

Ravyn fought in vain to grasp her mother's logic. Finally, she gave up. "So, what's going on, Mom?"

"Oh, the reason I called—Dad and I wondered if you'd come to church with us tomorrow morning. Lunch afterwards. Our treat."

"Sure." Ravyn didn't have to think twice. God wanted her time, and she could at least give Him a couple of hours a week.

"Would you like to ask Mark to join us?"

"No." Ravyn expelled a weary sigh. "You might as well know I told him I couldn't see him anymore."

Another pause. "Why on earth did you do that?"

Ravyn suddenly felt her temples begin to throb. "Mom, don't sound so panicked. There are other fish in the sea."

"Yes, but Mark is such a *nice* fish."

Ravyn smiled at the jest in spite of herself.

"What happened? Did you two have a spat?"

"No." Ravyn kicked off her shoes. "I can already tell that things between us aren't going to work out."

"What a shame."

"Yeah, it's a shame, all right."

Ravyn allowed her gaze to wander around the room, and suddenly the stark white walls seemed to have less potential. In fact, they looked more barren than ever.

In short, she thought, they resembled her heart.

❧

"So, how'd the date go?"

Mark backtracked through the kitchen and spotted his uncle in the den. "Oh, just fine." He wasn't in the mood to divulge the details.

Uncle Chet seemed to read right through him. " 'Just fine'? That's it?"

Standing at the doorway, Mark nodded out a reply and looked at the TV screen. The NBA semifinals were on. "Who's winning?"

"Miami over Detroit." Uncle Chet lifted the remote and turned off the basketball game. "I'm not really into it." He lazed back on the plump sofa. "I want to hear about your date with Ravyn."

Mark gave him a shrug as he entered the room and sat down. "It started off with an intoxicated co-worker at the steak house. She had a gash on her scalp, so we called an ambulance to take her to the hospital. But by the time the medics arrived, Ravyn needed to change clothes." Mark paused to explain. "Head lacerations can be messy."

Uncle Chet raised his hand, palm-side out. "Say no more. I get the picture."

"So Ravyn and I ended up leaving for another restaurant at the complex where she lives. Dinner was okay. We made it an early night."

"High drama at the steak house spoiled your romantic dinner, huh? That's too bad."

"No, actually, things went okay." Mark stood. He still didn't feel ready to discuss the particulars, and he certainly didn't want his uncle to assume his "investment" wouldn't pay out. Mark planned to keep his end of the bargain. After all, getting him through med school and onto the mission field had been Uncle Chet's and Aunt Edy's dream all along.

Uncle Chet drew his bushy brows together, looking serious. "How does Ravyn feel about you living overseas doing missionary work?"

Mark marveled at the older man's perception. "She respects my decision." He didn't add that Ravyn didn't feel it was her calling. "We'll see what happens."

His uncle lifted the remote and pointed it at the TV. "Keep me posted."

"Sure."

Mark left the den and jogged up the steps and into his bedroom. He changed into a pair of baggy gym shorts and a comfy T-shirt. After washing up in the bathroom, he collapsed into bed and thanked God for the work He was doing in Ravyn's life—and his own, too. He also prayed for wisdom. On one hand, he felt obligated to respect Ravyn's wishes regarding their relationship. On the other hand, Mark wasn't willing to give up on her yet.

He closed his eyes and placed the future in God's hands, determined not to take it back. But first things first. He had a residency to finish.

Chapter 12

The ER was abuzz with activity, and Ravyn found herself in the thick of it. Three sick patients demanded her attention, two of them critically ill. It was all she could do to juggle their care. As usual, she did her best to ignore Mark's presence, although she found it difficult to have to ask him to sign off on orders. Over the course of the last several days, he'd done his best to act aloof and professional toward her, but every now and then forgot himself and behaved as though they were best buddies. More often than not, he caught himself, though, and was quick to apologize. However, he had Ravyn's emotions swinging like a pendulum.

And then there was Carla. She went out of her way to avoid Ravyn, but she took advantage of every opportunity to sidle up to Mark. At one point, Ravyn saw the two engaged in conversation and she told herself she didn't care. Mark could talk with whomever he pleased, and since it was most likely clarification on an x-ray order that Carla needed, he *had* to discuss it with her.

Ravyn berated herself for her childish notions. What's more, she despised the fact that she'd gotten sucked into the ER drama.

At last the time came for Ravyn to punch out, and she hurried to leave the hospital. Fatigue weighted her every limb, and she couldn't wait to get home and crawl into bed.

As she drove uphill toward the west side of town, she passed a fast-food place and her stomach grumbled. Ravyn realized she hadn't taken a lunch break, and the last thing she'd eaten in the past twelve hours was a handful of pretzels from a bag that one of the unit clerks had opened. Pulling a U-turn, she maneuvered her car into the drive-through lane and ordered a breakfast sandwich and orange juice. Then she inched her vehicle toward the window, waiting her turn to pay for her food. She suddenly recalled how in their high school days she and Shelley would often hang out here with their other friends. Then one day she was gone. Vanished.

A rueful smile curved Ravyn's lips as she recalled how Shelley always talked about moving to California and becoming a famous actress. Perhaps she'd moved to the West Coast.

Ravyn completed her exchange with the cashier and drove off with her bagged breakfast. She continued to think about Shelley and, as she did, Mark's suggestion that she make peace with the past surfaced. Maybe it was time to look

73

up Shelley and give her a call. In talking to her, perhaps Ravyn would be able to put all the hurt, and even betrayal, behind her once and for all.

At that moment, it occurred to Ravyn that Mark's reentrance into her life might have been for the sole purpose of settling matters with him. Could be God never intended for her to develop a romantic relationship with Mark.

But if that were true, then why did she feel so glum?

🦋

"My friend Jen Taylor gave me this phone number. Her sister-in-law keeps in touch with the Jenkinses."

Ravyn set down the cardboard box containing the last of her belongings here at her folks' house, and took the proffered slip of paper. "Thanks, Mom."

"Somewhere along the line I heard they moved to Florida. Jen said the Jenkinses still live there."

"I'll try this number and see where it leads me. Might be that God doesn't want me to find Shelley."

"Follow His lead, honey."

"I will."

Ravyn lowered herself onto one of the worn kitchen chairs and watched as her mom sipped her iced tea. She thought Mom resembled a stereotypical gypsy in her colorful, frilly skirt and white T-shirt. Her dark hair was pulled back and carelessly secured with a large silver barrette. Sterling hoops swung from her earlobes.

"It's a hot one today, isn't it? I don't recall the month of June ever being quite this warm and muggy."

"It's always hot and muggy in June. How 'bout we go to my place and swim in the pool for a while?"

"Sounds nice, but no can do. I have to be at the university in a half hour to sit in on auditions." Her mother leaned forward. "Think you'd like to try out for a part in your father's summer play? It's air-conditioned in the auditorium."

"I'll pass. Thanks."

"Is that sarcasm I detect in your voice?"

"Me? Sarcastic?" Ravyn grinned at her own quip while running her finger over the scarred kitchen tabletop. The thing looked like it had gone through both World Wars. In fact, most of the furnishings in her parents' home looked either battered or outdated, although, thanks to Violet and Teala, the house was clean and the furniture dusted.

Mom laughed and lifted her glass. The ice cubes tinkled. "Mmm," she said, sipping her brew. "Green tea on ice is fabulous. Are you sure you don't want a glass?"

Ravyn shook her head. "Thanks anyway. I have to get going." She sent her mother a teasing grin. "My air-conditioned condo awaits me."

"Oh, go ahead. Rub it in. Pool, central air. . ." Her mother gave a flick of her wrist. "La-dee-da."

Ravyn laughed and finger-combed her hair back off her perspiring forehead. "Maybe I'll have some iced tea after all." She stood, walked to the fridge, and helped herself.

"So what do you hear from Mark these days?"

"Not much. I see him at work once in a while, but that's it." Ravyn replaced the pitcher in the fridge and then, glass in hand, reclaimed her seat at the kitchen table. "The last thing he said to me was, 'Can I borrow your pen?' and I haven't seen him or my pen since."

The glib remark caused her mother to laugh, although Ravyn didn't add how difficult it was to see Mark when their shifts overlapped. The sight of him tugged on her heart in a painful way, and when their eyes met regret filled her soul. Mark was probably the only guy she'd ever met with whom she'd connected in some odd, supernatural way. He could read her as easily as the daily newspaper and, likewise, she sensed what went through his mind. Their so-called telepathy came in handy in the trauma room last week after a patient was brought in with life-threatening injuries from a motorcycle crash. She had guessed what Mark was going to say before he said it, and Ravyn knew their faith in Christ was, of course, the cornerstone of that mystical connection between them.

Still, she couldn't accept his plans for the future, but at the same time, she found herself feeling like she had when Shelley disappeared. A sense of loss crimped her heart. The truth was, losing two friends in one lifetime proved almost more than Ravyn could bear.

As she drove back to her condo later that afternoon, she heard the Lord's still small voice from within say, *"I'll never leave you."* It brought tears to Ravyn's eyes and suddenly she felt immeasurably humbled. In spite of the fact that she'd neglected God all these years, He remained faithful and true to her.

❧

Mark watched Ravyn flit around the ER like a little hummingbird. She seemed to filter out the nonessential chatter and concentrate on her work, which was commendable for the most part. But he overheard Liz say she was concerned about Ravyn burning out. Apparently, she'd been picking up extra shifts, and she didn't take time out for lunch or her scheduled breaks. She assigned herself to the patients as they arrived instead of "sharing the wealth," as it were. Liz finally gave her a stern talking-to, saying, "What do you think this is? A one-nurse operation?"

And now, as Liz relayed the circumstances to a few of her friends, Mark felt saddened to hear it. In fact, he felt partially responsible. He suspected that Ravyn kept herself on the go so she didn't have to deal with her feelings for him. On the other hand, he could well imagine her calling him an egomaniac for assuming that he was the reason for her intense dedication to the ER. Perhaps it was wishful thinking on his part. For all he knew, she had a lot of debt to pay off—and she had talked about purchasing a new car.

Mark stood and made his way toward the exit. He couldn't stand listening to the gossip, especially since Ravyn was the subject matter. However, if the worst they could say about her was that she worked too hard, she wouldn't be their topic of discussion for very long.

Strolling down the empty hallway, he considered any one of a hundred things he could do to occupy himself, but his thoughts always came back around to Ravyn. He wished he could give her a little moral support, but he was trying to give her some space. Besides, Liz would straighten her out. Then once he finished his residency he wouldn't be around to antagonize her with his mere presence.

The thought saddened Mark. He had hoped that by now Ravyn would have changed her mind, and the two of them could at least be friends.

Talk about stubborn.

He paused by the glass doors that led out to the smoking deck. The rain poured down and lightning flashed in the distance. He recalled Ravyn mentioning her desire to do research at University of Wisconsin Hospital in Madison. She had lofty aspirations and they were every bit as important as his. She was all about her career. He was all about serving God overseas. Mark shook his head. They were hardly a match made in heaven.

Why, then, couldn't he just forget about her? *Lord, is it that You don't want me to forget about her?*

Over the last few weeks Mark had considered everything Ravyn had said when they'd had dinner together. Her remarks about medical school being wasted and him acting irresponsibly for gathering church support this summer were like scalpels slicing through to his soul. He began to wonder if she was right. After all, it was true that the health-care industry in the States would be far different when he returned from the mission field.

Are You refining my plans, Lord, to suit Your will, or is Ravyn a distraction?

The sound of rubber-soled athletic shoes squeaking against the polished floor signaled someone's rapid advance. Another staff member, he figured, due to the early hour. He straightened just as the object of his thoughts rounded the corner of the hallway, heading straight for him. He almost chuckled at the irony.

When Ravyn spotted him, her steps faltered. "Oh. . .hi." She hiked the strap of her vinyl lunch bag higher onto her shoulder in what Mark guessed was a nervous gesture. "I got banished from the ER for a half hour."

"Well, you don't want to sit on the smoking deck and eat your lunch. It's storming."

Ravyn swung her gaze to the window beside the doorway. Raindrops streamed down the glass pane. "Yeah, I guess it is."

Awkwardness hung between them like a thick velvet drape.

Mark turned to stare outside again. From the corner of his eye, he saw Ravyn pass behind him. He fought to hold his silence.

But he didn't win.

"Hey, wait."

She glanced over her shoulder.

"Can you spare a few minutes?"

"Sure." Ravyn pivoted to face him.

Mark stepped forward. "This isn't work related."

A little frown marred her dark brows. "Okay."

"Maybe it's sheer pride, I don't know. I haven't quite figured it out. All I know is I'm not handling getting dumped very well, not that it hasn't happened before. It has, but—"

"I didn't 'dump' you, Mark. I merely. . ." She paused as if searching for the right words. "I just don't think anything between us is meant to be."

"Really? Then how come we're both miserable?"

Ravyn blinked and Mark realized the question erupted from some hidden place inside his being, surprising them both.

He sighed and figured it was too late to turn back now. He might as well bare the rest of his heart. "You never gave 'anything between us' a chance."

A look of remorse spilled over her features. Her matter-of-fact facade seemed to melt away before Mark's eyes.

"Listen, Ravyn, I'm not sure what God's will is for us, but why don't we take things one step at a time?" He pushed out a smile for her benefit.

She stood there looking like she might go into shock at any moment.

Mark decided a bit of levity wouldn't hurt. Placing a hand on her shoulder, he steered her toward the cafeteria. "But first things first: If you want someone to help you eat your lunch, I'm more than happy to oblige."

Chapter 13

A moment of weakness. Mark had caught her in a moment of weakness. And now as she watched him devour her egg salad sandwich, Ravyn felt both amused and irritated. How could he have so easily finagled his way back into her life when she had fought so hard to shut him out?

Ravyn sipped her diet cola and decided she could, at least, act friendly. Friendly but distant. What would that hurt? Mark would soon be gone.

The thought nearly made her choke.

"I haven't had egg salad in years."

She felt oddly pleased that he enjoyed it. She'd whipped it up early this afternoon.

"So what's new with you?" he asked. "We haven't talked in about three weeks."

Ravyn chose not to remind him that it was on purpose they hadn't talked, other than business, of course.

"Not too much." As she regarded him, Ravyn decided Mark reminded her of her dad in many ways. They both were hardworking and strong-minded, possessed a good sense of humor, and had a cavalier outlook on life.

The latter trait, unfortunately, was a source of all kinds of problems, and Ravyn knew that to be true firsthand.

"You've been working a lot of shifts, huh?"

"Yes, but I did manage to find some time to play Sherlock Holmes."

"Oh?" Mark arched a brow, looking interested.

"I tracked down Shelley. I found out she's living in Chicago. She's got a talent agent and everything. She must be a successful actress."

"No kidding?"

"Yep. She goes by the name of Jeanne Shelley now. Those are her first and middle names reversed. Anyway, her agent said he'd get in touch with her and have her call me. That was two days ago." Ravyn peeled open the foil top of a yogurt carton while Mark snooped through the rest of her thermal lunch bag. He found her bag of potato chips.

"Mind if I eat these?"

"Go ahead. I eat enough junk in the ER. Somebody always has food to share."

"I think it's that way on just about every floor." Mark tore open the bag. "But

I have yet to find fruit and vegetables getting passed among the staff."

"That's because fruits and veggies are healthy." Ravyn laughed. "True comfort food is high calories, fat, and sugar."

"Thanks for the clarification." Mark grinned and tossed a few chips into his mouth. "So. . .back to Shelley. Do you think she'll call you?"

"No clue." Ravyn took a bite of yogurt and marveled at the peace she felt inside. "I've prayed about it and I'm leaving the matter up to God. I made the attempt and that's all I can do."

"You're a wise woman."

"It's elementary, my dear Watson."

Mark winced at her poorly feigned British accent.

"Sorry. Guess I'll leave the acting to Shelley."

He nodded, grinning all the while. "Good thinking."

Ravyn laughed. "And speaking of acting, my dad held auditions last week. His production of *Soul's Agony* will run from late August to Labor Day."

"Wish I had some time. I'd participate. Sounds like fun."

"My dad wrote the script himself, which is a first, and according to my mother, it's brilliant."

"Your parents are incredible people."

"I agree. They are." Ravyn finished her yogurt, then reached into her lunch bag and retrieved a sandwich bag filled with store-bought chocolate cookies.

Mark began helping himself. "It takes time and dedication to write and direct a play—might even be more work than being a doctor or nurse."

"I know where you're heading and you can stop right there." Ravyn took a bite of one of the sugary rounds. "I know my folks work hard. I never said they didn't. I just believe that there are times when God expects Christians to make use of what He's given us—like an able body and an intelligent mind—to earn a decent living."

"So where does that leave missionaries? Don't you think they earn a decent living?"

"I don't know. I'm sure some do—if they're practical."

"Practicality has nothing to do with it. Let's use Jesus as an example. He said birds had their nests, but the Son of Man didn't even have a place to lay His head. Jesus didn't have a job. He trusted God for everything, including His next meal."

"True. But He was also a carpenter before that, indicating He did, in fact, have a skill and hold down a job."

"I think that's kind of a stretch, Ravyn." Mark sounded a bit amused before turning serious once again. "Let's never forget He gave up everything including His life to preach the gospel. His disciples gave up their livelihoods as fishermen to follow Him. Likewise we're to do to the same."

"Yes, but on the other hand, we never read anywhere in the Bible that Luke gave up being a physician even though he wrote one of the Gospels."

Mark couldn't seem to find a comeback. Either that, or he gave up the argument altogether and all too easily.

Ravyn glanced at her wristwatch and realized a half hour had passed. She packed up her lunch bag. "Look, I don't have a problem supporting missionaries," she said at last, "as long as they're willing to support themselves if need be."

They stood and made their way out of the coffee shop.

"Kind of hard to find employment when you're in a foreign country."

"I'm not referring to foreign countries. I was thinking of my parents when I said that. My dad went months without earning a dime when, instead, he could have found a job and might have been a witness to his co-workers."

Mark listened without reply and Ravyn felt a check in her heart. She knew she wasn't much of a witness for Christ on the job. Was that what Mark thought, too?

They walked partway down the hall in silence before Ravyn spoke again.

"My dad used to say that if you work in the world, you get worldly. But, for myself, I don't see a way around it."

"I think it's all about one's personal, individual, and divine calling." Mark stuck his hands in the pockets of the long white coat that residents and MDs were required to wear over their scrubs. "Missionaries and Christians in full-time ministry highly respect those on the front line, working in the world." He chuckled. "They're the ones who support us."

"Good point." Ravyn couldn't find fault in that logic. "I guess I never thought of it that way."

She paused outside the women's locker room and held up her bag, indicating she wanted to stop and put it away.

"Thanks for the sandwich."

"You're welcome."

Mark gave her a charming smile. "Catch you later. I'll try to call you this week. Maybe we can find some time to get together."

"Okay. That'd be nice."

Ravyn entered the locker room and realized what she'd just agreed to. She smacked her palm against her forehead. *Oh, that man! He messes up my thinking!*

❦

Mark found his uncle sitting on a lawn chair in the backyard and walked outside to join him. "How are you feeling this afternoon?"

"Pretty good." Uncle Chet gazed at him and smiled.

Mark pulled up a white plastic chair and sat down beside him.

"I'm watching the weeds grow since your aunt won't let me pull 'em." Uncle Chet gave a disgruntled snort, but the wet stain covering the front of his striped

T-shirt indicated that, indeed, he had been gardening.

"You're not supposed to be exerting yourself. Your heart is still on the mend. At least Aunt Edy is following the cardiologist's orders."

"Bah!" Uncle Chet waved one hand at him. "I'm just fine. Besides, working in the garden is just as much work as walking—it's less of a bore, too."

Mark shook his head in disappointment. "I hope you're behaving. I'd like to have you around for a while."

"This subject is hereby closed—says me."

"Okay." Mark knew better than to argue with his obstinate uncle.

"So you're off work for a while now, huh?"

"Couple of days."

"Won't be long now and you'll be a full-fledged doctor."

"Yeah, and maybe then you'll listen to me when I tell you to take it easy."

Uncle Chet shook his finger at him. "Knock it off."

"All right."

Mark chuckled and glanced around the vibrant green yard. A month or so ago his aunt had planted the vegetable garden that Uncle Chet had been tilling when he suffered his heart attack. Already leafy plants sprouted from the dark, rich soil.

"So how's your little blackbird these days?"

"Ravyn?" Mark grinned at his uncle's silly nickname for her. "Funny you should mention her. I'm planning to drop in and see her."

"Never drop in on a woman, Mark. That's a dangerous thing to do."

He took a moment to consider his uncle's advice and recalled the last time he'd dropped in on Ravyn. She had seemed embarrassed about her less than perfect appearance, but Mark thought she'd looked fine. So she wasn't all dolled up. It had mattered little to him. On the other hand, if it was a big deal to her, then maybe he should call first.

"You serious about this young woman?"

Again, Mark digested the question. "Not sure yet," he answered in all honesty. "I've been focused on finishing my residency. First things first, I guess."

"You're not planning to be around this summer," Uncle Chet pointed out. "That's why I asked."

A wave of reality crashed over Mark. What was he thinking? He could hardly court Ravyn by cell phone—and that's assuming she agreed to be courted. So far he'd cajoled his way into her life.

He sat back in his chair and put his feet up on the adjoining plastic chair. Remorse permeated his being. Who was he kidding? He had no right to drop in on Ravyn today.

Chapter 14

Ravyn nibbled the inside of her lower lip as she waited for Mark to finish his conversation with another MD. Her conversation with Shelley weighed heavily on her mind, and with her parents in the throes of a new play and Teala absorbed in her romance, Ravyn decided Mark would make an efficient sounding board. He was, after all, the only other person who knew of the situation.

"Mark, can I talk to you?" She hailed him as he turned and started down the hallway.

He wheeled around at her question. "Ravyn." He smiled and walked back toward her. "I didn't see you standing there."

"I guess my scrubs sort of blend in with the wallpaper." She grinned at her jest. "Do you have a little time?"

He glanced at his watch. "A little. What's up?"

She sensed he was busy in spite of his willing reply. "It's kind of involved. I can try to catch you at a better time."

He paused but then his features relaxed. "No, this is fine. The ER's quiet. No guarantee it'll stay that way."

Ravyn agreed and she lowered her voice in case another staff member happened to be close by.

"I talked to Shelley. I had to call her agent back, and this time he gave me her number."

"And?" Mark folded his arms.

"Well, I think she might be in some sort of trouble. She sounded. . ." Ravyn searched for the right word. "I don't know—desperate. In a hurry. Like she didn't want to be overheard and there was a lot of noise in the background. She repeated her address about three times and practically begged me to visit as soon as I could. We had no time for chitchat. She said she had to go and hung up. That was it."

"Ravyn, if you're asking for my advice, I'd say stay out of it. If Shelley is in Chicago and in trouble, then it's probably way over your head to help her. Big city. Big trouble."

He spoke Ravyn's exact thoughts, but the niggling inside wouldn't abate. "I sort of feel like I should go."

"Then don't go alone." Mark checked his watch again. "Listen, I have to fly. Talk to you later."

He dashed off, leaving Ravyn to wonder at his aloofness. She realized they were at work and it wasn't the time or place to convey emotional sentiments, but that had never hindered Mark in the past. Besides, his response seemed rather harsh for a prospective missionary.

With her thoughts in a whir, she returned to the emergency room's arena area. She picked up her work right where she'd left off. In the early morning hours of the night shift, it was typically quiet, except on weekends when the bars emptied out. Ravyn much preferred a steady twelve hours to sitting around doing mindless paper shuffling.

Several feet away, a few nurses, the staff physician, and a security guard gabbed to pass the time. They talked shop and Ravyn's interest was piqued by a particular case they discussed.

Liz met her gaze. "Hey, don't just stand there and eavesdrop, pull up a chair and join us."

Ravyn smiled. By now she'd grown accustomed to Liz's boisterous antics. In fact, the day Liz called in sick, the ER didn't seem the same without her.

Unable to resist the invitation, Ravyn stepped around the parameters of the nurses' station and began conversing with her co-workers.

About an hour later, a patient with abdominal pain admitted herself to the ER. The chat group disbanded. At a physician's request, Ravyn hurried down the inner corridor in search of a piece of equipment. She passed unused exam rooms and a tiny break area where a coffeepot was kept along with a refrigerator and microwave oven. As she glanced in that direction, Ravyn did a double take and slowed her pace. She saw Mark and Carla sitting at the small round table, having, what appeared to Ravyn, an intimate conversation. Mark was leaning toward Carla, talking in such a hushed tone that Ravyn couldn't hear what was being said. Carla looked mesmerized.

Ravyn clenched her jaw. Now what was this all about? He'd acted curt to Ravyn—why? So he could rendezvous with Carla?

She chided herself for thinking the worst, but then it occurred to her that she never wholly trusted Mark because she never could quite believe that Shelley had lied so many years ago.

As she stood in the hall, memories came rushing back—Shelley's incessant prattle about how madly in love she was with Mark and then her tears when he broke her heart. As great an actress as Shelley might have been then or may be today, Ravyn didn't think anyone could feign such pain and despair.

So did that mean Mark was a philanderer with an incredible facade or had Shelley been a misguided teenager?

As Ravyn spied his ongoing discussion with Carla, she couldn't help but suspect he wasn't as upstanding and genuine as he appeared. Maybe there was something to his nickname "George" after all.

Disappointment rocked her soul. The Daniels and the Gideons of the Bible just didn't exist in this day and age.

Carla cleared her throat and Ravyn snapped to attention. Mark turned in his chair.

Ravyn avoided his gaze. "Dr. Thomas is looking for the portable ultrasound machine." She forced a sturdy tone. "Have either of you seen it?"

Both shook their heads and when Ravyn glimpsed Mark's expression, she noted he didn't even have the good grace to look guilty.

That's the stuff creeps are made of, she thought, turning on her heels and walking away. Continuing her search, she finally located the machine and wheeled it to the patient's room where she absorbed herself in her work. Mark's residency couldn't end fast enough as far as Ravyn was concerned.

But now she was more determined than ever to visit Shelley and hear the truth from her former friend's lips. Once and for all.

&

"You know she's jealous, don't you?"

Mark looked away from the now empty doorway where Ravyn had stood moments ago and regarded the smirk on Carla's face.

"Ravyn's a Christian, too," he explained. "Believers feel the same emotions everyone else does. But we have something more to help us overcome the destructive ones, like envy and jealousy. We have our faith in Christ."

"So what's your point?" Carla sat back in her chair.

"My point is, Ravyn will get over whatever is eating at her. And if you have questions in the future about what we discussed here, I hope you'll ask her."

"Why would I do that? She hates me."

Mark shook his head. "No, she doesn't. Ravyn was genuinely concerned about you the night you fell and hit your head."

Carla's blush surfaced through her suntanned cheeks. "Must you keep bringing that up?"

"Carla, from what you've told me, it sounds like you're teetering on a very slippery slope. Your behavior is going to get you hurt—or killed."

"I don't have a drinking problem, all right?" She folded her arms. "I just. . . like to have a good time. What girl doesn't?" A provocative smile curved her full lips. "And if you weren't so religious—"

"Time for me to go." Mark stood. "Just remember, everything I told you is in the Bible. You can look it up for yourself and you can ask Ravyn. She might seem like a tough cookie," he added with a grin, "but she's all marshmallow inside."

"For your sake, I hope that's true." Carla laughed.

Mark silently agreed as he made his way to the front of the ER. Ravyn hadn't exactly looked pleased, not that he took any pleasure in the fact she was jealous. However, it did affirm what he felt in his heart: he and Ravyn had strong feelings for each other.

Unfortunately, they were miles apart in their ideals and philosophies. Ravyn had pointed out that fact from the beginning.

Mark decided God had a lot of work to do and, humanly, it seemed impossible. In a matter of days, Mark would leave for the rest of the summer with only short stops at his great-aunt and uncle's place through the fall. He would, of course, see them during the Christmas holiday. Then come January, he'd be gone for what might as well be forever where he and Ravyn were concerned.

And by the looks of it, she wasn't speaking to him—at least not verbally. But the angry sparks shooting from her eyes might rival the upcoming Fourth of July fireworks.

Mark leaned against the counter near the unit clerk's desk where Ravyn wrote in a patient's chart.

"It's not what you think, okay?" he ventured.

"Okay."

Yeah. That was way too easy, Mark thought with a facetious bent.

He blew out a sigh but chose not to press the issue. Not here. Not now. He'd let Ravyn cool off awhile. He wanted to leave Dubuque knowing that at least the two of them were on good terms.

After that, it was all up to the Lord.

※

Ravyn packed her car, then slid behind the steering wheel and began her weekend trip to Chicago. According to the map she'd printed off the Internet, the drive would take about four hours.

Turning onto U.S. 20, she sped across the High Bridge, also known as the Julien Dubuque Bridge. It was a steel, arched structure that spanned the Mississippi River and connected the state of Iowa with Illinois. As she continued on toward the interstate, Ravyn marveled at how quickly she'd been able to make arrangements for this trip. She'd swapped a few shifts with two other RNs, and since everything came together so smoothly, Ravyn knew it just had to be God's will that she visit Shelley. She felt the Lord's leading in this. She rejected the inner nudging that she'd planned this trek in order to spite Mark and, regardless of his warning, she was going alone. She convinced herself, and not for the first time, that she didn't care what he said, did, or who he talked to.

No, what mattered now was that finally, after a decade, Ravyn would finally learn the *real* truth.

Chapter 15

After checking into a hotel and dropping off her belongings in her room, Ravyn climbed back into her car. She'd asked for directions to Shelley's place, and the clerk behind the front desk had warned her that she was heading into a rough part of the city. Tapping her fingers against the steering wheel now, Ravyn wondered if she should go. Obviously, Shelley wasn't as successful as Ravyn imagined.

But she's in trouble and I want answers. Ravyn decided that, in a sense, she and Shelley needed each other.

Her resolve gelled, and Ravyn stuck her key in the ignition. Within a half hour, she was maneuvering her car through downtown Chicago. Twice she turned right instead of left, but finally she found Shelley's address.

She stared through her window at the dirty, brown brick building that contained an establishment called The Sunset Grill on its lower level. Ravyn assumed Shelley's apartment was upstairs.

She got out of her car before she lost her nerve. Loud music blared from a car stereo somewhere down the street, and several feet away two shaggy-haired men in muscle shirts hovered beneath the hood of an automobile that had obviously seen better days.

Ravyn scurried to the brown wooden door at one end of the building and rang the doorbell. The smell of deep-fried food lingered in the air. She prayed for God's protection and tried not to second-guess her decision. Feeling nervous at no answer, she knocked on the door.

A waitress came out of the diner, wearing a grubby striped apron over a white tank top and red shorts. She was reed thin, and her dyed reddish blond hair was pulled back into a ponytail, exposing an inch or so of her natural light brown roots. Her hazel eyes sparkled with question—and then recognition set in.

"Ravyn!"

She blinked, fighting the shock. "Shelley?"

"Oh, thank God you came. I didn't think you would." Shelley stepped forward and wrapped her bony arms around Ravyn. She smelled of grease and cigarette smoke, and Ravyn almost choked.

She politely pulled back and stared up into her former friend's gaunt face. Words failed her. Shelley was a mere shadow of the healthy, vibrant friend Ravyn remembered. This woman looked twice her age.

"My son told me someone was at the door."

"Son?"

Shelley nodded. "I'll introduce you." She removed her apron. "Let me tell Flint I'm leaving."

"Flint?" Ravyn felt like an echo, but she could barely think straight. Was Shelley ill? Was she dying? She didn't look well.

"Flint owns this dive. Now, wait right here. Don't leave, okay? I'll be right back."

Against her better judgment, Ravyn complied. Moments later, Shelley returned, expletives following in her wake. Ravyn didn't think she'd ever heard such blue language.

"Ignore him. Flint's a creep. He'd have me working twenty-four hours a day if he could."

Shelley unlocked the adjacent door, then took Ravyn's elbow and steered her inside. The air in the tall stairwell that led to the second floor felt hot against Ravyn's skin, and that prevailing smell of grease seemed to ooze from the faded green walls.

When they reached the top of the steps, Shelley unlocked another door and bid Ravyn entry. Although tidy, the sparse living room had a dingy feel to it and smelled of stale cigarette smoke.

"Flint lets me rent this furnished apartment. He supposedly takes the money out of my paychecks, but in six months of working for him, I haven't seen a cent and when I asked about it. . ." She shook her head. "Let's just say things got ugly. So I'm living off the tips I earn and, believe me, that's not a lot."

"But you have an agent, so I thought—"

"He gets me gigs doing exotic dancing at nightclubs. He's a lousy agent."

Ravyn didn't know what to say.

"But I quit dancing years ago. I'm really trying to clean up my act, pardon the pun."

A husky little boy suddenly barreled into the room but stopped short at seeing Ravyn.

"Marky, this is the friend I told you about."

"Is she going to help us?"

"I haven't asked her yet." Shelley's tone held an incredulous note. "Give us a chance to get reacquainted, will you?"

The kid shrugged at the reprimand and eyed Ravyn. However, her mind hadn't gone much further than the child's name. *Marky?* Tension began throbbing at her temples as she took in his nut brown hair and chocolate-colored eyes. His face looked flushed and Ravyn thought the temperature in the apartment had to be nearing one hundred degrees.

"He looks like his dad," Shelley said, sounding chagrined.

Ravyn felt sick.

"Marky's ten. You can do the math and figure it out." Shelley waved a hand at her son. "Go in my room and watch TV so me and Ravyn can talk in private."

The boy wrinkled his face at the request, but he obeyed.

"I was pregnant when I left Dubuque."

Ravyn turned on her. "Why didn't you tell me?"

"Because you're so good, Ravyn. Whenever I watch *Gone with the Wind* I think of you. You're like Melanie, always looking out for everyone else—"

"Oh, please." Ravyn rolled her eyes. "There's no similarity. Trust me."

"But that's how I've always seen you, Rav. And, to the contrary, I'm a Scarlet O'Hara. I knew what I did was wrong, but I loved Mark so much that I gave in to what I wanted instead of doing what was right." She had the good grace to look ashamed of herself. "I've continued that pattern ever since, I'm afraid."

Ravyn's stomach churned.

Shelley expelled a weary breath. "When my parents found out I was pregnant, they sent me away to live with my dad's cousin in Florida. Mom and Dad were embarrassed and told all their church friends that I had some weird flu. That's why you took over my role in the play, remember?"

She nodded. How could she forget?

"I hated it at Aunt Petunia's house. That was her name. I'm not kidding. *Petunia.* But, unlike the flower, she wasn't pretty. She was a mean old biddy who arranged my son's adoption and never once asked me how I felt about it. So, before Marky was born, I ran away with a guy I'd met. He had some friends in Arkansas, so that's where we went. Then, after Marky entered the world, Pete dumped me and things have spiraled downhill from there." Shelley's laugh had a bitter edge to it. "As bad as it sounds, it got worse."

"I–I'm sorry to hear that." Ravyn struggled to process the information.

"I didn't dare go back to Dubuque. I figured everyone I knew hated me. Besides, by that time my parents had moved to Florida to be near Aunt Petunia, who was ailing with something or another. I forget."

"People in Dubuque would have understood and forgiven—even helped you. My family would have taken you in."

"Not according to my mother. She lived in constant fear her neighbors and church friends would discover she had an illegitimate grandson, and she had me believing I could never go back." Shelley's lips formed a grim line. "Incidentally, my parents disowned me a long time ago."

She motioned for Ravyn to sit down on the couch and then called for Marky to bring them each a can of diet cola and a glass filled with ice.

"I've been battling a, um, drug problem," Shelley further admitted. "But I've stayed clean now for over three months. It would have been longer, but Flint. . ." She shook her head. "Never mind. Let's just say he's not exactly a good example for me."

"He gives you drugs?" Ravyn felt outraged and appalled, although she'd heard similar stories in the ER and even before she'd started working at Victory.

Shelley nodded in answer to her question. "But a couple of guys from the rescue mission come into the diner almost every day. They've been encouraging me."

Marky reentered the living room, balancing the items his mother requested on a round serving tray.

"Want me to pour?" he asked, looking eager.

"No. Get back in my room—and don't try to listen in on our conversation, either."

The boy frowned at his mom before stomping off.

"Thanks, Marky!" Ravyn called to his retreating form.

"He's a good kid," Shelley said. "Takes care of me."

Ravyn found herself empathizing with the boy. After all, she'd taken care of her parents.

"I take it Mark doesn't know he has a son."

"Oh, he knows." Shelley took a long drink of her cola. "That's one of the first things I did is slap a paternity suit on him. He's supposed to send a check every month, but he doesn't have any money."

Ravyn tried to swallow the bile rising in her throat. "He knows? But. . .that can't be."

"It's true. Why are you so surprised? He's always been a womanizing jerk."

Disbelief showered over Ravyn. *Mark knows?*

A long minute passed in silence, then Shelley spoke again. "Look, I need some help. I've got to get out of here and I can't go to the mission. Not with Marky. Trust me, it's no place for a kid."

Ravyn blinked and tried to push aside her shock long enough to listen.

"All the friends I've made are—well, the wrong kind of friends, if you know what I mean. I just want to leave Chicago forever. I need to find a real-paying job and get Marky in a good school before he—he ends up like me."

"What do you want me to do?"

"Get me out of here, Ravyn. Please." Shelley leaned forward. "When you called last week I began to think there really is a God in heaven." She twirled the sweating glass in her palms. "I would have stayed on the phone with you longer, but Flint said if I did, he'd deduct the time out of my pay—which I still have yet to see. He just finds more ways to get me further indebted to him."

She wetted her lips. "Ravyn, let's get in your car right now and go—somewhere. Anywhere. Drop me off in a town that looks even remotely promising."

"And then what? Do you have any money saved?"

Shelley shook her head and lowered her gaze. A second later, she looked back at Ravyn. "But I'm sure I can find a job soon enough."

"At a sleazy nightclub or another greasy spoon?" Ravyn thought she might be naïve, but she didn't consider herself totally ignorant. "That won't help you. You'll end up falling back into your old lifestyle."

"Oh, but, please. I can't stay here." Shelley stared at her with wide and pleading eyes.

Ravyn pursed her lips, thinking about lending Shelley money. But, again, that posed a danger because Shelley could always use the borrowed funds to buy drugs.

"Okay, let's think over the situation. We need a plan." Ravyn had more or less spoken her thoughts and didn't expect a reply.

But Shelley set one hand on her shoulder and gave it a little squeeze. "Ravyn, it's Friday. It's a hot summer afternoon and there are going to be parties up and down this street tonight. Some friends might stop over with beer and drugs and I'm afraid that I might—"

"Okay, I understand." Ravyn sensed Shelley's hope was gone and her will was fading fast. "Then there's only one thing left for us to do."

"That is?"

"You and Marky are coming back to the hotel with me until we can figure out a practical solution."

Relief washed over Shelley's sunken features. "Thank you. It's at least a step forward." She sagged against Ravyn. "You're a true godsend."

❧

"Hey, watch this one!"

Ravyn turned just in time to see Marky jump off the diving board. His backside hit the water, creating a huge splash that reached both her and Shelley as they sat perched on the edge of the hotel's outdoor swimming pool.

"I'll have to nickname him Tsunami," Shelley joked.

Ravyn had to laugh in spite of all the drama earlier this afternoon.

After helping Shelley and Marky gather and pack their meager articles of clothing and miscellaneous items, they stopped at a discount store where Ravyn purchased some necessities for them. She had also bought swimsuits, thinking the pool would be a fun activity for Marky, and she'd been right: he now behaved very much like a typical ten-year-old boy.

It hadn't taken long before Ravyn realized she liked Marky. In fact, she liked him a whole lot more than she liked his father at the moment; however, she'd already noticed problematic behavior. Shelley had good cause for concern. Her son knew some colorful language and used it when he didn't get his way. He also tried to steal a portable CD player at the store, but Shelley caught him before they reached the cash register and made him put it back.

And Mark could have been a positive influence in his son's life. How can he think about helping people in a third world country when he doesn't even care about his own child?

Deep in Ravyn's soul she sensed something wasn't right, but she wrote it off as being in a state of shock and even denial. She immediately recalled Mark sitting with Carla alone in the break room and his nickname George in the ER. Maybe all the rumors were true after all.

What a scammer.

Ravyn felt heartsick. It seemed her suspicions about him had been right. Worse, he'd played her for a fool, and she'd fallen for his practiced charm. Then again, that's what she'd come to Chicago for: to learn the truth about both him and Shelley.

"I feel like I'm on a luxury vacation," Shelley said as she made swirls in the pool with her bony foot. "Marky and me—we're indebted to you big time."

Out of sheer politeness and nothing more, Ravyn pushed out a smile. The sight of Shelley in a bathing suit was worrisome. She looked rail thin. Her collarbone jutted out from beneath her onion-paper thin skin, and her ribs were visible with each deep breath Shelley took. Her knobby joints were equally as prominent, and her flamingo bird legs didn't look strong enough to even support her.

Ravyn glanced back at Marky. It was obvious to her that both mother and son had enormous issues to tackle. She felt overwhelmed, and not for the first time this afternoon. What would she do with these two? Shelley needed counseling—Marky did, too. They needed money and a safe place to live, and now Ravyn felt responsible for their well-being. On the other hand, if she wasn't careful these two might suck her time dry and deplete her savings account.

Lord, I've gotten myself into a real mess.

Just then Ravyn remembered Jace, the teen in the trauma room with the gunshot wound. She recalled her desire to help save his life and, later, her wish to help other teens before they found themselves in dangerous situations. On the path Marky treaded, he was headed for disaster. At least Shelley had the wisdom to see that fact before it was too late.

Ravyn drew in a deep breath and steadied her emotions. With God's help, she could think up a course of action.

"Okay, here I go again. Watch this one!"

Ravyn looked toward the diving board. Marky did another cannonball into the water, and she and Shelley couldn't help but laugh once more.

❧

Mark glanced at his watch. Three o'clock. He gazed around his aunt and uncle's yard where people stood mingling. He'd hoped to catch a glimpse of Ravyn, but it didn't look like she would show. Then again, what had he expected? He never did have another opportunity to talk to her since the shift she'd found him discussing the Lord with Carla and probably jumped to erroneous conclusions. Now his residency was completed, so he couldn't count on seeing Ravyn at the hospital again. He'd tried to call her all weekend, both at her condo and on her cell phone, but Ravyn never answered.

Oh, she was miffed at him, all right.

Or had she gone to Chicago by herself to try to find Shelley?

Mark wondered if he was right on both accounts. He had stopped by Ravyn's folks' house yesterday and no one had a clue as to her whereabouts, not even Teala. He knew from their lengthy discussions in the past that Ravyn was close to her younger sister. Why had she taken off, leaving the state, without telling someone about her plans? That was downright dangerous. If her intent had been to worry Mark sick, it worked, although he'd been careful not to upset her family with his questions and suspicions.

But what if something had happened to her?

The thought kept intruding on Mark's thoughts, and he didn't think he'd ever forgive himself if Ravyn was hurt—or worse.

At that moment, a couple of friends paused to congratulate Mark on "surviving" his residency.

"You made it, dude!" Andy Carey declared.

The two men balled their fists and knocked knuckles.

Mark chuckled and forced himself to relax and forget about Ravyn. She was, after all, an adult who could think for herself and make her own decisions.

Besides, Mark didn't know if he was even remotely welcome in her life in the first place.

Chapter 16

In the dark and quiet hotel room, Ravyn lay awake, thinking. She'd spent two and a half days with Shelley and Marky. She'd listened with a patient ear as Shelley told her one woeful tale after another. Her life thus far had been marred by one bad decision after another. Shelley claimed she was now more than ready to start anew.

The only question was where.

Ravyn ignored the answer that came to her time and time again. The last thing she wanted to do was take Shelley and Marky back to Dubuque and let them live with her. However, God's Holy Spirit seemed to prompt her to do exactly that.

But I don't want to support them. What if they steal from me? Where are they going to sleep? I don't want to give up my new bedroom set to Shelley. I worked hard for the things I have.

"Mom?"

Marky's whispered voice stilled Ravyn's thoughts.

"Mom, are you awake?"

"Shh." Shelley hushed him. Both she and Marky shared the queen-sized bed next to Ravyn's. Shelley said it was a far sight better than anything they'd slept on in years. "Be quiet or you'll wake up Ravyn."

"Mom, I don't think she wants to help us." Marky tried to speak in undertones, but it was like a foghorn trying to sound like a flute. Ravyn overheard him with little trouble, and the comment irritated her all the more. She'd been nothing but cordial and generous. She'd spent hundreds of dollars on them between buying new clothing and paying for all their meals. What else did the kid expect?

"Go to sleep, Marky."

"But, Mom, if Ravyn doesn't help us what are we going to do?"

"Will you quit worrying and go to sleep already?"

The silence that followed pressed in on Ravyn. She knew how Marky felt. As a little girl she had lost plenty of nights' sleep, fretting over what would become of her family.

"Walk by faith, Ravyn," her dad used to say. But it sounded so irresponsible to her young ears. She now knew the concept was one of God's commands. However, as a child, Ravyn wanted to find comfort in knowing her parents were in control and that they'd take care of her. In short, she longed for a sense of security.

And that's what Marky was asking for from his mother—security—except Shelley couldn't offer any. She battled her own demons and needed caring for herself.

Ravyn's heart softened. *Okay, Lord. For the first time in my life I'm going to walk by faith and take Shelley and Marky home with me. All I ask is that You help me each step of the way.*

"Okay, time for a meeting." Ravyn scooted upright in her bed, then reached over and flipped on the lamp.

Shelley and Marky squinted at her from the next bed.

"I've got a plan—and one that I honestly believe is God's will."

Marky bolted into a sitting position while Shelley propped herself up on one arm.

"Are you going to help us, Ravyn?" he asked. His dark eyes shone with anticipation.

"Marky, I've been helping you all weekend."

"Yeah, I know, but—"

"And we're very grateful," Shelley cut in before reaching backward and rapping her son in the shoulder.

He frowned and rubbed his arm.

"But I know what you're asking for, Marky, and I think I have the answer."

"What is it?" He appeared hopeful once more.

"You and your mom," Ravyn said, peering at Shelley, "are coming back to Dubuque with me and you're going to stay with me in my condo."

Shelley sat up a little straighter. "Back to Dubuque?"

"You'll have support there. My parents will help. No one is going to judge you. It's not as if you're the first single mother in the world—even though your folks forced that lie down your throat."

"I know, but—"

"And, Marky, where I live there's a pool and a golf course—"

Ravyn didn't even finish her sentence before the kid let out a whoop of happiness.

"Are you sure, Ravyn?" Tears glistened in Shelley's eyes.

"I'm sure but, um, there is one problem." The Dariens came to Ravyn's mind. They were so proud of Mark. Did they know he had a son?

She stood and pulled on her bathrobe. "Shelley, let's go out on the porch and talk so Marky can sleep and dream of doing super sized cannonballs in the pool at his *new home*."

"Yes!" He flopped onto his pillow. "But now I'm too excited to sleep. Can I watch TV?"

"No. It's late." Shelley turned out the light.

Ravyn crossed the room, pushed back the thick drape, and slid open the patio door. Shelley followed her outside. They stood on the small veranda that overlooked the hotel's parking lot.

"Thank you, Ravyn." Shelley enfolded her in a hug. "Thank you. I don't know what we would have done—"

"You're welcome." She stepped back. "I feel God wants me to help you out and I want to—trust and obey."

Shelley nodded, still looking grateful. "So what's the problem? I'll do anything you want. I'm trying to quit smoking. I'll sleep on the floor—"

"It has nothing to do with you." Ravyn drew in a deep breath, hoping for both tact and boldness. "It's, well, Mark has relatives in Dubuque. They're sweet people and, while I couldn't care less if Mark's reputation is soiled, hypocrite that he is, I don't want to hurt his aunt and uncle." She paused. "Do you think they know about Marky?"

"Mark has an aunt and uncle in Dubuque? I didn't know that. He's from out of state."

"Yes, but he's been living with his aunt and uncle—actually his great-aunt and uncle—while he finishes med school and his residency."

"Med school?" Shelley shook her head as if to clear it. "Wait a second—are you talking med school as in *Mark is a doctor?*"

"Yep, but unfortunately for you and Marky, he's bound for the mission field, so he still doesn't have any money." Ravyn tipped her head, thinking over the situation. "Unless he's lying about the mission field, too."

"Who's lying?"

"Mark." Ravyn stood arms akimbo and her anger mounted. "Oooh, that rat! I'll bet the whole medical missionary thing was a bunch of bunk so he could get out of paying child support."

Shelley gaped at her. "Mark is a *doctor?* No way!"

"Yes, 'way.' I met him in the ER when I started my job at Victory Medical Center. He just finished his residency." Ravyn thought back on the week. "His last day in the ER was Friday, and after he passes his boards, Mark will be a bona fide MD."

"Ravyn. . ." Shelley appeared confused. "I've done a lot of mind-altering drugs. I admit that to my shame. But I'm sober enough and sane enough to know that"—she shook her head again—"there is no way on God's green earth that Mark Leland is a medical doctor. No way."

"Who?" Ravyn felt her rage abate, only to be replaced by confusion. "Mark *Leland?* Who's that?"

"Marky's dad." Shelley regarded her askance. "Who are you talking about?"

"Mark Monroe."

Shelley scrunched up her face. "Who's that?"

Ravyn felt her throat go dry and humiliation flooded her being. "I thought *he* was Marky's biological father."

"Monroe?" Shelley shook her head. "Never heard of him."

"Yes you have."

The banter suddenly seemed comedic and Ravyn burst into a laugh, although nothing about the misunderstanding was funny. It had caused her much anguish this weekend, and it might have devastated Mark's plans for his ministry. But at the moment, Ravyn couldn't control the chortles bubbling up from somewhere deep inside her being.

Standing beside her, clad in the gray sweatpants and red tank shirt that Ravyn had purchased two days ago, Shelley regarded her with a frown. "Were you drinking at suppertime?"

"I don't drink." Ravyn tried in vain to suppress her ill-timed humor. "I'm sorry. I think I'm just so relieved."

"I feel like I just entered the Twilight Zone." Shelley combed her fingers through her shoulder-length hair, then set her hands on her bony hips.

Ravyn collected her wits. "Okay, let's start over. Who is Marky's father?"

"Mark Thomas Leland, formerly of Rochester, Minnesota, and currently a resident of St. Cloud. He flunked out of college and does odd jobs, but he's unemployed more than he works. Who are you talking about?"

"Mark Monroe. He was your leading man in my dad's summer production eleven years ago." Ravyn's mirth was replaced by a deep-seated sorrow. She'd believed the worst of him at every turn.

"Oh, yeah—him. I remember now. He was crazy about you, Rav. Remember how I said we were both going to end up with a guy named Mark?"

"Sure, I remember. But I thought you said that to imply I was getting in the way of your romance—*with Mark*." She tipped her head to one side and eyed Shelley. "Who is Mark Leland? Where did you meet him? When did you meet him?"

"That same summer—during the production. He was the light guy. He'd been going to school in Dubuque, taking summer remedial classes. Your dad somehow met him and convinced him to volunteer to work the spotlights for the play."

Ravyn searched her memory and came up empty. "I have no recollection of him."

"He wasn't a Christian."

She shrugged out a reply. She didn't know him.

"I talked about him all summer."

"I thought you meant Mark *Monroe*."

"Oh." Shelley halted and seemed to consider her answer. "Well, that's understandable. I was sneaking around with Mark Leland. I didn't want anyone to know. But you were my best friend. I couldn't help telling you about him."

"Right. And I always felt responsible for—for whatever made you leave Dubuque. Until two days ago, I never knew you were pregnant and your parents sent you away. I thought Mark Monroe broke your heart and you blamed me because..." She recalled the last scene of the play and Mark's kisses.

"Monroe was more interested in you than me."

Ravyn nodded and pulled her bathrobe tighter around her. The night was warm and humid, but with so many emotions pummeling her, she felt exposed and vulnerable.

"So you thought Marky was Monroe's kid? And what? Have you two rekindled that little spark from the past?"

"Sort of." Ravyn stared down at her bare feet.

"Hmm. I'm surprised you've been so nice to us all weekend. If our roles were reversed, I think I'd want to punch you in the nose."

"Thanks, *friend*," Ravyn quipped.

"Yeah, I'm horrible, all right." Shelley sounded serious as she gazed over the parking lot. At last she turned back to Ravyn. "But see how good you are? You've always been that way—always ready to help someone in need. I wasn't surprised when you told me you're a nurse."

She felt another jab in her conscience and looked up. "You're wrong, Shelley. I've been anything but good where Mark's concerned. I even went so far as to question his integrity and his character. He never once lost his patience with me. Instead, he told me he cares about me and he's phoned me at least four times this weekend. I've ignored his calls. I actually thought I—I hated him because I believed the worst-case scenario."

"There's a very fine line between love and hate, isn't there?"

Ravyn shrugged. With so many emotions bombarding her at the moment, she couldn't begin to identify her true feelings for Mark.

"Don't be so hard on yourself. Why wouldn't you believe the worst? You just admitted you can't recall meeting Mark Leland and it's not like I introduced you two or anything. I was off in my own little world, doing what I wanted to do. I gave no thought for anyone else."

"So every time you mentioned Mark, you meant Leland and I thought Monroe?"

"Sounds like it."

Ravyn tossed a glance at the stars that dotted the heavens. "Unbelievable."

Shelley folded her skinny arms and leaned against the wrought-iron rail of the porch. Next, Ravyn saw a silly grin curve her lips. "Wow. So, after all these years, you met up with *your* Mark again, huh?"

"Yes, but he's leaving the day after tomorrow, and we're at odds."

"Too bad." Remorse and wistfulness clotted Shelley's voice. "A good man is hard to find."

After having breakfast with a few friends, Mark returned to his great-aunt and uncle's house and began cleaning his bedroom. He sorted through his dresser drawers and closet. The chore didn't take long since Mark hadn't been home much during the last eight years. In fact, he hadn't experienced much of life outside the hospital, classroom, and, occasionally, church since he started med school and, after that, his residency program. Mark hoped he'd adjust to reality.

He moved to the large walnut-finished desk and emptied one drawer after another. Term papers, spiral-bound notebooks, admission letters, billing statements, handwritten comments and suggestions from professors—all were both useless and priceless mementos as he strove to achieve his goals. Mark could hardly believe that day had arrived.

His cell phone rang and he rushed to answer it but then reminded himself he wasn't on call anymore. He didn't have to jump. With a glance at the number on the external display, he felt more than a little surprised.

He flipped open his phone. "Ravyn. I didn't expect to hear from you *so soon.*" He cleared his throat after the pointed remark. He'd only been trying to reach her for three days.

"Very funny."

Mark grinned, stood, then stretched out on his bed while he talked. "So what's up?"

"This is going to take a while."

He glanced at his wristwatch out of habit more than anything else. "I've got some time. What's on your mind?"

"Well, first I want to apologize for not showing up at your party Sunday afternoon. I was in Chicago. I found Shelley."

"I figured. But I also know you weren't happy with me last week—"

"Yeah, I'm sorry about that, too. I guess I was puzzled when you were short with me in the hallway and then—"

"I had the neuro team hassling me about that patient we had in the ER, the one with the neck injury. As for Carla," he added, guessing her thought process, "I was witnessing to her, Ravyn."

"I'm not surprised."

Mark went from feeling defensive to defused by her agreeable reply. He'd fully expected her to challenge him. "Are you okay?"

"Yes. It's just been a rough weekend."

He listened as Ravyn began telling him about her friend Shelley, how she was in the throes of overcoming a drug habit, how she had a ten-year-old son—named Marky.

His gut lurched as possible allegations flitted across his mind. But an instant later, Ravyn quelled his mounting concerns. Shelley kept in touch with the boy's father, whose name just happened to be Mark.

Ravyn went on to explain how Shelley met the guy. "Do you remember him?"

"Vaguely."

"Well, that's more than I remember of him."

Mark pieced the circumstances together. On one hand, he could see how the case of mistaken identity occurred. On the other, he felt the sting of injustice and it wounded him to realize that Ravyn had struggled to believe him these last two months.

"I couldn't leave Shelley and Marky in that sweltering dump of an apartment. It was worse than any of the low-income units I lived in as a child. So I brought them back with me. Shelley really wants a chance at a new life, except— we already had an argument over cigarettes. I told her I wouldn't pay for them and Shelley's going crazy. She wants to smoke so badly that she's snapping at Marky and me. It's all I can do to keep my patience."

"There are over-the-counter remedies that might help Shelley."

"I know. I plan to pick something up for her when we go to the store this afternoon. She's making a grocery list right now. That's why I thought it'd be a good time for me to sneak out onto the deck and call you." A moment's pause. "Believe it or not, I didn't phone you to discuss Shelley and Marky."

"Oh?" He stared at the familiar white ceiling and wondered at the reason for her call. Did she need a favor?

Mark's pride cried out for retribution. *Hang up on her! Whatever she asks, refuse!*

However, the better part of him knew that if it were within his power, he'd help her any way he could. He cared about her and nothing she said or did would change the fact.

"What did you want to discuss?"

"Actually. I need to tell you something." Another pause. "I want you to know how truly sorry I am for—well, for jumping to conclusions and thinking the worst about you right from the start. I was so wrong."

The apology quieted his nagging indignation.

"I've done some soul-searching these past three days and God showed me that I've been selfish, angry, skeptical, bitter, and, well, maybe even jealous."

He grinned. *Maybe?*

"I hope you can forgive me."

His grin became a smile. How could he *not* forgive her? The Lord wouldn't allow it, and neither would his heart.

"All's forgiven."

He heard her expel a sigh. "Good. I know you leave tomorrow and—"

"Hey, how 'bout if I bring over a movie and a couple of pizzas?" Suddenly Mark didn't feel ready to wrap things up and say good-bye to Ravyn. He sensed their relationship could take a turn for the better, and he hated to miss an opportunity to see her again before he left Iowa. The fact she admitted to "maybe" feeling jealous encouraged him in a weird sort of way. "Do you feel like some extra company?"

"Sure. I could use some Christian reinforcement. And Marky will be happy with pizza. The kid eats nonstop."

"Good. Then it's a plan. I'll be over about six."

The conversation ended and in one swift move, Mark sat up and bounced off the bed. Pocketing his cell phone, he walked downstairs and informed his great-aunt that he wouldn't be home for dinner. Then, with renewed enthusiasm, he finished cleaning out his desk drawers.

Chapter 17

Sitting cross-legged on her sofa, Ravyn sent up a quick prayer while Mark explained the way of eternal salvation to Marky. After viewing a Christian movie about a boy with cancer who had one last wish to learn how to bull ride, Marky was full of questions. Even though Ravyn knew her walk with the Lord wasn't what it ought to be, she'd experienced the reality of her faith time and time again, and she prayed Marky would come to know Jesus in a personal way, too.

"God loved all of us so much that He sent His Son, Jesus Christ, from heaven to save us." Mark sat on the floor as he spoke. He appeared relaxed in his tan cargo pants and striped vintage-style cotton shirt, which he wore untucked; however, Ravyn sensed his zealousness. "Just like the character in the movie pointed out, we've all done things that are wrong and that's why we need the Lord."

"I thought *Jesus Christ* was a swear word," Marky admitted.

"Well, it's a sin to take God's name in vain," Mark explained. "People take God's name in vain when they use Jesus Christ as a swear word. But if we're talking about Him and how He's the One who saves us, then it's okay to say His name."

"Oh." Guilt reddened the boy's face before he looked over at his mom as if for confirmation.

"It's true." Shelley dabbed her eyes, wet, in part, from the movie's sad ending. "I should have told you about the Lord a long time ago, Marky, but I was—" She barely eked out the rest of her sentence. "I was living a life far away from God."

Marky appeared both uncomfortable and confused. He turned to Ravyn. "Can I have another piece of pizza?"

"Sure." She gave him a smile. "Help yourself."

He shot up from where he'd been sitting on the floor, grabbed his paper plate off the coffee table, and dashed into the kitchen.

"This is all foreign to Marky," Shelley said. "I don't think he's ever been to church in his entire life. And don't say it." She held her hand up, palm-side out. "I know it's my duty as his mother to teach him about God, but I haven't exactly been on my job and I take responsibility for it."

Mark stood. "I wasn't about to condemn you, and I doubt Ravyn would, either."

"She'd have good reason." Shelley stared at the tissue box in her lap. "You both would."

"Don't start in on yourself again." Ravyn reached across the length of the sofa and touched Shelley's shoulder. "You took a wrong turn in life, but you're headed in the right direction again."

"I agree." Mark stretched. "It's good you're willing to take responsibility for your actions."

Marky reentered the room. "Hey, can I see what else is on TV?" He picked up the remote with one hand and took a bite of his pizza with the other. A juicy piece of sausage tumbled onto the light-colored carpet. It bounced, leaving two blotches of greasy tomato sauce on Ravyn's expensive area rug.

"Oh, now look what you did," Shelley said. "Where's your plate?"

"I didn't think I needed it," Marky replied with his mouth stuffed.

Ravyn swallowed down her sudden impatience and steered the ten-year-old back into the kitchen. *This isn't the kid's first spill,* she reminded herself as she grabbed a handful of paper towels and pulled out the spray bottle of carpet cleaner from under the sink, *and it won't be the last.*

Without a word, she scrubbed out the spots before they became stains. Meanwhile, Shelley asked Mark various medical questions.

"I want to quit smoking for good, but I don't want to get fat. I heard people gain a lot of weight when they give up cigarettes."

Ravyn pressed her lips together and congratulated herself on her restraint. It was on the tip of her tongue to tell Shelley that she could use a few pounds on that bony body of hers.

Lord, I'm feeling bitter-spirited. Take it away and give me Your peace.

She reentered the kitchen and tossed the paper towels into the garbage.

"Sorry, Ravyn." Marky stared at her with wide, repentant brown eyes.

Her heart softened. "It's okay. It's just a rug." She tousled his dark hair. "When you're done eating, wash your hands, and then you can watch TV, okay?"

He nodded before taking another bite. His expression said all was right in his world again.

Ravyn realized, and not for the first time, that he was basically a nice boy. He just needed love and discipline—and lots of patience.

She stooped to put away the carpet solution and saw that Mark had followed her into the kitchen.

"It's after eight thirty. I need to get going. My plane leaves early tomorrow morning."

Ravyn stood slowly to her feet. She was surprised at the swell of disappointment mounting inside her. She pushed out a smile. "I'm glad you came over. Thanks for bringing the pizzas with you."

"You're very welcome." He inclined his head toward the door. "How about

102

if you walk me out?"

She had secretly hoped he'd ask. "Sure, but let me get something first." She traipsed to her bedroom and made her way to the dresser, where she lifted a small gift-wrapped box from its polished surface. While out grocery shopping this afternoon, she'd managed to stop at the mall and pick up a congratulatory present for Mark. It wasn't especially unique or expensive, but she hoped he'd like it.

She carried it in one hand discreetly at her side as she backtracked down the hallway.

"Keep the DVD," she overheard Mark say. "Watch it as much as you want to."

Marky shrugged a reply, seeming more interested in his cold pizza.

Meanwhile, Shelley climbed off the sofa and gave Mark a hug. "I wish you all the best."

"Thanks—and I'll be praying for you."

"Good. I need it."

Ravyn headed to the door, opened it, then she and Mark walked in silence to the elevator. Ravyn pressed the button to call the car to her floor.

"I've got to hand it to you," Mark said at last. "You're a brave woman to take on a Goliath of a project such as Shelley and her son."

"I'm not brave. I'm scared to death."

The elevator doors opened and they stepped inside.

"Could have fooled me."

Ravyn didn't reply but watched the illuminated numbers above the doors go from 3 to 1. When they reached the main floor, the elevator stopped and the doors opened.

"My advice, not that you've asked for it or anything. . ."

Ravyn grinned.

"Keep your eyes on Christ and you'll be fine. Remember Peter when he wanted to walk on water like the Lord? Jesus said, 'C'mon.' So he did. But the moment Peter doubted, he began to sink into the sea. Jesus had to pull him to safety."

Ravyn listened as they strode through the bright lobby. She remembered the biblical account.

"I think sometimes when God allows us to do great things for His glory, we start doubting and sink before accomplishing the mission."

She cast a glance his way. "Do you ever doubt your calling?"

"More times than I'd care to admit."

Ravyn suddenly regretted all the negative remarks she'd made. She certainly wasn't an encouragement to him.

"As for your situation, it looks like things have fallen into place. You have a plan, and Shelley seems both willing to go along with it and grateful for the help."

"Yes, she does."

Ravyn herself had much to be thankful for, particularly after her dad came up with "the plan" to which Mark referred. As of tomorrow morning, Shelley began her new secretarial position under the direction of Joan Drethers, the pastor's wife. Joan ran the office at the church Ravyn's parents attended and she needed assistance. She'd also earned a degree in biblical counseling years ago, so the setup seemed perfect. Meanwhile, Ravyn would continue her third-shift position in the ER and look after Marky during the day until school started in the fall. When Shelley came home in the afternoon, Ravyn would sleep and then Shelley would be home at night with her son.

Ravyn only prayed she could occupy a ten-year-old boy for eight hours a day.

They neared the lobby's front entrance and Ravyn touched Mark's arm. "Can you spare just a few more minutes?"

"Sure. In fact, I had hoped I'd get a little time alone with you."

Ravyn wondered at the remark while pointing to a corner where two printed-upholstered sofas and several coordinating armchairs had been placed near the impressive floor-to-ceiling stone hearth. The lobby in each section of this large condominium complex resembled an expansive great room which all occupants could enjoy. Tonight, however, the place was empty except for an occasional passerby.

Ravyn and Mark sat down on one of the couches.

"I bought you something."

"You didn't—"

"I know I didn't *have* to." She smiled at his look of embarrassment. "I wanted to."

"Well, thanks."

Ravyn scooted sideways and tucked her leg beneath her as she watched him open the gift. A smile curved his lips when he saw the gold-faced watch with its black leather band.

"I realize you might have a bazillion watches. I know I do. But this one is sort of special." Ravyn pointed out the smaller face within the large one. "It's like two watches in one, and now wherever you go and whatever time zone you're in, you'll always know what time it is in Dubuque, Iowa."

"Thank you, Ravyn." Mark leaned over and planted a quick kiss on her cheek. "I'll think of you when I wear it."

Now it was her turn at embarrassment, although it was short-lived. Torrents of remorse followed. How could she have misjudged him so completely?

"Mark, I'm sorry."

"For what?"

"I feel like I've wasted the last two months when, in truth, I could have enjoyed your friendship."

"If I hadn't ruined it by kissing you."

"Well, yeah." Ravyn fought off a smile and Mark sent her an amused grin. "But I've changed my mind about that—about our friendship."

"Oh?" Mark arched a brow.

Before she could explain, an elderly gentleman sat down in one of the nearby armchairs and opened the newspaper. With their privacy interrupted, Mark took Ravyn's hand and stood, pulling her up from the couch with him. He nodded toward the door, and she followed him out of the lobby and into the sultry June air. To the west, the horizon was aflame with the last of the sunset as they strolled through the guest parking lot.

"Now, as you were saying—you changed your mind?"

"Yes. It had to do with something Shelley said over the weekend. After hearing about her disastrous relationships, I came to the conclusion that any healthy, meaningful relationship develops from a friendship first."

"I agree."

"And, of course, the Lord has to be its foundation."

"That goes without saying."

They reached his car and Mark unlocked the door. He placed the gift Ravyn had given him inside and then turned back to her.

"I'm sorry I nipped our—friendship in the bud. But maybe it's for the best since you're—"

"Headed for the mission field," he finished for her.

"I was going to say *leaving*."

"Really?"

"Yes."

He gave a quick bob of his head, then lowered his gaze. When he looked up again, his gaze held a spark of mischief. He dipped a brow. "Of course there is the fact ye thought I was a black-hearted scoundrel."

Ravyn laughed at his antics.

"In that case, ye had good cause to sever our friendship," he continued.

She applauded. "Good pirate imitation, Monroe. My dad would be proud."

He took a bow.

Again the feelings of regret; they might have had fun together if she'd only given him the benefit of the doubt.

"Are you ever coming back?" The question rolled off Ravyn's tongue before she could stop it.

"Yeah, I'll be back." Mark stepped forward and gathered her into his arms. "Around Christmastime."

Ravyn wrapped her arms around his midsection. December seemed like a million years away.

"Will you wait for me?" His lips brushed against her temple and then he stepped back. "I'd like a chance to continue this conversation."

Looking up into his dark eyes, she barely got the chance to nod before Mark folded her into another embrace and pressed a fervent kiss against her mouth. Ravyn's senses took flight. Suddenly she felt sixteen again.

And then the moment ended.

"I'll call you."

Ravyn fought her disappointment.

"You have my cell phone number."

She nodded. "Take care of yourself." Her throat felt tight with unshed emotion.

He sent her a smile before climbing behind the wheel of his car. She walked away, unable to watch him go. She made her way to the lobby and, once inside, she strode to the elevators.

As she rode the car to her third-floor condo, Ravyn made a startling self-discovery: She'd fallen in love with Mark Monroe. Perhaps she'd loved him all along.

But now. . .was it too late?

Chapter 18

Ravyn walked down the maroon-carpeted aisle of one of the smaller theaters on the University of Dubuque campus. Her father's production would be held here this year, as were all rehearsals. From his vantage point, Dad saw her coming and waved.

"Okay, everyone!" he called to his cast. "Let's all take a fifteen-minute break!"

The people onstage set down their scripts and began conversing with each other.

Ravyn reached the front of the auditorium and hugged her dad.

"Hi. How's Marky been behaving?"

"Good. Your mother and I kept him busy." He chuckled. "Between helping us out and his baseball practice each morning, I'd say we're successfully taking the wind out of the boy's sails." Dad's gaze brightened. "It's smooth sailing from here on in."

Ravyn agreed. "I'll take him home now and let him go swimming and that should *anchor his ship in the harbor*," she teased, "at least for today."

Her father's jolly laughter rang throughout the empty theater. He slung his arm around her shoulders and gave her an affectionate squeeze. Then he planted a juicy smooch on the side of her head.

"Dad, please." She grinned and pushed him away.

He laughed again. As annoying as his shows of affection could be at times, Ravyn truly enjoyed them. What's more, she appreciated her parents' help these last two weeks with Marky. In ten short days, he'd morphed into a child again.

Shelley, on the other hand, seemed to struggle hour by hour, day by day. Sometimes Ravyn felt exhausted just getting Shelley to the church office where she worked six hours each day. As sad as it seemed, her friend hadn't worked an honest job in all her life. Rousing herself out of bed, showering, and getting dressed on time for her job each morning involved self-discipline, which was all new to Shelley. Even so, Shelley only had to recall the horror of her existence in Chicago, and all complaints were quelled.

Ravyn rounded up Marky, then said her good-byes to her mom and dad before leaving the redbrick building. Together she and Marky traipsed to the curb and climbed into Ravyn's car.

"Did you have fun this afternoon?"

"Yep. I was painting."

"I see that." Ravyn smiled as she noted the dried green and blue paint on his knuckles and under his fingernails. "A good swim in a chlorinated pool should fix that."

"Fix what?" He gave her a curious glance.

"The paint on your hands."

Marky seemed to notice it for the first time. "Oh, guess I didn't wash good enough."

Ravyn laughed. Typical boy.

They arrived home and changed into their swimwear. Ravyn grabbed a couple of towels and her cell phone. Minutes later, they were playing volleyball in the pool. Other children who lived in the condominium complex had seen them splashing and laughing and decided to join in on the fun. Soon the pool was filled with squealing kids.

Ravyn decided to take refuge in a deck chair on the sea-green tiled deck where other parents sat observing the ruckus. In conversing with her neighbors, she became better acquainted with them, and she realized what terrific social icebreakers kids could be.

Shelley had arrived home from work and showed up at the poolside in her denim skirt and T-shirt.

"I had a hunch this is where I'd find you." She pulled over a deck chair and sat beside Ravyn.

"You're home early."

"Joan had a dentist appointment, so she dropped me off."

"Oh, okay." Ravyn pointed at Marky. "Look at him over there. He's having a ball."

"So I see."

Shelley watched her son for several long minutes. Unidentified emotions played across her thin face before she turned in her chair and faced Ravyn. "I felt like quitting today. I got my first paycheck and the amount is laughable. I used to make better money in one night at the dance club than a whole week at the church office."

Ravyn grimaced. "You didn't quit, did you?"

"No. But I was going to. Except, now that I see Marky. . ." Shelley expelled an audible sigh. "I feel like God is showing me I'm doing the right thing. I won't get rich or famous, but I can do what's best for my kid. At this rate, he might actually grow up to be a decent human being."

Ravyn's heart went out to her friend. She reached over and set her hand on Shelley's arm. "Be assured. You're doing the right thing. You don't have to worry about money right now. You're my guest. Indefinitely. Maybe we should go to the bank and open a savings and checking account for you so if you need something—"

"I was hoping we could do that."

"But not cigarettes."

Shelley sent her a dark glance. "All right. No cigarettes."

"Cigars are off limits, too," she teased.

Shelley laughed. "I don't smoke cigars, you nut."

Ravyn grinned.

The next few minutes passed in silence as they watched the kids swim. Ravyn felt encouraged that Shelley mentioned the Lord showing her something and influencing her decision to stay at her job. It was progress.

"Did you hear from Mark today?"

Ravyn wagged her head. "Not yet."

"But you will. I noticed he's called every day since he left."

"Yes, he has. I keep thinking we'll run out of things to talk about, but we never do."

"If I were you, I'd hang on to that guy."

Ravyn reclined in her chair. "I'm trying to figure out how to do that."

"What you do you mean?"

"Well, as much as I love and respect my parents, I don't want to live the way they did, always relying on other people to support them financially. You remember how it was. And now I happen to fall for a guy who's going to be a missionary."

"Just for the record, I think you had it better at home than I ever did." Shelley crossed one slim leg over the other. "Your family was always laughing and having fun, but my folks were serious and worrying all the time about what the neighbors thought."

"I mean *financially*. Sometimes we didn't know where our next meal was coming from."

Shelley paused as if to digest the remark. "I don't recall you guys ever being in dire straits. Besides, missing a meal here and there never killed anyone. It's not like you, Teala, and Violet were starving to death."

"Shelley!" Ravyn couldn't believe her friend's lack of empathy.

"One time I went on a binge and I don't think Marky ate for days. He was just a little guy, too. I'm so ashamed." After a glance at her son in the pool, Shelley turned back to Ravyn.

"And your point is?"

"I guess what I'm saying is that your parents are human. Sure, they probably made plenty of mistakes. But they're good people who help others all the time, and you—well, you're the same way. Look at how you're helping me out. I cringe to think what could have happened to Marky and me if you hadn't stepped out of your comfort zone and come to Chicago."

Ravyn didn't know whether to bristle at the reprimand or feel flattered by Shelley's gratefulness.

She laughed in spite of herself. Then she rapped Shelley on the knee and stood. "Come on. Let's try to get to the bank before it closes."

❧

"So, what do you hear from George lately?"

Ravyn glanced up from a patient's chart to see Liz standing beside her with a teasing gleam in her eyes.

"We miss him around here. The new residents aren't nearly half as much fun to tease."

"I'll tell him that. I'm sure Mark will be flattered." Ravyn laughed.

"Seriously, what's he doing?"

"Right now he's at a large church in Wisconsin, helping with Vacation Bible School." Ravyn regarded Liz askance. "Did you know he's planning on being a missionary? This summer he's visiting different churches, hoping to gain their support."

"Yeah, I heard something to that effect. The two of you belong to the same church, right?"

"Sort of." Ravyn didn't have time to go into lengthy explanations about the big church forming a spin-off church on the other side of the city.

"Doesn't surprise me that you're religious." Liz leaned sideways against the counter. "I never heard you swear before, and you don't slack off like the rest of us."

"That hardly makes me religious, Liz. Anybody can stay busy and refrain from using curse words. What makes me different is. . ." Ravyn paused, realizing she'd never talked about the Lord at work before. While she would never push her faith on others, her co-worker was, in fact, probing for answers and at this point in her life, Ravyn felt comfortable enough and ready to share her knowledge. "It's my relationship with Jesus Christ."

An odd expression washed over Liz's tanned and freckled face. "You're one of those fanatics, eh?"

"Hardly. And I make my share of mistakes, so if you're going to suddenly expect me to be perfect, forget it."

"At least you're honest." Liz grinned. "I think that's why I've always liked you. Now back to George—he's going to the Amazon, right?"

"Um, no. Wrong continent. Try Indonesia."

"Oh, that's right. All I could remember was that it's someplace warm."

Ravyn smiled. "No wonder rumors get started around here."

"Yeah, no kidding. Once you hit forty, the memory goes." She took a step closer to Ravyn. "But, speaking of rumors, I found out Carla lied through her teeth about her and George. But you probably knew that already."

"Yes." Ravyn peered back down at the chart again.

"You could have said something. You could have at least told *me*." Liz's voice carried through the partially empty ER. "You should have confronted Carla for lying. She would have deserved it."

"Mark could have confronted her, too." Ravyn lifted her gaze once more and stared into Liz's blue eyes. "But he decided that a softer approach would be more effective, and I've come to realize he was right."

"Yeah, well, we decided on a soft approach, too—none of us are speaking to Carla."

Ravyn pressed her lips together. She refused to get mixed up in the mess.

"But next time you talk to your pal George," Liz said with a lilt in her tone, "tell him that the girls on third in the ER miss him."

"Will do. The news will make his day, I'm sure." Ravyn couldn't help feeling amused.

Then, out of the corner of her eye, she spotted Carla, who pushed a patient's gurney back into his room. Obviously the patient had come from having an x-ray. Ravyn wondered if the younger woman's feelings were hurt now that her co-workers shunned her. But perhaps she didn't care.

Flipping the chart closed, Ravyn checked on Mrs. Hiland, a stroke victim who'd suffered a setback. The neurology team had been summoned to evaluate and treat Mrs. Hiland's symptoms. Ravyn's job was to keep the sweet elderly lady stable until they arrived, and so far so good.

After seeing to her patient's needs, Ravyn exited the room and smacked headlong into Carla.

"I need to talk to you." Carla stuffed her hands into her smock's front pockets. "Can you take a break real quick?"

Ravyn thought it over. "Yeah, I guess now's okay." She thought Carla seemed anxious. "I'll let Liz know I'm leaving."

"Okay, I'll meet you on the smoking deck."

Ravyn went to tell Liz she was taking a break. Then, as promised, she met Carla outside. For the last week, an oppressive heat wave bore down on most of the Midwest, Iowa being no exception. The ER had been full today with people complaining of respiratory problems and other heat-related illnesses. Even now, at two o'clock in the morning, the temperatures were in the eighties, and the air felt thick and muggy.

"I've got to show you something." Carla took Ravyn's elbow and steered her under one of the halogen lamps. She lifted her top, revealing her midriff—and something more. A nasty purplish blue bruise spanned her entire left side.

"Ouch." Ravyn winced. "How did you manage that?"

"I fell backward off some bleachers. It was a pretty high fall. I'd been drinking and my friends thought I was dead because when I hit the ground, I knocked myself out cold."

"Did they call an ambulance?"

"No, someone just drove me home."

Ravyn gave her a momentary look of shock. "They didn't drive you to the hospital?"

"They'd been drinking a lot, too, so they didn't want to get involved."

"Carla!" Ravyn stood arms akimbo. "What kind of friends are those?"

Carla shook her head and thick strands of her blond hair escaped from the clip at her nape. "It doesn't matter. I probably won't see any of them again and, if I do, I won't remember their names or that we even partied together at the park." Carla held her top up higher. "Take a look, Ravyn. Did I break some ribs? I about died, pushing that patient back to the ER from radiology."

"If you're concerned about it, you need to get an x-ray."

"But everyone will talk—"

"Carla, if any co-worker reveals your personal health information just to gossip he or she will be in violation of the Federal HIPAA law."

"True, but you know how it goes."

"You have to think about your health first."

After a few more minutes of discussion, Carla finally made the decision to ask her supervisor if she could clock out early. Things weren't terribly busy, so Carla proceeded to check herself into the ER for an examination and x-ray of her midsection. Ravyn managed to work it out so she was Carla's nurse. She escorted her into one of the farthest curtained exam rooms on the opposite side of the nurses' station, so no one else paid much attention to the new admission.

"This is the second time you've come to my rescue," Carla muttered after she'd changed into a white and gray checked gown that wrapped around and tied at the waist. "Mark told me that I could always count on you."

Ravyn realized she'd been hearing the "count on you" comment a lot lately, from Shelley and now Carla, too. But, in truth, people had always relied on Ravyn for as long as she could remember. Her parents, sisters, friends, co-workers—and suddenly she didn't view it as a burdensome thing. She felt flattered. Needed.

"I'm so sick of this life."

"What do you mean?" Ravyn sat on the corner of the linen-covered gurney.

"My life. . ." Carla shook her blond head. "I just wish I could get it together."

"No one can do that for you, Carla."

"I know. But I can't do it alone, either." Tears filled her huge blue eyes, and she tried to blink them back. "I know there are a lot of support groups out there, but that's the problem. Which one do I choose?"

"Would you like to come to a ladies' Bible study with me and my friend Shelley tomorrow night?" The offer bounded out of Ravyn's mouth before she had a chance to really consider it.

"Bible study?"

Ravyn nodded, feeling amazed that twice during the same shift she'd been afforded the chance to share a snippet about her faith. "You'll find the truth about anything you're struggling with in the Bible. It's a great place to start."

Before Carla could answer, the staff physician entered the exam room. Ravyn left so the doctor could examine his patient's injuries, but she made a mental note to give Carla her phone number in case she decided to come to the Bible study. Ravyn had planned to go for Shelley's benefit but realized some time ago that she needed the fellowship and teaching from God's Word as much as anyone else.

Stepping over to the counter where she set down Carla's chart, Ravyn felt awestruck once more. Never before had she witnessed to co-workers. While she had never been ashamed to be a Christian, she'd never gone out of her way to present the Truth, either. It had been years since God used her as an instrument of His love and goodness, and Ravyn had to admit that it felt good.

Chapter 19

"Over here! Over here!"

Ravyn's gaze followed the voice to the front row where Marky stood waving his arms.

Shelley leaned closer to Ravyn. "Wouldn't you know he found us front-row seats? I was hoping for an inconspicuous spot in the back row."

Grinning at the comment and Marky's enthusiasm, Ravyn led the way down the carpeted aisle. Marky had seen her dad's production four times already, not including rehearsals, and she and Shelley had seen it twice, counting tonight—opening night and now the closing Labor Day weekend show. Since Marky had had a hand in the production, Ravyn's folks invited him to the cast party after the show. A more excited ten-year-old couldn't be found in all of Iowa.

"Hurry! Someone might get our seats!"

"Oh, Marky." Shelley said his name on a weary-sounding sigh as they reached him. "I doubt there will be a run on front-row seating. Besides, all you'd have to say is that you're saving these seats for your mom and your aunt Ravyn."

Without a reply, the kid turned and sat down. Then he bounced with anticipation in his padded chair.

Shelley deposited a program in his lap and sat beside him. Ravyn took the place next to her. The rest of the row stood empty, and she smiled at Marky's concern that someone might steal their seats if they hadn't acted quickly enough. Typically the Labor Day weekend show wasn't crowded; however, with the college students back on campus now, the small theater might hold a larger than expected audience. Ravyn knew if such a thing occurred it would please her father tenfold.

She stared, unseeing, at the program, which Violet had created on the computer, and thought about how far her dad's summer plays had come over the years. From a tent in the park and hand-typed, one-sheet programs to a beautifully renovated theater on the University of Dubuque campus with central air-conditioning and high-tech brochures that included pictures of each cast member inside. Sure, Dad's plays had been acted out in other theaters before, but sometimes the "theater" was a vacant church or a dark, dingy movie theater ready to close and be demolished. Other times churches lent him their auditoriums. But the time arrived at last when Dad's productions found a fitting home, since the university had offered him the use of this theater indefinitely. Dad was an alum and had, over the years, developed close relationships with several directors on the school's seminary board. They supported his ministry and during the school year Dad would begin teaching a class or two.

Ravyn felt so proud of him.

"Your father is living his dream of serving God in this way," Mark had said during a phone conversation several nights ago. "Your mom has been his perfect *helpmeet* to him."

Ravyn couldn't help the wry grin that tugged at her mouth as she recalled the discussion. She knew Mark was rubbing in the helpmeet part. But she had to admit her cynicism had waned over the summer. She'd seen the power of God in both Shelley's and Carla's lives and realized how complacent, even neglectful, she'd become in her walk with Christ.

In essence, Ravyn had evidenced the power of God in her own life, too.

"This is gonna be good." Marky squirmed in his chair. It seemed he couldn't sit still.

"You've seen this play a dozen times." Shelley shook her head at him in dismay. "Why are you so excited?"

Marky's brown eyes widened with exasperation. "I told you. It's a surprise."

"Oh, good grief." Shelley leaned into Ravyn. "I keep wondering if we should be worried."

"If my dad and your son are in cahoots, I think we should be very worried."

"I hear ya."

They shared a smile and Ravyn guessed her father had told Marky he'd mention his name and thank him publicly for all his hard work this summer. That would explain Marky's insistence on arriving early and claiming front-row seats.

The din in the theater began to grow with the number of people. Within a half hour, Ravyn guessed nearly three quarters of the theater had filled. Then, precisely at seven o'clock, the lights in the house dimmed and Al Woods took the stage.

"Good evening, ladies and gentleman." He spoke into the microphone and the audience quieted.

"Thank you for coming tonight. I trust you won't be disappointed with our production." He smiled and Ravyn thought he looked dapper in his dark suit. She marveled at how carefree he appeared while facing a couple hundred pairs of eyes. "Since this is our closing night, I'd like to take a few minutes to thank some very special people. My wife, Zann, for one. Paintress extraordinaire. She created our backdrops and selected the costumes. She also keeps me in line." With a chuckle he turned sideways and extended his arm. "Come on out here, Zann. Take a bow."

Ravyn applauded with the others as her mother waltzed onto the stage, waved to the audience, and then disappeared behind the thick red velveteen curtain.

"After the show, you'll meet our talented cast. At that time, I'll also tell you about our ministry—"

"Anyone sitting here?"

Her attention diverted for the moment, Ravyn gave the gentleman taking the seat beside her an annoyed look. "Um, no," she said in a hushed voice. She wondered why the guy didn't move down one, since there was plenty of room.

She glanced at him again and all at once she noticed his smile, caught the spark of amusement in his gaze, and smelled his zesty cologne.

"Mark!" She couldn't believe her eyes. She kept her tone low since her father was still speaking, but a mix of happiness and disbelief began pumping through her veins. "What are you doing here?"

He placed his arm around her shoulders and gave her a quick kiss. "I wanted to see your dad's play," he whispered. "Well, actually, I wanted to see you."

His words made her want to melt. "When did you get back?"

"A couple of hours ago, but I've been planning to surprise you for about a week. I had a church cancel on me—but I'll tell you about that later."

Ravyn nodded at the same time Shelley nudged her.

"Your dad just called Marky up onstage."

Ravyn grinned and watched as the boy sprang from his seat and made his way up onstage like a pro. When he reached Ravyn's father, he stared into the audience with an awed grin.

"So now, Marky, tell us what happened a few days ago." Dad removed the mike from its stand and held it close to Marky's lips.

"I got saved." His voice shook with mild trepidation.

"Tell our guests here tonight what that word *saved* means."

"Um. . ." Marky seemed stumped. "It means, like *saved*, like firemen save people and stuff."

"Rescued?"

"Yeah." The kid perked up.

"Well, who rescued you and from what were you rescued?"

Ravyn grinned at her father's dramatics.

"Jesus saved me, and I was saved from dying and spending the rest of my whole dead life away from God."

"Dead life? Hmm." Dad folded his arms and cupped his chin, looking thoughtful. "Do you mean eternal life?"

"Yeah, cuz when you die in this life you got another life and you either spend it with God or away from God." Marky used his hands to illustrate the two options. "God is like the sunshine, but the place that's away from God is all dark and nasty."

"Dark and nasty?" Dad shuddered. "Not for me. But, pray tell, how did you get rescued? How can anyone get rescued?"

"Well, it's like this." Marky took the microphone and Ravyn laughed at his sudden boldness. "Everybody's headed for that dark, nasty place because we've all done bad things in our lives. But if you're sorry about doing bad things, then you can get saved by Jesus."

"How?" Dad prompted.

"By asking Him, because Jesus is God's Son and He's got the power."

"A real live Superhero, eh?"

"Yeah, because God can do anything."

"That's right. So how do you feel now that you've been saved?"

"Good."

Ravyn had to laugh at the elementary reply.

"What would you tell others who are doing their own soul-searching?"

"I'd tell 'em to get saved and hurry up. And when it happens, you know it! It's like you can feel yourself get saved on the inside and then, when you open your eyes, everything seems different. Better."

Out of the mouths of babes, Ravyn thought as unexpected tears clouded her vision.

"Wow, that's terrific," Mark whispered near her ear. "He accepted Christ."

"It's a miracle." She smiled at him before glancing at Shelley, who had plump tears dribbling down her narrow face. Reaching under her seat, Ravyn took hold of one of the many tissue boxes strategically placed throughout the theater for times such as these.

She passed the tissues to Shelley. "Marky turned to Christ. He'll be all right now."

"But he's still a little boy who needs his mother," Ravyn reminded her. "Don't go writing yourself off as useless like you've done in the past. Marky needs you."

"Maybe so, but he's a Christian now and as long as chooses to walk with the Lord, he'll never end up in my footsteps."

Dad's voice boomed through the theater. "Well, Marky, that's quite a testimony. Folks," he addressed his audience once more, "this young man has been an enormous help to our summer staff and he's now been adopted into the family of God. Let's give him a big hand."

Ravyn applauded and even stood to give Marky a bear hug when he returned to his seat. "I'm very proud of you, my brother."

His pride and chagrin formed two rosy spots on his sun-tanned cheeks.

"Way to go, Marky." Mark extended his hand and the child gave his palm a smack.

"Are you surprised, Mom?"

"Am I ever! But I'm happy more than surprised." Shelley's voice was thick with unshed emotion. "Getting saved is the most important decision you'll ever make."

"And you, too." He took his mom's hand and sandwiched it between his two smaller ones. "Mom, if you watch this play tonight you can get saved, too. God doesn't care about all the bad things you've done. He forgives and you can start over."

Overcome with emotion, Ravyn swiped a few tissues from the box still in Shelley's lap. Marky loved his mother so much. The fact had been evident from the first day Ravyn met him. She listened now, wondering if Shelley would explain that she had been saved by grace years ago, but that she'd unfortunately become what the Bible calls in the book of Jeremiah "faithless" and backslidden. Shelley needed God's healing, but as far as Ravyn knew she'd asked Jesus to save her long ago.

Didn't she? Ravyn dabbed her eyes and wiped her nose. Well, that was up to God to judge. Not her. At the present, however, Shelley seemed to have little regard for herself. Instead, she appeared proud and happy with her son for his decision.

"I'll take you out for ice cream after the show, okay? We'll celebrate."

"Okay. Right after the cast party." The joy on Marky's face didn't fade until the lights in the house went down and the curtain opened.

Dry-eyed at last, Ravyn settled in beside Mark. The warmth of his presence and the weight of his arm around her shoulders lent her an assured, secure feeling. She wished this moment would last forever. Everything in the world seemed so indescribably perfect.

❧

The September night air had a nip to it. Ravyn scooted closer to Mark where they glided back and forth on a freestanding wooden swing that had been built on the edge of the park. From their vantage point, they could see the lights from downtown Dubuque sparkling off the Mississippi River.

"Are you cold?" Mark pulled her in tighter, right next to him.

"Not anymore."

He smiled. "Your folks have done a great job with Marky, and Shelley seems to be coming along, too."

"She hasn't missed a day of work all summer."

"I'm impressed. I know you've been keeping me updated on their situations when we've talked on the phone. But to actually see their progress is incredible— and it's all because of your willingness to be used by God."

"No, it's not. God worked in spite of me." Ravyn straightened and looked up into Mark's face. "I've witnessed the power of God like never before. What's more, I've come to respect my parents' ministry in a way I never thought possible. They hear the Lord's voice and obey Him. It sounds so simplistic, I realize, but to listen for God's still small voice above the din of life with all its trials and temptations isn't easy."

"How well I know that." He bobbed his head as if to emphasize the point.

"I'm ashamed of myself for putting them down for the work they do."

"Hmm. Do you feel that way about overseas missionaries, too?"

Ravyn opened her mouth to reply, but Mark cut her off.

"Before you answer, let me say that I don't know how far across the ocean I'll get at the rate I'm going. I'm only at 27 percent support. After practically knocking myself out at that Bible school program in Wisconsin, the church decided not to sponsor me."

"How disappointing."

"To say the least. Then the next church canceled my visit altogether."

"Well, we both know life's full of setbacks and letdowns, Mark. Why should the ministry be any different that way?"

"I don't know. I guess I just thought it would be. Maybe I've been rather arrogant to think God would hand me my support on a golden platter—just like my aunt and uncle paid my way through med school."

"I think you're being too hard on yourself." She leaned her head against Mark's shoulder again. His long-sleeved chambray shirt felt soft against her face and the side of her arm. "Your aunt and uncle might have paid the school bill, but you worked your backside off and you know it. You earned your MD."

"I worked hard, that's for sure." He kissed her temple. "But I made some phone calls in the last couple of days anyway, and I'm praying about whether to accept a job in an urgent care clinic here in Dubuque. If it's what God wants, I don't mind throwing some of my own money into the support pot."

"Really?" Ravyn turned on the swing to face him. "You're thinking of staying?"

"For now."

"I can't pretend. I'm elated."

"I kind of figured you might be." A half smile tugged at the corner of Mark's mouth. "But please understand that this in no way means I'm giving up my plans for the mission field. I view this as a temporary setback."

"I see it as a blessing. If you were to accept the urgent care position it'll buy us some time."

Mark regarded her askance, wearing a look of mischief. "And what kind of time are you seeking to purchase, madam?" he asked, feigning a French accent.

Ravyn laughed. "You are so crazy."

"That is because I am crazy about you."

He pulled her close to him again, but instead of a kiss, Ravyn felt a buzz when Mark's cell phone vibrated in his shirt pocket.

Startled, she jolted backward. Mark caught her arm before she could topple off the swing.

With one arm around Ravyn, he pulled out his phone. "You've got to stay away from those lattes, girl."

Ravyn caught her breath. "Excuse me. I thought I was being electrocuted by Pepé LePew."

Mark chuckled and answered his phone.

Grinning over the near mishap, Ravyn leaned back in the swing and stared up at the star-studded sky. Her smile faded, however, when she heard the sudden alarm in Mark's voice.

He sat forward, his forearms resting on his knees. "Did you call the paramedics?"

Ravyn moved to the edge of the swing and stared at Mark, wondering what sort of terrible thing had happened.

"Okay, tell them to transport him to Victory Medical Center. I'll meet you there. Did you try to rouse him? Is he breathing? Okay, okay—don't panic. Wait for the paramedics to arrive."

Ravyn's heart sank as she guessed the situation. Mark's uncle had likely suffered another heart attack.

Mark stayed on the line with his great-aunt, trying to calm her, until she announced the emergency medical personnel had arrived. When he finished the call, he confirmed Ravyn's suspicions.

"From what my aunt described, things sound rather grim." Mark's voice sounded tight with emotion as he stood. "I need to get over to the hospital."

"I'm coming with you."

He helped Ravyn off the swing.

"You sure? I have time to drive you home first."

"Nope, I'm positive."

Ravyn slipped her hand into his as they strode to Mark's car. There was no place on earth she'd rather be right now than by his side.

Chapter 20

With a cloud of disbelief fogging his mind, Mark stared at his great-uncle's casket. Had it really only been three days ago that Uncle Chet was pronounced dead at the hospital? Everything between then and now seemed a blur of calling friends and family members, meeting with the pastor and funeral director, and picking up relatives at the airport. But now reality struck: Uncle Chet was dead.

A tug on his arm reminded Mark of his aunt Edy. She clung to him as though her legs might not support her if she let go. He told himself to be strong. Aunt Edy needed him. Besides, as a physician, Mark had always been aware that death was a very real part of life. However, the fact hit him on a personal level, and it hit him hard.

The pastor read from the scriptures beneath gloomy skies, which seemed a fitting backdrop for this moment. Unable to concentrate, Mark stared across the gaping reddish brown earth and spotted Ravyn. Wearing somber garb, she stood alongside her family with Shelley and her son. Mark would have liked to feel Ravyn's presence beside him today. But his immediate family had arrived from New Hampshire, and they pressed in around him.

Ravyn. He didn't know how he would have managed without her these past couple of days. She had been a big help in consoling his aunt. Mark only hoped Ravyn understood that his neglect of her hadn't been intentional.

As if he'd spoken the illogical thought aloud, she glanced up and met his gaze. He saw only empathy in her expressive dark eyes. If he hadn't realized it before, he did now; he loved Ravyn.

She gave him a little smile before lowering her gaze. Mark, too, bowed his head as the pastor began to read the Twenty-third Psalm.

" 'The Lord is my shepherd; I shall not be in want. . . .' "

The graveside service ended and Mark lost sight of Ravyn, although he knew he'd catch up with her at some point. He focused on his duties at hand and helped Aunt Edy across the small country cemetery. They reached the parking lot, and he helped her into the car before walking around and climbing in behind the wheel.

"I invited the Woodses over to the small gathering at the house." Aunt Edy smoothed down the skirt of her black dress before she snapped her seat belt into place. "I didn't think you'd mind."

Mark started the car's engine. "Of course I don't."

"About time the two families meet each other."

"I agree." He sent his great-aunt a small smile and pulled out of the parking lot.

Silence spanned the next several minutes.

"Chet was very proud of you. He left a provision for you in his will. It's in the form of a life insurance policy, and its sum will take care of any funds you're lacking in church support."

"Let's talk about this later, all right?"

"Yes." Aunt Edy's voice sounded strained. "I just thought you should know about the money. Chet wanted very much to help you realize your goals to serve the Lord on the mission field, and that policy will help you get there."

"And what about you?" Mark braked for a stoplight and turned to his great-aunt. Her fawn-colored hair curled out from beneath the round black hat she wore. "I need to know you'll be well provided for."

"Oh, yes, I'll be fine." She held her hanky to her nose. "Chet made sure of it."

Mark's heart broke as she began to weep. He reached over and touched her shoulder and felt it shake beneath his palm. He felt like sobbing himself. It was hard to believe Uncle Chet wouldn't be at home when they arrived.

But of course, he was home—with the Lord in His eternal home in heaven.

Aunt Edy composed herself. "Nothing would make me happier than to see you marry Ravyn Woods and set off to Indonesia. She's a special young woman. Such a sensitive soul. She's been a comfort to me in the last couple of days, and she took in Shelley Jenkins and her boy. Why, she also brings that other young lady to our Bible study."

"Carla?"

"Yes, that's her."

"Aunt Edy, you don't have to convince me of Ravyn's big-hearted attributes. I've seen them for myself."

In spite of his comment, Mark's anguish mounted. He only had to recall how pleased Ravyn had been when he'd mentioned the position at the urgent care clinic. He hated the thought of disappointing her now. Worse, he didn't want to lose her altogether.

Nevertheless, he knew that if God provided the funds by way of Uncle Chet's will, then he had to go.

❧

"How can you eat tacos after all that food at the Dariens' this afternoon?" Shelley pulled out a chair and sat down at the kitchen table beside Ravyn.

"I'm starving. I didn't get a chance to eat. I was too busy meeting Mark's family." She sipped her cola. "All his sisters look alike. I hope I remember their names."

"They seem very nice." Shelley smiled and helped herself to a nacho chip, then dipped it in the warm and spicy cheese sauce. "His brothers are good-looking men. Too bad for me they're all married."

Ravyn grinned at the remark since her mouth was too full of taco to reply. But all kidding aside, she'd noticed how Mark's siblings went out of their way to befriend her. It went without saying that she and Mark were officially serious about each other.

"For a funeral gathering, it was actually an enjoyable afternoon."

Again, Ravyn bobbed out an answer.

Shelley tipped her head, looking rather bookish in her navy dress with its gold belt and her hair clipped up. "So why don't you marry Mark and live happily ever after?"

"Well, for starters," Ravyn said, swallowing her last bite, "he hasn't proposed. But, yeah, that is the goal."

Shelley laughed under her breath and ate another tortilla chip. She'd gained some weight this summer and didn't appear so sickly thin anymore. "I'll bet he'd pop the question in a heartbeat if he knew you'd say yes."

"I don't know if I'd say yes. That's why Mark and I are dating."

"Smart aleck. You forget I live with you. I know that missionary thing is holding you back."

"Not anymore. Mark might be the newest MD at the urgent care clinic across from the medical center."

"Oh, right. I sort of heard mutterings about that this afternoon. But I also heard it's not a done deal."

"It's not," Ravyn conceded, although she had been praying to that end. She had to wonder, too, how Mark's great-uncle's death might figure into his decision. She hoped he'd want to remain in Dubuque for his great-aunt's sake.

Shelley glanced at the clock on the microwave and stood. Strolling into the living room, she instructed Marky to turn off the TV and get ready for bed. After a few whines and complaints, he did as his mother asked and Shelley returned to her place at the table.

"This afternoon I saw a lot of people I hadn't seen in a decade or more. I felt overwhelmed at the flood of memories. I kept thinking about my parents. They were well-off financially and I was an only child and yet, they didn't love me the way I longed to be loved. I was a trophy of their marriage and only something to be seen and not heard. But in actuality, I think I would have done anything if my dad would have chosen to spend time with me rather than play golf or attend the men's club at church or go off on any number of his favorite recreations away from home."

Ravyn didn't reply. By now she could sense when Shelley needed to talk and rid herself of the past demons that continually haunted her.

"When we were kids, I used to relish going over to your house. Your folks might not have wallowed in material wealth, but they loved you and I felt that love through you. That's why I hung around."

"My parents liked it when you hung around because then they got two babysitters for the price of one."

"Ulterior motives, eh?"

"Uh-huh."

"Well, they still loved you girls. And now Mark loves you, too, Ravyn."

She lifted her gaze and peered at her friend. "Think so? *Love* is a strong word."

"I watched him today. His whole face lit up when you entered the room. He didn't notice anyone else. It was as if he totally zoned out and focused only on you."

"Really?" Ravyn felt a jolt of pleasure at the news. She hadn't noticed.

"When you weren't around, Mark's eyes searched you out—even while he was talking with other people." Shelley sighed. "I found it quite aggravating while trying to have a discussion with him."

Ravyn laughed.

Shelley glanced at the tabletop, running the side of her fingernail along the wood grain. "You are loved, Ravyn, and you don't know how lucky you are."

Ravyn reached out and set her hand on her friend's forearm. "Shelley, please don't—"

"I'm not saying this to make you feel bad. I'm telling you this, Rav, so you don't throw away something wonderful between you and Mark just because things don't stack up according to the way you've planned."

She retracted her hand as an inner wall of defense began to rise.

"Don't be angry with me. Hear me out, okay? Mark might be that one guy—the one chance at love you'll never have again. If you let it go you might regret it forever. I mean, if it were me in your place, I'd follow the guy to Timbuktu."

Ravyn held back a retort. Her mother and Teala had told her much the same thing. If you love someone, you ought to be able to follow him to the ends of the earth. But what close friends and well-intentioned family members didn't take into account were Ravyn's hard-earned career and her own plans for the future. Why couldn't Mark follow *her*?

A bit miffed, Ravyn collected all the wrappers from her fast-food supper and stuffed them into the paper bag. "You're forgetting that Mark has yet to mention the word *love* around me."

"He's probably scared. Think about it. Would you want to bare your heart to someone you thought might dump you if you decided to be a missionary?"

Ravyn tensed. "Shelley! You make me sound like I'm a shallow person. I'm not."

"Of course you're not. Look at all you've done for me and for Marky. Where would we be if it weren't for you?" She stood. "I didn't mean to offend you. But now I have to go tuck a certain ten-year-old into bed. He's got school tomorrow."

A forgiving smile played on Ravyn's lips, although as she watched Shelley leave the room, she couldn't seem to shake off everything she'd said.

In fact, the comments lingered in her mind all through the night. She thought and prayed and prayed some more.

Lord, what do I do if Mark makes the decision to go overseas?

The answer boomeranged back to her soul.

"Trust and obey."

❧

A hard rain splattered against the window as Ravyn stared out across the empty tennis courts. She stifled a yawn and turned back to Mark. He had called a half hour ago saying he needed to speak with her, that it was important. Now seemed the perfect time with Shelley at work and Marky at school. But, after working all night, Ravyn felt exhaustion creeping into her senses. The fact that Mark seemed at a loss for words only frustrated her.

She regarded him for several long moments as he sat on the edge of the sofa, which had doubled as her bed since Shelley moved in. His arms dangled over his knees. His expression looked solemn. In a word, he looked like one miserable man.

"Are you sure I can't get you something? I could make some lunch if you're hungry."

"No, that's okay." He stood and shoved his hands into the pockets of his tan casual trousers. He cleared his throat. "I'm glad you had a fun time shopping with my mom and sisters the other day."

"I did." She narrowed her gaze. "But that's not what you came over to discuss, is it? Our shopping trip?"

"No." He gave a slight wag of his head. "I'm working up to the real issue."

"Well, you're making me nervous. Maybe you should just spit it out and get it over with."

"Easy for you to say."

Ravyn wasn't amused by the quip. "Is it about your aunt?" She knew Mark had been preoccupied this last week with various legal matters. "Is it your family? They made it back to New Hampshire okay, didn't they?"

"Everyone's fine." Mark took a few steps toward her. "Look, I just wanted you to know I turned down the job at the clinic."

"Okay."

Ravyn felt a tad perplexed. She didn't know why he'd feel hesitant about telling her that, unless it meant—

Reality slammed into her. "Y–you're headed for that little island off of Indonesia, aren't you?"

"Yes, I am." Mark's brown eyes seemed so sad. "I'm sorry, Ravyn. I know this is what God wants me to do and where He wants me to go."

"Then why are you sorry?" She moved toward him. "You're trusting and obeying God. You're honorable and committed."

"Thanks, but—"

"Don't tell me you're leaving tomorrow!"

"No." A rueful grin tugged at the corner of his mouth. "In January. Like I planned. I need to do some healing after my uncle's untimely death, and I want to make sure my aunt's going to be okay."

"Understandable and. . .very gallant."

"You're very complimentary this morning, Ravyn, and you're, um, taking this a lot better than I expected. I don't know if that makes me feel good or bad." He flashed a bit of a smile before a stony expression washed over his face again. "What I want to know is, where does my decision leave us?"

Questions crowded her thoughts. Couldn't he tell she loved him? Why didn't he ask her to marry him? But then she recalled what Shelley had said about a guy not wanting to bare his heart if he thought he'd get dumped. Ravyn realized she had some explaining to do.

"Mark, I know I haven't been very supportive in the past of missionaries in general, but after a lot of dialogue with God, I've reconsidered."

"Oh?" He placed his hands on his hips and his expression seemed to soften.

Ravyn inched her way closer. "The truth is I love you. I think I've loved you since I was sixteen. I wish you wouldn't leave Dubuque, but if that's how the Lord is directing you, and it obviously is, then I want to go with you."

"You—what?" He looked stunned. "Wait a second. Let me get this straight. Are you saying you'll give up your nursing career and your future plans to go overseas with me?"

"Yes, that's exactly what I'm saying." Suddenly it all seemed so very simple. "All my well-laid plans won't mean anything if I'm unhappy. Besides, they're *my* plans and they have been all along. They're not God's plans."

Mark closed the distance between them and cupped her face with his hands. He urged her gaze into his. "Are you sure, Ravyn?"

"I'm sure. It means a lot to me that you're willing to follow the Lord and not cave in to external pressures. No matter what happens I'll be able to rest in the knowledge that your utmost desire is to walk with Christ." Tears blurred her vision. "Like my dad."

A smile grew wide across his face. "You'd have to marry me."

"Oh, well, forget it," she teased with an upward flick of her gaze.

His laugh filled the living room and a moment later, her feet left the carpeted floor as Mark twirled her around before wrapping her in a snug embrace.

"Of course I'll marry you, Mark." Ravyn felt his lips graze her temple.

"I love you."

"I know." With her head pressed against his heart, she smiled.

"You're perfect for me. You challenge and encourage me." He gently pushed her back and stared down into her eyes. "God filled my prescription for love—with you."

Ravyn felt special, cherished, and, yes, loved. And while it wasn't the proposal of marriage she'd imagined, she'd never experienced such joy. She knew at that precise moment she'd made the right decision.

And now she was about to seal it with a kiss.

Epilogue

O kay, everyone, look this way and smile!"
The photographer snapped several shots while the wedding party stood poised on the deep-red carpeted steps of the church's platform. Scarlet-leafed poinsettias were lined up in a row at their feet. The plants contrasted in seasonal fashion with the evergreen-colored dresses worn by the six bridesmaids. Mark and his groomsmen looked their dashing best in black tuxedos, although Ravyn's gaze never strayed beyond her handsome husband. Christmas had always been one of her favorite holidays, and now the celebration carried with it an extra special blessing; she'd just married the man she loved.

Ravyn pressed in a little closer to her husband.

A few more pictures were taken. Minutes later, the wedding party disbanded and made its way downstairs for the small reception, the happy bride and groom included. The pastor had agreed to marry Ravyn and Mark in the larger, founding church in order to accommodate the many guests.

As they entered the spacious fellowship area decorated with white paper wedding bells and streamers, family members and friends cheered. Then Ravyn and Mark cut their wedding cake amid more applause and pictures.

"Wow, I hardly recognize you two without your scrubs on," Liz said minutes later, after taking a sip of punch. "But I'll say this much, you make a perfect couple."

Ravyn felt Mark tighten his hold around her waist. She smiled. "We think so, too."

Liz set her punch down on a nearby table and gave both Ravyn and Mark a hug. "I'll sure miss you two. Make sure you e-mail me and keep me updated on what's happening overseas."

"We will," Mark promised.

Several other co-workers expressed their congratulations and then Carla approached them. Her cheeks held a rosy hue that matched her two-piece skirt and sweater.

She wrapped Ravyn in a sisterly embrace. "You look beautiful and the ceremony made me cry. It was so lovely." She took Mark's hand and gave it a congratulatory squeeze. "And guess what just happened? Mrs. Darien asked if I'd move in with her and I said yes."

"I'm so glad." Ravyn felt additional tears of happiness spring to her eyes.

Carla hadn't been in a good living situation for a long time. Her roommates liked to party in irresponsible, even dangerous ways.

"Aunt Edy discussed the matter with Ravyn and me," Mark said. "We were all for it from the beginning. I think you and my aunt will be an encouragement to each other."

"Thanks. She's pretty cool for an older lady."

Ravyn smiled and then more guests captured her and Mark's attention.

Finally Shelley made her way to them. Marky sat at a nearby table, eating cake and joking with other kids his age.

"I'll never forgive you for stealing my roommate." She flicked a teasing glance at Mark and hugged Ravyn. "I'm going to miss her."

"Well," Mark answered with a wry grin, "according to my aunt, wedding bells might be in your future, too."

"Oh, I don't know about that." Shelley actually blushed. "Trevor's a nice guy and everything and Marky certainly likes him, but. . ." She glanced over her shoulder and Ravyn followed her gaze to the stocky-framed man with light brown hair refilling his punch glass. "We'll see."

Ravyn had a hunch Mark was right: marriage lurked around the corner for Shelley. Shelley and Trevor had met during a junior high outing at church about the same time she'd found a new job as an administrative assistant at one of the city's many foundries. With the better salary, Shelley had decided she could assume Ravyn's monthly mortgage payments and take care of the condo while Ravyn and Mark were overseas.

"Oh, Ravyn, where would I be without you?" Shelley gave her another hug. "Sometimes I'm scared that you're leaving. I've relied on you for five months."

"And now it's time to rely on God. He's always with you."

"I know."

"Besides, my parents are just a phone call away."

"My aunt, too," Mark added.

Shelley nodded.

A moment later, Ravyn's father's voice commanded everyone's attention. "A special toast to the bride and groom," he said, lifting his punch glass. "May your ministry together be all God intended from the beginning of time, and may your lives be filled with special blessings."

"Yes, like lots of grandchildren!" Mark's mother exclaimed.

Everyone cheered and Ravyn rode out her wave of embarrassment with a smile. Then she looked up at Mark and he gazed into her eyes with unabashed love and desire before kissing her. Applause and laughter filled the room, and at that precise moment Ravyn knew she'd live nothing short of happily ever after.

COURTING
DISASTER

Chapter 1

Cadence Trent forced herself to remain calm even as a searing sense of urgency spread throughout her being. A natural gas explosion. A subdivision almost completely destroyed in Wind Lake. She had to hurry and call the others. Cadi glanced at her wristwatch. Wind Lake was a midsize village on the far northeast side of the county, not too far from where she lived in Waterloo. Still, time was of the essence.

Call Darrell, she reminded herself.

The thought of canceling her date with the handsome honey-blond caused Cadi to cringe. She hated to disappoint him for the umpteenth time. Tonight they planned to go to dinner followed by a concert. Darrell had purchased tickets, and they both had been looking forward to a fun evening out.

Oh, Lord, please help him to understand.

Somehow, in spite of her prayers, Cadi had a hunch he wouldn't.

Weeks ago, Darrell threatened to break off their relationship, stating she put her work before him. He felt Disaster Busters wasn't worth her time and effort. But Cadi knew otherwise. She had experienced the sheer joy of making someone's crisis less devastating. She'd helped victims of tragedy see the rainbow through the rain.

That was one area where she and Darrell disagreed.

Darrell said she had her head in the clouds if she thought Disaster Busters would be a successful venture. He'd given her countless business magazines, encouraging her to "do the math" when it came to Disaster Busters. Cadi knew he meant well, but she also knew her work made her feel needed. She fulfilled a purpose, and God provided and blessed the rest. So she forged onward. She never meant to take Darrell for granted, but like today, duty called and she had to go; there were people without homes, food, and clothing because of a natural gas explosion in their community. Her nonprofit organization, Disaster Busters, had been summoned to provide these victims with basic needs. How could she refuse?

Very simply, she couldn't.

The wooden steps of the old Victorian home creaked as Cadi took them two at a time. Upstairs, she hurried down the narrow hallway and into the bedroom. She grabbed the overnight bag she always kept packed with extra clothes and personal accessories and just about everything else. She picked up her purse, slinging its leather strap over her shoulder, and ran back down to the first floor.

"What's all the commotion?" Aunt Lou entered the foyer from the kitchen wiping her nimble hands on the colorful apron drawn about her thick waist. As always, her dusky gray hair was swirled elaborately around her head and at the sides of her face in a creation she called "Queen Elizabeth" fashion. Cadi had to agree the style made the older woman appear both regal and ageless.

"Sounds like cannonballs bouncing down the steps."

Cadi couldn't help the smirk tugging at the corners of her mouth. "You can recall what cannonballs sound like?"

"I was hardly referring to my age." Aunt Lou clucked her tongue. "Sassy girl."

She laughed. "Sorry about the noise. Another call came in."

"Oh. . ." A frown wrinkled her gray brows. "How long will you be gone?"

"Not sure. Just depends." Noticing her aunt's concerned expression, she added, "An explosion in Wind Lake. The building is a complete loss."

"How awful. Anyone hurt?"

"Several injuries, but no one was killed as far as I know. Emergency personnel are still on the scene."

"How dreadful." Aunt Lou's frown of concern gave way to an encouraging grin. "Well, I'll call Lonnie Mae and the other members of our prayer chain. We'll cover you."

"Thanks. I don't know what I'd do without you." Cadi kissed her aunt's cheek then dashed outside to her minivan. A gentle May breeze tousled her short hair and wafted through the budding treetops.

Opening the van door, she tossed her purse and overnight bag into the vehicle before climbing behind the wheel. She started the engine then slowly backed out of the driveway and into the street. She took one last look toward the house. Her aunt stood on the porch and waved. Cadi returned the gesture then put the transmission into drive and stepped on the accelerator.

Cadi felt a grin pull at the corners of her lips. Aunt Lou, bless her heart. The very thought of the woman caused a swell of gratitude to plume within her. Her aunt was the most giving and caring person in Cadi's life. What's more, Aunt Lou had been her parental figure since Cadi was eleven years old. Aunt Lou, in her seventies now and her great-aunt, actually, had taken Cadi in after her parents and younger brother and sister drowned when the Mississippi overflowed its banks. Cadi could still recall the tragedy vividly.

It had rained for days, but it seemed like a regular Sunday evening to Cadi when she and her family ventured off to the evening service at church. Minutes later their car stalled in a flooded intersection. The water kept rising and rising until Dad instructed all of them to climb up onto the roof of the sedan. Darkness fell hard and fast, making their predicament all the more harrowing.

There were others stranded, too, and the cries for help, the screams of fear, barely rose above the din of the rushing floodwater. Within a short period of time, Cadi and her family were swept off the car. Cadi had gulped for air and fought against the unmerciful current for what seemed like hours. Then, miraculously, a rescue worker plucked her from the surge.

The bodies of her parents and siblings were found a few days later.

Oh, Lord. . . Cadi closed her eyes, trying to quell the painful memory.

The driver in the car behind her honked, and she gave herself a mental shake. The past was just that: the past. No sense in reliving it, although Cadi's past was why she'd gone to school and become an emergency medical technician. Next she began the Disaster Busters organization. She wanted to help other victims of tragedies—like those in today's explosion.

The urgency of the situation caught up with her, and Cadi realized she hadn't called her colleagues, Bailey, Jeff, Megan, and Will. They had full-time jobs of their own but were still vital volunteers that kept Disaster Busters functional. Cadi tried to pay them with love offerings and donations that Disaster Busters received. Many times, paying them resulted in Cadi forfeiting her salary and, just as she had in the past, Aunt Lou came to the rescue. It was a sacrifice on her aunt's part, too.

Steering her van to the side of the road, Cadi fished her cell phone from her purse. Within minutes, she had placed the calls. All four assistants said they were available and could help, and Cadi arranged to meet them at the Disaster Busters office located inside Riverview Bible Church.

Next, it was time to call Darrell. She pressed in his number on the keypad of her phone and plugged in her hands-free device. She pulled away from the curb, sending up another silent prayer that he'd understand.

Darrell answered on the third ring. His reaction was just as Cadi feared.

"What? You're canceling on me again?"

She grimaced. "Sorry."

"We've got dinner reservations. I bought tickets for the concert afterward!"

Cadi imagined the angry sparks flashing in Darrell's hazel eyes. "Look, I apologize for backing out on our date, but the team and I—"

"The team. Right." Darrell paused. "Those friends of yours aren't going to help you make important contacts. Success means rubbing elbows with the right people. But I guess you proved to me once again that *the team* will always come before anything we might have together."

Cadi opened her mouth to refute his statements, but she couldn't. Aunt Lou's not-so-subtle remarks filled her mind. *"He's not a patient man, is he? Patience is a virtue, you know."*

Had Aunt Lou seen something amiss in Cadi's relationship with Darrell Barclay from the beginning?

"Cadi? Are you there?"

Darrell's deep voice rattled her. "I'm here." She squared her shoulders, remembering her mission at hand. She couldn't afford to let her emotions get in the way right now. She had a job to do, and she had to be strong—strong in the Lord. "Darrell, let's talk about this later, okay?"

"No need. As long as your loser business comes before me, I have nothing more to say."

She clenched her jaw. "Loser business?"

"That's what I said."

"I explained all this to you before."

"And I don't want to hear it again."

"Fine. If that's how you feel—"

"That's exactly how I feel. There are plenty of girls waiting in line to take your place in my life."

Shock enveloped Cadi. Had she heard correctly? Seconds later, she realized her hearing was just fine, and oddly enough the barb didn't sting as much as she thought it might.

"You know, if I'm that replaceable, Darrell, then you shouldn't be so irate that I'm canceling our date tonight."

"Yeah, whatever."

"I have to go." She paused. "Good-bye, Darrell."

She didn't wait for a reply. Ending the call, she removed her earpiece and set it and the phone on the console between the van's two front seats. She suspected it was the end of her short-lived romance with Darrell, and while she didn't feel heartbroken, exactly, she had to admit to a deep sense of disappointment. Someday she'd like to get married and have a family—a large family.

She quieted her straying thoughts and tightened her grip on the steering wheel. No time to fantasize about the future. There was a crisis at hand.

She forced her attention back to the present and turned her car into Riverview's vast parking lot. Almost a year ago, Cadi's pastor and the deacons agreed to lease her office space for Disaster Busters, and they encouraged her to fulfill her mission to help people in need. Remembering her pastor's kind words now seemed like a salve of comfort after Darrell's mean remark. "Loser business."

What does he know?

Cadi stepped down from her vehicle and shoved Darrell from her mind. She began forming a mental list of the supplies that she and her team needed to pack: blankets, clothing, nonperishable food items. . .

She crossed the parking lot and entered the side door of the large church. The soles of her white athletic shoes squeaked on the polished tile floor in the empty hallway. She reached the Disaster Busters office, and when she opened the door, the sight that greeted her erased any defeat she might have felt after her conversation with Darrell. There, packing boxes of foodstuff, were two members of her team.

"Bailey's gathering up some blankets," Jeff said as he lifted a box and handed it to Will.

"And I'll take this out to the trailer." Will motioned to the box with his head. "While I'm out there, I'll hitch it to the van."

"I'll come out and help," Jeff said.

"You guys are awesome." Cadi glanced from one to the other.

Then Will jutted out his narrow hip, and she tucked her car keys into the back pocket of his blue jeans.

Moments later she, too, set to task. She placed various items in crates and boxes. All the while she marveled at how close she and her team had grown since the inception of Disaster Busters just shy of a year ago. She had been a bridesmaid in Jeff and Bailey's wedding and attended Bailey's graduation from nursing school. Will acted like Cadi's big brother. They'd known each other since they were foster kids who'd wound up in the same home for almost two years before the state located Aunt Lou. Nevertheless, the joke remained that she and Will were siblings, although jest became reality in a spiritual way when Will asked Jesus Christ into his heart as a teenager. So when Cadi introduced him to Darrell, Will had light-heartedly said, "You be good to my baby sister, now, or I'll come lookin' for you."

Darrell had appeared confused as he peered from Cadi's Scandinavian, peaches-and-cream complexion to Will, whose African American heritage shone proudly from his dark brown eyes. "You're brother and sister?"

"Same heavenly Father." Will sported a broad grin.

"Oh. Right." Darrell had quickly changed the subject. Obviously he wasn't amused.

"No patience, no imagination, and no sense of humor," Cadi muttered as she folded and packed some clothing items from the clothes pantry in back of the office. The room was no bigger than a large closet.

"What did you say?"

Cadi whirled around and saw her best friend, Megan Buckingham, standing there with arms akimbo. Cadi shook her head. "Nothing. I mean, I didn't say anything worth repeating."

"Hmm, well let me take a guess." Megan tipped her head. Strands of her walnut brown hair fell across her preseason tanned cheek, evidence of the tanning booth she liked to frequent. "You canceled your date with Darrell, and he was anything but understanding."

"Bingo."

Meg flicked her gaze toward the dimpled ceiling. "Typical." She blew out a puff of air. "Well, he'll get over it."

Cadi shook her head. "Not this time, he won't. I think Darrell and I are through unless I beg and plead, which I won't. Not again."

Megan paused for several seconds. "Maybe it's for the best."

"I'm sure it's for the best. . .at least now I'm sure."

"About time," Megan quipped. "I thought you'd never come to your senses. I've said it all along: Darrell is a fake. I've been praying you'd see through his facade."

"Maybe you're right. It's just that I want a family of my own someday, and—"

"And Darrell's an eligible bachelor," Meg cut in. "He's good-looking, and he has a nice career going for him. But those aren't enough reasons to actually *marry* the guy."

"Meg, I see the positive in everyone. I can look beyond the. . .*the facade.*"

"Well, in Darrell's case, there's not much more to see, okay?" A teasing grin spread across Meg's face.

Cadi had to smile. "Seems I had to find that out the hard way."

Compassion filled Meg's iridescent brown eyes. "Oh, you're really hurt, aren't you?" She wrapped her long, slender arms around Cadi. "I'm so sorry."

She returned the hug. "I'm okay."

At that moment, Will strode back in from the parking lot. "I'm ready to take the next box to the trailer, and then I think we're all packed up and ready to go."

🐾

Black Hawk County sheriff's deputy Patrol Sergeant Frank Parker slowed traffic on the highway leading into town and directed motor vehicles and curious bystanders away from the emergency personnel. Wind Lake didn't get a whole lot of traffic, but most of its population, along with tourists arriving for the Memorial Day weekend, had come out to glimpse the devastation that the natural gas explosion caused. Homes in the newly constructed subdivision still smoldered, and debris littered the area.

"Stay off the street, folks," he said to the collecting crowd. "Move back."

A few people paused to ask questions, and some waved a greeting and called him by name. Frank took a special interest in this assignment. Born and raised here, he made his home in Wind Lake. In short, this village wasn't just the place in which he lived; it was his jurisdiction, along with the two adjacent townships. Placing sheriff deputies in their hometowns was all part of the county's Know Your Neighbors program.

Out of the corner of his eye, Frank saw movement and turned in time to see Erin Potter's red hair as she ducked around him. She worked for the *Village Gazette.* Frank watched her lift her high-speed camera then heard its shutter clicking as she snapped several photos. He gave her a good thirty seconds before calling her back behind the yellow plastic tape.

"You're a peach, Frank," she said with a wink. "I can always count on you to let me behind the barrier for a couple moments so I can get my pictures."

"Don't let that get around, Erin."

The slender, middle-aged woman chuckled and trotted back to the sidewalk, her ponytail swinging from side to side.

It wasn't but a minute later when a light blue minivan made its way down the street. Frank began shaking his head in a nonverbal warning so the vehicle wouldn't proceed further. The van continued on a few feet then rolled to a stop. Frank cautiously approached. The window slid down, and a young woman leaned her head out. His first thought was that she had the hugest sky blue eyes he'd ever seen.

"Disaster Busters reporting for duty."

And a sunny smile.

"They're expecting us."

Frank drew his chin back. "I beg your pardon?"

"We're the Disaster Busters team."

"Never heard of you." Frank noticed how the woman's layered blond hair flipped upward at the ends.

"We're a nonprofit organization out of Waterloo. We're here to help the victims of the explosion."

"We're a charity group!" the brunette in the passenger seat called to him.

The words "nonprofit organization" and "charity group" set off warning bells inside his head. "Got any ID?"

"Absolutely." The blond driver handed him her Iowa driver's license and a business card.

"Cadence Trent. Disaster Busters, eh?" He eyed the young woman and her passengers with skepticism. He knew firsthand the scams and schemes associated with tragedies. Victims were vulnerable, and part of his job was to protect them. "Sorry. I wasn't told you have security clearance, so turn the vehicle around."

"But—"

"You heard me. Turn around." He extended his hand to return the driver's ID.

"Officer!" A male voice hailed him. "Wait a minute, Officer!"

Frank wheeled around in time to see Harrison Elliot, Wind Lake's mayor, striding toward him.

"Is this the team from Waterloo? Five people in all? We've been expecting them." He sidled up to the minivan. "You must be Cadi."

"Yes. And you must be Mayor Elliot."

"I am he." There was a smile in his voice, but when he turned to Frank, he scowled. "Let this van pass, Officer."

"If you say so."

"I do, indeed."

Frank tensed in protest then returned the ID and took a step back. He observed the blond tuck the identification into a long, trim billfold before she gave him a smile. A semblance of a peace offering, perhaps, but Frank wasn't won over that easily.

"Pull forward, Cadi," Mayor Elliot said. "Park over there. Pastor Dremond is setting up some tables, and we're inviting those who are homeless because of this terrible tragedy to register."

At the mention of Adam Dremond's name, Frank's tension abated somewhat. He knew Adam personally, and he was a good man. The mayor, on the other hand, was more pomp than circumstance as far as Frank was concerned.

Meanwhile, Cadi drove forward.

"I summoned the Disaster Busters team," the stocky mayor informed Frank with a set to his jaw. "You had no business trying to turn them away."

"In all due respect, sir, if you had informed the sheriff's department of their expected arrival—"

"I did," he groused.

"Nothing came over the radio."

Elliot waved one beefy hand in the air. "Ooooh, I don't have time to argue the point. Just—just go about your business."

To his credit, Frank didn't even grin at the sputtered remark. Nevertheless, he bristled at the mayor's less-than-perfect handling of the situation. As for that little Disaster Buster, she might have clearance from Elliot, but that didn't mean her organization was really on the up-and-up.

Frank decided he'd better keep his eye on her.

Chapter 2

"She's all right, Frank."

"How do you know?" He watched Cadi and her crew from out of the corner of his eye. They stood behind a long, rectangular table set up under a blue, twelve-by-twelve tarp. The Disaster Busters registered the recently homeless and orchestrated temporary arrangements, courtesy of a local establishment called the Wind Lake Inn and several charitable residents. "What if they're rip-off artists?"

"I meet a group of local pastors for lunch every few months, and John Connor, Cadi Trent's pastor, is one of them." Adam grinned and finger-combed his thick, reddish brown hair off his forehead. "She comes highly recommended."

Frank turned toward him. He and Adam Dremond had known each other for years, ever since the reverend arrived in Wind Lake. Adam was something of a social activist, but he operated aboveboard and made it a point to get to know law enforcement officials. His cooperation paid off. The entire sheriff's department had come to respect Adam.

"So give me the lowdown on these Disaster Busters." Ordinarily Frank trusted his friend's word, but he still had his qualms about this group of strangers.

"Well, from what I understand, it's a faith-based organization, but it works with local government. I convinced the mayor to give Cadi's group a chance, and since there was a lot of bureaucratic red tape to cut through in order for county, state, or federal assistance to get here, Mayor Elliot was all for it."

"Hmm. . ." Frank tucked his thumbs into the thick belt strapped around his waist. He watched as Cadi's slender form bent and she wrote something on the paper in front of her. He had to admit she made a fetching sight, even in an ordinary pink polo shirt and faded blue jeans. Then, when she came around the table and placed her arm around the shoulders of a disheveled elderly woman, an odd sense of longing gripped him.

He shook it off and pulled his gaze away from Cadi. "She looks young."

"Midtwenties is my guess."

"I suppose that makes her old enough to be capable of an undertaking such as this," he muttered, even though at thirty-four he wasn't all that much older than she; however, he felt as if he'd lived an entire life—and that life ended some three years ago. Now his days were but twenty-four-hour capsules of existence—except around his two children. If it weren't for them, he wouldn't feel alive at all.

He wouldn't feel—period.

"I'm told Cadi is more than capable. So are her associates. Cadi is an experienced EMT, and there's a registered nurse in the group, along with a guy who's a family counselor."

"Sounds like they're qualified." After several pensive moments, he regarded Adam again and decided to voice his concerns. "Remember the tornado that hit a few years back?"

The pastor's usually jovial expression was replaced by a look of remorse. "Of course I remember. Who could forget it?"

Frank knew that *he* would never forget it. The storm had snuffed out the bright and beautiful life of his beloved wife and left him with two small children to raise. He was only too grateful for his extended family members who, between them, provided day care so Frank could keep his job. "There was a charity group that came in to help after the twister hit." He glanced back at the Disaster Busters group. "They seemed just as qualified and capable, but those guys looted our ravaged community and swindled the most vulnerable. To this day, there are those who haven't recovered."

"I'm well aware of that unfortunate incident, but Cadi's company isn't like that, okay?" Empathy shone from Adam's hazel eyes. "And maybe it's time you started trusting people again."

Frank guarded his reaction. "Maybe." He watched as Cadi conversed with two teenagers.

"We'd also love to see you in church again."

He swung his gaze back to Adam and noticed the twinkle in his eyes. "You've always got to work church into a conversation, don't you?"

Adam nodded. "It's my job."

"Yeah, I know." Frank couldn't help but grin, but just as soon as it appeared, he felt it slip from his lips. "Look, my relationship with the Lord is intact."

"Don't you want more than that? Don't you desire a closer walk with God and fellowship with other like-minded believers?"

"Sure, but attending church isn't easy."

Frank stopped short of admitting that on Sunday mornings when he thought of attending worship services, sudden memories of his wife, Yolanda, dashed his concerted efforts and left him feeling depressed and hopeless. In his mind's eye, he could see her preparing breakfast. He could practically hear her humming while she dressed the kids in their Sunday best. It was all Frank could do to keep from breaking down in front of his children. As if that wasn't bad enough, when he did manage to attend services, he was bombarded with sad, piteous stares from everyone who knew Yolanda. It was more than he could bear. So, typically, he waited until his mother-in-law picked up Dustin and Emily for Sunday school before he went to work early. Then he pushed his feelings into the farthest corner of his heart.

He cleared the discomfort from his throat. "I'm sure I'll get to church again eventually."

"If not ours then perhaps another solid, Bible-believing church."

"Yeah." Frank was amazed at how the man had divined his thoughts. "Maybe."

"Hearing God's Word will strengthen your faith. Fellowship with other believers will encourage you."

Frank smirked. "I get the message already."

Adam smiled and gave him a friendly slap between the shoulder blades. "All right. I've needled you enough for one day. Besides, I've got other work to do." He inclined his head toward the many explosion victims. "See ya later."

"Yeah. . .see you."

🕿

"What's with that sheriff's deputy?"

Cadi followed her friend's line of vision and glimpsed the tall, broad-shouldered man with short, jet black hair. He seemed to scowl at her and Meg.

"And why is he staring at us like we're convicted bank robbers? We're here to help."

"Maybe he's having a bad day," Cadi said. "Try to ignore him." Her suggestion belied the nervous anticipation winding its way around her insides—like the feeling that threatened whenever she spoke in front of large audiences. Now, as she did then, Cadi silently recited her favorite passage of scripture, Philippians 4:6–7. *"Do not be anxious about anything, but in everything, by prayer and petition, with thanksgiving, present your requests to God. And the peace of God, which transcends all understanding, will guard your hearts and your minds in Christ Jesus."*

"Um, I don't think we're going to be able to ignore that guy, Cadi." The warning in her friend's voice rang out loud and clear. "He's heading our way."

She glanced up from her yellow legal pad and met the gaze of the stern-faced deputy.

"Ladies," he said with a slight dip of his head when he reached them. "Anything I can do to assist you?"

Was he serious? Cadi sensed a measure of condescension in his tone. "We're okay, but thanks anyway."

The deputy shifted his stance. "I think maybe we got off to a bad start." He extended his right hand. "I'm Sergeant Frank Parker."

"Cadi Trent." She set her palm inside his much larger one. He gave it a firm but cordial shake that stayed with her long after he released her hand. Cadi turned toward her friend. "This is Meg Buckingham."

"Good to meet you both." Frank cleared his throat before glancing over his shoulder. He looked a mite uneasy, and it gave Cadi a small measure of comfort to think she wasn't the only one.

"Well, I'd best get back to work, unless there's anything you ladies need."

"There is one thing," Meg said before turning to Cadi. "Tell him about the two teenagers."

"Will and Pastor Dremond are taking care of them."

"Perhaps I can help."

Cadi regarded the man, noticing his large build and scrutinizing deep brown eyes. Along with his shadowed jaw, Cadi thought he made an imposing figure.

"Miss Trent? Or is it Mrs. Trent?"

"Miss." She felt almost mesmerized.

"Extremely *Miss* after today," Meg piped up, putting Cadi on sudden alert. "She and her boyfriend called it quits this afternoon."

"Meg!" She rapped her friend's upper arm. "I'm sure the officer here isn't interested in my personal issues." She felt her cheeks growing hot with embarrassment.

"Sorry to hear about the breakup, *Miss* Trent."

Awkwardness seemed to envelop her, but at least the man appeared sincere.

"Thanks." She managed a shrug and muttered, "It's for the best."

"Definitely for the best," Meg reiterated with a pointed look at Cadi. "Now about those kids; we're trying to locate their parents."

"What's the last name?" Frank pulled a small notebook from his back pocket and flipped it open.

Cadi looked at her pad of paper. "Jenkins. Their mom's first name is Loretta, and their dad's is Brett."

"Loretta and Brett Jenkins?" Frank wrote down the names, while shaking his head. "Don't believe I know either of them. They're obviously not locals. But I'll radio it in. We'll find 'em." With a nod and a small smile, he turned on his heel and took purposeful strides toward the white squad car with the words BLACK HAWK COUNTY SHERIFF painted across the doors in bold yellow letters.

"Maybe he's not such a crabby guy after all," Meg remarked, watching him go.

"Yeah, but you've got a big mouth." Cadi expelled a breath laden with aggravation. "How could you bring up my relationship with Darrell to a complete stranger?"

Meg faced her and seemed at a loss for words. "I—I don't know. I didn't mean to. It just tumbled out of my mouth. Once I'd blurted the news, I tried to make the best of it." She stepped forward and grabbed hold of Cadi's wrist. "I'm sorry. Will you forgive me? You know I don't make a habit of spouting off my best friend's personal information—or anyone else's for that matter. I'm usually very discreet."

Cadi couldn't argue. "Oh, let's just forget it, okay? Of course I forgive you!"

Meg beamed and gave her a quick hug. "I'll go tell Will and Pastor Dremond that we've got the sheriff's department helping us find the Jenkinses."

Cadi replied with a nod and resumed her post at the table. Bailey and Jeff were talking to another young couple. She listened in for a few minutes, and her heart broke to hear how the newlyweds lost almost everything in the explosion that damaged their home.

That's why I'm here, Lord, she thought. *I'm here to represent You with love and compassion and help lighten these people's loads.*

Her gaze roamed beyond the two couples and to the dark-haired sheriff's deputy standing next to his vehicle, its driver's side door wide open. He had placed his foot on the doorjamb while he penned something into his notebook, using his knee for a writing surface.

In the next second he looked up, and his dark eyes riveted her so that all she could do was stare back at him.

"Hey, Cadi, I'm looking for that box of men's clothes—Cadi? Yo, Cadi."

She felt a hand on her shoulder and the mild shake that followed.

"What?" She turned to find Will standing beside her. She collected her wits. "What are you looking for?"

"The deputy, huh?" A playful grin spread across Will's face. "Are you one of those women who can't resist a man in uniform?" He chuckled.

"Oh, hush." Cadi brushed his hand off her shoulder.

Will laughed again. "You're a free agent now, you know? Darrell is his-tor-eee."

She felt the deep frown creasing her brow. "Stop teasing me."

He shaded his amusement with feigned professionalism. "Have you seen the box of men's clothing? I'm working with several individuals who could use a few pairs of pants and several shirts."

Cadi pulled the minivan's keys from her jeans pocket and set them none-too-gently into Will's awaiting palm.

He gave her a gracious bow before walking away.

What a clown, Cadi thought in his wake. But what would she ever do without Will around to make her smile? He was like sunshine in the midst of the storm.

Or, in this case, *explosion.*

Cadi's musing came back around to the present tragedy, which, in turn, made her think about the nice-looking sheriff's deputy with the austere demeanor.

But when she looked his way again, she noticed that a different officer stood at the barricade, deterring onlookers. The squad car was gone, and Frank Parker was nowhere in sight.

Chapter 3

Frank squelched his impatience as Julie, an administrative assistant, ran a search on Cadi. Almost a half hour later, the plump brunette returned to the cubicle that surrounded his cluttered desk and shared what she'd found.

"The search came up empty."

"Good." Seeing Julie's curious expression, he immediately recanted his all-too-eager reply. "Um—it's good news for the community."

Her look of interest waned.

"I wouldn't want folks in Wind Lake to get swindled by con artists," he added. "It would be the nightmare of three years ago revisited."

"Oh, right. I remember that. My cousin and his wife were out their entire home insurance check because those supposed do-gooders helped them with the forms and conveniently had the check sent to them. They stole it."

"Exactly what I don't ever want to happen again." Frank, too, had lost more than his beloved wife. Stating they would "clean up" his damaged property, the phony charity group looted everything of value.

With a bob of her head, Julie headed for her own work area near the front of the sheriff department's satellite office.

Frank lazed back in his worn leather swivel chair. Out of habit he lifted a pen from the desk and tapped it against the metal finish while he pondered the situation. He had to admit to feeling relieved that Miss Cadi Trent had no criminal history. But why should he care if she did? And why couldn't he rid his memory of her arresting blue eyes? So what if she'd just broken up with her boyfriend? None of his concern.

Frank shook his head, disrupting his wayward thought process. What mattered to him was enforcing the law and protecting the citizens of Black Hawk County. Nothing more. Nothing less.

He stood and tossed the pen aside. He had work to do. No time for half-baked musings. Mayor Elliot had decided to hold a community barbecue in one of the county's many parks. This particular one, Lakeview Park, had a large, covered picnic area. The outing had been a spur-of-the-moment idea, and Frank supposed it was a good way of feeding those left homeless today and thanking all the volunteers who'd teamed together to help emergency personnel after this afternoon's explosion. Frank would be there; the park was part of his jurisdiction.

He collected his gear and strode outside to the patrol car. Expectancy pervaded his being. Would Cadi be at the barbecue?

It's none of my business unless she's doing something illegal.

He tried in vain to squelch further thoughts of the curvy blond with the enormous eyes. Okay, so he found her attractive. He'd admit at least that much. Except his emotions wanted to take a step further, and that was far from typical for him. He thought he'd become immune to feminine charm. What was going on?

It's the long hours I've been working. . . .

Seconds later, a very different idea struck. Maybe this was part of her plan. Distract the sheriff's department. Befriend the mayor. Disarm them all with her wiles and then—*bam!* Cadi and her Disaster Busters could scam poor, unsuspecting souls in no time.

A tight grin pulled at his mouth as he started the vehicle's engine. Now things made more sense.

❧

"It's five dollars for adults and two dollars for kids under twelve," Cadi informed the gathering crowd pressing in on her. She pointed at the sign she'd made earlier. "All the money raised will be divided and distributed to the victims of today's disaster."

A queue had already formed, and Will, Bailey, and Jeff collected the money. After people paid, they filed in under the large roofed picnic area and claimed tables for themselves and family members. Meanwhile, the grills, attended by volunteers, smoked outside the open-ended shelter.

Mayor Elliot told Cadi the village would take care of the cost of the hamburgers and hot dogs, while a local grocery store donated buns and condiments along with carrots, pickles, and potato salad. Cadi had never been so impressed with a community coming together to help each other. Even now several female residents of Wind Lake were arranging the food table in preparation for the huge buffet, and folks were beginning to help themselves to the fare.

"This was a great idea, Cadi." The mayor stood beside her and watched the goings-on. He puffed out his chest beneath the dark blue cotton dress shirt he wore tucked into his tan trousers. "I'm glad I thought of it."

"So am I. We've got a great turnout."

He nodded then snapped his pudgy fingers. "I almost forgot—I've made arrangements for you and your friends to stay at the Wind Lake Inn tonight."

"Thank you, but it's not necessary. We can drive back to Waterloo."

"No, no. I insist. It'll be dark and very late by the time our fundraiser ends tonight. I'm sure you and your crew will be exhausted, and the hotel is very comfortable."

"Well, then, all right." Cadi saw the wisdom in the mayor's decision. "Thank you. We appreciate it."

A glitter in the distance caught her eye and she turned in time to see

Sergeant Frank Parker making purposeful strides toward them. His shiny badge reflected the late afternoon sun. To Cadi, the deputy looked as daunting as an approaching thunderstorm.

The mayor must have noticed her sudden discomfort. "Some people take themselves far too seriously," he said with a glance in Frank's direction. "Don't let him cow you."

She laughed to cover her unease. "Don't worry. I won't."

"Good." Mayor Elliot gave her shoulder a pat of encouragement and sauntered off to greet several members of the media. He seemed in his element as he spoke to reporters.

Cadi grinned and moved to find something to do to help with the barbecue, but before she could inch forward, Frank Parker stepped into her path.

She sucked in a startled breath. When she last saw him, he'd been nearer to the street than the tent.

"Hello, Sergeant." She gathered her wits again, which she seemed to be having trouble keeping track of around this man. He seemed like a towering oak tree at this close proximity.

"Looks like a lot of money you're collecting there." He flicked a glance in Will, Bailey, and Jeff's direction. "I thought tonight was supposed to be a free event to thank the volunteers and emergency personnel."

She caught his meaning. "Oh, well, if it's the five dollars you're worried about, forget it. You can eat for free. After all, you helped this afternoon, too."

She stepped to the side and once more Frank blocked her way.

"That's not what I'm getting at."

"Oh?" Cadi felt confused.

"The money you're collecting. . ." A dark frown deepened his shadowed features. "I suppose it's for charitable purposes. Or is it to pay your expenses?"

"What?" She tipped her head then gave it a shake. "Listen, if it's a permit you're looking for, ask the mayor."

"The money, *Miss* Trent. Where's it going?"

The slur was unmistakable, and while Cadi could usually handle herself in a dignified manner, she felt close to losing her patience with this man. "If it's all right with you," she began facetiously, "we plan to divide up the money at the end of the night and give it to the victims of today's explosion."

"Oh, yeah?" He leaned forward, and Cadi got a whiff of some tangy scent he wore. "Well, I'm going to personally see to it that the victims get that money. Every last penny."

At first Cadi didn't understand, but then it dawned on her like a brilliant sunrise.

"Are you implying I'm some sort of thief?" She placed her hands on her hips and raised her chin.

"Maybe you are and maybe you aren't." He stood to his full height, which Cadi guessed to be well over six feet. "All I know for sure is that I'm here to protect the citizens of Wind Lake."

"Kind of like a vicious watchdog, eh?" Indignation sliced through her. "Well, I'll be sure to *whistle* for you when we're ready to count the money—unless you'd like to stand guard over it all night. We have nothing to hide, so whatever you decide is fine with me and my team."

He stood statue still as though stunned by her reply, and Cadi thought she saw a sparkle of amusement in his brown eyes—unless it was raw infuriation.

No. It was amusement. Definitely amusement.

Cadi felt her tense muscles relax somewhat, but in the next moment her attention was captured by the little girl dressed in a yellow, hooded sweatshirt and brightly printed corduroy slacks who'd flung herself around Deputy Parker's tree trunk of a leg.

"Daddy!" she squealed.

"Hi, Emmie." A smile lit his face like a flame in the darkness. He lifted the girl into his arms. Moments later a boy about eight or nine years old appeared. His greeting, like his attire, was much more subdued, and Cadi watched as he leaned against Frank's hip. "Hello, son." He tousled the boy's hair with his free hand.

Cadi watched in sheer amazement as the stony officer, who'd given her a difficult time since her arrival, morphed into some warm and fuzzy creature right before her very eyes.

She folded her arms. "I get the feeling that your bark is worse than your bite, Sergeant Parker." She grinned, feeling disarmed.

"These are my kids," Frank began proudly, despite the choke hold his daughter had him in. "Emily and Dustin."

"Nice to meet you both." She thought his children were beautiful with their golden-brown hair and amber eyes. "I'm Cadi." She glanced around, expecting to see a Mrs. Parker nearby. When the moments that ticked by didn't produce his wife, Cadi's curiosity mounted. The kids couldn't have appeared out of nowhere.

What do I care if he's married or not?

"Well, I need to get back to work," she said.

"Sure. Just *whistle* if you need anything."

The sarcastic quip wasn't lost on her. She grinned and busied herself with the numerous tasks at hand.

❧

After his mother fed the kids and took them home, Frank devoted his time to the steadfast scrutiny of the Disaster Busters team, particularly its leader, Cadi Trent. He had to admit he liked the way her short blond hair flipped up all over, matching her sassy personality. When he first confronted her about the dona-tion money, he thought he'd scared her, and his conscience pricked. But soon he realized they could match wits with little effort.

Vicious watchdog. Yeah, right!

Frank stifled the oncoming snicker and watched Cadi interact with the community. Most of the older citizens in Wind Lake knew each other, although the village had expanded. Cabins now lined the nearby lake, and novelty shops sprouted along Main Street. Soon tourists would be tying up intersections and crowding sidewalks. There would be boating accidents and petty thefts to inves-tigate, not to mention the bar fights to break up in the wee hours of the morning. The handful of police the village employed during tourist season couldn't keep up with the problems, and Frank knew from years gone by that the sheriff's department would be busy.

"Frank! Oh, Frank Parker!"

He turned and found Mrs. Corbin at his side. She'd been a schoolteacher in her younger days, and Frank knew her from church—when he used to attend regularly, that is.

The elderly woman placed her hand on his arm. "See that girl in the pink shirt?"

He followed her gaze to Cadi. "Yes, ma'am. I see her." He'd been watching her all night.

"Well, she's the nicest thing. She's agreed to help my friend Bettyanne file an insurance claim." A nippy gust of wind blew strands of her short white hair off her wrinkled forehead. "Bettyanne lost almost all of her belongings this after-noon. Such a shame. She'd just moved into that new duplex. She was renting, you know? Everything was so clean and nice. . . ."

Frank's ears had perked up at the mention of filing an insurance claim.

"And her antiques. . . Bettyanne loved to hit the antique shops on Thursday afternoons. Of course, the ones around here in town are far too commercial for her liking. Bettyanne prefers estate sales where she can find the true deals."

"Cadi offered to file an insurance claim for her?"

"Yes, that's right." The woman straightened her spindly frame. She stood all of five feet. "Cadi said she's staying overnight and she'd call the insurance company for Bettyanne tomorrow morning. They're meeting at the bank around nine o'clock. Bettyanne has her policy in a safe deposit box. Good thing that didn't go up in flames."

"Yes, ma'am." Suspicion reared its ugly head, and Frank clenched his jaw.

"Isn't that good of Cadi?" Mrs. Corbin prattled on. "She's a nice girl. Cadi asked Bettyanne if she needed housing, but she's going to move in with me for the time being."

"Nice girl, yeah." Frank's gaze burned into Cadi's shapely form. So the scamming had begun. He looked back down at Mrs. Corbin. "Thanks for letting me know."

"Oh, of course. Bettyanne's so relieved that she remembered she purchased a renter's insurance policy. I'm glad, too, that she might be the least bit compensated for her loss." Mrs. Corbin smiled. "But that's what insurance is for, isn't it?"

"That's right." He pushed out a smile for her benefit then meandered over to where Cadi stood over a box of clothing. She rummaged through its contents.

"I hear you've agreed to help an elderly lady file an insurance claim."

"What?" Cadi brought up her head so fast that she almost caught Frank right in the chin.

"Insurance claims—do you have experience filing them?"

She straightened. "Not really, but I can probably stumble through the process."

She tipped her head, and even in the dim lighting of the battery-operated lanterns, Frank could still see the curiosity that shimmered in her blue eyes. Then she shivered and looked back into the cardboard box.

"I know there's a clean sweatshirt in here...."

In spite of himself, Frank assisted her in locating the thick, zippered garment before helping her into it.

"Thanks."

"Sure." He cleared his throat. "Now, what's this I hear about an insurance claim?"

"Does someone need help filing one?"

Frank felt somewhat enchanted as she stared up at him. "Um, I understand you offered to help one of our senior citizens—"

"Oh, right. Mrs. Binder. Was there someone else?"

"No." He couldn't believe how clumsy and tongue-tied he'd become.

Cadi seemed to grow uncomfortable under his ogling. The truth was, Frank felt just as awkward, but he couldn't seem to help himself.

She glanced at her watch. "Well, I suppose we should count that money and divvy it up. Are you available?"

Frank bobbed his head in reply and cleared his suddenly parched throat. "Sure."

A teasing grin spread across her face. "Want to hear me whistle just for kicks?"

He drew himself up. "That's not necessary."

"Lucky for you," she retorted, spinning on her heel. "You and your eardrums, that is."

Chapter 4

I just have a little business to take care of, and then we can spend the day together."

"But, Daddy," Emily whined, "you said we'd go to the zoo."

"We will. Right after I finish my business."

"I thought it was your day off." Dustin took his spoon and poked at the cereal floating in his bowl.

"Look, you two, I just want to stop at the bank, okay? Then we'll go to the zoo as promised."

"Why can't we go to the bank with you?" Emily said, kneeling on her chair and then throwing her tiny frame into Frank's lap.

"One of these days you're going to miss and land on the floor." He sat his daughter back down in the kitchen chair. "Now, eat your breakfast."

"I don't want to go to Gramma's again," Dustin complained.

Frank blew out a breath of exasperation. His children were not cooperating this morning, and he needed to get to the bank in time to make sure the Disaster Busters didn't swindle an old lady out of her insurance money. Of course, he couldn't tell his kids that. What's more, he was off duty.

"All right. Tell you what. You can come to the bank with me, and then we'll go to the zoo."

"Hooray!" Emily shouted.

Dustin raised his arms, his fists balled in a silent victory cheer.

Pleased with the outcome, both ate their breakfasts, and the ambiance in the kitchen went from gloomy to bright and sunny. Then, while the kids dressed themselves and brushed their teeth, Frank threw together several peanut butter and jelly sandwiches. He placed them into a cooler, along with a cola for himself and juice drinks for the children. Minutes later they all were ready to walk out the front door.

Driving into town, Frank wondered how best to handle the situation at the bank. He couldn't very well come out and accuse anyone without proof, but he hoped his mere presence would deter Cadi and her cohorts from robbing a defenseless, aging widow.

He arrived at the bank after nine and pulled into its adjacent lot. After parking his vehicle, he killed the engine. The kids released their seat belts and hopped out of the sport utility vehicle, following Frank into the financial institution like a pair of ducklings.

Inside, Frank's gaze summed up his surroundings, and he spied Cadi seated at a long table in a glass-walled conference room just off of the lobby. The older woman who sat across from her was no doubt Mrs. Binder. He completed his own transaction at the teller window, keeping a watchful eye out; then he moseyed over and rapped on the pane.

Cadi glanced up and waved. Frank entered without further invitation.

"I had personal business here today," he said, his kids still on his heels. "When I saw you ladies, I thought I'd say hello."

Cadi smiled and turned to the woman sitting across the table from her. "This is Sergeant Frank Parker. He's a sheriff's deputy. He was on duty yesterday."

"Nice to meet you, Sergeant." The elderly woman seemed to force her polite smile.

"Frank, this is Mrs. Binder."

"A pleasure, ma'am."

"I phoned the insurance company this morning," Cadi said, "and they faxed over a claim form. Mrs. Binder is filling it out now. The bank manager offered to fax it back once she completes it and signs it."

"It'll never replace my valuables," she lamented, "but it's *something*."

Cadi agreed. "But just remember, Mrs. Binder, the insurance company said the check could take eight to ten weeks to arrive."

"I'll remember."

Frank decided to jump into the conversation. "And if you have any troubles after you submit your claim, come see me." He pulled out the business card that he'd strategically dropped into the breast pocket of his shirt. The county had cards printed up for all its deputies as folks often liked to know the name and business phone number of the responding officer, particularly in the cases of motor vehicle accidents.

"Thank you," Mrs. Binder said. "I'll remember your offer."

"You do that." *And if she doesn't get her check,* Frank added to himself, *I'll know just who to call.* He glanced at Cadi and grinned.

Moments later, he felt a collective presence behind him. He pivoted and found the four other Disaster Busters members standing behind his kids.

"We're going to the zoo," Emily told them.

"Great day for it," the brunette said. Frank thought he recalled her name being Meg.

"I haven't been to a zoo in ages," a woman with long, brownish-blond hair remarked. She stuck out her right hand to Frank. "I'm Bailey Schmid, and this is my husband, Jeff." She indicated the tall, slim guy at her side.

Frank shook his hand, too.

"I'm Will Angles."

Frank shook the African American man's hand and noticed the strong, firm

153

grasp despite the man's smaller, slender build.

"Nice to formally meet you all."

"Hey, Cadi," Meg said, "let's go to the zoo after you're finished here. It'll be fun."

"It's a small zoo. You might be disappointed," Frank said. "They've got a couple of bears and a farm animal section, and kids can take pony rides, but, like I said, it's small."

"Sounds fun." Bailey smiled in Dustin's direction. He tucked his chin, obviously overcome by bashfulness.

"Forget the zoo," Cadi replied. "I've got computer work to finish up, and you all promised to return to the explosion site and help several families scrounge up what's left of their belongings."

Frank immediately snapped to attention. He recalled how the last charity organization had looted the devastated properties. He decided to call the office and find out how many deputies would stand guard around the affected neighborhood while people picked through the area.

"We're helping folks this afternoon," Will put in. "I think it might perk us all up if we had some diversion this morning."

"Sure," Meg said. "Even if we spend another night here, it wouldn't be a big deal. We can attend services at Pastor Dremond's church tomorrow morning."

"Spend another night here?" Cadi shook her head. "I'd rather drive home."

"Listen, it's always good to have options," Meg said. "But I say we have a little fun before going back to work this afternoon. I also vote for an overnight stay so we can work right up until it gets dark if we want to and we don't have to worry about being tired and driving back to Waterloo."

"Yeah, Cadi, how 'bout it? The hotel is very comfortable," Bailey chimed in. She turned to Frank. "I never realized Wind Lake is so restful and resortlike."

"More the latter, I'd say. The tourist population is climbing each year."

"So what do you say, Cadi?" Jeff asked.

"I guess I don't care either way."

"Yes!" Will punched the air, acting as if he'd just scored the game's winning touchdown.

Frank chuckled at the man's exuberance.

Meg touched him on the sleeve. "Do you mind telling us how to get to the zoo?"

"Sure, but I still think you'll be disappointed."

"We have fun everywhere we go," Jeff interjected. He stuffed his hands into the pockets of his denim cargo pants and grinned. "We work hard and play hard."

"But Cadi mostly works hard," Meg said.

"Yeah, she's all work and no play," Will added.

"Oh, hush." She waved a hand at them while pointing to a place on the insurance form for Mrs. Binder with the other.

Frank grinned.

"She sounds like my dad," Dustin remarked. "All work. . ."

The growing smile slipped from Frank's face as he regarded his son.

"Well, it's nice that you're going to the zoo with him today, huh?" Meg looked from Dustin to Frank. "Is your wife going on the outing, too?"

"No. I'm not married." Regret and sadness accompanied the answer, although the pain had lessened over the years.

"My mommy's in heaven," Emily told them.

"How marvelous for her," Bailey said, hunkering down so that she was eye level with Emmie. "She's walking the streets of gold with Jesus, but I'll bet you miss her."

Emmie replied with several vigorous nods, but Frank knew she'd been too young to remember. A baby, just over a year old. However, his mother-in-law kept Yolanda's memory alive for the kids.

Frank cleared his throat, hoping for a subject change, although he had to admit to feeling impressed by the candid and empathetic way Bailey responded to his daughter.

"Now about those directions to the zoo," Jeff prompted.

"How 'bout if we just follow you there?" Meg tipped her head and regarded him, waiting for an answer.

"Um, yeah." Frank shrugged. "Sure."

Cadi cleared her throat. "I'm sure we'll find our way. We don't want to keep Sergeant Parker and his kids from their fun."

Frank couldn't help feeling curious when he noticed Cadi's sudden opposition. Was she hiding something? "You're not keeping me. The kids and I are happy to wait a few minutes." He pulled a couple of nickels from his pocket and told Dustin and Emmie to get a treat from the gumball machine by the front doors.

Cadi turned to the elderly woman sitting across from her at the rectangular table. "Mrs. Binder, do you need a ride someplace?"

"Oh, no." She waved a hand at Cadi then dabbed the back of her bluish-white cotton-candy hair. "My gentleman friend is coming to get me." A little pink blush crept up her powdered cheeks. "Don't tell a soul, but he's younger than I am."

Frank chuckled and glanced down at his athletic shoes.

Will made a *tsk-tsk* sound with the side of his mouth. "I'm afraid our Cadi will be pushing ninety-five before she has a *gentleman friend*."

Meg chuckled lightly, Will and Bailey laughed, and Jeff sported a wide grin.

Frank fought against any reaction, knowing it could be misconstrued. Next he saw Cadi's disapproving stare, although he didn't think she possibly could have heard the muttered remark.

"Well, listen, I'm going to take my kids outside," Frank said. "I've got a tan-colored SUV."

"See you in a few minutes." Jeff gave him a mock salute.

As Frank ushered his kids out of the bank, he had to admit he wasn't at all disappointed that the members of the Disaster Busters crew had imposed themselves on their zoo expedition. He thought he might even glean some important information that could come in handy later—like at their criminal trial.

Chapter 5

Cadi gripped the steering wheel of her minivan until her knuckles turned white. "I know full well what you guys are up to."

Whoops of laughter filled the vehicle, but Cadi tried to block it out and concentrate on her driving. This morning they had unhitched the trailer, and with the hotel manager's permission, they had backed it into a remote corner of the parking lot.

"I told you last night he wasn't married," Meg said, a smile still on her face. "See, I was right—as usual."

"He can't take his eyes off you," Bailey said from the backseat. "It's really a hoot."

"And what a coincidence that he showed up at the bank this morning," Will added.

"He's suspicious of us," Cadi pointed out. "He told me so last night."

"Well, what's he s'posed to do?" Will challenged. "A man's gotta test the water before diving in headfirst."

Cadi rolled her eyes at the analogy. "No, goofball, he's suspicious as in he thinks we're con artists."

"I think you're interested in him, too," Meg said. "I can tell. And we're just helping matters along. This zoo outing is the perfect way for you two to get to know each other."

"I don't want any help with my love life."

"What love life would that be?" Will retorted.

Every nerve in Cadi's body tensed. "Will, you know perfectly well that Darrell and I—"

"Should never have dated in the first place. Yeah, I know that."

She ignored the glib comment. "Look, I don't want another man in my life."

Cadi stopped at a red light and shifted in her seat. She refused to admit that she'd actually dreamed about the handsome deputy last night. *He stood in the misty distance, tall and strong, like a knight in shining armor.*

A car honked, and she jumped. Everyone in the van hooted.

"Like, who could you possibly be daydreaming about?" Jeff chuckled.

Cadi accelerated. "Look, you guys, this isn't funny."

Her friends couldn't have heard her over their laughter.

She tensed all the more.

"I remember you once told me that you wanted to find the right guy and get married," Bailey reminded her.

"I've mentioned that to all my trusted friends, but I was thinking of Darrell when I said it."

"*Urrnt.*" Will made a noise like a game show buzzer. "Wrong choice."

"Okay, I know that now," Cadi admitted, although she also knew she'd have to face Darrell and confirm that their breakup was official. The thought of that confrontation made her cringe.

"Maybe Frank's the right choice," Bailey said. "Find out if he's a believer. Give him a chance. He's definitely interested."

Cadi wanted to argue, but something inside her wanted it to be true. Nevertheless. . .

"I don't have peace about this."

"Oh, that's just because you're nervous." Meg readjusted in her seat belt. "Relax. Enjoy the day."

"Easy for you to say, Miss Matchmaker."

Her friend smiled back in reply. "You'll thank me for this someday."

"Yeah, sure I will."

The SUV up ahead slowed then turned left. Cadi followed it reluctantly, and within moments they drove onto the zoo's surface lot. Cadi pulled her van into the parking space across from the one Frank chose. She opened the door and climbed down from behind the wheel before sliding back the side door by which her friends exited. They traipsed behind Frank and his kids to the front gate where they paid meager entrance fees.

Once inside the zoo, Bailey and Jeff, still newlyweds, walked hand in hand along the stony walkway. Cadi strolled behind them, thinking they made the perfect couple. Their wedding had been an unforgettable collage of music, vows, and celebration of love.

Disappointment settled over her like fog along the Mississippi. She'd always wanted a family of her own, in addition to Aunt Lou. But considering her newly self-imposed condition of "terminally single," Cadi supposed she'd have to abandon the idea of satin and lace and a handsome knight.

She paused by a rough, split-rail fence and gazed inside its circumference. Harnessed ponies stomped and snorted while zoo employees lifted children into the saddles.

Children. Cadi figured that dream had imploded, too—just yesterday when she'd told Darrell good-bye.

Except Darrell had been all wrong for her. Once she'd overheard Darrell's two friends talking. One equated Darrell to patent leather and Cadi to buckskin. Darrell's other buddy remarked that Darrell was a polished gem and Cadi a diamond in the rough. Both had a few chuckles and walked away, never knowing Cadi was standing nearby and had heard every word. At first she took it as a sort of weird compliment, but now she realized Darrell's cronies pointed out what Cadi should have seen all along. There were so many dissimilarities between herself and Darrell.

A man behind her cleared his throat. Cadi started and swung around. Frank Parker and his kids stood there, staring at her. By the curious expressions on their faces, she knew something was amiss.

"What?" She looked from the kids to Frank. "What's wrong?"

"Are you in line for the pony ride or not?" he asked sarcastically. "If not, Dustin and Emily would like to make the next go-round."

Cadi felt her face flame with embarrassment. "Um, yeah. I guess I'll sit this one out." She stepped aside, and the kids ran into the corral.

She turned and leaned her forearms on the wooden fence. Frank did the same.

"So where did your friends take off to?"

"Excuse me?"

"Your friends."

Cadi glanced in all directions. No sight of Will, Meg, Bailey, or Jeff.

"Looks like they ditched me." She expelled a breath, heavy with exasperation. "They think they are so sly. This whole zoo thing is a setup, you know? They couldn't care less about spending the day at the zoo."

"I kind of figured." His gaze never strayed from his children.

Cadi blinked. "You did?"

Frank flicked a glance at her. "I might not be a rocket scientist, but I know a setup when I see it—particularly when it's *me* involved in the setup."

Cadi felt her heart sink out of sheer humiliation. "I'm really sorry. My friends didn't mean to—"

"Don't worry." He gave her a little smile. "I have well-intentioned friends, too." He took a sidestep and faced her. "I put things together on the way here from the bank. You broke up with your boyfriend. They found out I'm single. You're single. Need I say more?"

Cadi felt mortified but managed to shake her head in reply.

"Hey, don't take it so hard. Since my wife died, I have had more 'setups' than I'd care to count."

She could barely breathe. Her friends' practical joke now felt like a punch in the diaphragm.

"Were you two serious?"

"You two—who?" Seconds later, she grasped his meaning. "Oh, me and Darrell." She waved her hand. "No, we weren't serious, although I will confess to having serious delusions of grandeur." Cadi laughed at herself and her silly dreams. "Darrell disapproves of my career choice, and he can't get past it."

"Hmmm. . .so you're a devoted career woman?" Frank's gaze was still plastered to his kids as the horses clomped around in a circle.

"Well, I guess so. I mean, if I want my business to succeed, I have to put time and effort into it. It's just like with anything."

"So, what I'm hearing is that Darrell wasn't worth the time and effort."

"I guess you could say that." Cadi disliked the heartless way it sounded, but for all her hopes and dreams, Frank's summation was right on the mark.

He chuckled so hard that Cadi could feel the fence shake.

"At least you're honest." He stopped short and gave her a sideways glance. "Are you honest, Cadi?"

"I try to be." She frowned, bristling at his implication. "Are you honest?"

"Most of the time."

Cadi put a hand on one hip. "I'm not sure I understand where this conversation is going. Are you telling me you lie?"

Frank straightened. "Not long ago my mother-in-law asked me how I liked her new slacks outfit. She had taken Emmie shopping and found the pantsuit—or whatever you call it—on the bargain rack. I didn't have the heart to tell her I thought it was the ugliest ensemble I ever saw, so I told her she looked real pretty. Guess that's a lie by any measure."

"Maybe. Or maybe it's just saving face with your mother-in-law." She smiled and looked up into Frank's eyes. His dark gaze bore into hers, and her heart skipped a beat. She realized such a reaction had never occurred when she was in Darrell's company.

She averted her gaze, startled by her emotions, and wondered if she should leave the zoo and let her friends find their own way back to the hotel. It would serve them right if she did.

"Nice of you to help Mrs. Binder fill out all those insurance forms this morning."

Cadi sensed what he was getting at. "I'm not swindling senior citizens if that's what you're thinking. The truth is I like helping people."

"Is that why you started Disaster Busters?"

"It's part of the reason." She felt mildly annoyed by the interrogation, although she was familiar with answering for her business. In the past, numerous people had inquired about the hows and whys of starting Disaster Busters. She didn't mind fielding questions when the motives were right. She knew that if she expected people to trust her and her business, she had to be transparent.

But she could tell Frank openly distrusted her. She could read it in his dark eyes.

She fell silent for several long moments and watched the dust plume around the ponies as they clomped in a circle.

At last Cadi decided to take a chance and wear her heart on her sleeve.

"When I was a little girl, my parents, brother, and sister drowned in a flood," she began. "We lived in a small town along the Mississippi River. Actually, the neighborhood in which I grew up isn't even there anymore. It flooded so many times that the government demolished it. Anyway," she said, moving her arm back to the top rail of the fence, "after the tragedy of losing my family, I experienced a slew of bureaucratic horrors. I was in foster care for almost two years until my great-aunt was located and agreed to take custody of me. The entire situation wasn't handled well, from the emergency personnel who saved my life to the court-appointed social workers and presiding judges. When I was old enough to realize just how poorly my case was handled, I vowed to make a difference—to make it easier on victims of natural disasters—so they don't feel like society is kicking them when they're already down."

Frank stared at her, his expression teetering on disbelief.

"If my reply sounds rehearsed, it is to a point," she said, guessing his thoughts. "Sometimes I speak at churches so I can generate financial support for my organization. Disaster Busters is a business—but it's a ministry, too. Sort of like a pastorate."

He still seemed to be digesting the information.

"Something else about me, too." She smiled. "I'm a born-again Christian. That means—"

"I know what it means. I'm familiar with the biblical term *born-again*. The fact is, I made a decision for Christ when I was a kid."

"Oh." Her reply sounded rather lame to her own ears, but Cadi didn't like the way things were adding up. Frank Parker was a widower and a Christian who could make her heart skip and send her emotions reeling. Maybe her friends were right. Still, there was a gruffness about him that appealed to her about as much as this rough-sawn fence. The man of her dreams was kind and compassionate. Sensitive and caring. Those four words didn't seem to describe Frank Parker. What's more, he didn't appear to be friend material.

"I should be going." Cadi stepped away from the fence. "I'll walk out to the parking lot, and if I don't see my friends, they can either find their own way back to the hotel or call my cell phone."

Before Frank could answer, his children raced over after their ride.

"Daddy, you didn't see me waving to you," the little girl said with a pout.

"I've been talking with Miss Trent, honey. I'm sorry."

"Oh." Emily's gaze slid from her dad to Cadi.

Cadi replied with a guilty smile. She hadn't meant to steal Frank's attention from his children.

Then Dustin looked at Cadi, almost as though he were seeing her for the first time. Was that a glint of enthusiasm in his honey-colored eyes?

"Do you cook dinners like Miss Paige?"

"Or bake cookies like Miss Nicole?" Emily asked with wide, hopeful eyes.

"Paige? Nicole?" Puzzled, Cadi looked at Frank.

"Remember the well-intentioned friends I mentioned? Those two women were, um, setups."

"Ah." Cadi grinned. "And a way to a man's heart is through his stomach."

"Something like that."

She couldn't help a laugh. "Well, Emily," she said, turning to the little girl, "I've got no time for baking. I don't cook, either." She looked at Dustin. "In fact, I'm a terrible cook. I burn everything. Seriously."

Frank looked as though he were holding back a guffaw while the kids scrunched their faces, unable to follow the conversation. At least, Cadi thought, she had quelled any romantic notions he might have.

"Well, have a fun day." She took several steps backward, smiled at the trio, then whirled around and strode to her van as fast as her legs could carry her.

Chapter 6

I'm telling you, she's up to no good!"

Adam heaved another sigh. "You have no proof."

"It's a gut feeling—and I trust my gut."

"Sure it's not heartburn?" The pastor swatted at the circling gnats. "Listen, can we talk about this another time? I have a sermon to prepare."

"I realize that—and I'll only keep you a minute." Frank knew from when he used to attend regularly that it was Adam's habit to arrive at church on Saturday evenings and research, rehearse, and pray over his next day's message. Adam had done this for years, which was why Frank chose to meet him here... and now.

He glanced around the parking lot, empty except for his SUV, just as Dustin opened the door to the vehicle.

"Dad, tell Emily to be quiet. She won't stop singing."

Emmie's impish voice wafted on the thick summer air. "La-la-la..."

"Dad, make her stop. She's plugging her ears. She won't listen to me."

"La-la-la..."

"I'll be right there, Dustin."

"Frank, I have my sermon to practice, and you have kids to take home and put to bed."

He swung his gaze back to Adam, who grinned, but Frank had yet to speak his piece.

"I'm telling you, something's up. Cadi's jittery around me; she avoids looking me in the eye." He paused. "She's hiding something."

"I talked to Cadi last night at the barbecue, and she didn't seem jumpy to me. What's more, I spoke with her—"

"Dad!" Dustin's voice cut into the conversation and held a tone of unmistakable aggravation. "She's singing *again!*"

"Okay, son. I'll be there in a sec." Frank turned back to Adam. "Look, about Cadi—"

"She and her team are the real deal, Frank. Go home," the pastor advised. "Relax. Pray about things. We'll talk again tomorrow. I think that when we do you'll agree that Cadi and the Disaster Busters are in Wind Lake to help." An idea lit his gaze. "Hey, come to service, and then you and the kids can come over for lunch. What do you say?"

"Appreciate the offer. I'll consider it." Frank was amazed at the way Adam always worked in the invitation to hear one of his sermons.

"We'll be seeing you later," Adam said as he began to make his way across the almost deserted parking lot. "G'night, kids. Be good for your dad and make Jesus proud."

Frank strode to the SUV and settled the matter between his children, knowing full well that they were exhausted. After the zoo this morning, they went to his parents' condo in a retirement community on the outskirts of town. His folks still worked full-time jobs, but because they were older than fifty-five, they qualified for a condo in the newly constructed retirement center. Both Mom and Dad loved it, as the amenities seemed like luxuries to them after years of living in a century-old farmhouse, but Frank had been sad to see the old place go in order to make room for a strip mall.

"Can't stop progress," Dad had said, and Frank supposed it was true. Besides, his folks' new low-maintenance home meant they had more time to spend with friends and family. This afternoon, for instance, Dustin and Emily splashed and played in the retirement community's indoor pool, under adult supervision. Later, Mom made one of Frank's favorite dinners: spaghetti with meatballs. He ate so much he thought he'd bust, and thankfully, Mom put in a children's video for the kids to watch so the adults could laze around, talk, and allow their meals to digest. Now, however, Dustin and Emily were beyond tired—which accounted for their squabbling.

Pulling alongside the curb in front of the townhouse he rented from his in-laws, Frank parked his vehicle. When the tornado had destroyed his home and killed his wife three years ago, he needed a place to go, and his in-laws just happened to need tenants in the unit adjacent to theirs. So he moved himself and the kids into this two-story place, and he just never bothered to leave. He figured it gave Dustin and Emmie a sense of home, since their grandparents lived right next door. What's more, his mother-in-law, Lois Chayton, ran a day care in her home, which benefited Frank greatly.

"Hi, Gramma! Hi, Grampa!" the kids hollered through the screen door before Frank unlocked their identical front entrance and ushered the pair inside.

He called his own hello to his in-laws before stepping into the sparse living room area. His mother and Lois had tried to spiff up the place by hanging pictures on the wall, and his sister brought over knickknacks, setting them here and there. But the fact remained: Frank didn't give a hoot about decorating his home, although he managed to keep it fairly clean. That was the best he could do, and Lois stepped in and took care of the rest. She knew as well as he did that life hurled issues at him that were much more pressing than housekeeping—issues like taking care of his kids and working sometimes eighty hours a week.

Dustin and Emily took their turns in the shower, and then Frank tucked them into their beds. With each child in his and her respective room and the house now still and silent, Frank moseyed out onto the narrow cement slab of a front porch. He lowered his tired body onto one of the hard plastic lawn chairs and kicked up his feet, setting his athletic shoes on the metal rail.

The night air had a nip to it, but it felt pleasant enough. Refreshing.

He forced himself to relax. His eyelids grew heavy.

"We are so totally lost."

The voice coming from the sidewalk sounded vaguely familiar.

"But that guy said the hotel is this way."

"It's the other way. I'm sure of it."

Frank sat up in time to see two males and two females making their way past his home. Beneath the glow of the streetlamp, he recognized them at once.

"Hey." Frank stood. "Disaster Busters."

They stopped and looked his way.

"It's me, Frank Parker." He stepped off the porch and walked over to them. They greeted him.

"Have you seen Cadi?" Meg asked. "We've been trying to get ahold of her, but either (a) she's turned off her phone because she's, like, really mad at us or (b) her battery's dead or (c) her phone's in her monster purse in which she carries almost everything and she can't hear it ringing."

"If this is multiple choice," Frank said with a grin, "I'm choosing (a)—she's really mad at you." He chuckled in spite of himself.

"So, um, you're on to our matchmaking efforts, huh?" Bailey asked, holding her husband's hand. She looked at her friends. "I guess it was a bad idea."

"Seemed like a good idea at the time," Will retorted; then a broad, mischievous smile lit his expression.

"Except now we're worried about Cadi," Meg informed Frank. "You wouldn't happen to know where she is, would you?"

He shook his head. "She left the zoo right away—as soon as she found out you all took off on her. She mentioned you'd call her cell phone." He rubbed his stubbly jaw. "I don't think she thought the whole setup thing was amusing." He sensed the foursome's embarrassment and discomfort. "If it's any consolation, I took it all in stride."

"Frank, we're sorry if we put you in a bad position," Jeff said, sounding sincere. "Hopefully we'll find Cadi back at the hotel and we can make it up to her somehow. Can you point us in the right direction?"

"What hotel?"

"Wind Lake Inn."

Frank shook his head. "That's on the other side of town. How'd you manage to get so far off course?"

"We were at the explosion site all afternoon, digging through the rubble,"

Jeff said. "We were able to help one family recover a good number of their possessions."

Frank tried to fight off the doubt and suspicion seeping into his heart.

"Afterward we were invited to eat dinner with a family who will be staying with relatives until their home can be rebuilt," Bailey added. "The Neumanns. Do you know them?"

Frank nodded. "I know them well." He made a mental note to follow up with the Neumanns once the Disaster Busters team left town.

"So after our huge meal," Meg put in, "we all decided the walk back to the hotel would be healthy, and we were told we had a short distance to go, but—"

"But somehow we must have gotten turned around," Will interjected.

Muttering ensued, and he chuckled again.

"This might sound like a stupid question, but did anyone call the hotel and ask for Cadi?"

"We've been calling all day." Meg sighed. "No answer in our room, and all they could tell us is she didn't check out."

"Hmm."

"Frank, are you available to drive us to the hotel?" Jeff asked. "We've been told Wind Lake doesn't have public transportation."

"No, it doesn't."

"Ordinarily we'd never dream of imposing," Bailey added quickly, "but we're exhausted, and I, for one, can't bear the thought of walking across town."

"Sure, I can give you a lift." He supposed his in-laws could watch the kids for a while. "Wait here while I grab my keys."

❧

Cadi sat back on the queen-sized bed in the hotel room and smiled at her laptop. She'd been working all afternoon on creating a Web site for the victims who'd lost everything after the explosion. It had turned out perfectly.

After leaving the zoo this morning, Cadi had returned to the bank and talked with Leslie Pensky, the branch manager. Together they set up an account, and Pastor Dremond agreed to be the signer, overseer, and disperser of the funds. Cadi would give him the signature card tomorrow after the worship service, and the pastor would drop it off at the bank on Monday.

And now, with the Web site up, people everywhere could make a donation.

Lord, I guess it was Your will for me to spend an extra day in Wind Lake.

Cadi glanced at her gold bracelet watch. It was nearly ten o'clock. Where were her friends?

She scooted off the bed and searched for her cell phone, only to realize she'd left it out in the van. No wonder she hadn't heard from them!

Taking strides for the door, the latch clicked, and it opened just as she reached for the handle.

"Where have you been?" Cadi asked as Meg stepped into the room.

"I was just about to ask you the same thing."

Cadi had the good grace to feel chagrined. "I just realized I left my phone in the van and was headed outside to get it."

"I knew it." Meg snapped her fingers. "We've been trying to get ahold of you all afternoon. I knew you wouldn't purposely ignore us."

"I didn't. Honest. Sorry you couldn't reach me."

"We actually wondered if maybe you'd gone home, but we knew you wouldn't leave us stranded."

"Not a chance, although. . ." Cadi paused. "I thought about it." With a grin she padded to one of the two beds in the room and sat down. "I'll admit that your little prank upset me, but when I left the zoo, I came up with a great idea." She smiled. "I stopped back at the bank, met the branch manager, and set up an account for the explosion victims. Then this afternoon, I created a Web site, just like we planned. Come and look."

Cadi pulled her computer onto her lap and showed Meg the Web pages she'd put together.

"The digital photos Will took this morning before we went to the bank turned out great."

"Absolutely. And they transferred onto my computer and the new Web site with no problems."

Meg sighed. "Well, your Web site is impressive even if your memory isn't." She shook her head. "I'm going to attach that cell phone of yours to idiot strings and make you wear it around your neck."

"That's an idea." Still smiling, Cadi shut down her computer. "So how did things go for all of you this afternoon?"

"We worked as hard as you did. You would have been proud of us."

"I'm always proud of you—my friends."

A wide grin spread across Meg's face before her expression turned serious again. "We made progress, but there is still so much left to do. And so much damage! At one point I had to sob right along with a woman whose cherished family photographs had been destroyed. But then I reminded her that she and her husband are both alive and unhurt, and we both started crying all over again—but crying tears of joy."

"You helped her see the rainbow through the rain. That's important—and that's what Disaster Busters is here for."

Meg nodded and sighed wearily. "When it got too dark to keep searching and sorting, we had dinner with some other volunteers before heading for the hotel—except we somehow got our directions crossed and wound up on the other side of town. Our friendly neighborhood sheriff's deputy gave us a ride."

"Frank?" Cadi stared at her friend, amazed. "How'd you manage to run into him?"

"Sheer coincidence—if you believe in coincidence, that is."

Cynicism wound its way around Cadi's heart. "He was probably following you all day. He thinks we're lowlife scum who'd rob senior citizens." She stood to ready herself for bed.

"Frank doesn't think ill of us. In fact, he asked all kinds of questions about Disaster Busters while driving us back here."

"He's asking questions because he's suspicious." Cadi searched her overnight bag for her nightshirt and toothbrush. "He's interrogated me at least twice."

"Let him interrogate. We've got nothing to hide."

"I agree. But Frank takes his suspicions way too far."

"Uh-oh. Sounds like you're angry with him." Meg tipped her head. "Or are you angry with us for trying to set you up with Frank?"

"I'm not angry with anybody." Cadi turned her back to Meg, hoping to mask any telltale emotions. "It's just rather insulting to be treated like a thief when you're really trying hard to help other people."

Meg seemed to think it over. "Look," she said at last, "I'll admit Frank has some rough edges." She flopped onto the adjacent bed with its colorful floral spread. "But those edges are probably due to his wife's death. I wonder how it happened."

Cadi strode to the bathroom and closed the door behind her. She told herself she didn't care about Frank Parker or his adorable kids—or how his wife died. But she immediately regretted her harsh attitude. It belied her values, her very being.

Closing her eyes, she prayed for God's peace that surpasses all understanding. Perhaps by morning her tumultuous feelings would be back under control.

Chapter 7

D addy, why are you coming to church with us?"

Frank winced. His daughter shouldn't have to ask such a thing. Rather, attending worship services with their dad ought to be a regular event in his kids' lives.

He glanced at Emmie in the rearview mirror of his vehicle. Pigtails in her hair, she sat belted into the backseat, looking darling in her Sunday best, thanks to his mother-in-law's helpful hands. Once more it pained Frank that accompanying his kids to church was such a rarity.

"I'm coming today so I can hear God's Word with you and Dustin. It's the right thing to do. I should have been attending services with you more often."

He spoke from his heart but didn't add that after hearing that the Disaster Busters team would be in church today, he had decided to use his attendance as a great excuse to check them out one more time. He had dual motives, it was true, and he admitted them to God and himself. But at least he was actually on his way to the small, quaint house of worship again, and for the first time there were no tears stinging the backs of his eyes and no lump of sorrow in his throat over having lost Yolanda.

No doubt the reason was because he felt serious about his self-appointed undercover mission. Those Disaster Busters were up to something. Particularly Miss Cadi Trent. Frank just knew it. Why else would he have lost sleep last night thinking about her?

He pulled into the parking lot and slowed his vehicle to a halt. He shut off the engine and climbed from behind the wheel of the SUV, then helped his kids out.

On the way into the building, he greeted several people he knew and tried to ignore their expressions of shock and surprise at seeing him here again. Inside, he managed to pay little attention to the pity-filled stares. Many in this congregation had known and loved Yolanda, and now they saw him as her unfortunate, lonely widower in desperate need of female companionship.

Ridiculous notion.

Strolling up the center aisle of the sanctuary he bobbed a curt greeting to Paige Dunner, Dustin's Sunday school teacher.

"We missed you today." She waved, and Frank noticed her gray eyes weren't on his son as she spoke. He glimpsed her inviting expression, but he wasn't interested in anything the skinny brunette had to offer.

169

A few pews later, Dustin halted.

Frank set his hand on his son's shoulder before he could slide in and sit. "Let's go up in front."

"But, Dad, we always sit here with Gramma and Grampa. They'll be getting outta Bible study any minute."

"That's fine, son, but I prefer to sit up front today." Frank had already spotted Cadi's blond hair in the front pew. She might be more hesitant to follow through with any rip-off schemes if she knew he was watching her every move.

"But—"

"Follow me, Dustin."

The boy obeyed, albeit reluctantly. Moments later, Frank and the children slid into the pew directly behind the Disaster Busters. The team greeted him with cordial smiles, but Frank sensed Cadi's unease at once.

She's up to something, all right.

Frank settled into the pew and stared at the back of Cadi's head. He couldn't help noticing that she'd fixed her hair so the usual sassy flips were smoothed under today. He had to admit the style looked more conservative and quite appropriate for Sunday morning service.

His gaze moved down to her slender shoulders concealed by the teal and black printed jacket she wore.

Then suddenly she turned to hear something one of her friends said, and Frank glimpsed the dangly silver earrings that hung from her lobes. The movement sent a waft of her delicate scent in his direction. She piqued his interest, all right, in more ways than one.

Which makes her even more dangerous, he told himself, folding his arms across his chest.

Cadi wanted to groan out loud when Frank and his kids took occupancy of the wooden pew behind her. She had nothing against those two precious children, but she felt Frank's molten gaze burning into her being. She had a hunch he meant to intimidate her, and she fought to overcome the destructive emotion. After all, no one could intimidate her unless she allowed him to do so.

Besides, Lord, I have nothing to hide. Drawing in a deep breath, she forced herself to relax.

"Dad, did you come to church with us today because of *her*?"

The boy's question reached Cadi's ears. Next she heard Frank's whispered reproof. Meg and Bailey, sitting on either side of her, began to laugh.

"Oh, for pity's sake," she muttered, feeling her friends' shoulders shake in amusement. Couldn't her friends see that Frank viewed them as potential prisoners, not friends?

Lord, please show this distrustful deputy that Disaster Busters is run with integrity.

I'd never want to bring shame to Christ's name.

"Thanks again for the ride to the hotel last night," Will said.

Cadi turned in time to see him twist around in the pew and face Frank.

"Glad I could help."

"As you can see, we found Cadi." Will chuckled. "The little workaholic was so intent on building that Web site for victims of Friday's explosion that she forgot her cell phone in the van and never knew we were trying to reach her."

"Web site, huh?"

Cadi thought she could hear the distrust in his tone. She whirled around. "That's right. Web site." But the sight of Frank out of uniform and dressed in a black suit with a periwinkle shirt and coordinating necktie gave her pause. He looked like a model who had just stepped out of the glossy pages of a magazine.

She cleared her throat. "Pastor Dremond is going to announce the site—and explain its purpose."

Before turning back around in the pew, Cadi smiled at the little girl who looked as precious as a baby doll. But not wanting to leave out Frank's son, Cadi reached toward him, palm up. Dustin whacked it. Next she balled her first, and they knocked knuckles.

"What happened to a handshake?" Frank asked facetiously.

"Handshake?" Cadi rolled her eyes. "That was so yesterday."

Frank narrowed his dark gaze at her, but she saw a light of amusement in his brown eyes. She laughed and gave Dustin a mischievous wink.

The boy smiled back at her.

Music suddenly filled the air as the organist and pianist began to play. Cadi turned in her seat just as the choir began filling the loft behind the platform. Minutes later, the ensemble sang a soul-stirring rendition of the hymn "Be Thou My Vision."

Then Pastor Dremond strode to the podium. The coffee-colored suit he wore complemented his reddish brown hair. He read the announcements and moved on to the Web site Cadi created yesterday.

"The Internet has many dangers," he said, "but it can be used for blessings, as well. This site will be a blessing to those in need after Friday's tragedy because it allows those who feel led to do so to donate funds that will in turn be used to provide basic necessities. None of us is rolling in money, but if each of us gives a little, the sum will accumulate into a lot. And that leads me to my sermon this morning. . . ."

Pastor Dremond began by reading from the Gospel of Luke, chapter twenty-one, beginning in verse one, which illustrated sacrificial giving. "As he looked up, Jesus saw the rich putting their gifts into the temple treasury. He also saw a poor widow put in two very small copper coins. 'I tell you the truth,' he said, 'this poor widow has put in more than all the others. All these people gave their gifts out of their wealth; but she out of her poverty put in all she had to live on.'"

The reverend looked out over the congregation. "Some folks want to hang on to every last coin," he said, "but in the end, they miss out on the best things in life. Likewise, some people don't want to return love and affection or friendship because they're too busy hanging on to their hearts. In a word, they're *afraid* to give."

The pastor asked his congregation to turn in their Bibles to the Gospel of Matthew, chapter ten, verse thirty-nine. "Jesus said, 'Whoever finds his life will lose it, and whoever loses his life for my sake will find it.'"

Again, Pastor Dremond glanced up from his Bible. "I think this verse illustrates how the more we try to hang on to something in this world, the more prone we are to losing it. Including, as Jesus said, our very lives."

The pastor went on to make a few more comparisons and then closed his message with prayer.

When the service ended, members of the congregation crowded around Cadi and inquired about the new Web site. She directed them to her Disaster Busters site, through which they could log on to the Wind Lake Explosion Victims' page. Many thanked her for her service, and Cadi felt blessed, as though she'd truly made a difference in this community.

Once the churchgoers continued on their way, Cadi collected her purse and Bible and headed down the center aisle toward the door.

"You're very innovative, aren't you?"

She recognized the voice at once—but more, she recognized the cynical tone. Glancing to her right, she spied Frank Parker standing several feet away.

Cadi paused and regarded him. "There's hardly anything innovative about creating a Web page. It's done all the time, and anyone can do it."

"Guess that's my point." He took a few steps forward and narrowed his gaze. "There are a lot of scams on the Internet, and at face value most of them appear on the up-and-up."

"Are you insinuating that I'm trying to scam people using the Web page I created?" Cadi asked indignantly, as heat filled her face and spread down her neck. She glanced around for the reverend. "And do you think Pastor Dremond would be in on such a scam?"

"I merely made a comment, that's all. Do you think you might be overreacting, perhaps out of guilt?"

The remark struck her like a slap across the face. Tears threatened, but she fought to keep them at bay. She drew in a calming breath and held it, knowing she had no good, Christian thing to say to this man.

She brushed past him and left the church. Meg, Bailey, Jeff, and Will were waiting for her in the parking lot next to the van.

"Hey, we've got directions to the Dremonds' house!" Jeff called. His light brown hair was so short it didn't move in the gentle wind.

Cadi pushed strands of her hair off her face. "I'd rather go home. We can pick up some food on the way."

"Fast food compared to a home-cooked meal? The latter has my vote," Will said. "Mrs. Dremond said she prepared pot roast. Mmm-mmm. That's my kind of noonday supper."

As if in reply, Cadi's stomach rumbled. She hadn't eaten breakfast this morning.

"You look upset." Meg peered at her and tilted her head. "What's wrong?"

Cadi momentarily closed her eyes to regain her composure. "Another run-in with our friendly neighborhood sheriff's deputy. He accused me of setting up the Web site so I can steal donations."

"Shut *up!*" Will replied in disbelief. "Maybe you should file some kind of complaint against him. I mean, he has no proof, and his behavior borders on harassment."

Cadi considered it.

"In the meantime, let's drive over to the Dremonds' and eat." Will rubbed his palms together.

"I just want to go home."

"Oh, c'mon, Cadi," Bailey said. "It'll be fun."

"All right. But just remember, we need to get home today. I don't have another change of clothes."

"I'm out of clean clothes, too," Meg said. "Besides, it seems our work is done here."

"I agree, but a few hours at the Dremonds' place won't set us back too far," Jeff reasoned. "It won't take us long to get home."

A moment later the heavy entryway doors of the small country church closed with a bang. Cadi turned in time to see Pastor Dremond exiting the building along with Sergeant Parker and his two children.

"Want me to go talk to him, Cadi?" Will stared in the deputy's direction with a firm set to his jaw. "I'll straighten him out about everything."

"No. Just leave the matter alone. With any luck we'll never see the guy again."

"See you at home in a few minutes!" the reverend called to the Disaster Busters team. Then he shook hands with Frank.

Cadi's gaze met Frank's dark eyes. Tumultuous emotions made her stomach flip while an infinite sadness filled her being. *He thinks I'm out to cheat people.* She looked away and told herself to feel thankful that she'd seen the last of the hypercritical sheriff's deputy. After lunch with the Dremonds, she could retreat to Waterloo and, she hoped, out of his jurisdiction.

Chapter 8

The Disaster Busters team piled into the van with Cadi at the wheel. They rode to the Dremonds' single-story ranch-style home, located a mile up the road from the church. With the trailer hitched again to the van, Cadi carefully maneuvered the vehicle up the winding gravel driveway.

All jumped out, and after a hearty welcome from the Dremond kids and Simon, the family's dog, Cadi, Meg, and Bailey offered to help Lindsey Dremond in the kitchen. There wasn't much to do, however, as the trim, dark-haired woman had things under control. So the women chatted and got acquainted while the last of the lunch preparations were made. Then Meg and Bailey went outside to set up the picnic table for the children.

Minutes later, while Cadi carried a porcelain bowl filled with steaming roasted meat, potatoes, carrots, and celery to the dining room table, she heard laughter coming from the next room. She thought she recognized the deep guffaw that certainly didn't sound as if it came from mild-mannered Pastor Dremond.

Oh, Lord, no—not him.

"Cadi, you'll never believe who just arrived with his kids." Meg rushed over to her. "It's that nice officer you like so much."

She had to smile at her friend's sarcastic wit. "Great. I'll look forward to being interrogated while I try to eat."

"Bring it on," Meg said with a smile. "He's outnumbered."

Cadi relented. "True enough."

"Between all of us, maybe we can put that guy's suspicions to rest once and for all."

She nodded in agreement. Her friend made a good point, and with a new perspective, Cadi's nerves felt less jangled.

Until she was seated beside the brawny man at the dinner table. His shoulders were so broad that his arm brushed against Cadi each time he moved.

Pastor Dremond prayed over their food and concluded with a hearty "Amen." Everyone began eating while Lindsey set off to check on the kids and make sure they were behaving outside. She made a quick return and announced that all was well. They didn't mind eating their pot roast under the budding apple blossoms.

"Gorgeous afternoon, isn't it?" Pastor Dremond remarked. "Perfect day in May."

"I love this time of year, but summer is my favorite season." Meg cut into a piece of meat. "Can't wait until it arrives."

"How do you like to spend your summer days?" the pastor inquired. "When you're not responding to disasters, of course."

"Well, I do have a full-time job, and I'm working on my master's degree in Christian counseling. But when I find free time, I play volleyball on a team at church, and Cadi and I enjoy watching the guys play softball."

Cadi gasped at the remark's implication, choking on the iced tea she'd just sipped. Will clapped her between the shoulder blades.

"Gracious me!" A pinkish hue crept into Meg's cheeks. "I, um, didn't mean anything by that comment. We just enjoy the evening games. We mostly sit and talk with our girlfriends in the stands."

Beside her, Frank chuckled.

"We do tend to gab more than we watch the game, I'm afraid," Bailey added.

"My mouth ran ahead of my brain," Meg said apologetically.

"Sure did," Will quipped.

Cadi finished her coughing fit. "Excuse me for getting all choked up."

Chuckles flitted around the table.

"Quite all right," Adam said. "My wife makes strong tea."

Cadi smiled and cast a quick glance in Frank's direction. He was smiling, and he seemed so disarming—so likable—that she wished they could be friends.

"And evening softball games are a favorite pastime of mine, too," the pastor continued. "My oldest son is on a Little League team."

"Awesome," Meg replied, sending a look of apology across the table to Cadi. She accepted with a smile.

"If I recall, you used to play some softball, Frank."

"That was a long time ago." He shifted in his chair, and his elbow bumped Cadi's. He murmured an apology.

"Your son's close to the right age to join Little League."

"Maybe next year. Dustin has expressed an interest in softball. I guess I could sign him up."

"Great. We can carpool." Pastor Dremond grinned at his wife.

Cadi took a bite of the seasoned beef and savored its rich flavor.

"So, what kind of disasters has this group responded to lately?" Frank asked, changing the subject.

Cadi felt Frank's stare, but with her mouth full, she dared not reply. Instead, she looked across the table at Meg, Jeff, and Bailey, silently urging them to respond.

"You name it, we've been there," Jeff said. "Probably similar, that way, to your line of work, Officer."

"Hmm."

"Feel free to check out our credibility, if you haven't already," Will told him. "We play by the book."

"The Good Book," Bailey added. "Disaster Busters is a Christian organization."

"I ran a check on both the organization and Cadi, and everything came back squeaky clean."

Cadi swallowed. "You ran a check on me?" Stunned, she turned toward him.

"Just doing my job." He peered at her with an unwavering gaze.

Cadi felt more than offended. She was hurt—hurt that someone would dislike and suspect her when all the while her intentions were honorable.

Lindsey cleared her throat. "Well, if you don't mind, I'd prefer if you all didn't exchange disaster stories during lunch. I can barely watch the local news channels. But I'd love to hear what God is doing in your lives."

Bailey replied first, then one by one, they shared miraculous accounts of the Lord's mercy and goodness—all except Frank Parker who, Cadi noticed, didn't contribute to the conversation. What's more, he had the nerve to settle back in his seat and drape his arm over the back of her chair. Cadi, however, refused to be intimidated. The thought of filing a complaint against him, as Will suggested, somehow grew more and more appealing.

After lunch, the reverend cleared the dishes, and his wife served dessert. The children came in, and the boys began begging to play a game of catch with Will, Jeff, Frank, and the pastor. The men declined, but Cadi decided throwing around a ball with the kids sounded better than sitting under Frank's scrutiny a moment longer.

"I'll play with you. In fact, I have a mitt in my van."

"You do?" Frank's son looked awed.

"I'll go get our mitts!" the oldest of the Dremond boys called over his shoulder as he dashed away.

Cadi smiled and turned back to answer Dustin. "Yep, but it's quite by accident. We were in such a hurry to leave Waterloo on Friday that I forgot to remove the box of sports paraphernalia I borrowed from a few friends for the Teen Challenge the church sponsored last Saturday."

"I wondered what was in that box," Will said, kneading his jaw.

"That's right, Cadi. You volunteered to referee, didn't you?"

"Yep. And the kids had a great time."

"Do you have an extra mitt for me?" Dustin asked. "Mine's at home."

"I think there's probably an extra mitt in that box." Cadi smiled at the boy's eager expression.

After excusing herself from the table, Cadi strode outside to her van with the little boys in tow. In spite of the trailer hitched to the van, she managed to retrieve two brown leather mitts and a softball. She handed one glove to Dustin, and in no time a game of catch commenced on the Dremonds' wide, neatly mowed front lawn.

She tossed the ball to one of the Dremond boys. He caught it and threw it to Dustin. Next Dustin pitched the ball to the second Dremond boy who missed the catch and had to go scrambling after it. With ball back in hand, he then threw it to Cadi.

"Dustin, that mitt's too big for you. Pastor Dremond says to use this one."

The deep male voice caused her to make a sharp pivot once she caught the ball. Frank was making his way from the house. He'd shed his suit coat and tie, and now the sleeves of his blue dress shirt were rolled to his elbows. He held a small mitt in one hand.

"That's my old mitt," the oldest Dremond boy said. "You can use it."

Frank made the switch. "Well, as long as I have a mitt, too, I might as well play with you and the kids."

The boys let out a whoop, with Dustin cheering the loudest.

"Sure." Cadi's answer belied the dread she felt inside. But perhaps a simple game of catch would lighten him up and allow Frank to see that she wasn't the villain he assumed.

He stepped in several feet away from Cadi, and Dustin threw the ball to him. Frank caught it easily and tossed it to a Dremond boy. The child, in turn, threw it to Cadi. She hurled it in Frank's direction. Unfortunately, her aim was off and he had to duck before chasing the ball several yards.

Cadi laughed. "Oops. That was an accident. Honest."

He gave her one of his amused scowls.

To his credit, Frank didn't try to retaliate, nor did he pitch the ball over her head so she'd have to run for it in her long, layered skirt and leather flats. But when Dustin missed a catch and scampered to fetch the ball, Frank stepped in closer to Cadi and out of the kids' earshot.

"Know what you are? A pretty little package of trouble, that's what."

"I don't recall asking for your opinion, Officer."

The tart reply caused Frank to grin.

She narrowed her gaze. "Lucky for the both of us, I'm returning to Waterloo and we'll never have to see each other again."

"Unless I have to make an arrest. Waterloo is my department's jurisdiction, too."

Cadi stared at him askance, unsure she understood the connection. "An arrest?"

He nodded. "It's illegal to scam folks off the Internet."

"Of course it is, but I'm not skimming or scamming. And, I must say, you're the biggest bully I've ever met!"

His dark gaze smoldered. "Bully or not, be warned, Cadi Trent. If I find out you're stealing donations off that site you put up on the Internet, I'll make sure the legal ball starts rolling, and I'll gladly see you behind bars."

Cadi was more than taken aback, not so much by the threat, itself, but by the malice dripping off each word. "What did I ever do to make you hate me? I came to Wind Lake to help people after an explosion leveled most of their neighborhood. I was summoned here by the mayor at the request of Adam Dremond. But somehow you decided you could take out all the hatred in your heart on me. Why?"

"Your point is?" His stony expression said her words had little to no affect on him.

Again a wave of incredulity struck her. A second later, she shook her head, realizing how futile it was to plead her innocence to a man who'd already judged her as guilty.

In one smooth motion, she reached out and pulled the glove off his hand. Next, she moved to retrieve the ball from Dustin.

"I have to go home now," she explained to the boy.

Disappointment dropped over his features as he relinquished the ball. Then he looked over at his dad with questions in his golden brown eyes.

"It was nice playing catch with you." She gave a wave to the other kids in forced politeness. She even managed a smile. After all, they hadn't done anything wrong.

She made her way to the van, climbed in the side door, and tossed the sports gear into the cardboard box filled with other odds and ends. Opening the door on the driver's side, she reached in for her cell phone that she'd mistakenly left inside the vehicle. She refused to walk past Frank again and give him another chance to intimidate her. She'd call Meg on her cell phone and let her know it was time to leave. Meg would inform the others, and Cadi felt certain they'd understand.

She leaned against the side of the vehicle and tried to press in Meg's number, but her hands were shaking so badly from her encounter with Frank that she kept misdialing.

"Everything all right?"

Cadi started as Adam Dremond came around the van.

"Um. . .yeah. Everything's fine," she fibbed. Tears of anger and humiliation pooled in her eyes, and Cadi realized how totally astonished she was by Frank's outright meanness. Her emotions were tangled in knots, and it was all because of *him*. He had her feeling weak-kneed and giddy one minute then horrified and scared the next.

"Your friends are gathering their things and will be out shortly."

Cadi sent the pastor a curious glance.

"We saw you and Frank talking. We couldn't hear what was being said, but judging by your expression, followed by your collection of the ball and glove, we figured something's amiss."

"He threatened to arrest me," Cadi blurted.

"He—what?" A deep frown shadowed the pastor's features.

"He thinks I'm a rip-off artist, and he said he'd 'gladly' see me behind bars." She felt her chin quiver. "I've never even gotten a speeding ticket."

Adam shook his head. "It's not you, Cadi. It's Frank. He's fighting demons from his past. I'm not defending him or his actions. I'm just trying to put things in perspective for you. It's nothing personal against you."

"I beg to differ. Threatening to arrest me is very personal."

An expression of regret settled over the reverend's face. "I'm sorry this happened. And, trust me, Frank won't arrest you. I'll talk to him."

"Well, I have a good mind to contact his superiors."

"Will you give me a chance to speak with him first?"

Cadi mulled over the request then nodded. Pastor Dremond had been kind and gracious from the start, and she was content with leaving the situation in his capable hands.

The rest of the Disaster Busters team showed up, and without a single joke or complaint, they climbed into the van.

"Please thank your wife for a delicious lunch," Cadi said as she slid behind the wheel.

"I will." Pastor Dremond waved good-bye. "Thanks for coming."

After starting up the engine, she pulled away from the curb and pressed her foot against the accelerator. She couldn't leave Wind Lake and its despicable sheriff's deputy fast enough.

Chapter 9

"You beat everything, you know that?"

Frank sat back in the sofa and awaited the rest of Adam's scolding, thankful the kids wouldn't be privy to their conversation. Lindsey had taken them to the ice cream parlor in town.

"The least you owe that young woman is an apology."

"I was just doing my job."

"Baloney." Adam ceased his pacing across the carpeting and pulled up a chair. "You were wrong, Frank. Admit it."

"Look, how was I supposed to know that you're the signer on the bank account connected to Cadi's Web site? She could have clarified the situation. Or you could have told me last night when I approached you with my concerns in the church parking lot."

"Had you asked, I would have told you. What I did say was that Cadi isn't up to anything sneaky and underhanded. I knew that—and know that—to be true." Adam looked exasperated as he raked his fingers through his hair. "And if you would have asked Cadi for some specifics, instead of threatening her, I'm sure she would have told you the facts, as well. Your approach was all wrong." He paused and glared at Frank. "You made her cry, you big galoot."

An arrow of regret struck him in the heart.

"The poor girl thinks you're out to get her. She's scared."

He frowned. "Did she say that—that she's scared?"

"She didn't have to!" Adam flung his arms in the air. "It was written all over her face!" He paused. "She's also angry. She threatened to contact your superiors."

"Now that I believe." Frank stood and hardened his inner core. Feminine tears and fears might bend the will of some men, but he happened to think Cadi was a stronger-minded woman than the good pastor made her out to be. Adam's last comment drove that notion home. "Cadi will get over whatever's bothering her, and she can contact whomever she wants. It's her word against mine."

"And yours against mine," Adam reminded him. "My voice will be heard even if you prejudice any higher-ups against Cadi."

Frank knew he had a point since Adam was well-known and respected in the area. His social activism had swayed media personnel and citizens alike.

He turned slowly back around and placed his hands on his hips. He weighed his options.

"Checkmate, my friend." Adam grinned.

Frank raised his hands in surrender. "All right. But don't come whining to me if something goes wrong."

"So you'll apologize to Cadi?"

"I didn't say that."

Adam folded his arms and narrowed his gaze. "You know who you remind me of? My oldest son, Paul. He liked to pull a certain girl's ponytail while they were both at recess. He thought it was fun because he liked her and, at seven years old, he was unsure of how to display such affection." Adam's expression said he was only half amused. "The truth of the matter was, he hurt his classmate each time he pulled her hair."

"You're comparing me to a seven-year-old?" Frank clenched his jaw in irritation. "Thanks a lot."

"You're missing the point. I've watched you all weekend. It seems to me Cadi's gotten under your skin in a way that feels uncomfortable to you. You're lashing out at her, but it's not her fault. You own your emotions."

"Oh, please, spare me the psychoanalysis, okay?"

Adam continued on, undaunted. "Many widowers I counsel tell me they feel guilty for being attracted to other women, even though their wives would have wanted them to remarry and be happy."

Frank moved to leave the living room area and put an end to this whole preposterous subject when Adam, having risen from his chair, sidestepped into Frank's path.

"Consider what I've said, will you? Please?"

"Look, I really don't have time—"

"Make time. Forgiveness—or lack thereof—can steer the soul in the right or wrong direction. The Bible illustrates this truth time and time again."

Frank didn't reply but walked around the pastor and exited the living room. Next he made his way out to the front porch, wishing Lindsey would hurry up and return with the kids so he could collect his two and head for home. He sensed Adam meant well, but Frank didn't care for him or anyone else second-guessing his thoughts and feelings.

Adam strode from the house and stood beside him. "I still think you owe Cadi an apology. You sought her out, Frank. I saw you, and I would have stepped in had I known of your less-than-gentlemanly intentions. I assumed you were getting to know her and quelling your suspicions. Instead, you hurt Cadi, and your abrasiveness was uncalled for."

"Abrasiveness, huh?" He was hardly the steel-wool Brillo-pad guy whom Adam just described. He wasn't a bully, either, as Cadi had accused.

"I have her phone number. Why don't you call her?"

"I know how to find her."

"Okay. I trust you'll contact her, then, and make this right."

Frank glanced at Adam. "I'll think it over, but I'm not making promises."

Adam didn't reply. The subject was dropped. A few minutes went by and small talk ensued.

Sometime later, Lindsey finally pulled the large van into the driveway. The children jumped out, and Frank steered Dustin and Emmie into his SUV.

He drove home, listening to his children prattle on about how much fun they had this afternoon. Dustin mentioned Cadi and said he wished she would have played ball longer. Frank's heart wrenched, and he battled against everything Adam said to him. But it was true: Frank had sought out Cadi for dubious reasons.

So now what do I do? He hated the thought of swallowing his pride and apologizing. There was a chance, after all, he still could be right about Disaster Busters.

Pushing the matter from his mind, he chose to deal with it later.

He pulled into the driveway, and once inside the house, he prompted Dustin and Emily to shower, get their pajamas on, and brush their teeth. He was met by a whiny resistance from his daughter and a few complaints from his son, but by nine o'clock, both kids were in bed for the night.

Frank flipped on the TV and tuned in to a local cable news show. Then he collapsed into the soft, black leather sofa and pulled the Sunday newspaper onto his lap. He had just found the sports section when Dustin padded into the living room.

"Dad?"

"Hmm?" He glanced up from the newspaper. "What is it, son?"

Dustin hedged but then stepped forward. "Dad, how come you were mean to Cadi?"

"What are you talking about?" Frank saw his son flinch at the harsh tone, and he softened it at once. "When was I mean to Cadi?"

"When we were playing ball. I heard you say you'd be happy if she was locked up in jail. You scared her."

"Oh, I was just kidding around," Frank fibbed for his son's sake. "Cadi just got mad at me, that's all."

"But I saw her face. It turned a funny color—like when Emmie was sick—and then she took her stuff and went home."

"Don't worry, son. I didn't scare Cadi. In fact, she had some choice words for me, too. Everything's fine." Frank fought the aggravation rising inside of him. He felt like accusing the Dremonds of somehow brainwashing his kid, but he knew no such thing occurred—unless Lindsay had mentioned the situation when she took the children for ice cream.

"Did Mrs. Dremond say that I scared Cadi?"

The look of surprise, followed by the shake of Dustin's head, told Frank the boy hadn't been influenced.

"Well, look, Cadi's a grown woman. She can handle it." He pulled Dustin in beside him on the couch and kept an arm around his shoulders.

"I like Cadi," the boy said.

"That's nice." Frank felt his jaw tense.

"She's pretty." Dustin twisted around to peer up at Frank. "Do you think she's pretty, Dad?"

"Sure." He hoped his reply sounded uninterested.

"Maybe you should ask her on a date."

He shook his head. "Dustin—"

"Dad," he said emphatically, crawling up on his knees to be face-to-face with Frank, "*she's got her own mitt.*"

"Oh, well, in that case. . ." He sent a glance sky-rocketing and chuckled.

"Da-ad." Dustin's lips curved downward and his golden-brown eyes glimmered with unshed irritation.

"I'm not laughing at you, son," Frank quickly put in. "I'm grateful for your opinion. I'll think about it, all right?"

"Okay." The eight-year-old appeared satisfied for the time being and took off up the steps and back to bed.

Alone in the living room, Frank had his own private laugh. *Typical boy. A pretty lady plays catch with him and right away he thinks I should ask her on a date. What a hoot. Funnier yet is that Cadi would never go out with me. She probably rues the day we met.*

He recalled her question: *"What did I ever do to make you hate me?"*

Remorse stung his very soul. He opened the sports page and tried to shake off the feeling, but it continued. Could he really have been so wrong about her? Was her work genuine, as she maintained? Or was Cadi just the best liar on the planet? Of course, Adam supported her, and he wasn't easily fooled. Or was he?

Frank decided to do some more digging on her and the members of the Disaster Busters. If the info he found—or didn't find—proved he'd been wrong about her, he'd apologize. But only then!

❧

"You can't be serious."

Cadi sent Meg a sideways glance as she drove home. It had been nearly eighty degrees today and she and Meg, along with a host of teenagers from church, had washed cars, vans, and trucks all afternoon. The event was a fund-raiser for the teen mission team and they'd raised quite a bit of cash, but now Cadi felt the effects of her labor. Worse, she'd picked a poor time to inform Meg of her decision to reconcile with Darrell.

"That guy is the rudest and most condescending man I've ever met. What's more, he's conceited."

"He knows his faults. He's working on them. Besides," Cadi said, "I can think of worse rude and condescending men." Frank Parker's swarthy image flitted across her mind.

"You know, Meg, I've come to realize I didn't give things between Darrell and me a chance. Darrell and I talked on the phone several times this week, and I decided to actually work at our relationship now. Maybe my influence will somehow make Darrell a better person. He said I'm like a reality check for him."

Meg didn't seem swayed in the least. "You're making a huge mistake, but it's your life."

Cadi didn't appreciate how Meg dismissed the subject so quickly. On the other hand, they'd had this discussion before and Meg never had cared for Darrell.

"Let me ask you this," Meg blurted. "Does he make your knees weak and your heart sing?"

Again, the image of Frank Parker loomed in Cadi's memory. "That's ridiculous. You can't trust emotions when making important decisions about a relationship. Emotions can be totally deceiving."

"Maybe, but when my knees get weak and my heart sings, I'll know I've met the man of my dreams."

"Well, just to warn you, every warm and fuzzy emotion went off while I was near that deputy last weekend, and he was the meanest person I've encountered in a very long while."

"So you admit your attraction to him, eh?" Meg turned in her seat despite the seat belt across her slim body. "Is that why you're getting back together with Darrell? You're fighting your feelings for Deputy Parker?"

"No and no." Cadi regretted her sudden harsh tone. She softened it at once. "I mean, of course I'm not."

"Look, I'm the first to agree that last weekend was full of unfortunate experiences for you, but I don't think the guy is, as you say, 'mean.' I think there's a lot of misunderstanding going around." Meg paused. "While you were out playing ball with the kids last Sunday, Pastor Dremond told us about that bogus charity organization that came to Wind Lake a few years ago."

"What are you talking about? What bogus charity organization?" Cadi ran a hand through her hair after stopping for a red light.

"You mean you don't know? I assumed Pastor Dremond told you long before he ever mentioned those creeps to us."

"No, this is the first time I'm hearing about it."

"Well, apparently several men said they were in town to help after a bad storm, but they looted damaged property and stole jewelry and other valuables. In short, they were a bunch of thieves."

"Hmm." Things started making sense to Cadi. "No wonder Sergeant Parker distrusted us from the start." She shook her head. "Why weren't we told about this?"

Meg rotated her shoulders in uncertainty. "I thought you knew about it already, and I guess no one else in Wind Lake was suspicious of us except for Frank. While he was outside playing ball with you and the boys, Will told Pastor Dremond about Frank's interrogating you. That's when the pastor told us about the fake charity group." Her tone of voice softened. "He also said Frank's been through a lot these past few years."

Cadi refused to feel sorry for the guy. "I'm sure he has, but that fact doesn't excuse bad behavior."

"I agree, but—"

Cadi didn't want to hear any "buts." She wanted to forget about it—and about Frank Parker.

She glanced at her watch as the light turned green. "I've got to hurry and drop you off and get home so I can shower and change. Darrell is taking me to his older brother's thirtieth birthday party tonight. He's picking me up at six. I'm going to have to hurry."

Cadi watched as her best friend folded her arms across her chest and pressed her lips together in taut disapproval. What's more, Meg didn't utter another word the rest of the way to her apartment.

Chapter 10

Balloons of every color streamed from the ceiling along with a banner that read OVER THE HILL. Cadi thought the black-lettered proclamation was premature for Darrell's older brother; however, she agreed that turning thirty was a benchmark in a person's life, and she couldn't help wondering where she'd be in five years. Would she be married? Have children?

She smoothed down the multicolored challis split skirt she wore beneath a matching top. She chanced a look at Darrell, who stood beside her, polished and suave from the top of his honey-colored hair to the tips of his expensive leather loafers. Again she wondered what her life would be like in the future, and suddenly, she couldn't quite imagine herself married and sipping her morning coffee with him.

He smiled down at her, and Cadi pushed out a grin before glancing around the crowded living room. People were talking and laughing, having a good time. She, too, had enjoyed talking to different folks for most of the night, and she'd sung choruses of "Happy Birthday to You" with them, filling the entire ranch-style home with merriment.

"Having fun?" Darrell moved closer and slipped his arm around her waist. Cadi tensed. Why did his touch feel unwelcome? All evening she'd thought about what Meg said earlier, and she wished her knees would weaken and her heart would "sing" whenever Darrell was near. Instead, Cadi's heart seemed to recoil.

Lord, what's wrong with me?

Cadi immediately sensed her heavenly Father's reply. Had she prayed about getting back together with Darrell? No. So what was she trying to prove? That she wasn't a sap for a certain sheriff's deputy who'd rather see her in jail than on the other side of the table from him in an upscale Italian restaurant?

Practical. Love is practical, she reminded herself.

She turned and regarded Darrell once more, but this time she caught him staring off in the distance. She traced his line of vision across the room to a petite blond in a slinky black dress. The woman's long hair hung to her waist.

Cadi cleared her throat and nudged him with her elbow.

Darrell looked down at her. "You should grow your hair long," he muttered after flashing the other woman a cosmopolitan smile.

A myriad of emotions filled Cadi's heart, the foremost being irritation. "I *should*, huh? You don't like my hair?"

"Oh, listen, I didn't mean anything by it. Let's not argue. We've just gotten through all that other nonsense."

"Nonsense?" Cadi tipped her head expectantly. "What nonsense?"

He gave her a patronizing grin. "All our broken dates because of your business."

"Are you blaming me?" Cadi felt her face begin to flame. "Darrell, for your information—"

"Shh." He kissed the side of her head, and Cadi resisted the urge to slap him away. "We'll talk about it later."

Cadi bristled, and the overwhelming notion that reconciliation with Darrell was an impossibility filled her being. The man of her dreams wouldn't want to make her something she wasn't.

Grow my hair long. Yeah, right, she fumed.

She watched as Darrell stood ogling the blond across the room. The man of her dreams wouldn't have roving eyes, either!

Although she'd vowed to give their relationship a second chance, she never said she'd change her appearance for him simply because he admired a certain feature on another woman. Truth be told, his wandering gaze wasn't exactly a new practice. But when she'd agreed to work at their relationship, Darrell had promised to kiss his playboy ways good-bye forever.

So much for Darrell keeping his end of the bargain.

Meg was right. I should have listened. What was I thinking?

A sense of betrayal gripped her. Disgusted, she shrugged out of Darrell's hold. She felt the need to get away from him, so she strolled over to a group of young women chatting by the porch door.

Keep calm, she told herself. *Darrell and I can discuss this matter in private.*

She recognized Liza Redelli from church and sat down in the maple dining room chair beside her. Out of the corner of her eye, Cadi watched Darrell head for the shapely blond.

In that moment, Cadi knew without a doubt that she and Darrell would never be a couple.

"Hi, Cadi." Liza turned her way. "Good to see you. What's new?"

Cadi swallowed her emotions.

"Hi, Liza." They conversed for a few minutes and, before long, Cadi was overcome by a fierce determination to find another ride home. She'd come with Darrell, but there would be blizzards in Bermuda before she climbed into his sports car tonight and allowed him to behave as if nothing had happened again.

She glanced his way, and as if in affirmation, she spied him and the other woman steeped in what appeared to be an intimate chat. Chances were he'd never know Cadi even left the party.

"Liza, I need a ride home," she blurted. "Can you give me a lift?"

Liza shook her head, and her nut brown hair brushed against her plump shoulders. "I came with three other people in a compact car. There's no room for one more."

"Okay. I understand. Thanks anyway." Cadi weighed her options.

"I'll give you a lift home."

The voice caused Cadi to turn in her chair. There, behind her, stood Ross Hinshaw. A heavyset guy with nondescript brown hair and acne lesions on his chin, it appeared Ross hadn't changed a lot physically since Cadi last saw him. She'd gone to high school with him, and although he wasn't a Christian back then, she remembered him as a nice enough guy.

"I'm actually leaving in a few minutes," he said. "Let me just tell my buddy. He's going to another party after this one."

"Great. Thanks." She gave him a smile, noticing a slight dip in his gait as he walked away. She wondered if he had knee problems or perhaps a bad back.

In either case, Cadi just felt grateful for the ride home.

He returned a few minutes later, and they walked outside to his shiny black pickup.

"Didn't you come here tonight with Darrell Barclay?" Ross asked as he put the transmission into gear.

"Yes, but—well, it was a mistake. That's all I can say about the situation."

"Oh yeah? His loss might be my gain." Ross chuckled.

Cadi gave him a curious glance and noticed his lopsided grin as they drove under the glow of a streetlight. The comment made her nervous, but she brushed it off by telling herself Ross meant it as a backhanded compliment, nothing more.

"You still live in that old Victorian house on Daisy Drive?"

"Yes. With my aunt. You've got a good memory."

"Yeah, well, my folks still live about half a mile from there."

Cadi recalled the general vicinity of the neighborhood in which Ross grew up. "I hope you don't have to drive too far out of your way."

"Naw, it's okay."

"I appreciate the ride home." She chose her words with care so as not to encourage him in any way. "What have you been doing since graduation from high school? Did you go to college?"

"Some."

As Ross started talking, Cadi noticed something odd about the way he pronounced many of his words. He didn't exactly slur them, but Cadi had the impression something wasn't right.

"Are you feeling okay?" she asked as Ross pulled onto the expressway.

"I'm fine." He cracked his window then turned up the vehicle's stereo system.

Heavy metal music filled the truck's cab.

Ross lit a cigarette, and Cadi wondered if she wouldn't have been better off going home with Darrell—even with his wandering eyes and flirty ways.

"What about you? What do you do for a living? I heard you were a nurse or something."

"An EMT. Emergency medical technician." Cadi had to practically shout over the blaring noise. Worse, the vulgar lyrics pulsing from the stereo made her cringe. "Can we turn this down a little?"

"Sure." Ross obliged.

Cadi expelled a breath of relief.

"Where you working?"

She began explaining about her business, Disaster Busters, how it functioned, and her position, but soon she realized that Ross was driving at an increasingly excessive speed. They'd turned off the expressway and were traveling a remote stretch of highway that led into Waterloo.

The truck's tires squealed as the vehicle rounded a curve.

Stay calm. Twenty minutes, tops, and I'll be home, Cadi thought in an attempt to placate herself. Then, several miles later, she saw the familiar bend in the road.

"Hey, Ross, you might want to slow down. I see Suicide Hill up ahead."

"Suicide Hill." He laughed and lit another cigarette. "It's not dangerous. I've driven this road a million times. Relax. I'm in control." He turned and grinned at her.

"But. . .you're going way too fast!"

Just as Cadi finished the last syllable, the truck went onto the shoulder. Dirt and gravel pelted the vehicle's underbody. Ross snapped to attention and yanked on the steering wheel, making a sharp left. His correction sent the truck careening over the centerline. Headlights from an oncoming car flashed through the windshield.

"Ross, watch out!" Cadi screamed.

He fought for control as the truck fishtailed. Again the tires screeched beneath them. Then another jerk on the wheel and the truck sailed down a hill. It sped across a yard before slamming head-on into a wooden stockade fence. The air bag in front of Cadi deployed on impact, ramming into her chest and face, stealing her breath away.

She gasped for air and battled to inhale. Then, before she could utter a prayer, she submerged into total darkness.

🐝

"What do we have here, Marty?" Using his Maglite, Frank surveyed the crash scene from the side of the road.

"Other than the obvious, I'm not sure yet," the other officer replied. "A passerby made the 911 call. Fire truck and ambulance are on the way."

"Victims? Survivors?"

"Like I said, I don't know. I just arrived on the scene myself."

Muted moans of distress in the near distance spurred Frank and his colleague down the hill.

"Careful. There might be downed wires, Marty."

"I'll keep a lookout for 'em."

Following the tire tracks into the undeveloped acreage, they stumbled upon a man lying prostrate on the damp ground, groaning in agony.

Marty bent to assist him.

Frank continued his survey of the area. "Anyone else in the truck?" he asked the injured man.

"Yeah, but I think she's dead. And—and she was driving. It wasn't me. She was driving."

Frank set off toward the mangled pickup. He mentally braced himself for the sight he might find. He'd seen it before, and it wasn't pretty. Never was.

A patch of brightly colored fabric caught his eye, and several strides later, he found a woman heaped on the ground near the rear of the truck. Her position, closer to the passenger side than the driver's, raised questions in his mind about who had really been at the wheel when the truck crashed.

Arias of sirens from oncoming emergency vehicles sang in the distance. Meanwhile, Frank hunkered down beside the female and found a pulse.

Good news.

He searched her swollen, bloodied face and red-stained blond hair. A slow recognition seeped its way into his thoughts, but he figured he had to be imagining things.

He checked the woman for obvious fractures and found none, but her height and body shape matched that of a certain Disaster Buster he'd recently met—and couldn't seem to forget.

Again, he shone his light into her face. By the looks of it, her nose was broken.

"Cadi?" He set his hand on her shoulder to prevent her from moving in case of a head, neck, or spinal cord injury. "Cadi, is that you? Can you hear me?"

Her eyes fluttered open, and he glimpsed their blue depths. He knew without a doubt it was her.

"Oh, it's you."

Her less-than-enthusiastic reaction was like a knife in his heart.

She stirred.

"Be still. The paramedics will be here in a few minutes."

"I need to sit up. I—I can't breathe."

Frank tried to stop her from moving, but she was in obvious distress. At last he propped her up the safest way he knew how and hoped her injuries weren't worse than they appeared.

"That's better," she panted. "I felt like I was suffocating."

"Stay still, Cadi. You might have internal injuries or broken bones."

"I managed to crawl out of the truck by myself and make my way this far."

Frank felt both impressed and amused. "Do me a favor and stay still, okay?"

"Or what? You'll arrest me?" She tried to stand.

"Cadi, you're hurt. Let's call a truce so I can help you."

She replied with a half groan and half cry.

"Let me help you."

She didn't protest further, and Frank tried to make her comfortable. The seconds passing seemed like hours. He couldn't imagine what was taking the paramedics so long to arrive.

Cadi began to struggle again.

"Take it easy."

"Is the truck going to blow up?"

"I doubt it." Frank shined his flashlight on the mangled vehicle. He detected no signs of danger.

"I heard Ross say—say the truck was going to blow up. I was so freaked out."

Incensed, Frank silently summed up the situation. *So the guy took off running and left Cadi inside—what a jerk.*

"Is he okay? Ross? Is he hurt?"

His anger toward the man pulled Frank's nerves taut. "Don't fret over him. He's not worth the energy, Cadi. Trust me."

"I fret about everybody. I've made helping others my—my whole life."

"Relax, Cadi. You don't owe me any explanations."

She quieted.

"That's better."

"Why aren't you telling me about—about Ross? Was he killed? I want the truth."

"He's alive." Frank directed his flashlight off into the distance. He saw that Marty had helped the guy to his feet. They were slowly making their way up the hill. "In fact, my guess is your boyfriend will make a full recovery."

Frank wanted to add that the guy had left her for dead—that he'd lied about which one of them was driving when the crash occurred. But he refused to upset Cadi further. He was outraged, however, that she cared about someone so obviously self-absorbed. Was this her boyfriend? The one she broke up with? Or was this someone new? Either way, it was obvious to Frank that she sure knew how to pick the losers.

Then, suddenly, his rationale did a 180-degree turn. He felt like King David when the prophet Nathan proclaimed, "You are the man."

Contrition enveloped him. If any mutual attraction had existed last weekend, it made Frank little better than any other "loser" in Cadi's life. What's more, his brutish behavior clinched the title for him.

Loser.

The paramedic squad and fire truck finally arrived, and the red and blue lights illuminated the starlit night.

"Cadi, everything's going to be all right. I promise you."

She caught his wrist and murmured something, but with all the approaching noise, Frank couldn't make it out.

"Say it again; I didn't hear you." He knelt closer.

"Ross is not my—my boyfriend," she said with a labored breath.

"Glad to hear it." *In more ways than one,* Frank added to himself.

"Will you help me stand?" She began to struggle.

"Good grief, Cadi. Don't move any more. You might be doing more damage to yourself."

"But I can't breathe."

"Relax." He shrugged out of his lightweight jacket and carefully placed it behind her head and over his knee, propping her even higher. "Is that better?"

"A little."

He brushed the stained and matted hair off her face. "Just relax," he repeated.

In the distance, the emergency personnel gathered their gear and headed toward them.

"Frank?" Cadi's weakening voice reached his ears. The way she said his name did something crazy to his insides.

"What is it?" In that moment, he thought he'd do just about anything to help her.

"I—I hate to tell you this, but—"

"Tell me what?"

"I—I. . ."

Frank wondered if a confession of some sort was on the way. "What is it, Cadi?"

"I—I think I'm going to be sick!"

Chapter 11

The hospital room's stark ceiling blurred before it came into focus again. Cadi blinked and fought the effects of the pain medication she'd been given. Over the course of the last several hours, she'd had every x-ray imaginable, and the worst of her injuries seemed to be a broken nose and a fractured rib as well as multiple bumps and bruises.

She touched the swollen and throbbing center of her face. The specialist on call had finished packing and setting her broken nose; then he'd spoken about the possibility of plastic surgery.

The entire situation seemed so surreal. Had Frank really been the responding officer, or had she dreamed up their verbal exchange? She had almost convinced herself that the latter was true. After all, Frank Parker thought she was a swindler and said he'd gladly see her behind bars. But it was a totally different man—a sort of hero—who had knelt over her and tried to help her tonight.

Cadi's eyelids grew heavy and fluttered shut. She allowed the fantasy of her knight in shining armor to play out in her head. She knew the morphine had a lot to do with her delusional state, but she was too exhausted to fight it.

Minutes later, she heard the glass exam room doors slide open then close again. She sensed a presence and opened her eyes. The dream vanished, and she watched in chagrined awe as the very object of her thoughts neared her hospital bed. She blinked, wondering if she'd somehow conjured him up.

"Hi."

"Hi."

"Mind if I ask you a few questions?"

"Sure, I—I guess not." She struggled to sit up but found it hurt too much. She then maneuvered the head of the bed to more of an upright position. Frank quickened his strides and assisted her.

"I would have come in to talk to you sooner," he said, "but I, um, had to shower and change my uniform."

"Oh?" Cadi didn't understand his meaning at first and decided that in his spotless beige shirt and green trousers, he looked like a real-life version of the fabled rugged, tall-dark-and-handsome hero.

And that's when she realized the unfortunate reason for his just-pressed appearance.

She closed her eyes and winced. "Oh, I'm so sorry—"

"You couldn't help it."

She peeked at him and found him leaning his muscular forearms on the side rail. His presence seemed too close for comfort.

He smiled and shook his head. "Girl, you look like you were in a boxing match and lost."

"Thanks a lot." Cadi almost laughed, but the pain shooting through her body stopped her cold. "No jokes." She wrapped her arms around her midsection.

"Fair enough."

Cadi marveled at how disarming Frank was when he smiled. But soon the amusement disappeared from his face.

He glanced at his clasped hands, and she thought his fingers looked strong and capable. "Cadi," he said gravely, "I have my assumptions, but I need to hear it from you. Were you driving that pickup tonight?"

He looked back up at her, and his dark gaze bore right into her.

"No, I wasn't driving." She wished she didn't feel so vulnerable. She hiked up the white sheet covering her gown-clad body and tucked it under her arms. "Ross was driving."

"He swears up and down that it was you."

Cadi swallowed hard and willed away the tears of indignation forming behind her eyes. "Well, you already think I steal and cheat disaster victims, so I'm sure you think I'm a liar now, too."

"Slow down." He placed his hand over her forearm. "I'm not thinking the worst of you, all right?"

When he paused, Cadi glanced his way.

"The fact is, I thought about calling you and apologizing for my boorish actions last weekend, but I sort of lost my nerve."

Cadi arched one bruised brow. "You? Lost your nerve?"

She watched him wrestle with a grin. "Believe it or not, us macho guys have fragile egos."

Cadi laughed and groaned in agony at the same time. "Frank, that was *so* not nice!"

"I wasn't trying to be funny." He smiled in spite of himself.

She caught her breath then gave him a withering glance.

"Seriously," he said, his tone resonating with sincerity, "I'm sorry I acted like—to use Adam's words—'a big galoot.'"

So Pastor Dremond spoke to him just as he promised.

"I hope you can forgive me."

"I can—and I do." It certainly wasn't difficult while he was being so charming.

"Good."

She stared at him, trying to figure out this man. She recalled Pastor Dremond saying Frank wrestled with something from his past. Was it more than his wife's death?

"I'd rather have you as a friend than a foe," she murmured.

"Ditto."

The light in his eyes made her heart melt.

"But, for now, let's get back to business. For the record, I'm going to ask you again: Were you driving?"

"No."

"Were you drinking tonight?"

Cadi gasped then winced at the lightning bolting through her ribcage. "I don't drink," she managed through gritted teeth.

"Did you know Ross was intoxicated when you got into the truck with him tonight?"

Cadi gaped at the question. "He was intoxicated?"

"I'll take that as a no." Frank straightened. "How do you know this guy?"

"I don't really know him. I mean, I know who he is because we went to high school together. I was at a birthday party and needed a ride home. Ross offered, and I accepted."

"Cadi, he was drunk." Frank leaned in again.

"I had no clue. There was no alcohol served at the party. The Barclays are Christians who don't believe in celebrating with liquor, so it never occurred to me that Ross—"

"Okay, I get the picture." Frank stood to his full height. "How'd you get to the party?"

She hedged, not wanting Frank to know the many wrong choices she'd made in the past seven days. But then again, if her answer was too vague, he might find grounds to mistrust her again.

She decided to shoot straight from the hip. "Darrell picked me up."

"Darrell. . ."

She could see his mental gears turning.

"Is that the guy you broke up with?"

"Yes." She gazed up at the ceiling tiles again and chastised herself for not heeding Meg's warnings about Darrell. "I thought we could reconcile, but things will never work between us. If that fact wasn't obvious to me before, it certainly was tonight."

"Hmm, and how did you come to that conclusion?"

"His roving eyes."

"Ah. That'll do it."

"And when Darrell became engrossed in the company of another woman— whose long blond hair is not that impressive, if you ask me—I decided to find my own way home." She looked at Frank. "You know the rest of the story."

She watched her explanation play across his shadowy features. He seemed to ponder the logic, or lack thereof. "Are you finally through with this guy now, or what?"

She couldn't help a grin. "Is this on or off the record?"

Frank had the good grace to look embarrassed for asking. "Off."

"We're really through."

"Good." Frank gave her a nod of approval.

"Good?" Cadi felt a tad bewildered by his emphatic reply.

"Well, look. . ." He cleared his throat. "I'll give Marty, the officer in charge, all the information. It's customary for us to do an investigation, particularly since Ross was intoxicated when he got behind the wheel. But I think you should know that I'm requesting to be taken off this case after tonight."

"Why?" She stared into his face, almost losing herself in the depths of his velvety brown eyes. "Am I in trouble?"

He stared back at her. "No, but. . ." He paused. "I think maybe I am."

"Oh?" She hadn't filed any complaints.

She watched in puzzlement as a grin spread across his face.

"I feel like I'm too close to this case, personally, to be objective."

The explanation made sense.

"I need to get going." After a parting smile, he strode toward the door then stopped. "Oh, and your aunt is anxious to see you. I apologize for keeping her waiting, but I needed to speak with you first. All the evidence backs up your story and. . . Cadi?"

"Yes?"

"Just to warn you, Ross Hinshaw is going to jail. His recklessness could have killed him, you, and countless others on the road tonight."

"You're right." The realization that so many lives could have been lost gave Cadi a jolt, and in that moment, she gleaned a sliver of insight into Frank's world. Obviously he often dealt with the worst side of humanity. Little wonder that he'd developed such a granitelike demeanor.

Except she'd glimpsed his softer side, too—like when his children were around and in the way he'd tried to help her tonight.

"Thanks, Frank. Thanks for everything."

He replied with a smile and an amiable wink then left the room.

❧

Except for sending her flowers and talking to her on the phone a couple of times, Frank refrained from contacting Cadi. Instead, he allowed the first few weeks of June to pass before entertaining thoughts of a bona fide courtship. He figured she needed time to get over her failed romance and recover from her injuries before he approached her and asked her out.

Still, he kept himself abreast of the goings-on in her life by logging on to the Disaster Busters Web site almost daily. He read Cadi's blog, and it gave him a clearer view of her character. In a word, she impressed him. He read her account of the car crash and her recent campaign against drunk drivers. He silently applauded her for taking action, and each time he saw Cadi's photograph on the site—and her blue eyes and smiling face—the notion of dating her made his mouth go dry.

Did he have time to cultivate a relationship? Could he make time? What would the kids think? What would his parents and in-laws think? Would they approve of Cadi? He hated the thought of what might happen if they didn't. Losing Yolanda had been devastating enough, and Frank didn't think that he or any of his family members had the energy for more drama.

So, did he dare set off on this romantic pursuit? He had a hunch Cadi wouldn't be opposed to it. But what if things wouldn't work out? She was a career woman and a crusader. He was a workaholic with two kids.

Maybe he shouldn't bother.

Frank expelled an audible sigh. He stood from the kitchen table where he'd been sitting, contemplating. He stretched and glanced out the patio doors and into the backyard where Dustin and Emmie played with their friends. Convinced all was well outside, he moseyed over to the sink and washed the supper dishes while rehashing the situation over in his mind.

Before long, his children's friends had gone home, the kitchen was clean, and dusk had settled. Frank called the kids into the house, and once they were washed up and in their pajamas, they settled on the couch to watch their favorite TV shows. Frank sat between them, one arm around each child. He relished quality time like this, so when a nature program came on one of the cable channels, he allowed the two to stay up late and enjoy it.

Then it was time for the local news.

"Okay, time for bed." Frank stood and stretched.

The kids moaned in unison.

"No arguments." He was just about to recite his infamous obedience lecture when Dustin's exclamation filled the room.

"Dad, look!" He pointed to the television. "It's her!"

Frank followed his son's gaze then stared in disbelief. There on his twenty-seven-inch color screen was the woman who'd occupied his thoughts for the better part of a month.

"Dad, it's Cadi."

"So I see." He was amazed Dustin remembered her name. "Quiet down so I can hear what's going on."

But it was too late. The interview with her had ended.

"And there you have it," the female reporter said. "Flooding and a tornado have devastated much of Cass County. But as you just heard, it's volunteers like these from Disaster Busters who can really make a difference in victims' lives, helping them literally find shelter in the time of storm."

"Dad, a tornado!"

"I heard, son, but the twister touched down days ago." Frank had been well aware of the flooding in that part of the state, too. "No more bad storms are in the forecast. I suspect Cadi's just helping with the cleanup."

"I hope she doesn't get hurt."

Frank glimpsed his son's fretful expression. He smiled. "She looks none the worse for wear to me—and that's after her car accident."

"Cadi was in a car accident?" A worried little frown creased Emmie's forehead.

"Yes, but she's all right. You just saw it for yourself." He clapped his hands together. "Okay. Enough TV. It's bedtime."

Frank headed for the stairs, leading the kids up toward their bedrooms. Emmie slipped in beside him and took his hand.

"Daddy, I'm scared."

He looked at his daughter. "Of what?"

"Of bad things like on TV."

"You're perfectly safe." He wanted to promise to protect her always, but hadn't he made that same vow to Yolanda and failed to keep it?

"Just trust in the Lord," Dustin spouted.

The reply seemed almost effortless and served as a rebuke to Frank.

" 'Trust in the Lord with all your heart and lean not on your own understanding,' Proverbs 3:5," Dustin recited proudly.

"That's Bible truth," Frank said. "Do you feel better now, Emmie?"

She bobbed her head. "Daddy, do you still like Cadi?"

"Sure." He hoped he sounded nonchalant. "But how do you know I even liked her in the first place?"

"I don't know," came the impish, singsong reply.

"It's 'cuz you get a funny look on your face sometimes," Dustin amended. "And once you left the computer on and I saw her picture."

Frank winced. He usually took precautions to safeguard his kids from the Internet. "I'll be more careful in the future."

They reached the top of the steps.

"Is she still mad at you like that day after church?"

"No, son, that's all taken care of now."

"Are you friends?"

"I suppose so."

"How come you don't ask Cadi on a date?"

"Maybe I will, Dustin. What do you think about that?" Frank chuckled at his son's surprised expression. But in the next moment, he saw this as an opportune time to find out his kids' opinions on the subject of his possibly dating Cadi. "Maybe I'll ask her out to dinner or something."

"Goodie. Can we come, too?" Emmie asked. "I've never been on a date before."

"And you won't be for another twenty years if I have my way." Frank laughed and swung the pixie into his arms.

She squealed with delight.

"Hey, Dad, how 'bout if we ask Cadi to our church's Fourth of July picnic?"

"We?"

"Yeah. She can be on our softball team."

"Aha, the true motive comes to light." Frank chuckled and deposited his daughter on her bed. "We'll see, okay?"

After tucking Emmie under her covers and giving her a kiss good night, Frank walked Dustin into his room.

"Think you'd kiss Cadi good night, Dad? She's pretty."

Frank put his hands on his hips and watched his son crawl in between the bedsheets. "How old are you?"

"Eight." Dustin rolled his eyes. "You know how old I am."

"Right. And I know you're too young to think about kissing girls, so keep your mind on sports, got it?"

"Got it." Dustin grinned.

Frank placed a kiss on his forehead and turned out the light. He rubbed his whiskered jaw as he made his way back downstairs. It encouraged him to hear his kids weren't averse to his asking Cadi out.

Perhaps it was time to take his relationship with her one step forward.

Chapter 12

Cadi stared at the note Aunt Lou had left: "*Call Deputy Parker at your earliest convenience. No hurry.*"

Aunt Lou had also penned his phone number along with the date and time the message had been taken.

"Frank called?" Anticipation plumed inside of her.

"Yes, he did." Aunt Lou peeked around Cadi's shoulder. "It didn't sound like business."

"Cool." She pocketed the message. "I'll call him back."

"Call him now if you'd like. I have wash to do."

"I'll call him later, after I unpack."

A wry little smile played across Aunt Lou's face. "Officer Parker said he saw you on television."

"He did?" Cadi hoped that wasn't the only reason for his call. She'd been praying about getting to know Frank better, but she wanted the Lord to do the work in his heart. She figured she'd know that was happening if Frank initiated the relationship. The last thing Cadi wanted was to force something that wasn't God's will—as she had with Darrell.

"I must say, I'm very proud of you and your organization."

Cadi hugged her aunt. "Thanks for your prayers and encouragement. What would I ever do without you and your prayer chain?"

Releasing Aunt Lou, she lifted her duffel bag and lugged it upstairs where she began to unpack.

Aunt Lou followed her into her bedroom.

"I heard on the news that no one was killed or injured by the tornado," the older woman said, smoothing the skirt of her printed housedress. "That's good news."

"Actually, there was one injury, but the guy is going to be all right. He broke his arm getting his dog out of the house when the flooding began." Cadi managed a smile for her aunt, but the truth was floodwaters frightened her to the point of sheer panic.

"I trust the dog is all right, too."

Cadi nodded.

"Well, thank heaven for that." She collected Cadi's dirty clothes.

"Oh, Aunt Lou, don't pick up after me. I can throw my own clothes into the washing machine."

"You hush. I'm glad to do it." Aunt Lou headed for the doorway. "What would you like for supper tonight?"

"Anything's fine."

"Then it's cold chicken and potato salad."

"Yum." Cadi's stomach rumbled with anticipation, and she realized she hadn't eaten much all day.

"Oh, and..." Her aunt paused, and a huge smile spread across her face. "The car is going to be delivered tomorrow morning. I'm so excited."

"Hooray!" Cadi raised her hands and cheered. "You deserve it, Aunt Lou."

"Well, I don't know about that." An apple-red hue filled her cheeks. "But I'm very grateful for your generosity."

Cadi didn't feel she was particularly giving. Her aunt had, after all, taken her in as a child and brought her up to the best of her abilities. She'd nurtured Cadi's walk with the Lord and sacrificed through the years, showing true Christlike love. Now Aunt Lou's old clunker could barely chug its way to the grocery store and back. Cadi figured buying her a new car with the settlement she'd been awarded by Ross's car insurance company was only due reward.

"I never had a new car before. Never." Aunt Lou shifted the clothes in her arms. "And, of course, you can borrow it any time."

Cadi chuckled. "Thanks, but so far God has kept my van running, and now that it's paid off, thanks to the insurance money, I have one less financial burden."

Aunt Lou clucked her tongue and wagged her head. "Imagine Ross Hinshaw hiring an attorney because he thought you'd sue him. You're not that kind of a person—even though there was pain and suffering on your part and the accident was due to Ross's negligence."

"Yes, I suppose it is fair that I received some recompense." Ross's attorney had contacted her with the offer, hoping to stem future claims and possible losses, and a lawyer at church who specializes in family law helped seal the deal. "I'm just glad my medical bills were paid for."

"And then some! But Lonnie Mae said you could have gotten a lot more had you pressed the issue."

"Aunt Lou, we've discussed this before, and—"

"I know. I know. You're too good-hearted." Her aunt grinned affectionately. "To think you'd spend your money on an old goat like me. Lonnie Mae and the entire prayer chain couldn't believe it. A new car! For me!"

Cadi arched a brow. "I thought you were supposed to be praying on that prayer chain."

"We do pray, you sassy thing. But every so often we have to update each other on all the miracles that God has done."

Cadi replied with a grin. She didn't have anything against the prayer chain, but she certainly enjoyed teasing her great-aunt.

"Well, I'm off to the laundry room," Aunt Lou announced. "Come down to the kitchen when you're ready to eat. Everything is already prepared."

When her aunt left for the lower level, Cadi extracted Frank's message from her pocket then dug through her purse until she found her cell phone. She said a quick prayer for wisdom and calm for her sudden nerves then pressed his number into her keypad. She half expected to get a recorded message.

"Yep, Frank Parker here."

"Frank? It's Cadi. I'm returning your call."

"Well, hi—hang on a second."

She heard muffled voices before he returned.

"I sent my kids outside to play."

"You're home? I thought maybe I called your office."

"Cell phone."

"Ah." She sat down on the edge of her bed and folded one leg beneath her. "How've you been?"

"Good. What about you? How are you feeling?"

"Just great, actually."

"Glad to hear it. You were pretty banged up."

"I'll say."

That night was still pretty much a blur for Cadi; however, she and Frank had discussed it a couple of days later when she called to thank him for the beautiful bouquet of sunflowers, mums, daisies, and phlox. Two huge balloons and a box of chocolates had accompanied the arrangement. Aunt Lou took one look at the gifts and remarked that Frank certainly knew how to get a woman's attention.

"Cadi, do you have plans on Saturday night?"

The question shook her. "Saturday?"

"If you're available, I'd like to take you to dinner."

She couldn't contain her smile. "Why, Officer Parker, are you asking me on a date?"

"Oh, man. . .you're going to make me squirm, aren't you?"

Cadi laughed.

"Are you free or not?"

She decided he was rather fun to tease, but she chose not to push it. A date with Frank was what she'd been hoping and praying for!

"Dinner sounds nice. Thanks for the invite."

"I'll pick you up about six."

"I'll be ready."

When their call ended, Cadi stared at her cell phone, replaying their conversation in her mind. She couldn't wait to call Meg and tell her.

Then she flopped back on her bed and smiled. *And just wait until Aunt Lou and her prayer chain hear about this!*

Chapter 13

Cadi heard car doors slam and rushed to peek out her bedroom window. She glimpsed Frank emerging from his SUV followed by his two children.

He brought his kids? Frank never mentioned bringing his kids!

Cadi wondered if maybe he planned to drop them off at a babysitter's house. In the next moment, she noticed Frank's casual attire and knew at once that she'd overdressed for the occasion.

She hastened into the hallway and called downstairs to her aunt. "I'll be down in a minute!" Then she flung off the black dress and kicked off the heels. She grabbed a flattering khaki skirt out of the closet and pulled a teal sleeveless shirt over her head. Next she slipped her feet into brown sandals and grabbed her trim leather purse.

Finally she began to make her way down the steps, trying not to sound winded as her guests came into view.

Frank's daughter met her at the foot of the wide stairwell. "We came to take you on a date."

Cadi veiled her disappointment. She had envisioned a quiet, romantic evening alone with Frank.

"I never been on a date before," the girl added.

As she stared into the upturned, cherubic face, Cadi's regret vanished. The girl was baby-doll adorable. How could she resist?

Very simply, she couldn't.

"And I brung you these." Enthusiasm shone from her golden-brown eyes as she held out a bouquet of colorful but wilting flowers. "I picked 'em in my gramma's garden. My daddy said it was okay."

"How sweet. Thank you."

Making her way down the rest of the steps, Cadi accepted the flowers and gave the little tyke a hug. Aunt Lou was ready with a small vase and quickly placed the blooms in water.

"Thank you for asking me on your. . .date."

Cadi glanced at Frank and noticed his obvious chagrin.

"You remember my daughter, Emily, don't you?"

"Of course."

"And my son, Dustin."

Cadi smiled at the boy. "Hi, Dustin."

"I've never been on a date, either," he said, appearing embarrassed. "We're taking you out for pizza and then renting some movies. We can watch them together at our house."

"Sounds like—like a fun time." Cadi forced the upbeat inflection into her voice, unsure if the evening would be as eventful as she imagined.

She glanced at her aunt. "You've all met my aunt, Lou."

Everyone nodded, and her aunt sent her a curious look before seeing them to the door and walking them outside.

The humidity hung in the air like a thick drape, and Cadi felt beads of perspiration forming on her brow. As they ambled down the cement walkway, graced by multicolored petunias on either side, Frank nodded to the slate, four-door sedan parked in the driveway. The sticker was still on the rear window.

"New car?"

"Yes. Cadi purchased it for me," Aunt Lou replied. "Isn't she a beauty?" The excitement in her voice was unmistakable. "And she drives like a dream."

Cadi couldn't help smiling at the gleaming sedan. She felt pleased that she'd been able to purchase the car for her aunt. "She deserves it after all she's done for me."

"Nonsense." Aunt Lou bent over and plucked a weed from the flower bed. "You all have a good time now."

"We will," Dustin replied.

He and Emily raced to the curb.

Reaching his SUV, Frank opened the door for Cadi then helped his children into the backseat and saw to it that they were buckled in.

"Why are cars always referred to as 'she'?" Cadi asked when Frank climbed behind the wheel. She fastened her seat belt and then gave her aunt one last wave.

"Motor vehicles, like women, are unpredictable," he retorted, "especially in bad weather."

Cadi glanced over her shoulder at Emily. "Did you hear what your dad said? He said we women are 'unpredictable.'"

A little frown creased Emily's brow. "What does that mean?"

Frank chuckled and started the engine.

"It means wishy-washy, like you never know what they're going to do next," Cadi said and aimed a look at Frank. "But I can think of a few men who are unpredictable, too."

"Me, too," Emily said with a weary-sounding sigh. "My grampa is unaddict-able. First he wants to play checkers with Dustin, but he really promised to take me to the park."

"The voice of experience," Frank muttered with a grin. "All four, almost five, years of her life."

Cadi laughed and decided that at least this evening would be entertaining.

❦

Sitting in the armchair with his feet up on the ottoman, Frank couldn't shake the embarrassment numbing his body. He'd never seen his children behave in such an obnoxious manner, the little show-offs.

At the pizzeria, they shouted over each other, trying to impress Cadi with their many talents and attributes. Then they argued over movies at the rental store, attempting to drag Cadi into the middle of it. Once they'd arrived home, the two fought over who got to sit next to Cadi on the couch, and Dustin actually plopped his pillow in her lap and lay his head down, stretching out on the rest of the piece of furniture. This sent Emmie into a hissy fit until Cadi assured them both that she had plenty of lap for both kids.

So now there they were, Dustin reclined and Emmie curled up on Cadi while Frank sat in the adjacent leather chair. He'd be lucky if she ever spoke to him again.

"Oh, wasn't that a touching story?" Cadi said when Emmie's movie ended. "The princess shared her riches with her kingdom."

Emmie regarded her with wide eyes, looked back at the TV, and then at Cadi once more.

"It's a blessing to share the things God gives us, isn't it?" Cadi remarked.

Frank watched his daughter nod, and he had to admit feeling somewhat impressed that Cadi found a way to emphasize a moral in the story that hadn't been an obvious theme. In fact, Frank had seen this flick about five times, and he hadn't picked up on the giving aspect.

"Now we watch my movie," Dustin said, getting up and changing the DVD.

Emmie inched her pillow forward, and Frank could see fireworks coming.

"Emily Marie—"

Before Frank could say more, Dustin returned to the sofa. "Hey, move over!" He shoved his pillow into Emmie's.

"That'll be enough." Frank stood and clenched his jaw. His beautiful children had morphed into unrecognizable little brats. "Any more bad behavior and you'll go to bed without a second movie."

Dustin clamped his mouth shut, and Emmie didn't make a peep.

Well, maybe it's good that Cadi finds out right away what my life is like with two kids, Frank thought. *Now she won't have lofty expectations.*

He looked back at her and his children. They vied for her attention and, sitting together, they made a cozy sight that sent an odd sense of longing zinging through him. Still, he hoped Cadi didn't feel too imposed upon.

Standing to his feet, Frank realized he needed to be more of a host. He caught Cadi's eye and smiled. "Can I get you a soda or something?"

"No, thanks."

"I'll take a soda," Dustin said. "How 'bout some popcorn?"

"Yeah. . ." Emmie perked up.

"No soda or popcorn for you two." Frank lowered himself back into his chair. "It's too close to bedtime. Besides, I was asking our *guest*."

The kids groaned in disappointment, and Frank shook his head at them.

They continued to watch the movie. Before long, Emmie fell asleep, and Frank took her upstairs to bed. When he returned, he took a seat on the couch on the other side of Cadi. He listened as Dustin talked her ear off about how he could ride his bike faster than the neighbor kid. Frank thought it was gracious of Cadi to act so impressed.

Stretching his arm across the back of the sofa, his gaze met hers, and he offered an apologetic look. Then he glanced at his son once again. "If you're not interested in this movie—that you picked out, I might add—we can turn it off and you can go to bed."

"Okay, okay." The boy took the hint, although his silence didn't last long. "Hey, Cadi, know what you smell like?"

"Dustin!" Frank could only imagine the forthcoming comparison, not that his son would intentionally insult Cadi.

She pulled her chin back. "I hope I don't smell bad."

"Uh-uh." Dustin grinned. "You smell real good. Like cake."

"Thanks." She smiled.

Relief poured over Frank, and he had to admit his son was right. He had been reveling in the sweet scent Cadi wore from the moment he sat beside her.

"Actually, you do smell good," he conceded, deciding to make light of Dustin's remark.

"I thought you'd never notice," she quipped.

"Haven't had the opportunity."

Their gazes met again, and they shared a laugh.

Suddenly Frank's mood lifted. The entire room seemed brighter.

❧

Cadi watched Frank trail his son up the steps. When his bedtime came, Dustin had protested, but his dad overruled, and now the boy all but stomped his way to the second floor.

She couldn't help smiling. Typical kid. She knew that from babysitting throughout her high school years and doing her share of nursery duty at church. Folks always said she had a special, God-gifted way with children; they took to her immediately, and judging from the way Dustin and Emily behaved tonight, she hadn't lost her touch.

Still wearing a grin, she stood and stretched as she glanced around the living room. Not for the first time, she became aware of the sparse décor in Frank's home. Even with a few odds and ends here and there, and several framed pictures on the oak entertainment center, the home had an impersonal feel to it. Cadi was hardly an expert on interior design; however, Aunt Lou tinkered and toyed with her decorating all the time and almost every corner of the old home had been filled with unique charm and loving touches.

Cadi's gaze lingered on the framed photos. Stepping forward, she paused to inspect the family shot. She picked it up and studied it. What impressed her most was Frank's demeanor. Gone were the hard angles and planes in his face. His features were softer in the picture. Beside him, a slim, auburn-haired beauty cradled a baby in her arms, and Cadi guessed the infant was Emily. Dustin looked no more than four or five, and he stood on the other side of his mother's wicker chair.

Cadi's gaze kept returning to Frank's smiling face. His dark eyes held sparks of happiness in their depths. In short, he looked altogether like a different man.

Hearing him clear his throat, she lifted her gaze.

Frank stepped toward her. "Thanks for being a good sport tonight. When my kids learned that I'd asked you out, they both begged and pleaded to come along. I gave in against my better judgment, and I'll admit it probably wasn't the smartest thing to take two rambunctious children with me on a first date." He shrugged his broad shoulders. "Then I figured you might as well see me—us—just as we are."

"I'll admit to feeling confused at first and maybe even a bit disappointed." Cadi smiled and shook her head. "But I think everything turned out fine. I love kids, and you should be proud of yours. Emmie's a sweet girl and Dustin is a nice, very thoughtful boy."

"I don't know how 'sweet' and 'nice' they were tonight." Frank moved closer and peered at the picture that Cadi still held in her hand.

"I hope you don't mind my looking at your photographs."

Frank wagged his head. "I don't mind."

"Is this your wife?"

"Was," he both corrected and confirmed. "She's been dead for over three years."

"I'm sorry to hear that." Cadi regarded the photo again. "She's beautiful. What was her name?"

"Yolanda." A rueful smile played across his lips. "She was the model domestic engineer. We owned a house outside of town, had a few acres of land, and Landi always had some project going on, whether she was planting flowers or wallpapering a bedroom. And she sure knew how to cook."

"I'm quite the opposite." Cadi set the picture back into place. "Maybe *hopeless* is the word to describe my domestic abilities. I've tried to cook and failed. My aunt attempted to instruct me, I've watched culinary shows on TV, and still it seems that every time I even go near the stove the smoke alarm goes off."

Frank's smile grew. "Well, if it's any consolation, the way to this man's heart isn't necessarily through his stomach." He chuckled. "Can I get you something to drink? Cola? A diet drink?"

"Um, sure."

Cadi was still trying to figure out what the way-to-this-man's-heart comment meant. But then she recalled their conversation at the zoo. His well-intentioned friends had set him up with women who cooked and baked.

Amused, she followed him into the kitchen. The decor was functional but unimaginative, like the living room.

"What'll it be?" Frank extracted a clear plastic bottle. "How 'bout a raspberry-flavored carbonated water?"

"Good enough." She took the proffered drink then eyed Frank. For some odd reason she couldn't imagine him taking a swig of this particular beverage.

He selected a diet cola for himself. Then, as if divining her thoughts, he said, "My kids' grandparents live next door, and when Lois, Yolanda's mother, found out that we were having a guest over, she straightened up and stocked the fridge."

"Nice gesture on her part."

"I'll say. I'm grateful to her." A sheepish grin accompanied Frank's reply. "I didn't think about cleaning the house."

Smiling, they reentered the living room.

"I suppose you're going to tell me that it's evident I need a wife."

Cadi took a seat on the couch, and Frank lowered his sizable frame beside her.

"Well, if cleaning and shopping is why you need a wife," she said, "I'm no candidate for the position." She saw no point in pretense. "And I already told you that I can't cook."

She sipped her carbonated water and watched Frank chuckle. Relaxing, he sat back, crossed his legs, and stretched his arm around Cadi's shoulders. She liked feeling his warmth and his strength, and she couldn't help but snuggle into him just a little.

"I must admit I find you both delightful and refreshing, not to mention pretty—and, as Dustin said, you smell good, too."

"Thanks." Cadi felt a blush creep up her neck and into her cheeks. "So, tell me about you."

A surprised look crossed his face. "Me? You already know about me."

"No, I don't. I know very little about you, really."

Frank took a gulp of diet soda. "What is it you want to know?"

"Well. . ." She paused in thought. "What's your favorite color?"

"Favorite color?" A half smile curled his full lips. He looked deep into her eyes, causing Cadi to blush. "Blue. How's that?"

She felt flattered. "What do you do for fun?"

"What do you have in mind?"

"I'm not suggesting, Sergeant Parker." She arched a brow. "I'm *asking*."

"Oh."

Cadi flicked a glance upward. When she looked back at him, she noted his mischievous grin.

"Do you like football? Baseball? Hockey? Snowmobiling? Skiing?"

"Do you like those things?"

"Uh-huh." She nodded. "Number one Hawkeye fan."

He replied with a rumble of laughter before adding, "No shopping at the mall all day for you, eh?"

"Well, I do shop occasionally," she admitted. "But I'm hardly a mall rat."

Frank's grin was contagious.

"I don't ski, though."

"Ah. Well, neither do I. And the fact is I don't have much of a life apart from my kids and working."

"I may be able to help if you'd like to change that."

"Oh?" He appeared thoroughly amused.

"Sure." She couldn't pass up another chance to tease him. "Next time my friends and I plan to go somewhere fun, we could probably find it in our ever-so-gracious hearts to ask you along."

"Hmm."

Cadi watched the smile work on his lips as he fought it off. She, on the other hand, didn't even try to hide her grin.

At last he gave in and chuckled. Then he took another drink of his cola. "I read your blog," he said, changing the subject.

The statement surprised Cadi. "You did?"

He nodded. "I found it interesting." He paused. "I think the work you're doing to draw attention to the devastating effects of drunk driving is commendable. If the sheriff's department can be of any help, let us know."

"I will. Thanks, but. . ." She regarded him askance. "We're talking about you, remember?"

"Cadi, there's nothing to say about me." He balanced his soda can on his knee and stared at it.

She mulled it over. "Mind if I ask how your wife died?"

"No, I don't mind." He took hold of his soda can again, sat forward, and swung his gaze to hers. "Remember the tornado that ripped through this part of the state a few years back? It almost completely wiped out Rogan's Hill, a subdivision not far from here."

Cadi remembered. "That was a horrendous storm."

Frank agreed. "Yolanda was home with the kids when it hit. She did everything right. She grabbed the kids—Dustin was about five at the time and Emmie was only an infant—and took refuge in the basement. But when the house was destroyed Landi. . ." He swallowed hard. "Well, she was killed. Neighbors found the kids crying, and Dustin was confused, but otherwise they were both unharmed." He paused "Before the twister hit, Landi begged me to come home. She said she was frightened but I—I told her she'd be okay. I felt I was needed on the job, not at home. I regre my decision to this day."

Although he spoke in a matter-of-fact way, Cadi saw the remorse in his eyes She recognized the pain and guilt pooling in their depths. She knew it well.

"I'm so sorry."

"Me, too." He forced a smile. "But life goes on for those of us left behind even when we might feel dead inside."

"I can relate all too well," she said emphatically. She shifted so she could see him better. "I wondered for years and years why I survived and my family didn't I felt guilty for being alive."

His gaze met hers, and he appeared to be digesting everything she said Then he reached out and touched her cheek.

They stared at each other for a long moment, and then Frank leaned forward and placed a light kiss on her lips. Cadi allowed her eyes to flutter closed, relishing the moment.

"Frank?"

Cadi started, hearing another female's voice followed by the thud of a closing door. She drew back and stared at Frank with wide eyes.

"My mother-in-law." He grinned. "She promised to sit with the kids."

"Oh." Cadi blinked.

Frank chuckled at what had to be her bewildered expression. "You didn't think I'd let you hitchhike home, did you?"

Chapter 14

Frank made the introductions, and Cadi smiled. "Pleased to meet you."

"Likewise." The bone-thin woman with short blond hair flicked a glance at her before looking back at Frank. "Are you ready to drive her home now, or do you want me to come back later? But not too much later. Church tomorrow, you know?"

Cadi sensed an immediate dislike coming from Lois Chayton and felt both puzzled and troubled by it. Did the woman resent her presence and think she'd come to take her daughter's place?

"We can go now." Frank's gaze shifted to Cadi. "Ready?"

"Sure."

It seemed an abrupt ending to an already peculiar first date. But as Cadi plucked her purse off the oak coffee table and made her way to the front door, she sensed Frank's former mother-in-law disapproved of her. She must have seen them kiss and drawn the wrong conclusions.

Frank opened the door of his SUV for Cadi, and she got in. He walked around and climbed behind the wheel.

"I don't think Lois likes me." She pulled the seat belt across her chest.

"It's nothing personal. That's just Lois. It takes her a while to warm up to people." He started the engine then pulled away from the curb. "I should add that I, um, don't do a lot of dating."

"Hmm. Well, for what it's worth, I don't date a lot, either."

"I figured."

Curious, Cadi peered over at him.

"Will made a comment about you being ninety-five before having a gentleman friend."

"He said—what?"

Frank chuckled. "At the bank, the morning you were helping Mrs. Binder fill out the insurance form. . .well, she mentioned her 'gentleman friend' would pick her up. That's when Will made the comparison."

Cadi told herself she shouldn't be surprised by the antics of her wisecracking friend. "Oooh, just wait until I get my hands on him!"

Frank's hearty laugh made her smile, and the rest of the drive back to Waterloo passed with more quips and chuckles. Quite pleasant, given that most of the time Cadi regarded it as a tedious ride across the county at night.

All too soon, Frank slowed and parked his SUV in front of Cadi's house.

"On a serious note," he began, turning in his seat to face her, "I'd like to apologize once more for thinking the worst of your intentions when we first met."

"I accept this apology just like I did the last one." She tried to make out his expression in the darkness.

"Thanks." He killed the engine.

"I had a lot of time to think when I was recovering from the car accident," she added, "and it did cross my mind that in your line of work you almost have to be suspicious of everyone to a point."

"I do. That's true."

Releasing his seat belt, he unlatched his door and got out of the vehicle. Cadi did the same. Only too late did she realize Frank had intended to open the door for her. She smiled to herself and made a mental note to allow him that bit of gallantry in the future.

They traipsed up the walk, swatting away mosquitoes. The humidity hadn't abated, and no breezes stirred the moist, heavy air.

"The truth is, apart from my displaced notions," he said, "I liked you from the start. I guess that's what makes my initial actions even more regrettable."

"I'll admit to having my feelings hurt, but..." Cadi shook off the recollection before it had time to seed. "Let's just forget it, all right?"

"Sounds good to me."

They reached the front door.

Cadi looked up at him. She could just barely make out his features under the dim porch light. She glimpsed an expression of gentleness on his face. Maybe even something else that she couldn't quite put a finger on. "I had a nice time tonight."

"I'm glad. A little embarrassed, but glad you had a good time." A moment passed, and then he took a step forward and, placing his hand behind her head, he drew her lips to his.

A thought winged its way across Cadi's mind: *He makes my knees weak and my heart sing.*

The kiss deepened and senses took flight. But a moment later, the heavy wooden door swung open.

"I thought I heard you."

Aunt Lou's voice jolted Cadi back to the here and how. She stepped back while a self-conscious smile worked its way across her face.

"Why don't you two come inside? The bugs'll eat you up alive out there."

"Thanks, but I need to be on my way." Frank caught Cadi's hand and gave it a squeeze. "I'll call you."

"Okay. Bye. And thanks again."

She watched him go and entered the house. She closed the door behind her then sagged against it, marveling at the effect Frank had on her senses.

"Have a nice time tonight?"

"Um, yeah." She smiled at her aunt who had her hair wrapped in pink curlers that matched her short-sleeved pastel housedress. One of her favorite shopping channels lit up the TV screen.

"You could have asked him in, hon. I was on my way to bed."

Cadi waved off her aunt's suggestion. "Frank left his kids with their grandmother, and she asked him to hurry back."

"I see. . .and how was the date?" Aunt Lou lifted the sleek, black remote and turned off the television. "I like Frank a whole lot more than I ever liked Darrell."

"Me, too." Cadi laughed at her own reply.

"There's a genuine sparkle in his eyes. I had no qualms about you going off with him tonight. I sensed he was trustworthy."

"I'd have to agree with that." Cadi kicked off her sandals and set them on the steps. "His kids are sweet, too."

"I guess I didn't realize he had children until tonight when they walked into the house."

Cadi relayed the entire story to her aunt. About halfway through, they both got comfy on the classic-styled caramel-colored sofa.

"Oh, mercy! She was killed during that awful tornado?" Aunt Lou shook her head, mulling over the matter. "That was an awful storm. Iowa gets its share of twisters, you know, but that one was a doozy."

"I remember." Cadi had been taking classes at the technical college. When the tornado warning came, all staff and students were required to take cover in the stairwells.

"I just realized, Cadi, it appears you and Frank share a common denominator. You both have suffered tragic losses."

"I saw that connection. I recognized the pain in his eyes."

"That man does have expressive eyes, doesn't he?"

Cadi nodded, stood, and padded across the tapestry-styled carpeting and into the kitchen where she took a bottle of spring water from the refrigerator. Reentering the living room, she sat back down on the couch and took a long drink.

"By comparison, Darrell's eyes struck me as being cold and calculated. They looked like hazel-colored glass. No depth to them, you know?"

Cadi stifled a yawn. "Were you watching those goofy movies on that women's channel again? The heroines are always victims. I can't stand it."

Aunt Lou neither admitted nor denied it, much to Cadi's amusement. Instead, her aunt stood from the couch and stretched.

"Time for bed. Church in the morning."

"I'm just going to finish my water. Then I'll turn off the lights and lock up before I go upstairs."

"Very good." She bent to kiss Cadi's cheek. "Sweet dreams."

She hadn't a doubt about that. She smiled at her great-aunt. "G'night, Aunt Lou."

❧

"Did you kiss her, Dad?"

Frank's jaw tensed as he sat at the breakfast table with his kids. He was tempted to tell Dustin it was none of his business whether he kissed Cadi or not. But then he figured he might as well be honest about it.

"Did you, Dad?" Emily asked. Her spoon hung in midair, halfway between her cereal bowl and her mouth. "Did you kiss her?"

He looked from one to the other. "You two are really something." He couldn't help a grin. "Yeah, I kissed her, all right? And I liked it, too. What do you think about that?"

Dustin grinned, and Emmie giggled and wrinkled her nose. "Ewwww."

Frank shook his head at them.

"Did Cadi like kissing you?" Dustin asked eagerly.

Frank recalled her starry-eyed expression. "Yeah, I think she liked it just fine." He shook off the pleasant memory and narrowed his gaze at his son. Frank didn't know whether to be concerned over Dustin's recent preoccupation with kissing or not. Was it merely a boyhood curiosity? Should he address the issue, or would it pass on its own?

"Did you ask her to the picnic, Dad?"

"No. To tell you the truth, I kind of forgot about the picnic. I might have to work that day, anyhow."

The boy's expression fell. "But I thought we were all going—like a family."

The comment cut Frank. "Let me see what I can work out." He sensed the picnic carried more importance to his son than he'd first thought. "And I'll call Cadi and invite her. But let's get one thing straight: The three of us *are* a family. If someday I remarry, that lady will just be added to the family that we already have."

"But we're not a real family," Dustin muttered into his cereal bowl.

Frank leaned closer to his son. "Excuse me?"

Dustin lifted his chin and looked Frank in the eye. "We're not a real family. My Sunday school teacher said so. She said a real family has a father *and a mother*."

Frank clenched his jaw. He knew Dustin's Sunday school teacher. Paige Dunner. She enjoyed barging into Frank's life whenever she could drum up an excuse. To this point, he'd politely tolerated the meals she brought over to the house and the goodies she baked up for the kids on their birthdays or Valentine's

Day and at Christmastime. But Frank wasn't about to allow Paige to manipulate his son so she could get to him.

"You're done with that Sunday school class. Hear me?"

Dustin's eyes grew wide. "But, Dad—"

"No exceptions."

Frank glanced across the table and, glimpsing the startled expression on Emily's face, softened his tone.

"I'm not punishing you, Dustin. I'm trying to protect you. That's my duty as your father. So we'll stop Sunday school for a while and I'll speak with Miss Paige, but you can still go to church."

"Will you come with us, Daddy?" Emmie asked, a pleading light in her amber eyes.

Frank paused, thinking it over, then expelled an audible sigh. "Oh, I don't know." He felt a sort of dread when he thought of attending the small church.

"Does Cadi go to church?" Dustin asked, his mouth stuffed with toast.

"Don't talk with your mouth full, son; and, yes, she goes to church."

"We could go to Cadi's church today," Emmie suggested on the sweetest note Frank ever heard, "and then you can come with us."

"Yeah, Dad, you came with us the time when Cadi was at our church."

"What is this? A conspiracy?" Frank stood and took his dishes to the sink. His entire body felt tense. His children were working his last nerve. He felt close to losing his patience.

But as he rinsed out his coffee mug, it occurred to him that perhaps his kids were starving for his attention. He tried to spend quality time with them on his days off, but perhaps it hadn't been enough.

He forced himself to take a deep breath, relax, and think things over.

Church? Attend services at Cadi's church this morning? No one there would regard him as the unfortunate widower struggling to raise two very precocious kids. What's more, he wouldn't have to withstand piteous stares from folks who knew and loved Yolanda. And, if he visited Cadi's church today, he wouldn't have to put up with overzealous unattached females like Paige Dunner. Of course, being with Cadi again would be a boon. Then again, she might have other plans.

He swung around and looked at his children. They stared back at him with expectancy glimmering in their eyes.

"Okay, I'll call Cadi and find out some things about her church—like the name of it and where it's located."

He glanced at his watch and decided they could very possibly make a later service.

Regarding his kids once more, he added, "This is a last-minute thing, but maybe it'll work out."

They let out a happy whoop.

"But I'm not promising anything." Frank had to raise his voice above their victorious cheers to add, "So don't get your hopes up."

In reply Dustin and Emily peered into their cereal bowls and grinned.

Chapter 15

The wind shifted, bringing in a cooler breeze and a reprieve from the hot, humid air. Cadi decided it was perfect weather for the first of July.

She drew in a deep breath as she stood outside the church's front entrance waiting for Frank and his children to arrive. She'd been surprised by his phone call at eight thirty this morning, during which he asked to visit her church. He didn't give a lengthy explanation, and Cadi felt puzzled. Was he just checking her out further, making sure she belonged to a church whose pastors preached the same biblical beliefs as Adam Dremond? Cadi had no worries there, although Riverview Bible Church was about ten times larger than Pastor Dremond's quaint little church in Wind Lake. Regardless of the reason, Cadi felt a swell of anticipation at seeing him again.

"Are you waiting for me?"

Hearing the familiar voice, Cadi suppressed a groan and glanced to her left. Darrell Barclay stood on the sidewalk, a few feet away, wearing an expensive suit and a lopsided grin. He'd never called to see if she was all right after the car accident, and even though she saw him here and there at church, they hadn't spoken to each other. Now Cadi wondered how he could have the nerve to approach her and be so arrogant—and so wrong.

"No, I'm not waiting for you, Darrell." She looked away.

He stepped forward. "I thought perhaps you wanted to apologize."

She arched a brow and regarded him again. "Apologize for what?"

"For humiliating me at my brother's birthday party, of course." Another step closer and Cadi got a whiff of his temple-throbbing cologne. "What kind of girl are you to leave my parents' house with some *lowlife* like Ross Hinshaw?"

"I'm a girl who makes mistakes like everyone else," Cadi replied in her own defense.

In the next moment, she caught sight of Frank and his kids walking across the parking lot, heading for the entrance. She realized she already possessed stronger feelings for Frank—and amazingly felt closer to him—than Darrell.

"Our dating relationship was one of my biggest mistakes," she added with a quick glance in his direction. "Now if you'll excuse me, my visitors have arrived."

She marched off to meet the Parkers, slowing her strides as she neared. When the children saw her, they raced to meet her.

"Hi, you guys." She noted Dustin's striped, short-sleeved dress shirt and navy slacks and Emily's frilly yellow dress. "You both look so nice."

"So do you." Emily hugged her around the waist.

"Thanks." Cadi tousled Dustin's sandy-colored hair then turned to Frank, who was dressed in tan slacks and a blue Oxford shirt with a coordinating necktie. She was about to remark on his dapper appearance when she noticed the dark glance he flicked toward the entrance doors.

A quick peek over her shoulder, and Cadi saw Darrell disappear into the building.

"Everything all right?"

Cadi looked back at Frank and smiled. "It is now." She took Emily's hand and slipped her other arm around Dustin's shoulders. "Come on. Let's go inside. We don't want to be late."

They reached the glass-paned doors and entered, then strode through the bustling foyer and into the expansive sanctuary. People milled about as the pianist played a medley of up-tempo hymns.

"I saved some seats for us," she told Frank. "And I have a big surprise for you," she said to the kids. "You're invited to attend children's church today as two very special guests. You'll even get to pick a prize out of the guest box if you attend. But you don't have to go. It's up to you and your dad."

They found their places. Cadi picked up her Bible and notebook from one of the padded, dark green chairs and explained Riverview's children's program to Frank and the kids.

"What do you think, Dustin and Emily? Would you like to go to children's church today?"

Both kids turned to their dad for permission.

"You can go if you want," he said.

"We'll come and get you right after our service up here is over," Cadi promised. She looked at Frank, sitting to her right. "Afterward, my aunt insists you all come over for lunch."

"Can we, Dad?" Dustin's eyes sparked with eagerness.

"Yeah, can we?" Emily maneuvered her way onto Cadi's lap.

"We're sort of intruding on your day," Frank said with a note of contrition in his voice.

"Yes, you are—and I'm rather happy about it." She noticed his whole demeanor seemed to relax.

Next she watched him take in his surroundings. Cadi sensed that not much escaped his scrutiny. She felt suddenly very safe, even protected, in Frank's presence.

The service began with the choir singing a soul-stirring number. Then, while an appointed member of the congregation stood and read from the book of Luke, Meg and Aunt Lou filed into the row. Cadi, Frank, and the children moved down to accommodate them. After the choir sang again, Pastor Bryant dismissed the children. Moments later, Meg's younger sister, Beth, showed up to escort Dustin and Emily downstairs.

The kids appeared tentative at first, but Beth soon won them over, and they followed her out of the sanctuary.

The aisles filled up with children from ages four to twelve and, during the din of the exodus, Cadi leaned over to Frank and explained, "Meg's sister is one of the volunteers who helps with children's church."

He nodded in understanding, although Cadi sensed he had already figured out that much.

"Tell me something else," he said.

"Okay."

With another incline of his head, he indicated down the row of seats. "Do I have competition?"

A little frown tugged at her brows as Cadi peered around Frank's muscular frame. She spotted Darrell sitting at the end of the aisle, and annoyance filled her being.

She straightened. "No competition there. Believe me." While she didn't dare hope they'd be friends someday, she did wish that she and Darrell would eventually develop a mutual respect for each other. They were, after all, both Christians. But until Darrell got over himself, a platonic friendship seemed impossible.

At this point, Cadi merely wanted to put some distance between them. In fact, she had assumed that distance already existed. She couldn't imagine why Darrell decided to approach her this morning, unless it was to goad her. Except she didn't think he was speaking to her. He never called once to check on her recovery from the car accident and, with regard to that fateful night, she supposed she did owe Darrell some sort of apology. She'd made some wrong choices and paid the consequences. What's more, Cadi regretted her harsh words to Darrell earlier.

She opened her mouth to relay all this to Frank, but before she could utter another word, Pastor Conner began his sermon.

Cadi sat back and made a mental note to explain things to Frank later. In the meantime, she opened her Bible and tuned in to the preaching of God's Word.

❧

"I love you, Cadi."

The words hit Frank like a sock in the jaw. Next he watched his little daughter throw her arms around Cadi's waist and hug her good-bye. Dustin was quick to get in on the action, and Frank heard his son repeat Emily's phrase. "I love you."

Cadi laughed. "I love you guys, too." She helped them climb into the SUV while Frank stood by feeling dazed.

Kids don't know what they're saying, he rationalized. *They just met Cadi. They can't possibly love her.*

Except the same words had been on the tip of his tongue all afternoon.

He gave himself a firm mental shake. This relationship was moving way too fast.

"I'm glad you could come today." Cadi stood in front of him, her slender chin tipped upward, and she searched Frank's face. "I had fun."

"It was nice. Thanks for inviting us over after church. We didn't intend to stay so long."

The remark came out a bit more stilted than he intended. He watched as the smile slipped from Cadi's face.

"Anything wrong?"

"No." He wagged his head. "I just need to get the kids home."

"Oh, sure. I understand." She glanced into the SUV's open window and waved.

"Don't forget the Fourth of July picnic!" Dustin called.

"I won't."

Frank cleared his throat. "Cadi, about the picnic. . ."

She turned toward him. Her eyes were as blue as the sky and her smile as brilliant as an evening sunset. She wore an expression of both expectancy and hopefulness, and he hated to disappoint her.

"I might have to work," he muttered, averting his gaze.

"No big deal. Just let me know. Unless there's a disaster somewhere calling my name, I've got no plans yet for the Fourth."

Frank grinned in spite of himself. He threw a glance over his shoulder at the porch where Cadi's great-aunt, along with two neighbors who had stopped by, sat on white wicker furniture chatting. He wanted to kiss Cadi before he left, but not in front of an audience.

He settled for a quick hug and figured it was probably for the best anyway. He had a feeling he needed to take a step back and examine this relationship with a cool head filled with common sense before moving full throttle ahead. So much had happened both last night and today that Frank felt like he'd lived an entire month in less than twenty-four hours.

"Thanks again for everything." He walked around his vehicle and climbed in behind the wheel. The kids shouted good-byes to Cadi as he pulled away from the curb.

As he drove the distance back to Wind Lake, Frank had plenty of time to reflect on everything that occurred from this morning until now. After a stirring but pride-splitting message from the pulpit, he had retrieved Dustin and Emily from children's church. The first question to leave their lips was, "Can we come back next week?"

Next, Cadi's great-aunt had served up one of the tastiest luncheons Frank had ever eaten. They watched a little football on television, and he chuckled to himself now, thinking how both Cadi and her aunt enjoyed the sport. Unconventional women—that they were. Refreshing, actually, as far as Frank was concerned. He found it amazing, too, that Dustin and Emmie took to Aunt Lou almost as fast as they'd taken to Cadi. They had two sets of grandparents who loved them and aunts and uncles and cousins—why did they think Cadi and her aunt were so special?

Frank kneaded his whiskery jaw and went back to his unconventional theory. He couldn't recollect ever seeing his mother, mother-in-law, or sisters watch sports on television—at least not voluntarily. Making it even more incredible that Cadi and her aunt enjoyed a good ball game was the fact that Iowa laid no claim to any major league teams. Today they cheered on the Green Bay Packers and Milwaukee Brewers. And then the truth emerged: Aunt Lou admitted having grown up in Wisconsin. Her bias had rubbed off on Cadi.

Frank grinned as nighttime fell down around his vehicle. A glance into the rearview mirror revealed that his children were dozing. They'd had an action-packed day.

And they're enamored with Cadi.

And so am I.

Now what do I do?

Frank had to admit to feeling wary, if not downright petrified. Cadi had captured his heart the day he met her. Was such a thing really possible? Could it be real? The last thing he wanted was to get hurt—and for his kids to get hurt. Things just seemed too perfect. There had to be a catch.

He thought over the conversation he had with Cadi this afternoon when they took the kids for a walk to the park. She said she'd babysat all through high school, almost every weekend, which, Frank concluded, explained her practiced way with children. He heard the story of Cadi's two years in foster care and how by God's divine guiding hand of grace, the state had located and contacted Aunt Lou who, of course, stepped up to claim her only heir. Cadi knew the heart-twisting, soul-searing pain of tragically losing a loved one. She related to the guilt that sometimes followed. She understood when he mentioned feeling dead inside for the last few years, and Frank saw the tiny tear that formed in the corner of her eye when he confessed that she made him feel alive again.

"I'm touched, Frank," she'd said as they sat on the park bench. "Thanks for telling me that."

But now he felt like an imbecile. He should have kept his mouth shut. He'd shown Cadi his weakest, most vulnerable side this weekend, a part of himself he hadn't revealed to anyone since Yolanda's death.

Not even to God.

Frank reached the townhouse he rented from his in-laws and parked his SUV. He got out then woke up his children and helped them from the vehicle. Once they were in the house, he helped the two wash up and get ready for bed. After tucking the kids in, he gathered their dirty clothes and carried them to the basement laundry room. He threw a load in the washer then trudged back upstairs. Returning to the living room, he heard a knock on the back door and answered it. His mother-in-law stood there wearing a fuzzy blue bathrobe.

"Can I come in? I'd like to talk with you."

"Sure." Frank let her in and closed the door.

"Kids in bed?"

"Yep."

"They were up awfully late tonight."

He knew Lois didn't mean anything by the remark, but it irritated him just the same. Stepping away from the door, he walked farther into the kitchen and leaned against the kitchen table.

"Is that why you came over? To reprimand me?"

"Of course not. I was just. . .well, concerned when I didn't hear from you or see the kids this morning." She paused and regarded him askance.

"We visited Cadi's church. I should have told you so you wouldn't have expected the kids. I apologize."

"You took Dustin and Emmie to another church this morning?"The dismay in her voice was evident. "What's that supposed to mean? Our church isn't good enough for you anymore?"

Frank shook his head. "Not the case."

"Let me remind you that it's the very church Yolanda grew up in. Dad and I still attend there. Your parents attend there, too, now. Our friends and—"

"And that's the problem," Frank cut in, fighting to keep the impatience out of his tone. "Whenever I step inside that church, I feel suffocated by the past and by everyone who loved Yolanda."

"When did you reach that conclusion? After you met Cadi?"

"Yes, although it's been coming for a while." Frank stared, unseeing, at the oak cupboards. "Adam Dremond brought up the subject months ago."

Lois folded her bony arms. "Have you been dating Cadi since she and her colleagues came to town to help with that gas explosion?"

"No, but that's when we met. We just started seeing each other." It galled him to give an account to his deceased wife's mother. On the other hand, he depended on Lois for so many things involving the kids and his home. To that degree he figured he owed her an explanation.

"I suppose if you marry this woman Dad and I will never see the children again."

"What?" Frank swung his gaze at her. Her remark seemed irrational. "What are you talking about? Marriage? I just started dating Cadi."

"Well, I suppose it's bound to happen sooner or later—your getting remarried, that is."

"Lois, if I should remarry, I promise never to stand in the way of your relationship with Dustin and Emmie. They love you very much. You're an important person in their lives." He shifted his stance. "Look, it's too soon for me to be confident in where my relationship with Cadi is going, but I do know I have to start living again. I think she's pretty, I admire her tenacity, and I enjoy the way she makes me feel when we're together."

"Hmm, sounds serious." Lois tipped her head. "I wonder what Yolanda would think."

"Landi would want me to be happy."

"What about Paige Dunner? I thought you liked her. She's pretty, too, and Yolanda thought the world of her." A faraway gleam entered Lois's hazel eyes. "She always said Paige would make an excellent wife and mother."

"I'm sure she will, but I'm not the guy who'd make her an excellent husband."

"What about Nicole Russell? She goes to our church. She's single. She and Yolanda went to high school together."

"I know who you're referring to, but there's no. . .no chemistry there with either of those women."

"Yes, well, I already saw a bit of that, um, chemistry you feel for Cadi."

"I kissed her. Big deal." Frank grew increasingly uncomfortable. His so-called "love life" was none of Lois's business, and he preferred to keep it that way. "Listen, it's late, and I need to get some shut-eye."

He walked around Lois and left the room. No more than a minute later, he heard her leave through the back door.

Chapter 16

Rain pelted the window of the Disaster Busters office then dribbled down the pane like so many teardrops.

Cadi released a blasé sigh and stared out over the almost empty parking lot. Puddles formed on the black asphalt. It had been gloomy and rainy for a good part of a week, and Cadi was beginning to feel a bit dreary herself. Her mood, she acknowledged, was not only due to the weather but the fact that she hadn't heard from Frank in over a week.

On the Fourth of July he'd called to say the picnic had been rained out, and he hadn't called again. Then, two days ago, she phoned him to ask if the kids wanted to attend children's church. Frank said he had to work and Dustin and Emily were spending the day with their grandparents. He ended their conversation soon after that, leaving Cadi no choice but to wonder if she'd offended him somehow. Either that or Frank was put off by what he had termed his "competition."

Cadi had meant to explain about both her run-in with Darrell as well as their nonexistent relationship on the day Frank and his kids came to the house for noon dinner, but she never got the opportunity. Even so, Sergeant Frank Parker didn't strike her as a guy who would be deterred that easily. It had to be something else.

Lord, You know his heart. You know all things. I don't have peace about calling Frank again. Is it best that he and I don't contact each other? Is this Your will? I'm hurt and disappointed, but I know that Your will and not mine is and always will be best.

She squared her shoulders, leaving the matter in the hands of her heavenly Father, and moved away from the window. She glanced at the clock on the walnut credenza. Four thirty. She was tired and listless, and with the dismal skies outside, it felt like the time should be much later.

Her gaze shifted to the accumulating paperwork in need of filing, and Cadi decided to make a pot of coffee to infuse some artificial enthusiasm into her system. A short while later, with a mug of rich-smelling brew beside her on the scarred desktop, she began sorting the documents she'd allowed to pile up.

About an hour later, she was just finishing up when a knock sounded. Her office door stood ajar, and glancing in that direction, she saw Darrell standing in the threshold.

He walked in without waiting for her reply. "Some of us are going to the steak house for dinner. We decided to meet here. Want to come?"

"No, thanks." She was puzzled by the invitation.

"I can see you weren't expecting me."

"To say the least." Cadi closed the filing cabinet drawer and walked around the desk. Sitting on its corner, she folded her arms and regarded him askance. "What are you doing here?"

"Well. . ." He stepped toward her. "I decided I'm ready to hear whatever it is you have to say."

Oh, don't tempt me. She fought against the mounting cynicism.

"I'm ready to accept your apology." He stuffed his hands into the side pockets of his crisp navy slacks. "I wasn't ready before. Now I am."

"I'm so flattered, Your Highness." She bowed.

"Oh, quit the theatrics. I'm serious."

Cadi smiled at his retort.

"Did you ever think of how embarrassed I was the night of that party when you left with Ross Hinshaw of all people? You chose him over me?"

Her amusement vanished. "No, I guess I didn't consider your feelings—because you were rather preoccupied with a certain woman with long blond hair."

Darrell rolled his eyes. "So you left with Hinshaw because you were jealous?" He nodded. "I suppose that makes more sense."

"I left with Ross because I was hurt," she corrected. "All I wanted to do was go home, and he offered me a ride. It was a bad choice on my part, even though I had no idea Ross was drunk."

"Hmm." Darrell strode to the desk and sat on its edge next to Cadi. She refused to encourage him and walked to the door.

"I admit my actions that night bordered on irrational," she said, "and I'm sorry for any embarrassment I caused you." There. She'd apologized.

"Apology accepted." He flashed a practiced grin, and Cadi wondered how she'd ever found him charming. "Now, how about dinner at the steak house?"

"I'm not hungry. Thanks." She set her hand on the doorknob, hoping Darrell would take the hint.

"Our friends say we look good together, Cadi."

"Our friends?" She couldn't imagine to whom he referred. "I don't believe we share the same friends."

He chuckled at the remark. "We're all brothers and sisters in Christ. Your friends are my friends and vice versa. It's just that my friends are climbing the social ladder and gaining respect—earning money."

Cadi thought about her closest friends—Meg, Will, Jeff, and Bailey. They climbed a different "ladder of success"—one of service to God and helping other human beings in their time of need. Of course, Christians in positions as bankers, lawyers, and corporate executives were needed, also, but Cadi couldn't imagine fitting into that social circle. She saw that fact clearly now.

"It's true that you've disappointed me on several occasions," Darrell said, "but I'm willing to give our relationship another chance. I've discussed the matter with several godly individuals here at church, and each of them persuaded me to cultivate, not terminate, our relationship."

She gaped at him, noting the one-sidedness of his logic. *God, help me here. Give me patience with this man.*

"What do you say, Cadi?"

She shook her head. "Darrell, seriously, our relationship was terminated months ago. I just didn't realize it then. But I do now."

He appeared taken aback. "Months ago?"

She softened. "We're all wrong for each other. Let's face it: You want and need someone different than who I am. You want a woman who is polished, sophisticated." She stopped herself before adding "arm ornament" to the list.

Darrell stuck out his lower lip and sort of shrugged in silent agreement. "You polish up rather nicely."

He meant it as a compliment, and to a certain extent she was flattered. But Cadi would never forget his wandering eyes at the party and the fact that he hadn't felt concerned enough about her even to make one quick phone call to check on her recovery after the accident. What's more, he considered Disaster Busters a waste of time and nothing more. And then there was his walk with the Lord to consider. In Cadi's opinion, it appeared perfect, almost superficial, although she didn't doubt that Darrell was a Christian.

"You have possibilities, Cadi."

"So do you." She smiled. "But we're not right for each other." She glanced down at her attire. "I wear a sweatshirt and blue jeans to work."

"Yes, but—"

"I'm an EMT, and you can't stand the sight of blood."

"A lot of couples have vastly different likes and dislikes—"

"Darrell, I'm in love with somebody else."

Cadi couldn't believe the statement had flown out of her mouth with so little effort.

Darrell, however, didn't appear too surprised. "The guy with the two kids? He was in church a couple of Sundays ago?"

"Yes." She was still reeling from her admission. Had she really said "love"? When did that happen? How could it have happened? Frank confused her most of the time. Love him? Impossible.

Then she recalled how she felt in his arms, all weak-kneed and her heart singing like a bird in the springtime. He shared a side of himself that made her feel special and needed. His children were well-adjusted despite losing their mother so tragically. They looked up to Frank, respected and adored him, and that alone told Cadi a lot about the man, even though when they talked that Sunday afternoon, he'd admitted to wrestling with his relationship with God.

Nevertheless, the fanciful workings of her heart dared to hope in love and a happily-ever-after with Frank.

"Must be divorced, huh?"

"Widowed." She blinked and gathered her wits. "Darrell, I think you need to leave. I—I've got some errands to run."

"What does he do for a living? Does he make more money than I do? I hope you're considering these important questions."

She ignored him and crossed the room. She saw no point in discussing Frank any further—especially with Darrell. Opening the bottom drawer of her wooden desk, she lifted out her purse.

"I should get going, and you don't want to miss your friends. The steak house gets really crowded."

Darrell glanced at his pricey gold wristwatch. "Yes, I suppose."

He sauntered to the door in a way that exuded self-confidence. She followed him out, turning off the lights before closing up the office behind her.

"Well, have fun tonight." She forced a polite inflection into her voice.

When Darrell didn't reply, she paused and regarded him with a curious frown. He just stood there, statue still and staring over her shoulder. What had seized his attention?

Oh, well, none of her concern.

She whirled around and took a forward stride, instantly colliding with none other than the elusive deputy himself, Frank Parker.

❧

Frank had dropped in to see Cadi on a whim. Purely a whim. He'd had business at the courthouse, and the idea of her being a mere couple of miles away nearly drove him to distraction.

For the last nine days, she'd occupied his thoughts almost every hour, and when she didn't, Dustin or Emily served as a reminder each time one of them mentioned her name.

Very simply, he wanted to see her again. He *had* to see her again.

But when he entered the church and neared the Disaster Busters office, after asking directions, he was brought up short by what he first believed to be some sort of lovers' quarrel. He recognized Cadi's voice and felt pinned to the tile floor, unable to breathe, let alone move.

Then he heard what he could only describe as an answer to his deep-down, most personal prayers.

A sign. He had longed for a sign. Move forward or turn tail and run?

He now felt confident in taking the next few steps ahead.

And, as Cadi stood just inches away, having fallen right into his arms, he watched her face turn from pink to a very pretty crimson. Her eyes, on the other hand, held that proverbial deer-caught-in-the-headlights stare.

"You okay?" Frank steadied then released her. "I hope you didn't reinjure those ribs when we crashed just now."

"I–I'm fine," she stammered.

She looked flustered, and Frank resisted the urge to chuckle. Instead, he held out his right hand to Darrell and introduced himself. Under the circumstances, he had no qualms about being cordial to the guy.

The other man replied in a brisk but polite manner and quickly excused himself, saying he had a dinner engagement.

Frank stifled a guffaw and peered at Cadi.

"This isn't what you think," she said in a whispered tone. "Darrell stopped by to—well, you see, I did sort of owe him an apology, and—"

"Cadi, relax. I wasn't eavesdropping or anything, but I heard enough to know that there's nothing going on between you two, okay?"

"How much did you hear?" A mix of suspicion and dread swept over her features.

Frank was so encouraged he felt almost giddy. "I heard you tell him to leave."

"Oh." Cadi tried in vain to hide a grimace.

"I also heard you say something about running errands. I just got off duty. Do you have time to grab a bite to eat?"

Her blue eyes searched his face. "I was beginning to think you didn't want to see me again."

He noted her wounded expression and took hold of her hand. "Let's talk over supper. How 'bout it?"

Chapter 17

C adi toyed with the handle of her stoneware coffee mug as she sat across the table from Frank. She watched him eat the last of his honey ham sandwich, complete with thick slices of cheese, lettuce, tomatoes, mustard, red onions, and cucumbers. It resembled the salad she'd eaten except it'd been stuffed between two fat pieces of whole wheat and herb bread.

She grinned as he polished off the last of his meal. A couple of weeks ago Aunt Lou had commented that Frank and his kids were fun to cook for because of their hearty appetites.

He pushed his plate to the end of the long, narrow table. "So, you see, I never wanted to hurt you," he said, wrapping up his explanation for not contacting her sooner. "I just thought maybe things between us were moving too fast."

She hid a wince and dared not ask if he still felt that way. She suspected he'd heard her blunder while speaking with Darrell earlier. Should she explain? Maybe she didn't mean "love"—if not, then what *did* she mean?

"I have to protect my kids," Frank continued. "They adore you, and I don't want them to get hurt. I don't want any of us to get hurt."

"Me, either." She did wonder, however, what point he was trying to make. Did he want to see her more? Less? Not at all?

She allowed her gaze to wander around the rustic coffee and sandwich shop, admiring its old-time Western decor. From her vantage point, she could see through the front windows, and she noticed it had begun to rain again.

"So what do you want to do about. . .things?" She looked back at Frank. He still wore his uniform—the tan shirt and green trousers. He'd mentioned that he knew his shift would end after his business at the courthouse was completed, so he'd driven his own vehicle from Wind Lake, but he hadn't found time to change clothes.

He rotated his broad shoulders in response to her question. "What's there to do?" He wiped his mouth with a white paper napkin then set it on the table. "Would you like some dessert?"

"Um, no. . ." Cadi felt so confused her head spun.

"I talked to Adam Dremond last week. He told me there are folks still struggling with housing issues as well as other basic needs while they wait for their insurance to cover their losses. He said in some cases it can take up to three months—or longer—to get a claim paid."

Cadi marveled at the lengthy time frame and figured it depended on the insurance company. Her allotment from the car accident had been issued immediately, it seemed.

"Anyway, donations are still coming in from the Web page. Adam is pleased."

"Excellent. I'm glad the site proved to be a helpful tool."

Their gazes met and, as always, Cadi felt like she could lose herself in Frank's deep brown eyes. Next she watched as a smile worked its way up his face.

He reached across the table and placed his palm over the top of her hand. "It's good to see you, Cadi. I'm glad I gave in to my impulse and dropped in on you."

"I'm glad you did, too."

They lingered at the table a few more minutes then pushed back their wooden chairs. Frank had already paid for the meals, so they strode out of the restaurant and ran through the downpour to his fawn-colored SUV.

Inside, they shook off the rain and buckled up; then Frank started the engine.

"Thanks for dinner."

"You're welcome, except you didn't eat much."

"I've got a lot on my mind."

"Nothing to do with your verbal exchange with—what's his name? Darrell?"

Cadi laughed. "No. I actually hadn't given him much thought at all." The truth was she'd been working up her nerve to ask Frank where she stood with him.

They rode in silence for several long minutes.

"You sure everything's okay?"

"Yep."

She watched the rain stream down the windshield as the wipers kept time with the instrumental light jazz playing on the radio. They drove through one puddle and then another.

"I hope the streets aren't affected by all this rain." She craned her neck, trying to view what lay ahead. This section of road had flooded in the past.

"Roads are fine, Cadi. I know them as well as my own reflection."

"Then I'll take your word for it." She forced herself to sit back and relax.

"We've had bad weather lately, but nothing like the other parts of the state."

"Don't I know it! Some places looked like war zones."

"That's what twisters can do." Frank grew pensive.

Regret filled Cadi. "I hope I didn't trigger painful memories for you."

"You didn't. It actually helps to talk to someone like you, someone objective, outside the family, and who can identify with my intense loss." She saw him flash a smile as they passed under a streetlight.

"I feel the same way."

"I can tell."

A little grin tugged at her mouth as she realized how bittersweet their connection was. A natural disaster.

"Well, I must admit that responding to the flood situation in Cass County was frightening for me, but Disaster Busters was in charge of finding folks temporary lodging. Had I been part of the rescue efforts, I might have had serious issues."

"Did you ever learn to swim?"

"Sure, but in chlorinated pools. You and I both know the best swimmers can be rendered defenseless in floodwaters."

"True enough."

"The currents alone can be deadly."

"Agreed."

"Swimming in pools, I can handle." She repositioned herself in the leather seat. "But floods. . ." She didn't finish her sentence, distracted once more by the weather outside. "I just wish it would stop raining."

"Cadi, don't worry. We're safe," he said as if reading her troubled thoughts. "I'd know it if we weren't. There aren't any flash flood warnings in effect around here, and I'm familiar with the highways, even the side roads, prone to flooding in this county. This isn't one of them."

She considered his words and felt somewhat reassured.

She settled back in her seat and took a deep breath. "Thanks. I feel better."

"Good." There was a smile in his voice. "Tell you what, I'll drive you home now, and your aunt can take you over to church tomorrow to pick up your van. I'm sure it'll be safe enough in the parking lot overnight."

Cadi shook her head. "I'm a big girl. I shouldn't have burdened you with my childish insecurities."

"Listen, we all have them, childish or not. Let me help you out. It's no trouble."

His offer put her at ease all the more. "Really? You'd do that for me?"

"Of course I would." He stretched his arm across the distance between the seats and took her hand. "I'd consider it an honor."

How gallant, Cadi thought. Suddenly her thoughts about the rain dissipated.

Frank drove the rest of the distance to her home. He parked and they exited the vehicle then ran through the rain and up onto the front porch.

She faced him. "Can I ask you something? I mean—I just want to make certain I heard you correctly at the coffeehouse."

"Sure." He leaned against one of the round, vertical posts that adjoined the spindled railing.

"What I think I heard you say," she began again, trying to be as diplomatic as possible, "is that our relationship is moving too fast and that you want to back off."

"That was my mind-set initially." He chuckled, perhaps at himself. "But the truth is I don't want to back off. I'd like to see you every day if I could."

She smiled, feeling encouraged. "That would be fine with me. But am I to understand that you don't want me to see Dustin or Emily because you're afraid they'll get hurt?"

He looked down at his boots before returning his gaze to hers. "It's almost too late for that, and it's my fault. The reality is my kids will be hurt if they *don't* get to see you."

"I'll be a little hurt, too, but you're their father, and I will, of course, abide by whatever you decide."

Frank regarded her in a kind of thoughtful awe. "You'd really be hurt? You're that fond of my kids?"

"Of course I am." She laughed. "I mean, they really feed my self-esteem because they think I'm so wonderful. How could I not adore them right back?"

Frank chuckled. "You've got a point there."

"All kidding aside, you've got a couple of wonderful, thoughtful, sensitive children, and that says a lot about you as their parent."

"I can't take all the credit. I get a lot of help."

"I don't think you give yourself enough credit."

He shrugged, and a faraway look entered his eyes as he stared off somewhere over her head. "I feel like I've been living life on autopilot until now."

"And God knew it, and He protected you by enabling you to raise your kids and maintain your job."

Frank's gaze returned to Cadi, and she glimpsed the intensity in his eyes. "And now God brought you into my life."

Cadi felt like cheering. Frank was coming back to life in more ways than one. His spiritual life seemed to be returning, too.

Taking a step toward him, she stood on tiptoe and kissed his rough jaw. His arms enveloped her, and in that moment, she knew in her heart her dreams would become reality.

Chapter 18

The weekend arrived, and Frank took Cadi out for dinner—without his children. The kids would have kicked up more of a fuss if Frank hadn't promised they'd attend Riverview with Cadi the next morning. After services and children's church, they drove to his folks' condo for lunch, Cadi and her aunt Lou in tow. The fact that Cadi was undaunted about meeting his folks impressed Frank, and everyone seemed to get along just fine. When they left, Mom hugged and kissed him good-bye before whispering, "It's good to see my boy happy again."

Frank gently reminded her that he was hardly a "boy," although Mom had the rest of the statement correct; he felt happy again.

In the days following, Frank found himself lost in his thoughts of Cadi more often than not. His co-workers took note of his distractedness, and one guy asked why he suddenly volunteered for every trip to the courthouse in Waterloo that arose.

"Gotta be a woman."

Frank didn't deny it, which fueled the jibes and snickers, but he tried to act less obvious—and stay out on patrol a lot more.

Good grief! He never remembered behaving so love struck in all his life!

Then, almost a week later, on a rainy August morning, Bettyanne Binder paid Frank a visit. He had just finished a night shift, and he planned to get home, catch a few winks, then gather up the kids and visit Cadi this evening. He hoped whatever the elderly woman required wouldn't take loads of his time.

Frank stood as the secretary showed her to his cubicle.

"Hi, Mrs. Binder. What can I do for you?"

She held up his business card and waved it. "I have a crime to report."

"All right." He helped her into a chair, wondering if the same teenagers he'd busted for underage drinking and disturbing the peace recently were wreaking more havoc in town.

"What happened?"

She removed her plastic rain bonnet and shook it out before smoothing down the skirt of her pale-blue-and-white-checked dress. "I was robbed—that's what happened. Just look at this!"

Frank sat on the edge of his desk and watched as the older woman pulled a folded piece of paper from her ivory canvas purse. She handed it to him.

He took and examined it. "This is a copy of a canceled check."

"Exactly. Now look at the back of it. That hen scratch doesn't belong to me!"

He arched his brows. "You're telling me this isn't your signature?"

"Precisely. Why, I have lovely penmanship, always did, and it certainly doesn't resemble that—that scribble on the back of the check!"

Frank studied the copy again before glancing up at Mrs. Binder. "Maybe you should start from the beginning. How did you obtain this copy?"

"Well, when the insurance money from that dreadful explosion didn't come and didn't come, I finally called. The company told me the paperwork was initially misplaced but that they had found it and my claim finally got processed. I waited awhile longer and called again. But the gal on the phone said the check was issued and that it had been cashed. Needless to say, I was astonished." The woman's vein-lined hand fluttered to the base of her slim neck. "I insisted I never received the money, and that's when they sent me the copy you have in your hand."

"Looks like the check was cashed at the First Bank of Wind Lake." He stood and walked around his desk. "Did you speak with the manager over there?"

"No. I just picked that up at the post office this morning. I haven't had a chance to speak with anyone." Her hands trembled. "I'm just so very upset."

"I understand. Let me make a phone call or two."

Opening the drawer, he pulled out the phone book, found the number, and called the bank. Leslie Pensky, the manager, couldn't recall who'd cashed the check over a month ago. When Frank asked about the cameras positioned in the lobby, she told him they were self-rewinding devices and only caught and retained a week's worth of activity at a time.

He thanked her for the info then ended the call.

"Well..." He rubbed his jaw in contemplation. "This is going to take further investigation."

"Deputy, I already know who stole my money." She shifted her slight frame in the chair. "It was that girl who helped me fill out the insurance forms. The blond from Waterloo."

"Cadi?" Frank shook his head. "No way."

But a moment later, the image of her aunt's new sedan fluttered through his mind. He recalled that Cadi had purchased it for her, and when he'd first seen the sleek gray car, he remarked on the generous gift. He meant to inquire about it further because his curiosity got the better of him, but then he became distracted by the kids, along with his own emotions, and forgot all about it. The fact was, whenever he was with Cadi, all he could think about was her. What's more, he thought about her even when they weren't together.

"She's the thief, I tell you!"

"Impossible. Cadi isn't capable of committing a crime." He tamped down his suspicion and inspected the canceled copy again. "Besides, how would she have gotten ahold of your check?"

"Maybe she drove into Wind Lake and asked for it at the post office."

"Did you ask Stan about that?" The Wind Lake post office wasn't large, and everyone knew Stan Smith, the postmaster.

"I haven't had a chance to ask him." Tears formed in the older woman's eyes. "But I often have other people collect my mail for me. Sometimes they are out-of-town friends whom Stan doesn't know. They're visiting me and want to go into town for some reason, and I ask them to pick up my mail. They give Stan my name, and he hands it over."

"Probably not a good practice."

"Apparently not." Mrs. Binder's chin quivered. "A body can't trust anyone these days. Which brings me back to the reason I'm here. Cadi could have pretended like she was doing me a favor and gotten my check at the post office. I'm sure she stole it."

Frank shook his head. "Cadi wouldn't steal your check."

"Well, I want to press charges!" She balled a fist and did her best to slam it into the palm of her other hand. "I heard from a reputable source that this kind of thing happened in this town once before."

Frank winced, knowing full well Mrs. Binder was correct.

"I won't stand for it. And if you won't help me, I'll take this matter to your superiors."

"Mrs. Binder, you have no proof." Frank sensed her fear and frustration and made a special effort to soften his tone. "Now look, Cadi's my—my friend. Let me talk to her and look into this matter further and I'll get back to you, okay?"

"But I've been waiting for my money."

"Pressing charges won't get you your money any sooner. But I promise to speak with Cadi right away, and I'll pursue any leads that might result from our conversation. In the meantime, you let me know if there are any new developments on your end. All right?" Frank helped her up from the chair. "Let's be in contact on Monday morning. And I strongly suggest that from now on, you don't let anyone collect your mail for you."

Mrs. Binder replied with an exasperated sigh but eventually agreed to Frank's terms and left the office.

Once she'd gone, he lowered himself into his desk chair and contemplated the situation. He was tired from working all night, and he hated how his fatigued mind conjured up all kinds of questions and doubts about Cadi. He could rationalize almost everything except that new car she had purchased for her aunt. That suspicion was hard to shake.

Then Mrs. Binder's words echoed in his thoughts. *I heard from a reputable source that this kind of thing happened in this town once before.* Frank remembered, all too well, the cheating, the looting, and the devastated citizens who were left with nothing after the bogus charity group left town. He refused to believe Cadi was in the same category as those now-convicted thieves. She was the most honest, genuine woman he'd ever known.

But had he been duped? The thought sent a chill through him.

Dear God, not again!

🐾

Cadi finished her phone calls to Meg, Jeff, Bailey, and Will; Disaster Busters had been summoned across the state again. This time to Fort Dodge where heavy rains caused rivers to rise and neighborhoods to flood. Rescue efforts were under way.

Cadi thought of the upcoming weekend and her plans with Frank. She hated to leave town. She'd been so looking forward to seeing him and his kids again. That, combined with the fact this emergency was flood related, tempted her to refuse the request for Disaster Busters' assistance. The memory of what happened to her family in a flash flood caused a renewed sense of panic to surge through her.

But, no. She couldn't give in to fear and back out. People needed her help. She had to go—and time was of the essence.

She punched in Frank's office number. When she reached his voice mail at work, she tried his cell phone. Another recording picked up, and this time she left a message. She explained the details of Disaster Busters' latest recruitment and cited its location. She knew she was babbling, but she hoped it kept the mounting trepidation out of her tone.

At last she disconnected the call and glanced at her watch. She'd have just enough time to go home and pack up her things before she met the team back here at church.

Locking up the office, she walked through the empty halls and out into the parking lot. The rain had slowed to a drizzle. She reached her van and felt both pleased and surprised when she spotted a squad car pulling into the lot. She knew it was Frank. With a smile she waved and watched as he pulled alongside her vehicle.

He opened the door and got out. Cadi walked around the front of her minivan to meet him.

"Got a minute?"

"Sure." She noted his somewhat gruff demeanor. "Anything wrong?"

"Can we talk inside?"

"Sure, but I don't have a lot of time." Cadi led him back into Riverview's large facility. "Did you get my phone message?"

"No, I haven't had a chance to check messages."

Judging by his tone, Cadi knew she hadn't imagined his brusqueness. "Bad day?"

"Sort of." He released a weary-sounding sigh. "I'm exhausted."

"I can tell." She unlocked her office door and let him inside. "Want some coffee? It's a couple of hours old, but it's in a thermal pot."

"No, thanks. Cadi, look, I'm here on business, and I'm afraid it's not pleasant."

"What's going on?"

He pulled a piece of white paper out of his back pocket, unfolded it, and handed it to her. "Take a look at that."

Cadi took the proffered document and noticed the obvious. She held a copy of a canceled check made out to Bettyanne Binder for a large sum of money. She remembered helping the elderly woman fill out the insurance claim form.

"Mrs. Binder must be pleased."

"She would be—if she had been the one to cash the check."

"What?" Cadi felt a puzzled frown dip her brows.

"See the signature on the back of the check? Mrs. Binder insists it's not hers."

Cadi looked at the back side of the copy before glancing up at Frank again. "I don't understand."

He sat down on the corner of her desk, one leg dangling over the side. "Mrs. Binder believes someone managed to steal her check, forge a semblance of her signature, and get the cash." He paused, and Cadi saw his gaze flick over her. "She's sure that 'someone' is you, and she wants to press charges."

"What? But that's ridiculous."

"I know."

Cadi didn't think he sounded convinced, and a sickening dread fell over her. "You think I stole it, too?" The words came forth with significant effort.

"I don't think you stole it, but—"

"But?" She shook her head, remembering how he'd falsely accused her when they first met. It pained her to think he still didn't trust her.

"Cadi, look—"

"Oh, don't waste your breath. I can see the guilty verdict written all over your face."

"Bear with me, okay?" A muscle worked in his jaw, and Cadi wondered if he was about to lose his patience. "Since Mrs. Binder named you, specifically, I wanted to bring this to you myself. I didn't want one of the other officers to come to you with her complaint."

"Well, I don't know who cashed this thing." She gave back the copy of the check. "It certainly wasn't me."

Frank folded the paper and stuffed it into his pocket again. "So, you never did tell me—how were you able to purchase your aunt's new car?"

"How was I. . . ?" She blinked. "You never asked until now. What a coincidence." She stepped closer to him. "You think I stole that lady's money, don't you?"

"No, I'm not accusing you of anything. I'm inquiring."

Cadi shook her head to the contrary. "You're investigating. There's a major difference." She placed her hands on her hips and narrowed her gaze. How could she love a man who seemed so ready to convict her of a crime?

"Investigating is my job. Just for the sake of discussion, would you mind answering my question?"

"Yeah, I do mind—but I'll answer it because I have nothing to hide."

A stony expression, but one that seemed mixed with regret, settled over his features.

"I received a settlement from my car accident. You're brilliant enough to figure out the rest."

"Can you prove it?"

"Do I have to?"

He appeared to weigh his reply, but before he could actually answer, Cadi backed down. She didn't have time for this. She made her way to the file cabinet and opened the drawer in which she kept personal documents because she had nowhere to lock them up in her bedroom at home. She pulled out a folder containing the legal documents in question. Then she strode back to Frank, and it was all she could do to keep from flinging it at him.

He leafed through the file then handed it back.

"Satisfied?"

"Yeah. Thanks."

He stood to leave, and as he opened the door, Cadi's heart twisted. How could he accuse her and walk away? Just like that?

"Frank. . ."

He paused, glanced over his shoulder, then turned his body toward her.

"I can't fathom how you could even imagine that I'd steal something like another person's insurance check and forge their signature. It was one thing to be suspicious of me before we knew each other, but you and I. . ." She couldn't finish for fear she'd choke on the rest of her sentence.

His features softened. "Cadi, I *had* to ask—"

"But you should have *known*."

He shook his head. "I was acting on Mrs. Binder's accusations."

"Which are nonsense." Cadi fought back her tears. "You believed her, not me. You suspected the worst of me. How could you?"

"How?" He took a step forward. "Because I'm good at my job. I know *anyone* at *anytime* is capable of *anything*, given the right circumstances. If you don't believe me, read the Bible. King David comes to mind. He was an anointed man of God, yet he committed adultery and murder."

"That much is true, but you missed the point. I'm talking about a fundamental premise here. Trust. All good relationships are based on trust. Even the foundation of our faith is based on trust; we trust Jesus Christ and His work on the cross for our eternal salvation. We trust God with our present. Our future." She raised her arms, palms up, in an emphatic shrug. "If you don't trust me, what kind of relationship can we ever hope to have? Nothing. We have nothing."

"Nothing, huh?" His expression hardened. "I'm sorry you feel that way."

He wheeled around and left the office, pulling the door closed with a finality that shattered Cadi's heart.

Chapter 19

Frank fumed all the way back to Wind Lake.

Nothing. She said we have nothing. I suppose she thinks the last couple of months have been a waste of time, too.

Frank refused to admit Cadi's reaction might have been legitimate. He'd *had* to ask her about the insurance check. He'd merely been doing his job.

Hadn't he?

He shook off any doubts. He was in the right to question her, especially after Mrs. Binder went so far as to name Cadi as the one who stole her insurance check.

Except, in his heart, he'd known Cadi was innocent all along.

His grip tightened on the steering wheel of the squad car. Perhaps he should have told her from the start that he'd defended her to Mrs. Binder. Maybe it would have prevented those angry sparks he'd seen in her blue eyes. Sure, he had questions. But she'd answered them—right before she said they had "nothing."

Does she really feel that way?

Frank stopped at the office, dropped off the squad car, then drove home in his own vehicle. Knowing his kids were with Lois today, he walked into the adjacent townhouse to say hello. The noise level in the finished basement rec room was off the charts because rain had forced Lois to move the day-care center indoors. But Dustin and Emmie were having fun, and since Lois didn't mind, he decided he'd leave them there so he could get a few hours of sleep. His limbs felt weighted from exhaustion.

"Don't worry, Dad, we'll be sure to wake you up when it's time to go to Cadi's house."

Frank refrained from growling at his son. Hadn't this been exactly what he'd feared? Cadi's calling it quits and his kids getting hurt?

He made his way next door. His brain felt muddled from lack of sleep.

Did she really say to call it quits?

Fatigue clouded his ability to reason, although one thing he knew for sure: His life would never be the same without Cadi.

❧

"The Des Moines River continues to rise. Experts say it will crest four feet above flood stage. Many roads have already become impassable, so motorists are advised to take precautions."

Cadi turned up the radio in the minivan.

"In low-lying areas, floodwaters have submerged street signs and carried away everything from ice machines to netted soccer goals. It's reported that as many as twenty thousand people are without power."

"Great," she muttered. "Just great."

"We're going to live up to our name this weekend," Will quipped from where he sat in the passenger seat. "Disaster Busters."

"Do you want me to drive, Cadi?" Jeff called to her from the backseat.

"No, I'm okay."

"Well, at this speed, we'll never get there. I don't think I've ever seen you drive so slow."

She wrestled with the idea of giving up control of her vehicle, but in the end she knew Jeff was right. In this instance, her anxiety made her overly cautious, and she sensed her team's growing impatience.

Pulling over onto the shoulder, Cadi allowed her friend to take the wheel. She crawled into the bucket seat across from Bailey, secured her seat belt and shoulder strap, then forced her taut nerves to relax. Will tuned the radio in to a Christian station, and Cadi forced herself not to think about what lay ahead or dwell on the heated verbal exchange she'd had with Frank. But it was no use. She couldn't shake either subject from her thoughts.

"You're so quiet, Cadi," Meg said. "Aren't you feeling well?"

"I'm fine. I—I just have a lot on my mind right now."

"Did Frank pop the question?"

"Oh, he 'popped' several, but none was the question you're referring to— that's for sure." Cadi turned in her seat and regarded her best friend. She noted the teasing gleam in Meg's hazel eyes, but Cadi wasn't up to the goading. Or the banter. "Seriously, I'd rather not talk about it."

Meg searched her face then nodded. "Okay."

With the subject of Frank now dropped, Cadi tried again to push aside her tumultuous emotions. She focused on prayer in preparation for the flooding situation that she and the rest of the team would soon encounter.

An hour later, Jeff pulled the van into the parking lot of the New Elk Lodge, a huge facility and part of a campground. It had opened its doors to rescue personnel and those seeking immediate shelter. After checking in, they were directed farther down the highway. They walked the rest of the way beneath a gloomy sky.

"At least the rain stopped," Meg said, sounding cheery.

"For now," Will added. "More is on the way."

Cadi suppressed a groan.

When they arrived on the scene, they were met with controlled chaos. Many residents had been able to evacuate while some refused to leave their homes.

Others, however, were trapped.

After speaking with the fire chief, one of the men heading up the rescue efforts, Will approached Cadi and the rest of the Disaster Busters team. "Okay, here's the scoop. We're going to help get folks out of their houses. We'll cover this cul-de-sac." He gave a nod, indicating to the area just over his shoulder. "It's about a quarter of a mile long, and as you all can see, it goes downhill and curves to the left. We're standing on the high end." He looked at Cadi. "Since the water is overflow from the river and not due to a flash flood, most rescuers are wading in. Every boat, other than those privately owned, is being used to evacuate elderly and handicapped residents."

"We can walk. Let's go," Jeff said eagerly.

"One last thing." A serious expression spread across Will's face. "We've only got a few hours until dark, and more rain is on the way. The water level on the street is expected to rise."

Cadi looked down the flooded, tree-lined neighborhood and squelched her fears before they could resurface. *I can do this, Lord. With Your help, I can do anything.*

"Are you going to be all right, Cadi?"

She turned and found Bailey regarding her with a concerned expression. "I'll be fine," she said with more confidence than she felt. "This is nothing like the horrible rushing water that my family and I were caught in when I was a kid." She glanced at the gray sky. "I just hope the rain holds off."

"We've got to be done by the time it's dark," Will repeated. "There's no power in this area. We'll need to take flashlights."

Jeff clapped his hands then rubbed his palms together. "Let's get our gear and go."

After pulling on protective waders and collecting their flashlights, the Disaster Busters team made its way into the deluge. Cadi's pulse raced with each step she took, but she kept reminding herself that people needed her help and that an almighty God walked right along with her.

❦

After four hours of sleep and two cups of strong coffee, Frank felt like a new man. While the kids ate supper at their grandparents' next door, he opened his Bible and read several chapters. He was amazed at the way his skewed world righted itself once he allowed God's Word to steer his thought processes.

He phoned Cadi, intending to begin with an apology, but only reached her voice mail. Either she was really angry, Frank reasoned, or she couldn't hear her cell phone. Knowing Cadi, he figured it was more the latter since she was forgiving to a fault. But would she agree to continue their relationship, or had he finally crossed the line with the way he'd handled the Binder insurance check situation?

Lord, I hope I didn't do permanent damage here.

He mulled things over and remembered Cadi saying this morning that she'd left a message for him. Locating his cell phone, Frank accessed his messages. He listened to her lengthy recording in which she canceled their plans this weekend because of the flood situation across the state. He heard the apprehension in her voice, and his chest constricted at the thought that he'd let her down. Instead of encouragement, he had most likely added to her stress. He wondered what he could do to make it up to her.

He paced the living room floor and shot up an arrow of a prayer for wisdom. Flowers and candy wouldn't do the trick, because Cadi was out of town. She couldn't be reached by phone.

I'll just have to find her and tell her in person.

Tell her what?

Frank stopped and placed his hands on his hips. He figured he'd start off by apologizing for his boorish behavior this morning. He'd let Cadi know he was wrong for questioning her integrity and that he—well, he just couldn't imagine his life without her.

His home phone jangled, and he answered it at once, hoping it might be Cadi. Instead, it was another sheriff's deputy.

"Hey, listen, I know you're off duty," the officer began, "but I've got this lady here—Mrs. Binder."

"She's there? At the office?" Frank felt a heavy frown settle on his brows. "What's going on?"

"She says it's urgent that she speak with you. She says you know the situation."

"Yeah, okay. Put her on." Frank drew in a deep breath and lowered himself onto the couch. Moments later, he heard Mrs. Binder's gentle but determined voice.

"Deputy Parker, I won't need to press charges. I have my money."

Surprised by the turn of events, Frank sat forward and prompted her to continue.

"Well, you see, on the day my check arrived, I had a hair appointment. The post office closed at noon, seeing it was a Saturday, so my, um, gentleman friend," she said, sounding suddenly bashful, "offered to pick up my mail. When he saw that my check had come, he walked over to the beauty parlor and had me sign it. Then he dashed to the bank to cash it because the bank also closes earlier on Saturday. Well, I suppose you know that. Anyway, he gave me the money, but I scarcely recall him doing so because I was engrossed in a very important conversation with Lorna Flores. She heads up the committee for our quilting club."

Frank couldn't help a small grin.

"Needless to say, that explains my chicken scratch of a signature. I wasn't paying attention to what I was doing. Later on, after I arrived home, I changed purses, although I never did see the envelope with the money that I had zipped into the side pocket for safekeeping."

He cringed, imagining the scenario. "Just a word of warning for the future, Mrs. Binder: You should never carry such a large sum in your purse or keep it in your home."

"Yes, I know. You're absolutely right. The bank is the safest place. But, you see, my account isn't with the bank in Wind Lake. My gentleman friend does his financial business there and the girls all know him. They call him Grampa Grapes." She laughed. "His last name is Grapenwald."

Frank recognized the name immediately. "Are you referring to Harold Grapenwald? He worked as a janitor and general handyman at the high school until he retired. He's known around town as a guy who'll help anybody and who can fix almost anything."

"That's Harold." Mrs. Binder sounded both pleased and proud. "Anyway," she said, her voice growing solemn once more, "the long and short of it is, he thought he was doing me a favor even though I could have just as easily taken the check to my own bank that following Monday."

"I see." Frank saw no reason not to believe her, as careless and ridiculous as it might seem to him. After all, he'd heard stranger explanations in his line of work. He'd learned truth was definitely weirder than fiction.

"I told Harold about my visit to your office today." A short pause. "He's been on a fishing trip in Canada and just got back. I haven't talked to him in weeks—until this afternoon. When I mentioned pressing charges against Cadi, he reminded me that he'd cashed the check for me."

"You understand, Mrs. Binder, that's it's a serious thing to accuse someone of theft and forgery." Frank felt as if he were reprimanding himself as well as the older woman.

"I realize that, although it's not like I dragged Cadi's name through the mud. I've only discussed this matter with two close friends, one being Harold. They're both aware the incident is no fault of Cadi's."

Frank felt appeased.

"I'm terribly sorry for any trouble I caused," she continued. "Chalk it up to an old man's good intentions and an old woman's less-than-perfect memory."

"We all forget things, even important things. Doesn't matter what age we are." He felt immensely relieved that the money had been found, but now he was doubly determined to speak with Cadi as soon as possible.

"Thank you for your understanding," Mrs. Binder said. "I'm very embarrassed, and I'll have you know I deposited the money into my bank account this afternoon."

"Good. Thanks for calling. I'm glad everything worked out."

The phone conversation ended, and Frank sat back on the sofa, forming a plan. He fired off another quick prayer that Lois would agree to babysit for the weekend. His parents could probably help out, as well.

He raked his hand through his short-cropped hair. His mind was made up. He stood and walked next door, letting himself into the house. The kids came running to greet him.

"Are we going to Cadi's now?"

Frank saw the excitement in his son's eyes and hated to disappoint him. "Cadi's not home this weekend. She got called out of town on business."

A frown of disappointment furrowed the boy's sun-streaked brows. "But she bought a new video game for me."

"There'll be time in the days ahead to play it, I'm sure." Frank saw that Lois had entered the room. He looked her way. "Cadi is assisting with the rescue operations near Fort Dodge. Major flooding over in that area. I'd like to go find her and maybe lend a hand."

"Can we come, too, Daddy?"

"No, Em." He swung the little girl up into his arms. "It's too dangerous. But I'd like to go. . . ." He looked at Lois again.

"If you're asking in a roundabout way if I'll watch my grandchildren this weekend, you know I will." She stared at him with tight-lipped acquiescence. "I know how important this woman is to you."

"Yes, she's important to me."

Lois shifted her stance and slipped her slender hands into the pockets of her denim slacks. "I guess she's a nice enough person."

Frank smiled, feeling both shocked and elated by the positive remark. "How did you come to realize that?"

"She won *you* over, didn't she?"

"Sure did." He smiled.

"The biggest thing I noticed," Lois said, "is that she's succeeded where we, your family, and friends have failed. God used her to draw you back to church and back into His Word. For that reason alone, I've decided Cadi's a special person."

"She is. She's very special." Frank felt like his mother-in-law's comments were affirmation for tonight's plans. He knew he was doing the right thing, even if it meant driving hours in the rain in order to talk to Cadi.

He looked at Dustin and Emily. "You two behave for your grandma. I've got my phone, and you can call me." He hesitated for a moment. "Maybe you can talk to Cadi, too, if she's not busy."

And if she's still speaking to me, he added silently.

Chapter 20

Cadi glanced up just as large droplets of rain fell from the darkening sky. By now the floodwater was hip-high in some areas on the street, and every muscle in her body ached. Her legs felt waterlogged. For a good part of the afternoon, she and her team helped people pack some of their belongings and cajoled others who insisted on staying. So far as Cadi knew, everyone on the cul-de-sac had evacuated.

All except the Manskis, who'd changed their minds at the last minute. They'd been bent on staying until their neighbors convinced them otherwise. And now, as Cadi carried boxes out of their house and loaded them into an aluminum rowboat that Mr. Manski had stored in his garage, she prayed they'd finish before the last of their daylight vanished.

"Okay, is that it?" She heaved a box over the side of the small, floating craft.

"Well, let me think. . . ."

Cadi suppressed a groan as the middle-aged woman began to ponder for the umpteenth time. She sat in the boat while her husband stood in the water at the helm, ready to pull his wife and property to higher ground. Unfortunately, his better half was having trouble making up her mind about what to take and what to leave behind. Cadi felt trapped between Mr. Manski's impatience and his wife's indecision.

"Mrs. Manski, there's really no time left." Cadi knew that, at the request of the fire chief, the Disaster Busters crew, along with the last of the emergency personnel, had vacated the cul-de-sac almost forty-five minutes ago. None of the Disaster Busters team knew she had stayed behind to help, and she could only imagine how frantic Meg, Will, Jeff, and Bailey would be as they searched for her. It didn't, however, match her own escalating fear of being in floodwater after dark.

"Look," she told the Manskis, "this is our opportunity to get out of here safely. We need to go."

A bolt of anxiety shot through Cadi when she thought again of the late hour, the rain, and the murky river water. Even so, she felt sure she'd manage if she held on to the boat and the Manskis were with her.

"Maybe I should take—oh, wait—I guess those items can stay, too."

"We're leaving Anita," her husband said. "No more stuff."

"I agree." Cadi peered down the long street, but because of the bend in the road and the encroaching darkness, she couldn't see the other rescue personnel.

"Wait." Anita Manski began to push to her feet.

"Don't stand up!" Cadi's heart did a flip as she imagined the petite woman falling overboard and cracking her head on some unseen object.

"Honey, I moved a lot of stuff upstairs." The man pulled off his baseball cap and rubbed his balding head. "You can make a list of what you want and I'll get it tomorrow."

Cadi wanted to encourage that call to action. "Good plan, Mr. Manski." She grabbed hold of the stern. "I'll push, you pull."

"Oh, my purse. I've got to have my purse." Anita Manski swung her gaze from Cadi to her husband. "My medication and my wallet are in there along with my cell phone and address book."

Sam Manski fired off a string of obscenities that burned Cadi's ears. "If you think I'm going to fetch it," he added, "you're out of your mind."

"Well, maybe we should have just stayed put."

"Too late for that now!"

"Please, stop bickering. I'll go back into the house and get the purse." Cadi realized it might be foolish to waste already borrowed time, but if Mrs. Manski required her medication, *someone* had to retrieve it.

"You'll need the keys," the older woman said. "Sam, give her the house keys."

He trudged around and placed his thick key ring in Cadi's palm. "Make it snappy, okay?"

"You got it."

"My purse is on the dining room buffet. It's a fawn-colored, leather handbag."

"It's a suitcase," her husband groused.

Maybe we should have used it as a floatation device. Cadi tried not to huff about it as she waded through the water and climbed the wooden porch steps. Inside the Cape Cod home, she strained to see in the unlit rooms. Only too late did she realize she'd left her flashlight in the boat with the Manskis. She hadn't been able to carry the large flashlight and boxes, too, so she'd set down the battery-powered light and then forgotten it. Unfortunately for her, there wasn't time to go back out to the boat and retrieve it. She'd have to fumble her way through the place and find Mrs. Manski's purse.

She gazed around. Everything was unfamiliar, yet she recalled glimpsing the dining room to the left of the front door.

She felt her way to what she believed was the buffet and knocked into an object that clanged against the floor. She winced, hesitated, then moved on.

Hurry. I have to hurry.

She continued to feel her way through the room.

No purse.

She touched her way to the other side and tried again, but this time she tripped over something and fell. Unhurt, she pushed to her feet. Seconds later, she recognized the object over which she'd just stumbled: the leather handbag!

Relief engulfed her as Cadi lifted the heavy purse, slinging its strap over her shoulder. She picked her way back through the house. When she reached the porch, the dense downpour combined with the water lapping against the steps gave her great pause. She tried to see beyond the sheets of rain but couldn't make out a single thing, and she wasn't about to wade into the blackness of the floodwater on her own.

"Mr. and Mrs. Manski? I found the purse!"

She listened for a reply.

Nothing but the din of the falling rain.

She called again, but no one answered.

Once more. But no response.

In the next moment, Cadi came head-to-head with her worst nightmare: She was stranded, alone, with darkness surrounding her, and the river rising.

❧

"Cadi's missing!"

"What?" Frank exited the SUV and pulled the hood of his rain gear over his head. He stared at Meg. He could see she'd been out in the elements for some time, and her plastic poncho was of little use anymore. "What do you mean she's missing?"

"We were helping with the evacuation," she said, throwing a thumb over her shoulder. "We were supposed to quit when it got dark, and we agreed to meet at the checkpoint, but Cadi hasn't shown up. Jeff was the last one to see her. He said she was at the end of the block, on the cul-de-sac, helping people gather up their stuff. He thought she was right behind him, but apparently she wasn't. Next we located the folks she'd been assisting, the Manskis. They said they assumed she'd followed them to higher ground." Meg's voice strained from unshed emotion. "Obviously she didn't, and now we can't find her!"

"She's not in the lodge?" Frank had been in the facility but hadn't bothered to look around. He'd been told emergency personnel were downhill a ways from the campsite.

"We've searched the lodge twice. No sign of Cadi. But I was just on my way up there again for another look when I ran into you."

"Here, take my vehicle; don't walk." He handed her the keys. "Where's everyone else?"

Meg turned and pointed to her distant left. "Jeff and Will volunteered to hunt for Cadi, but the cops won't let them beyond the barricades. Orders from headquarters and all that."

"That seems odd. Why wouldn't they form a rescue party to locate Cadi?"

"Because it's not a mandatory evacuation situation. Some residents chose to stay in their homes, flooded or not. The cops feel Cadi's safe until morning, but. . ." Meg almost choked on her words, and Frank knew she was extremely upset. "But they don't know Cadi's history. If she's out there, even if she's safe, she's got to be terrified."

"I agree." Frank wiped the rain out of his eyes and reran the information through his mind. It pained him to think of Cadi trapped in what was obviously a frightening situation for her.

Lord, please protect her.

Frank urged Meg into the shelter of his SUV and suggested she drive to the lodge and dry out for a while.

"And don't worry," he added. "We'll find Cadi."

He walked the rest of the way down the road and spotted the three remaining Disaster Busters members. They filled him in, stating, just as Meg had, that Cadi was still somewhere out in the flooded area.

"It's my fault." Jeff had to raise his voice to be heard above the downpour. "I told her earlier this afternoon to face her fears. She was probably trying to prove something and pushed herself further than she should have."

"Well, let's not jump to conclusions." Frank noticed none of them laid any blame on him for Cadi's disappearance. He wondered if they knew about this morning's confrontation. He felt responsible for her, and he realized he'd never forgive himself if the unspeakable happened to Cadi. He had to find her.

He eyed the officers standing guard at the barricades. He wondered if he knew any of them. Often enough he crossed paths with state troopers, police, and other sheriff's deputies, both within Iowa and out of state. A unique camaraderie existed among officers of the law, and Frank felt fairly confident he could enlist their help.

He looked at Bailey. She had obviously assumed his thoughts.

"When we last saw her, Cadi was unharmed, so they said if she's stranded, we'll have to wait until morning to get her. Emergency crews say there's no imminent danger, such as ruptured gas and electrical lines. All power to the area has been shut off. Even so, they won't let anyone back into the area because of safety concerns. Sounds like an oxymoron to me."

"Well, I can see their point," Frank said, although he understood Bailey's side, too. "Someone might slip and fall and drown, and then the family could sue the city, county, and state for not protecting its citizens."

"I get it, Frank. But I can't handle the thought of Cadi cold and wet and scared to death all night. We have to do *something*."

He heartily agreed. "How deep is the water down there?"

"Not too bad," Will replied. "Maybe three feet high."

"That's bad enough," Bailey argued.

Frank rubbed his jaw, contemplating. "And you're sure Cadi's down this particular street?"

"Yep. I saw her carrying boxes from the last house on the right," Jeff said.

An idea formed. He glanced at the officers again and then back at the trio beside him.

"Listen, why don't you all head to the lodge, warm up inside, and give me some time? Say, an hour? I'll meet you up there, and maybe I'll have more answers."

❧

Cadi sat just inside the front entrance of the Manskis' home. She shivered and watched the veil of rain pour from the sky. She leaned her aching back up against the wall and, as she mulled over the events of the last ten hours, she deemed it a bad day all around.

She concluded she'd overreacted this morning with Frank. Why didn't she soothe away all his doubts instead of becoming defensive? Now she could only hope and pray he'd believe she was innocent and forgive her childish fit of temper.

Next she'd let the Manskis manipulate her, and then she'd defied the law by lingering in an area that was off-limits after nightfall. Now she faced the consequences. She hated to think how worried her friends were—and all because she didn't do what she knew was right!

Assessing her present situation once more, Cadi wondered if she could work up the courage to duck into the rain and walk up the street. Sounded easy enough. But then the gravity of the situation struck her and she envisioned the pitch-black night and the water swirling around her, and she decided there was no amount of courage on earth that would propel her through all that. She could scream for help, but no one would hear her above the rain, and she'd likely drain the last of her energy, just upsetting herself further.

She reached into her sweatshirt pocket and pulled out her cell phone. She tried to place a call again, but just as before, it was no use. No signal.

So, now what? Ride it out and wait until morning?

Cadi closed her eyes and prayed. She willed herself to relax. Breathe. Think of something positive. A picnic with Frank and his kids on a gorgeous summer day. No rain. Just sunny, cloudless skies. No angry words. Only mutual adulation.

"Cadi!"

She snapped to attention. She listened. Had she imagined it?

"Cadi!"

The voice was unmistakably Frank's, and moments later she flinched as a bright beam shone in her eyes. It moved away then returned, illuminating the open entryway of the home.

She squinted. "Frank, is that you?"

"Yep." His voice grew closer.

Disbelief and joy swept over her. She shielded her eyes from the blinding light as he approached. "What are you doing here?"

"Courting disaster. What does it look like?"

Cadi almost laughed.

Almost.

Instead, she stood and hurried onto the porch. She met him on the stairs and threw her arms around him. She pressed her cheek against his cold, wet jaw. "I've never been so happy to see anyone in my life!"

"I was hoping you'd say that." She felt his strong arm close around her waist as he held her.

She took great comfort in the fact that he didn't seem angry. Nevertheless, she owed him an apology.

"I'm sorry about this morning. I have such a hotheaded temper. My mouth runs off without my—"

He silenced her with a kiss. "Cadi, I'm the one who should be saying I'm sorry. I never should have doubted you—you, of all people."

"You trust me? You really do?"

"Yes, Cadi, I do."

Sudden tears obscured her vision, and her pent-up emotions gave way.

"Shh, don't cry." He held her for several long moments more before moving back a few paces. "I think we'd best finish this conversation later."

She sniffed.

He pulled an orange floatation device off his forearm. "I managed to get this life jacket, and I could have waited while some officers rustled up a boat for me to use, but I figured by the time they found one, I could have fetched you and been back on higher ground." He slipped the preserver over her head and secured it.

"Ready?"

"No, wait." Cadi remembered Mrs. Manski's purse and Mr. Manski's keys. She ran into the house, grabbed the items, and returned to the porch steps.

"All set?"

"Yes."

He took her hand and led her down each step; however, she made the mistake of glancing across the ominous body of water. Panic gripped her as memories of her childhood disaster overwhelmed her common sense. She froze and looped her arm around the last rung of the rail.

"What's the matter?"

"I—I can't do this," she stammered.

"Yes, you can. I've got a secure hold on you." He gave her hand a squeeze.

"And a few yards away, the water's shallower. This is the deepest part." He paused and gently tugged at her arm. "Come on. You'll be fine."

Cadi's mouth felt parched and her throat tight, making a reply impossible.

Frank stepped in beside her and placed his lips close to her ear. "There's no way I'll let anything happen to you." He placed a kiss on the side of her head. "I can't imagine my life without you, Cadi, and that's the honest truth. I don't know when it happened—maybe the first minute I saw you in Wind Lake, but I'm in love with you."

Her fears dissipated. She turned to stare at him while happiness swelled inside of her. She'd dreamed of hearing him say that he loved her, and now her dream had come true.

She let go of the railing and clung to him. "I love you, too, Frank."

She wanted to say more, much more, but he suddenly moved with lightning speed. He whisked her off the step, into the blinding rain, and through the water. Before she could react, they'd reached the shallowest section of the flooded street. Several more steps and their feet were no longer submerged, but on wet pavement. The last of her fear evaporated, although her limbs felt weak from the hours of physical labor and the chill from the water.

She stopped to catch her breath. "That was some kind of trick, but it worked. You got me off the porch."

He caught her gaze and held it. Cadi could just barely see the meaningful glint in his eyes.

"Just for the record, I meant every word."

Her joy was renewed.

"Let's get out of this rain. Think you can make it up the hill?" Frank shined the flashlight toward the wet asphalt highway.

She smiled and nodded. "With you at my side and God in my heart, I think I can make it anywhere."

She clutched Frank's hand, her fingers entwined with his, and she held on tight as they made their way to the lodge.

Epilogue

Fresh, springtime floral arrangements stood in cut-glass vases near the altar, and pleated white paper wedding bells hung from Riverview Bible Church's vaulted ceiling. The pews filled with enthusiastic friends and relatives who had come to share this special day, uniting for life Frank Allen Parker and Cadence Renee Trent.

In one of the back dressing rooms, Cadi smoothed the skirt of the white satin and lace gown, a creation her great-aunt had taken pleasure in sewing.

"You look absolutely stunning," Aunt Lou said, tears brimming in her eyes.

Cadi hugged her great-aunt long and hard. "Thank you—thank you for everything."

"I'm as proud as any mother of the bride."

Pulling back, Cadi dabbed her own eyes. "Let's not start crying now. We'll look all puffy for the pictures."

"You're right." Aunt Lou sniffed and swatted an errant tear.

The prelude began, the music wafting through the church's elaborate sound system. Lois Chayton, Dustin and Emmie's grandmother, appeared at the door.

"Everyone's ready." Her eyes twinkled with happiness.

Over the months, Cadi had gotten better acquainted with Lois. Despite her gruffness, Cadi discovered that Lois had a caring nature and a genuine love for the Lord. Children adored her, so Lois's in-home day care was both a fitting and successful business venture. What's more, Cadi felt pleased she'd included Lois in the wedding party. She made a fantastic wedding director, and she wasn't shy about ordering people into their places.

"You're on," Lois said.

Cadi took Aunt Lou's arm, and they strolled through the hallway and into the expansive lobby. Bailey and Jeff, the last of the bridal party to walk down the aisle, were already halfway to the altar.

The wedding march began to play, and Cadi couldn't believe the moment she had dreamed of for so long was finally at hand. Her groom awaited her, looking dapper in his dark tux. Dustin and Emmie stood beside him, looking like miniature versions of the bride and groom.

An usher laid out the white bridal runner, and then Aunt Lou escorted

Cadi to the front of the sanctuary. Cadi hardly noticed their friends and family crowded into the many rows of padded seats as her gaze affixed to Frank's. He seemed to fill every one of her senses.

They reached the altar, and after her aunt "gave her away," Cadi slipped her hand around Frank's elbow. Both Pastor Dremond and Pastor Connor took a turn challenging Frank and Cadi in their new life together. Next they recited their vows, and finally the pastors pronounced them united in matrimony.

Pastor Dremond gave Frank a wry smile. "You may kiss your bride."

Frank turned and cupped Cadi's face with his hands. "My beautiful, sassy bride," he whispered with a mix of adoration and amusement shining in his dark eyes.

"My handsome hero."

They kissed, and Cadi decided her weak knees and heart's song were more than part of a fairy-tale finale to a perfect wedding ceremony. Rather, they signified her entire happily-ever-after as Mrs. Frank Parker.

THE SUPERHEROES
NEXT DOOR

Chapter 1

*P*erfect.

Ciara Rome scrutinized the row of two-story, red brick townhouses that spanned an entire block and concluded she'd made the right decision in renting the fourth home from the corner for the summer. A quiet neighborhood in a gated condo community was exactly what she wanted.

Several birds twittered in a nearby treetop, and a breeze caressed her face and neck. Only the gentle rustling of leafy branches could be heard.

Just perfect!

Gathering her belongings from her compact car, Cici's mind fast-forwarded to August when she anticipated handing in her master's thesis, all spit and polished, to an extremely pleased professor. How proud Professor Agnes Carter-Hill would be of her work. It had taken Cici years to nurture her theme and collect the evidence to support it. In all diligence, she'd persevered, completing the master's program at a university here in Iowa. She'd honed her supposition and then, with Aggie's guidance, she'd refined it. *The inconsequential effects of paternal absence on infants, preschool children, and teenagers.*

Essentially her hypothesis surmised that the male gender was unessential to quality childrearing, and it, of course, reflected Cici's personal belief as her mother had raised her single-handedly. Her father had left them when Cici was twelve. He moved away, never to be seen or heard from again. But who needed him, anyway? She and Mom had done all right for themselves. Mom had a decent-paying job as a supervisor for a housekeeping company in Nevada, and Cici was on the verge of attaining her master's degree.

She just needed to force herself to sit at the keyboard and write up her thesis. And this peaceful subdivision would provide the perfect sabbatical in which to write it.

With the thick strap of her pink and black leather laptop case slung over her shoulder, Cici traipsed to the front door of the condo. She pulled her wheeled luggage behind her, then stopped and fished the key out of her jeans pocket. She could hardly wait to settle in and get started. She felt suddenly glad that her friend Jennifer Hargrove decided to rent out her condo while she celebrated her graduation with a trip across Europe with her fiancé and a few other couples they knew from their church. Cici had felt jealous that Jen earned her degree first, but the short-lived negative response soon gave way to genuine happiness and, once her own thesis was completed, Cici would celebrate her graduation. Then with any luck, she'd acquire a great-paying position within the Iowa Department of Education. She loved children and cared deeply about their welfare. She didn't need to trudge through foreign countries; a job with the Iowa DOE would be reward enough for her.

"Um, excuse me. . ."

Cici stood poised with the key in the door and was about to turn the lock when she heard a woman's voice coming up behind her.

She turned with a start and watched as a middle-aged woman with a stocky frame ambled up Jen's walkway.

"Pardon me. I didn't mean to give you a fright."

"Oh, um, no problem." Cici ran a hand over the top of her head, wondering if the woman had put a few gray hairs in its natural auburn color.

"I'm Roberta Rawlings. Welcome to Blossomwood Estates." She smiled and lifted her chin. Her gold and black animal print outfit seemed to accentuate her coppery eyes. "I'm the community director."

"Nice to meet you." Cici smiled politely. "I'm Ciara Rome. Cici for short. I'm renting Jennifer Hargrove's townhouse for the summer."

"Yes, I know." The older woman carefully tucked a lock of her chin-length brown hair behind her ear. "It's my job to know the comings and goings around here. It's what makes our community a safe one." Her smile grew. "And a fun one. I organize all the events, too."

Cici arched her brows. "Events?" Jen never said anything about organized events.

"Yes. We call it our Condo Club, and we have various social functions within our little community at least once a week. Practically everyone attends the functions."

"I see." Cici noticed the gleam of expectancy in Roberta's brown eyes and tried not to shudder. The last thing Cici wanted—or needed—was a social function forced upon her. Not when she had a thesis to write by August.

"I hope you won't be a stranger."

"I guess I can try to show up." Cici didn't want to seem unsociable and inadvertently tarnish Jen's good name with her neighbors.

"The Condo Club's next get-together is Friday evening."

Cici had a hunch the woman wouldn't take "no" for an answer.

"We'll have food and some fun games for the kids," she persisted. "I imagine you're eager to meet your neighbors. I mean, a woman should always know who's living next door." Roberta stepped closer. "For security purposes, of course."

"Oh, right."

"A woman can't be too careful these days."

"I suppose that's true enough."

Roberta replied with a curt nod as if to say, "Of course it is." Next, she shifted her stance. "Well, here's your welcome packet. The dates for all the events are listed in the folder."

"Thanks."

Cici watched Roberta turn and sashay down the walk, her skinny high-heeled shoes smacking on the cement with each step. With a sigh, Cici returned her attention to the front door and unlocked it. Cool, still air met her as she entered the condo.

Alone at last!

She took in the familiar surroundings and missed her friend all over again. She and Jen met in college at Iowa State University, located north of the city of Des Moines. They were best friends and did everything together, from adjusting to dorm life to making a home out of their first apartment. They'd studied, occasionally double-dated, and even spent holidays with each other's families. Cici's family consisted of only herself and Mom, but Jen made up for it because she was like the sister Cici never had.

Closing the door behind her, she walked through the adequately sized living room and made her way up the carpeted steps. Seeing the framed collage of Jen's family members and friends, Cici remembered back to that happy day when she and Jen had earned their bachelor's degrees. Later, they each decided to go on for their master's. However, something weird happened to Jen about two years ago: She found religion. Things just hadn't been quite the same since. Suddenly Jen no longer enjoyed frequenting their favorite nightclubs. Instead she found pleasure in going to church, of all things! Cici had visited a few "worship services" with her friend and found it inspiring in many ways, although it certainly wasn't her idea of a good time. She mentioned the experience to Aggie, who took an intellectual approach to Jen's finding faith in God. "Religion is a crutch upon which weak and narrow-minded people need to lean."

Cici wondered over her professor's remark ever since. Jen never seemed "weak and narrow-minded" before. But was she really? Had friendship blinded Cici to the fact?

Still deep in thought, she ambled into the master bedroom where she deposited her luggage. The yellow room felt bright and sunny. The beautiful multicolored quilt Jen had purchased at a local craft fair covered the queen-size bed. Cici took note of the large framed artwork hanging above it. Where had Jen found the atrocious thing? The print depicted a host of angels, warring in the heavens, while below an entire town went about its business, oblivious to the battle going on beyond the clouds.

Dramatic. Wonder what Aggie would have to say about it. Cici felt her lips curve upward in a smirk. Her distinguished professor would, no doubt, liken the artwork to some sort of cartoon.

But would she be right?

Cici shook off her musing and gazed around the bedroom. She paused at Jen's mirrored dresser. Several framed photographs adorned its polished oak surface. Making her way over, Cici lifted the picture of Jen standing beside her fiancé, William. Not Bill. Not Will. *William.* He was a husky, blond, Bible-quoting and -toting guy, and Jen was head over heels in love with him.

With a long sigh, Cici set the photo back in its place. As dogmatic as William could be about his faith, he seemed like a decent human being. What's more, her best friend loved him, so that was all the reason Cici needed to like the man. In fact, she looked forward to standing up in their wedding in October.

My thesis will be done long before then. I'll have completed another goal in life. . . .

Leaving the bedroom, she walked across the hallway and entered the second bedroom, which served as both a guest room and Jen's office. An oak-framed daybed was pushed against the length of one wall, and the rest of the space was occupied by a desk, bookcase, file cabinet, and built-in shelves on the wall. It looked completely functional. But best of all, it would be quiet, unlike the apartment Cici shared with two other friends. Jen had been the fourth roommate until she purchased this condo over a year ago. Cici often teased her, saying that she'd never forgive her for moving out and leaving Cici to fend for herself against Bridget and Tanya, two fun-loving females who enjoyed attending parties and nightclubs more than their classes at the university. However, they were honest, caring, loyal friends, and they paid their share of the rent on time. Even so, Cici understood Jen's need for her own place—a place she could call home. She'd found it here in this condo. . . .

And someday, Cici vowed, she'd have that, too. A home of her own—

Just as soon as she wrote her thesis.

❧

Luke Weldon sat on the edge of the bathtub, helping his three young sons dry off and get into their pajamas. Exhaustion weighted his every limb, every muscle. He felt as though he'd melt down the side of the tub and land in a pool of fatigue all over the ceramic tile floor. He'd worked all day, trying to keep clients happy with their software products, but he still had more to do. His sister-in-law had only been able to watch the boys for a few hours this afternoon, and while he was grateful for the help, it hadn't been long enough. Now he'd be forced to work all night—once he got the kids to sleep, that is.

Another all-nighter. That was the trouble with a home-based business. A guy couldn't pack up and leave the office at the end of the day. Instead, his business followed him day and night.

He glanced at the happy, earnest expressions on his kids' faces as they raced to be the first one in their pj's. Devin, of course, would win—as he usually did. At the mature and responsible age of six and a half, he was eighteen months older than his twin brothers, Aaron and Brian. He was his daddy's helper—but they all were. They'd had to be—ever since that tragic night when Alissa was killed.

He squeezed his eyes closed. *Why, God? Why did that accident have to happen? Most of all, why couldn't I have been enough for her—me and our babies?*

Luke stymied his thoughts. He'd asked those questions a million times since Alissa's death, and he knew from experience that such inquiries only brought on a selfish pity party. Luke had no time for those. Not anymore.

Father, forgive me for questioning Your sovereignty. Silently Luke added Job's words. *"I know that You can do all things; no plan of yours can be thwarted."*

"I win!"

Luke snapped his attention to dark-haired Devin, who stood with his arms up in victory. He was in his Spiderman pj's while Brian and Aaron tied for second place, one wearing Batman pajamas and the other, Superman.

"Come on, heroes," Devin declared, bolting out of the bathroom. "We've got work to do."

The younger boys followed, arms stretched out, pretending they were flying.

Luke grinned and sopped up the water that had spilled over from the "rub-a-dub-dub, three men in a tub" bath time and hung the wet towels over the ceramic wall racks to dry. He gathered up the plastic toys and put them in a netted bag hooked over the faucet.

Then he sucked in a breath and blew it out again. His sons were whooping it up, and he knew what they were up to.

"Better not be jumping on my bed." Luke had to grin in spite of himself.

Laughter turned to whispers and giggles.

Praying for a second wind, Luke made his way down the hallway and into his room where precious faces peered up at him. He recognized the mischief shining in all three pairs of deep brown eyes.

"You were jumping on my bed, weren't you?" Luke placed his hands on his hips, trying to act stern.

The boys just looked at him.

"Won't fess up, huh? Fine. Now you're all going to get it."

He inched forward and feigned a menacing expression. All three boys grinned in anticipation. They knew what was coming. When Luke reached the bed, he shot out his hands and tickled them all at the same time while flinging his own body over the width of the king-size bed. The boys jumped all over him like puppies, squealing in delight.

Ignoring the protests from his weary body, Luke laughed and played with abandon.

Chapter 2

All she wanted was some peace and quiet! Was that really too much to ask?

First Roberta Rawlings' phone message this morning, reminding her about the get-together on Friday and then these kids next door.

Cici lazed back in the tan leather chair and tossed her silver-plated, monogrammed pen onto the desk. Frustration caused her temples to throb. She'd put up with the noise next door all day; she was tempted to contact Roberta Rawlings—or even e-mail Jen—and complain. Cici had wanted a sabbatical and now here she sat, making corrections on her printed copy before she typed them into her laptop computer. The only problem was the rambunctious children next door. Jen had also failed to mention her noisy neighbors.

The boisterous laughter reverberated from behind the shared wall of the connected homes. She imagined at least a dozen of them over there, jumping on the beds and throwing pillows and toys. It sounded as though they'd soon come bursting through the plaster and land in her office.

A thunderous *boom* sounded, rattling the picture on the wall above the desk. Then Cici heard a horrendous *crash*. Sudden silence followed, and she figured the kids must have broken something. Where in the world was their mother?

Things on the other side of the wall remained quiet, and the opportunity to get back to work presented itself, but Cici's concentration had been hopelessly broken. She stared, unseeing, at the computer screen in front of her and forced herself to imagine how terrific she'd feel when she handed in her completed thesis. She envisioned reaching her goal.

I can do this. Cici tried to psych herself up and dive into her work again. However, she couldn't keep from wondering if the children next door were all right. What if they'd been left alone? She'd heard countless reports about parents leaving their kids unattended. What if the youngsters burned the place down?

Fear gripped her. What if that really happened and her computer was damaged in the fire? What if she lost her thesis and all her research?

A sense of urgency shot through her, and Cici stood. As she made her way downstairs, she became engaged in self-debate. Was this really a good idea? She didn't want to be a busybody neighbor. Then again, she didn't want the children's welfare endangered, not to mention anyone else's if something disastrous did occur.

It's about being responsible, she finally reasoned.

Her mind made up, she opened the back door and stepped out onto the cement-slab patio. Cici inhaled the fresh air and noticed the sky was a perfect blue. The sunshine spilled into the spacious yard and glittered off something on the wooden play structure with its swings, bright yellow slide, and colorful awning. The kid in Cici begged for release, but she squelched it like she'd done ever since she was twelve. After her dad left, Cici grew up fast. She'd had to.

Painful memories threatened, but she quickly shook them off and focused on her thesis—and the very reason she was trekking over to her next-door neighbor's house.

She walked around the cedar partition that separated the two patios and provided a bit of privacy from the adjoining two-story condo. She reached the neighbor's white-paneled back door and rang the bell. A full minute ticked by during which she swatted at several pesky flies. Pressing the doorbell again, she continued to wait until, finally, a dark-haired child with large, curious brown eyes opened the door and peered through the crack.

"Hi." Cici cleared her throat. "I'm living next door, and—"

The door opened wider and a taller but similar-looking child stared back at her. Cici spotted their blue jeans, shirtless chests, and then noticed the blankets tied around their necks. She hid a grin.

Suddenly another little fellow appeared, shouting, "We're defenders of the universe!"

He ran back inside, disappearing as fast as he'd shown up.

Cici's amusement fled as she glanced at the two remaining caped crusaders. She imagined the lack of control in the house. "Who's watching over you kids?"

"Jesus!" the smaller boy shouted out as if he were answering a Sunday school quiz question.

Cici refrained from rolling her eyes. Things here might be worse than she imagined. "Is there a *real* adult in the house?" If not, she planned to call Social Services.

"Can I help you?"

A man, tall with a medium build and the most incredible mahogany brown eyes Cici had ever seen, suddenly stood at the door. His dark hair fell over his forehead and ears, spilling onto his neck in a stylishly mussed but masculine fashion.

The two boys scampered away and the man, who appeared every inch a "real adult," stepped forward. He wore a light blue button-down shirt that hung over faded jeans.

"I'm Luke Weldon. What can I do for you?"

"Well, um, I just moved in next door. I'm—"

"Ciara." A broad smile split Luke's suntanned face. "Jen told me you were coming for the summer." He unlocked the screen door and swung it open. "Come on in."

Stunned, Cici fought the invitation. She'd come over here to complain about the noise, after all. "I'm working on my master's thesis, and—"

"Yeah, yeah, come on in before the flies do." Lightly touching Cici's elbow, he steered her toward the kitchen. "My kids have been eating their frozen juice treats outside, and I haven't had a chance to hose off the patio, so the flies are fierce."

"So I noticed." Cici forced a polite smile. She took in her surroundings, noticing the dishes piled in the sink and the partially eaten peanut butter and jelly sandwiches left on paper plates on the round kitchen table. "How many kids live here?"

"Three."

Only three?

Luke seemed to follow her gaze. "Pardon the mess. I've been repairing a software program all morning. It's not doing what I designed it to and, needless to say, the company that purchased it hasn't been pleased. But I think I've got it up and running now. I could use a little break." He made his way to the refrigerator. "Want a soda?"

"No, thanks. The truth is I've been working on my master's thesis all morning and—"

"So you could use a break, too, huh?" He flipped open a soda can and took a swig. "I'm glad you came over to get acquainted."

"Well, to tell you the truth, I—"

The volume on the television suddenly soared to a deafening blare. Cici jumped. One of the kids ran into the kitchen, his little face masked with concern as if a true crisis were at hand.

"Dad, Aaron's playing with the remote again!" He ran back into the living room.

"Scuse me." Luke set down his soda and followed the boy out of the kitchen.

Scenes from the flick, *Mr. Mom,* flitted through Cici's head as the volume on the TV went down. She laughed to herself, recalling the countless times she'd watched that movie. One of her roommates owned the DVD. But, however funny the story line, the premise reinforced Cici's theory that a guy just couldn't run a house single-handedly, raise well-adjusted children, and maintain a career.

But a woman could. In fact, women didn't need men at all when it came to raising children, and kids survived just fine without a father.

She had.

Minutes passed, and finally Luke strolled back into the kitchen. "Sorry about that. I had to deal with my son."

Cici arched a brow. "Deal with him?"

Luke smiled. "Discipline him. He's not allowed to play with the television or the remote and he disobeyed."

"Hmm. . ." Cici found it interesting that she hadn't heard any sort of scolding. "Well, I'll bet you'll be glad when your wife gets home."

Luke took another swig of his canned soft drink. "I'm not married."

"Oh, so you're divorced? Your day to have the kids?"

He shook his head. "My wife died a few years ago."

His reply stunned her. "I–I'm sorry. . ."

"Thanks." A mix of discomfort and gloom settled over his features.

"I'm sure you miss her very much."

"Yeah." He sucked in a breath and blew it out again. "But I can't change the past. What's more, I have three sons to raise and a business to run, so I can't very well sit around feeling sorry for myself."

"No, I suppose you can't." She regarded him askance. "Are you raising your boys on your own?"

"Yes, but I have help from my in-laws and friends at church."

Cici had to admit she admired his candor. However, his mention of "friends at church" gave her an uneasy feeling.

"In fact, Jen and William babysat for me so I could attend a seminar."

"They did, huh?" Her suspicion mounted. "So, you've met William?"

"He's one of my best friends."

Cici hid a grimace. Her inkling had been correct. Another religious kook. She should have figured—except Jen never mentioned the single father next door. Unless. . .

She tamped down the sudden swell of enthusiasm. Luke Weldon might be living proof that her master's theory was correct. It was sheer brilliance on Jen's part. Obviously it had been her plan all along. Except. . .it didn't quite make sense given that Jen heartily disagreed with Cici's viewpoint.

Unless Jen had another plan in mind.

Cici squared her shoulders. "Just so you know, William has already preached to me, so you can save your breath."

A frown furrowed his dark brows. "What are you talking about?"

"You know very well what I'm talking about. If you know William and you've got church friends, then you're one of them. You're a Christian. And Christians feel some kind of need to convert the world to their narrow-minded way of thinking. But I have my own way, my own religion."

"All right." He lifted a shoulder. "I can respect that."

Cici brought herself up, fully expecting more of an argument out of him. When none came, she relaxed and reminded herself why she came over here in the first place.

"Um, getting back to the reason I came over. . ." She placed her hands on her hips. "As I said, I'm writing my master's thesis." Cici noticed the kids were trickling into the room, one by one, and watching her with their gorgeous, wide brown eyes. She saw the intelligence in their depths, and she saw something else, too. Something she couldn't quite explain. "So, like I said, I was working on my thesis, and I had to stop because of. . ."

She paused again, unable to complain about the noise while the boys stood by staring at her. She decided she could never hurt their feelings. "Well, I heard kids playing, and I wanted to come over and say hello. I like kids." She brought her gaze back to Luke. "I hope to get a job with the Iowa Department of Education once I've completed school. I just have my thesis left to write and then I'm finished."

"Good for you." His gaze traveled over the tops of his children's heads. "Let me introduce my boys. This is Devin." He placed his hand on the tallest boy's shoulder. "He's six."

"Almost seven," Devin corrected. "My birthday is October seventeenth, and I'll be in first grade this year."

"I'm impressed." Cici smiled at the boy.

"I'm Aaron." One of the twins stepped forward, and with the light blue blanket still caped around his neck, he raised both arms as if showing off his muscles. "I'm a superhero!"

And the one who likes to play with the TV's remote control. Cici grinned.

"I'm a superhero, too," the other twin added before shyly ducking behind Luke.

"Tell Miss Ciara your name," he prompted. "She's going to live in Miss Jenny's house for the summer."

"Brian," the boy blurted before hiding his face again.

"The twins are five years old."

"I'm a superhero, too," Devin informed her. "But I do more superheroing around here cuz I'm the oldest."

"I'm a superhero, too," Luke mimicked, earning perplexed stares from his children.

Finally the little firecracker spoke up. "Da–ad," Aaron said, "you can't b'tend you're a superhero, cuz you're big." He gave Luke's hip a playful shove.

Not to be outdone, the other boys copied their brother.

"Hey, don't beat me up. I'm not a bad guy." He tickled the kids and they dissolved into fits of giggles.

Cici couldn't help smiling as she looked on.

"Okay, that's enough goofing around. We have a guest, remember? That means we're on our best behavior."

The boys righted themselves and looked back at Cici.

"Listen, it's nice to meet you superheroes. All of you." She locked her gaze with Luke's. She had to admit he was an exceptionally fine-looking man, and she admired his good-humored manner. Clearly, his kids adored him. However, those traits alone didn't qualify him to be a sole parent. Children needed a mother's nurturing and real discipline, coaching, and encouragement in order to become productive citizens and lead successful lives. They didn't need to grow up parented by Peter Pan, and she hoped to prove it in her thesis.

"So tell me." She copped a sassy attitude and folded her arms. "How do you know I'm a 'Miss'?"

"What?" Luke appeared confused.

"You've introduced me as *Miss Ciara*."

"Oh, that's easy." His lips curved upward mischievously, and he gave her a charming wink. "Us superheroes know everything."

Chapter 3

Hands on hips, Luke stood at the large picture window in his livin room and peered out at his new neighbor. She was speaking with To Evenrod from the condo across the street, and Luke couldn't drag h gaze away from her.

Ciara. She had the most beautiful name he'd ever heard and it fit her. Sh was altogether unforgettable.

Luke expelled a disappointed sigh as he watched the slender redhead con versing on the walk. That gorgeous, thick, wavy hair of hers was piled on he head, secured with some sort of clip, and she wore faded blue jeans and a sleeve less white shirt.

Don't look too close. She's not a believer, Luke reminded himself. Neithe William nor Jen had mentioned whether Ciara was a Christian or not, but sh had made it clear enough to him yesterday. She said she had her "own religion.

I've got no business entertaining my attraction to this woman.

In spite of his self-reproof, he couldn't help staring. She stood close enoug so he could see her blue eyes widen at something Tori said, and he recalled th freckles sprinkled across Ciara's pretty face and slim arms. She had the kind c skin that seemed like it would sunburn easily.

Luke shook himself and captured his wayward thoughts before turnin from the window. "What am I thinking?" He smacked his palm to his forehea He had work to do, and here he stood, wasting time, gawking at his neighbor. I only a few hours, the kids would return home from the public pool. They'd gon swimming with friends this afternoon.

Taking the steps two at a time, Luke made his way up to his office. H decided it might be a good idea for him to stay away from Ciara Rome—as fa away as possible.

❧

Cici dragged herself to the Condo Club's Friday evening get-together. She'd neede the break from working at her computer all day, and she figured it wouldn't hurt t meet a few more of Jen's neighbors. So far she liked Tori Evenrod. She found th woman amusing, and Tori had the scoop on everyone in her little community.

Cici was particularly interested in getting the lowdown on Luke Weldor After meeting him, she'd decided to act on her idea that he and his adorable bu incredibly rambunctious kids would make perfect examples, serving as furthe roof her thesis was correct. Now she planned to set about obtaining her data. Of course that meant hanging around with a religious nut for a while, but Cici figured she could handle it, seeing as how she loved Jen as a sister and she could tolerate William. What's more, according to Tori, Luke was a "good guy" and a target for several of the single women in the neighborhood. Cici understood she had stiff competition in vying for Luke's time.

She smiled. Nothing like a good challenge.

"Hey, I haven't seen you around before."

Cici turned to see a blond, burly guy standing to her right. He wore tight-fitting jeans and a white T-shirt that bore the name of a popular beer across the chest.

"You must not come to these things often." He gave her a lazy grin. "Either that or you just moved in."

"Both, actually." Cici pushed out a polite smile. "I'm renting a friend's condo for the summer."

"Oh." A curious light sparked in his blue eyes, and a smile split his weather-worn, tanned face. Then he stuck out his right hand. "The name's Chase Tibbits."

"Ciara Rome." She slipped her palm into his and noticed his hand's calloused texture. She imagined he was some sort of contractor. "Nice to meet you."

"Hey, same here."

"What do you do for a living, Mr. Tibbits?"

He guffawed and several heads turned. "I'm no 'mister.' Call me Chase." He chuckled once more. "I do roofing, siding. You name it, I can do it."

"Can you knit? Crochet?" Cici couldn't seem to stifle the quip.

"Everything except those things." Chase laughed. "Needles scare me. Nails don't—unless they're fingernails."

"Funny." Cici grinned.

He grunted out a laugh before glancing over at the food table in a shady part of the condo clubhouse's yard. "Hey, would you like a beer?"

She tipped her head, noting that he enjoyed using the word *hey*. "No, thanks." She wanted to get back to her thesis, and she knew an alcoholic beverage would only cloud her thinking.

"Well, I'm going to get another one. I'll be back."

"Take your time."

Chase strode off to get a drink and, moments later, Cici spied Luke and his boys. The kids appeared well-groomed, each attired in a brightly colored shorts outfit. She couldn't help noticing that Luke, also, looked nice in his khaki slacks and tan polo shirt. His dark hair had been neatly combed, although a few rakish strands hung over his forehead.

Smiling, she made her way toward him. "Well, hi, neighbor."

"Hi, Ciara." Luke gave her a warm smile. He prompted his boys to tell her hello, which they immediately did.

"Daddy, we're hungry," Devin complained.

Before Luke could reply, a beautiful woman with Mediterranean features cut in. "I'll get the kids some food." Her almond-shaped brown eyes darkened with an unspoken but suggestive invitation. "You know how much I adore your kids. . . ."

Cici guessed the woman was ready and willing to move into the wife and mommy role at the Weldon house.

"And Roberta outdid herself with the snack table tonight. There's all sorts of food that your boys will love."

"No, thanks, Michayla, but I appreciate the offer." He took hold of his two youngest sons' hands. Then he introduced Cici.

"If you'll excuse me now, I need to feed my children."

"Of course." Cici watched the Weldons walk away before returning her gaze to the black-haired woman.

"Nice to meet you."

"Likewise."

Michayla Martinelli relaxed her stance, although she maintained a certain measure of aloofness. "New in the neighborhood?"

"Yes. I'm renting a friend's condo for the summer." Cici wished she could have pasted a sign across her forehead so she wouldn't have to repeat the same information over and over.

"Only for the summer?"

"Right."

"What a shame." Michayla's tone rang with gentle sarcasm. Then she feigned a little smile. "Although, fall is my favorite time of year."

Cici ignored the subtle insult. She couldn't care less what the woman thought about her and whether she had targeted Luke Weldon as her next conquest. Cici had moved into Jen's condo for one thing and one thing only: to write her thesis.

Chase returned with a drink in his hand.

"Hey, Mic, how's it going?" He hugged her around the shoulders.

In reply, she gave him a withering glare before shrugging out of his hold and striding off.

Chase chuckled. "She idolizes me."

"I can see that," Cici quipped, although she couldn't help wondering if Chase was for real. Was his ego the size of Montana or had he purposely goaded the lovely Michayla Martinelli for sheer entertainment?

Cici rather suspected the answer to her question was both ego and entertainment. She also had to admit that Chase was attractive in a rather brutish sort of way.

"Hey, you never did tell me what you do."

"What I do? As in my career?"

"Yeah." The dimple in his right cheek winked at her as he smiled. "Let me guess: You're a teacher."

"No, but I've done some teaching, right before I managed a day care center. Now I'm finishing up my master's thesis."

She expounded on her topic but soon realized Chase's mind, as well as his gaze, had wandered. Cici didn't waste another word on him. Instead, she strolled over to Tori Evenrod, conversed for a bit, and met several more individuals.

Then, as fate would have it, she ran into Luke Weldon again.

"Having fun?"

"I don't know about 'fun,' but it's been a pleasant evening." She glanced at her wristwatch, contemplating leaving the party and heading for Jen's condo.

"Did you get something to eat?"

"Not much." Cici had indulged in a diet cola and a few crackers with cheese spread, and that had kept her hunger at bay. She figured she'd eat back at Jen's condo. "What about you?"

"The boys are eating. They loved those miniature meatballs." He grinned and glanced around at the mingling crowd. "I see you met both Michayla and Chase."

"Sure did."

"And you're not running for cover?" Luke stuck his hands into the pockets of his tan trousers. "I'm impressed. They're two of the neighborhood's more, um, volatile residents."

Cici couldn't help teasing him. She folded her arms and grinned. "Why would I be intimidated with *Superman* here?"

The retort earned her one of Luke's captivating smiles. "And, speaking of superheroes, I s'pose I should get mine home."

"I was just leaving myself. Can I walk with you?"

"Absolutely."

Luke swung around and Cici followed his gaze to where his sons were sitting with other kids. Next, without warning, Luke blew out an ear-ringer of a whistle.

Cici cringed, but the Weldon boys came running. They stood before their dad like soldiers awaiting orders from their commander in chief.

"Time to go home."

They moaned, but the well-mannered superheroes didn't actually complain.

She fell in step beside Luke, feeling more convinced than ever that a woman was responsible for instilling such admirable character traits in the kids. Surely Luke just benefited from what she'd done—whoever "she" was.

"You mentioned getting a lot of help with your boys. Female help, huh?"

Luke seemed to mull over the question for several seconds. "Well, my sister-in-law watches the guys if she's got a day off, and, like today, Nancy Smith, a neighbor, took my kids to the public swimming pool along with her brood."

It wasn't quite the answer Cici was digging for and, as if sensing her dissatisfaction, Luke added, "I don't have a harem, if that's what you're asking, and I certainly would never use my kids in order to get a woman to date me."

Cici replied with an ambivalent shrug, telling herself she wasn't impressed either way. She'd known her share of lying, cheating men—men like her own father—and she wasn't convinced Luke couldn't be lumped into that category.

"And if it's Michayla's solicitousness that prompted your question," Luke continued, "I'm not interested in accepting her offers, kind as they may sound, because I know there are strings attached. Strings I have no intentions of getting tangled up in. I might be a simple Christian man, but I'm not stupid."

"Guess time will tell, won't it? I mean, I don't think any man can refuse a woman like Michayla forever." She nudged him with her elbow and grinned. "Not even a superhero like you."

"You're totally wrong." A smug smile curved his lips and he shook his head. He kept his gaze up ahead at the kids who skipped, jumped, and ran in front of them. "And, if you must know, I don't find Michayla Martinelli particularly attractive."

Cici laughed in disbelief. "Okay, so maybe you're not stupid, but you must be blind."

"I'm neither, thank you very much." He slid a glance to her and then back at his sons.

A slight frown pulled at her brows. "Are you in a committed relationship with someone else?" she asked—as part of her research, of course.

"Nope. How about you?"

"Not at this time, no." The truth was, Cici hadn't ever been all that committed to any guy. Her education and furthering her career had taken precedence her entire adult life. Her roommates even went so far as to label her a "workaholic."

"So, um, what about Chase Tibbits?"

Cici peered over at Luke and glimpsed his mischievous grin.

"The women around here swoon over Chase just because he owns a lot of power tools, but I noticed you didn't seem too taken with him."

"I wasn't. He's not my type."

"Well, see, the same goes for me and Michayla. She's not my type." Luke halted in midstride, causing Cici to do the same.

"Did I get too personal? If so, I apologize." Cici meant it sincerely.

"No, it's not that." Luke shook his head, but Cici saw the curious gleam in his brown eyes. "I'm just wondering why in the world we're discussing Chase and Michayla, two of my least favorite neighbors."

"Oh, well I can explain my questions about Michayla." She cast a self-conscious smile at her sandals. "Let me explain. You see, I'm curious about the women who have impacted your sons' young lives. I'm still researching my master's thesis."

"Got it." Understanding lit Luke's eyes, and he began walking again. "Research. Okay, well, in that case..."

Once more Cici fell into step beside him.

"The boys' grandmas, Sunday school teachers, friends, and even neighbors—with the exception of two who, for research purposes, shall remain nameless..."

Cici couldn't help grinning.

"They've all impacted my kids in some way."

She and Luke reached their connecting units and strolled up the side walk-way and around to the back. Cici decided that, in spite of herself, she found Luke quite engaging.

"Can I help you get the kids settled?"

"No, I can't ask you to do that." He paused at the end of the fence separating the two patios and handed the house key to Devin. "Especially not since I spent the last block convincing you that I don't use my kids as bait in order to capture a woman's interest." He tossed a glance skyward as if to emphasize the ridiculousness of the notion.

Cici laughed. "Well, then, it's a good thing you're not asking. I'm offering. Besides," she added, stepping around him, "I'm not interested in you. I like your kids."

"Oooh..."

Cici caught his playful wince.

"You sure know how to chink a superhero's armor."

Chapter 4

The place is a mess. I wasn't expecting company."

"I completely understand." Cici scanned the sink full of dirty dishes, the cluttered countertops, and the uncleared table. The apartment she shared with her roommates, Bridget and Tanya, could look this bad and, sometimes, worse. "Not to worry."

The boys ran into the living room and suddenly the television's volume boomed.

Cici jumped.

Devin bolted into the kitchen. "Dad!"

"I know, son. Aaron is playing with the remote again." Luke followed his son out of the kitchen.

In that moment, Cici experienced a sense of chaos like she'd never before imagined. But just as quickly, the TV's volume went down and Luke seemed to regain control of his household. The next thing Cici heard was the sound of three pairs of sneakers thundering up the carpeted steps. How could three little boys be so noisy?

Luke reentered the kitchen looking none the worse for wear. "I'm going to help the boys get into their pajamas. If you'd like to read them each a story before bedtime, that'd be appreciated."

"I'd love to." She cast a glance at the sink. "How 'bout if I start working on your dishes while you help the kids upstairs?"

"No way. You're my guest." He motioned to the living room. "Please. Have a seat, get comfy, and the kids will be down with their books in a few minutes. While you read to them, I can get the kitchen cleaned up."

"Okay, if you're sure. . ."

"I'm sure." Luke nodded toward the living room and gave her a quick grin before heading upstairs to tend to his boys.

Cici watched him go then strode out of the kitchen and sat down on the blue, white, and green plaid sofa. The upholstery had obviously seen better days and the pale blue carpet looked worn in places, too. But, overall, the living area seemed clean.

She listened to the commotion upstairs. The boys were fussing at each other. She heard Luke's mild-mannered tone reminding them there was a guest present and that they should be on their "best behavior."

She looked around, taking in her surroundings. Across the room, the television was encased in a cherry wood wall unit. An assortment of framed photographs and knickknacks occupied adjacent shelves. Just when she felt tempted to walk over and get a closer view, two of the three kids ran down the stairs, storybooks under their arms.

Devin, the oldest boy, sat to Cici's left and dropped his hard-covered book in her lap. "Can I go first?"

"Sure." She glanced at the book's title: *The Truck Book.* She looked at Devin. "You like trucks?"

He replied with a vigorous nod.

Brian, the shy twin, sat on Cici's right side. He slipped his book onto her legs and stared up at her with probing brown eyes. They held a depth that seemed beyond his years, and Cici felt a tug on her heartstrings.

She turned her attention to the title of his book. *"The Oak Inside the Acorn."* She gave the boy a smile. "Sounds interesting."

He replied with a nod and a shy smile.

"Where's your other brother?" she asked the two beside her.

"Aaron's getting a talking-to because he played with the remote again." Devin wore a serious expression. "But he and my dad will be down pretty soon."

"Okay, we'll wait."

A *"talking-to,"* huh? Cici was curious and decided to quiz the children. "A 'talking-to' doesn't sound like much of a punishment. Do you ever get a time-out or lose privileges?"

"Sometimes." Again, Devin was the one to reply.

But before she could dig further, Aaron bounded down the steps, followed by his father.

"I'm going last." Aaron held up his book. Cici only glimpsed the title. Something about pirates who didn't do anything.

She frowned, wondering what the story could possibly be about.

"Dad said after the story we can watch the movie. That's why I don't care about going last."

"Movie? Yay!" Devin cheered and Brian was quick to join in.

Luke grinned and sat down in the dark blue upholstered armchair adjacent to where Cici sat on the sofa.

"Well, I guess I should get started so the kids can watch their movie." She looked his way for affirmation.

He gave her a nod.

"You don't have to read my book." Devin withdrew his choice from her lap. "I know how to read most of it myself anyhow, and I want to watch the movie."

"All right." She glanced at Luke to confirm the decision.

He shrugged in acquiescence.

Cici began reading Brian's selection. The story was all about how people have specific purposes in life and, therefore, they needed to be "the trees" that God made them to be.

Nothing wrong with the story's overall message, although Cici picked up on the religious propaganda sprinkled throughout its contents. She told herself she shouldn't be surprised.

"Well, wasn't that nice?" She closed the book.

"Yeah, and I think if I was a tree, I'd be like that oak tree," Devin remarked.

"Thank goodness you're a superhero instead," Cici teased with a look at Luke. He smiled back, and she had the feeling he wasn't at all interested in cleaning his kitchen. Instead he appeared thoroughly relaxed, enjoying story time as much as his kids.

"So, Devin"—she returned her attention to the soon-to-be first grader—"do you think God really cares what happens here on earth?" She wondered if Luke would object to her challenging his son's faith.

He didn't, and Devin was quick to answer.

"Yeah, He cares. He made us and I care about stuff I make, so why wouldn't God?"

Cici weighed the candid reply and found she couldn't argue with it. After all, she cared about things she created. . .like her thesis.

"What about you?" she asked Aaron, who sat at his father's feet. "Do you think God is really up in heaven somewhere, worrying about what's happening here on earth?"

"Yeah."

"How do you know?" She glanced at Luke again but didn't get the feeling that he minded her questions. She'd cease at once if she thought he objected.

"I don't know." Aaron raised his narrow shoulders. "I just know."

Because it's what you've been taught, and you haven't learned any differently.

"I know," Brian said.

Cici turned to regard him.

"He's real because God is love." Brian's brown eyes shone with earnestness. "My dad loves us like God does."

"Except God is perfect," Luke added, "and I'm just a regular guy."

"In heaven we'll be perfect kids," Devin said. "Aaron won't always get in trouble in heaven."

Aaron nodded as he peeked over his shoulder at his dad who sent him an affectionate wink.

Cici grew uncomfortable with the subject, although she couldn't say why. She'd discussed God, the Bible, and various Christian beliefs with Jen and William plenty of times in the past. Occasionally she and William would verbally spar over a particular point, mostly because Cici enjoyed razzing him. Jen always knew what she was up to, but William took the challenge each and every time. However, no matter the outcome, he never held a grudge. That spoke volumes about his character, in Cici's mind. But she scarcely knew Luke, and he didn't strike her as a guy who loved a good debate. He seemed more the peace-keeping kind, and she'd hate to offend him in his own home. "Okay, well, I think it's time to move on to the next book."

"I just wanna watch the movie." Aaron turned to look up at his dad again.

"Me, too," Devin said.

"Me, too!" Brian exclaimed.

The vote was unanimous, so Luke stood, strode across the room, and inserted the DVD into the player located beneath the TV. As he did so, he gave Cici a brief history of the VeggieTales animated characters. The kids expounded on his explanation with a high-spirited synopsis about the pirate movie. They had obviously seen it before.

"Basically it comes down to this. . ." Luke wrapped it up. "A hero doesn't have to be the bravest or the smartest. A hero just has to want to do what's right in God's eyes." He eyed his sons. "Right, guys?"

"Yeah, superheroes!" In all his excitement, Aaron stood and started running around the room until Luke cleared his throat.

"He's gonna get another talking-to," Brian whispered, wide-eyed, to Cici.

She said nothing. She just observed the boys and Luke and made mental notes as she watched them interact.

Finally Luke sat on the floor and pulled Aaron into his lap. He still wiggled and squirmed, although his dad's restraining arms kept the little bundle of energy contained so he couldn't disrupt his brothers during the movie.

Cici watched the DVD while surreptitiously observing Luke and the kids. The kids sang along with the vegetable-like characters dressed as pirates—and she concluded the flick smacked of more religious propaganda, albeit subtly. She couldn't deny, however, that it was cute, and the children appeared to thoroughly enjoy what they saw and heard.

When the movie ended, Luke directed the boys up to bed.

"Thanks for allowing me to barge in on you." Cici rose from the sofa. "I don't feel like I was much help to you."

"I've got a decent routine down when it comes to bedtime, but the boys are always excited to have someone besides me read them stories."

"Good. It was fun." Cici gave him a smile.

Luke returned the gesture as he stuffed his hands into the pockets of his khaki trousers. "Did you gain any new info for your research?"

"Yes, actually."

"Cool. I'm happy to answer any other questions you have on kids, not that I'm a huge expert or anything." He shifted from one foot to the other.

"Thanks." Cici pushed out a grin. Without the kids around as a buffer, things between her and Luke felt suddenly awkward.

"Well. . ." He bobbed his head and pursed his lips. "Um, I'd better get the kids into bed. But you're welcome to stay. Feel free to grab a cola or something out of the fridge."

Cici thought over the invitation. However, before she could reply, a thunderous crash sounded from above.

She glanced at the ceiling before sending Luke a wide-eyed stare.

He remained calm. "That would be Aaron, parachuting from his top bunk."

"Parachuting?"

Luke was halfway up the stairs already. "That's what he calls it. He throws his pillows and blankets onto the floor and then leaps off the top bunk. *Parachuting.*"

The idea made Cici gape while riotous laughter filled the second floor. No doubt the little daredevil and his brothers never thought of the dangers associated with such a stunt.

From where she stood, rooted to the carpet, she couldn't wait to see how Luke handled this situation. Would he yell? Spank? She knew what she'd do if she were in charge. She'd see to it the child lost some privileges beginning tomorrow morning!

She listened. Things upstairs didn't sound amiss. No angry voices. No crying. But the silence was deafening. Cici wondered what was happening and debated whether to leave or stay.

Within moments, the latter won out. She'd offered to help, after all. Besides, she was much too curious to go back to Jen's condo now.

Making her way into the kitchen, she opened the dishwasher and started loading it. She'd only rinsed a few sticky cups and set them in the top rack when Luke suddenly appeared.

"Hey, what are you doing?" He caught her wrists.

She looked up at him and their gazes locked. Cici felt pinned by his deep brown eyes. She saw them travel down her face and pause at her mouth, as her insides seemed to flip with anticipation while he gently held her wrists. Was he about to kiss her? In that split second, Cici didn't think she'd mind it at all. His nearness overwhelmed her senses in a dizzying way, and she felt certain he could hear her heart banging inside her rib cage. Whatever the intriguing, nameless, electrifying current was between them, it was mutual. Cici felt sure of at least that much.

But then Luke stepped back, dropped her hands, and the magic vanished.

Cici was both puzzled and disappointed.

"You're my guest." His tone sounded serious and his gaze backed it up. "I don't make my guests clean my kitchen."

"Make?" She shook her head. "Don't be silly, Luke, you're not forcing me to do dishes. I'm glad to help out. That's why I came in tonight after the get-together."

"I won't hear another word about it." Placing his palm beneath her elbow, he led her away from the sink, gave her a dish towel to dry her hands, and guided her into the living room.

"Luke, honestly—"

"I'm starved," he said, changing the subject. "How 'bout you?"

"I'm—"

Before she could reply, he added, "I didn't eat much at the get-together tonight because I was too busy making sure the boys ate enough food. What do you say we order a pizza?" He picked up the phone book and leafed through it. "The boys will love cold pizza for lunch tomorrow."

Cici wrinkled her nose. She wasn't much for cold leftovers. Nevertheless, her stomach growled, and a hot, fresh pizza sounded marvelous.

"What do you like on your pie?"

"Just cheese and veggies. No meat."

Luke glanced at her with a twinkle in his eyes. "The movie made you hungry for vegetables, eh?"

She laughed in spite of herself and sat on the sofa. She listened as he ordered one "veggie delight" and one sausage and pepperoni.

"That's a lot of pizza," Cici remarked as Luke took his place in the armchair.

"My sons and I can down an entire pizza by ourselves."

"On second thought, that's not hard to believe." Tim, John, and Andy, a few of her guy friends, came to mind. They never seemed to fill up, especially when it came to junk food.

"So, tell me," Cici began, "how did you reprimand Aaron for his 'parachuting' tonight?"

"I just explained to him, again, about the possible catastrophes. For instance, if he lost his footing when he jumped, he could crash into the window and cut his arm. Then he'd need stitches and he might not be able to go swimming for weeks." Luke lazed back and crossed his legs. "Or, if he landed wrong, he could break his leg and he wouldn't be able to ride his bike or play outside for the rest of the summer."

She bobbed her head in understanding. "Teaching him to consider the consequences of his actions."

"Exactly. My kids aren't bad. They're just boys. And I'll admit that Aaron is my wild child, but I can reason with him—even at his young age. The other two are intent listeners so they learn from my explaining things to Aaron." Luke shrugged. "It works. At least it works for now."

"Good." Cici folded one leg beneath her and faced Luke.

"Have you heard from Jen?"

"No. Have you heard from William?"

He shook his head.

Cici shrugged. "I don't expect we will, to tell you the truth. Jen is with the man she loves, and they're traipsing across Europe together with other friends. If it were me, I wouldn't give my friends back home a single thought."

Luke chuckled. "Maybe you're right. I remember feeling that way once." He seemed momentarily wistful, but then shook it off. He sucked in a breath and blew out a sigh. "After seeing Europe, William and Jen are scheduled to tour the Holy Lands. I'm envious."

It sounded as if Luke was envious of more than just Jen and William's trip abroad; however, she decided to avoid probing into his deep, innermost feelings. It wasn't her business anyway. "That's somewhere you'd like to visit? The Holy Lands?"

"For sure. It would be such a thrill to walk where Jesus did."

Cici stiffened. *Here it comes,* she thought. *He's going to question my beliefs and tell me why his are better.*

But to her surprise the conversation didn't stray in that direction.

"Have you done much traveling?"

Cici shook her head. "No. I've never left Iowa."

He laughed. "No kidding? How come?"

"Lack of funds." Cici felt herself relax since it appeared the topic of religion had been dropped. "Any extra money I earn has gone toward my education. It's been that way since I graduated from high school. I worked my way through college, earned my degree, and now I'm about to earn my master's—that is, if I ever finish my thesis."

"And, as you mentioned, your research tonight has been for your thesis because it pertains to child development."

"Exactly." Cici was glad he'd brought up the subject of her thesis again. She never tired of discussing the topic.

"What about your family? Younger siblings? Nieces and nephews?"

"No. It's just my mom and me. My dad ran off with another woman when I was about twelve." A familiar bitterness mounted inside her. "After that, all my ideas about what a real family is evaporated into thin air. I learned early on to have a general distrust of men."

"I can relate. After my wife died, I went through a time where I had a general distrust of women. Sometimes I wonder if I still do."

"Oh?" This time Cici's curiosity got the better of her.

He sat forward. "Didn't William or Jen tell you about it?"

"About what?"

He regarded her with a thoughtful expression for several long moments.

"My wife left a nightclub with some guy I'd never met or seen before. It may have been a lapse in judgment on her part, or she might have been having an affair with him. I guess I'll never know. She died in an accident that night. They were in his car, he was behind the wheel, and he died, too. He had no family in the area so they weren't much help in providing me with any clues. Thus my general distrust."

Cici hid her grimace. She couldn't imagine how painful the situation had to be for him. "I'm sorry. I had no idea."

He replied with a simple shrug. "I've had a lot of love and support from friends and family, and I muddled through the grief. I came to realize that I had to focus on the future and let God heal the past. I have three young boys to bring up. They depend on me."

"You must hate her."

"Who? My deceased wife?" Luke shook his head. "I could never hate Alissa. I loved her."

"You're serious, aren't you?"

Luke nodded. "Yes, I am."

Cici could tell he meant every word, and she was amazed that he didn't harbor any ill feelings for his departed wife. "Still, you must miss having a woman around—for your sons' sakes."

"Well, sure I do. I'm not as unfeeling as a streetlamp."

Cici grinned.

"This is a season, and God is aware and on top of my situation. He has my sons' best interests at heart, more than I ever could."

"I'm not sure about that, but you're right about everything being in constant change. The earth itself. . .life is cyclical. But without a mother figure in your sons' world, I can't help wondering who's going to hold them through all the disappointments in grade school? Who will nurture them into their adult years?"

A mischievous smirk pulled at the corner of his mouth. "Are you volunteering for the job?"

She rolled her eyes. "Of course not. I barely know you." She averted her gaze, willing away the memory of what took place in the kitchen just minutes ago. His touch affected her, and she hated to admit it.

He chuckled. "Seriously, God knows the future, and I trust Him to bring the right woman into our lives when He sees fit."

"Until then?"

"Until then, I'm a single dad."

"Well, that's where we differ. You see, my belief is that fathers can't nurture children the way mothers do. Women can single-handedly raise kids to become well-adjusted, productive citizens while men fall short of the mark time and time again."

Luke sat forward and placed his forearms on his knees. A frown furrowed his dark brows. "How do you know?"

She leaned toward him. "I've done years of research on the subject of child rearing. My professor considers me an expert in the field."

"Well, I applaud you for all your work, but I think I can probably blow your research right out of the water."

"Oh?" Cici raised her brows and excitement pulsed through her veins at the sound of his challenge. "And how do you propose to do that?"

"See, my God is bigger than all the knowledge in the world. My God confounds even the wisest of men—and women."

"Please." Cici held up a forestalling hand, unimpressed. "Don't keep dragging God into this."

Luke sat back in silent acquiescence.

"On a human level, I still don't understand how you intend to prove me wrong. Especially when I intend to use you to prove my theory right."

"You intend to *use* me?" Luke seemed amused.

"I do, so consider yourself fairly warned."

"Okay. Then I'm going to pray that God will show you the truth about fathers raising their kids—and, yeah, I'm dragging God into this because He's in every part of my life. I'm going to trust that He'll show you that we, single dads, are equally as competent in every way as single moms."

Cici opened her mouth to retort, but the doorbell rang, cutting her off.

Luke stood and grinned. "Pizza's here."

Chapter 5

Luke sat alone on his patio, enjoying a rare interval of peace. Several doors down, a neighbor's wind chimes tinkled in the breeze, and across the yard, on the adjacent property, some older kids laughed and splashed in an aboveground pool. Raucous sounds of summer—and, oddly, they helped Luke relax. He had tucked his boys into bed an hour ago, but the present respite was bittersweet since he'd had an extremely rough day. The boys had been at their naughtiest, and he hadn't gotten any work done in his office.

Lord, I'm praying that You'll show Ciara how I can be both a good father and mother. But the way I feel right now, I'd quit fatherhood if it were a regular paying job.

He sighed and allowed his thoughts to stray to his interim next-door neighbor. He liked her, from her curly auburn hair to her vivacious blue eyes and contagious smile. He wished she would have stayed longer last night, but she'd eaten one slice of pizza before leaving, saying she had more work to do on her thesis. While it irked him that she admitted to "using" him to prove her theory correct, her honesty was refreshing. He felt like he could let his guard down since her intentions were anything but romantic. Disappointing, yes, but he had no business romancing her anyway because she didn't share his faith. So, as far as he was concerned, she could bring on the research. Luke was confident in who he was: a Christian man who made his share of mistakes, but one who loved his children more than his own life.

Images of his sons scampered across his mind. Those little rascals—they'd been devilish today!

He released an audible sigh and shifted his weight in the lawn chair. Darkness was falling rapidly around him. Leaning his head back, he heard mosquitoes buzzing close to his ear, but he was too exhausted to even swat them away. He closed his eyes. . .

🐛

Cici stepped out onto the patio for a quick breather. She inhaled deeply, allowing the cool night air to fill her lungs. Then she exhaled. After repeating the deep-breathing exercises several times, she felt the day's tension begin to seep from her body.

This morning she'd met with her professor, Agnes Carter-Hill, to talk about her thesis. Aggie was particularly interested in hearing about Cici's "living example" next door and encouraged further study. But she cautioned Cici not to get too personally involved.

How could I possibly get personally involved with Luke Weldon and his kid. First of all, he's not my type and secondly. . .

Her musings came to a halt at the sound of a man's light snoring on the other side of the fence. Her first thought was that someone's grandpa must be paying a visit next door, but when she peeked around the fence post she saw Luke sprawled out in a lawn chair, sleeping.

Cici swallowed a laugh and shook her head at the man. Then her smile slipped from her lips and a wave of empathy washed over her. Poor guy. He had his hand full with those three boys of his. Cici thought back on how exhausted she'd felt after eight hours working at a day care center. She could scarcely imagine how Luke managed 24/7 with his boys—and with his own business to run, also.

She stepped off the patio and onto the lush grass. She felt inexplicably drawn closer, as if she'd never seen a guy taking a catnap before. The university campus was littered with sleeping students at times. Still, she couldn't help wanting better glimpse of him. As she crept closer, she saw his shadowed jaw beneath the moonlight. He wore jeans and a T-shirt. Cici watched his chest move slowly up and down with every snore.

She put her hand over her mouth, squelching a giggle. The sight of him seemed amusing and somehow endearing, as well.

Seconds later, a wail wafted through the second floor window. She froze and looked up at the house.

"Daddy. Daddy. . ."

One of the boys was crying. Probably one of the twins, Cici guessed. Casting aside all tentativeness, she strode toward Luke, placed her hand on his shoulder and gave him a shake.

"Wake up, Luke."

He peeled open one eyelid. Seeing her, he bolted upright. "Ciara." He finger combed his hair back off his forehead. "What's going on?"

He seemed embarrassed. "I hear one of the kids crying."

"Oh?" He pushed to his feet and they both listened.

It came again. "Daddy. Daddy. . ."

"You're right. Thanks for letting me know."

Concern made her follow him into the house. "Do you think he had a bad dream?"

"Not sure."

Cici trailed Luke up the steps. The layout of his condo was similar to Jen's next door, but the second floor had three bedrooms and a full bathroom.

At the doorway, Cici leaned against the wall and watched as Luke lifted the boy into his arms. "Is that Aaron?"

"Brian."

The boy whimpered.

"He's soaking wet. I think he's got a fever."

"What can I do to help?"

Luke carried the child out of the room, and Cici moved to close the door so as not to disturb the other boys. It was amazing they were still asleep.

"I'll get him out of his wet pajamas if you'll start a tepid bath for him."

"Tepid?" The word seemed so formal that it sounded odd coming from him, Mr. Laidback-and-casual.

"You know, lukewarm."

"Of course. . .sure. . ."

Cici hurried down the short hallway to the bathroom where she sat on the side of the tub and turned on the faucets. While waiting for the tub to fill, she took note of the net of plastic toys hanging from a corner hook. She also saw the dirty ring around the tub, and in that moment she realized Luke hadn't asked her in; she'd barged in and not for any sort of research, either. It's just that it had felt so natural.

Before she could dwell on it further, Luke entered the bathroom with Brian in his arms. She tested the bath. Its temperature definitely felt "tepid."

"It's full enough."

Cici shut off the water and stood to get out of his way.

"This isn't going to be pleasant." Luke's tone held a warning note while both worry and regret shone from his deep brown eyes. "He's burning up, and he's going to scream when I force him into this bath. Even though it's not cold, it'll feel like ice because his body temp is so high. But this is the only way I know to cool him down."

Cici paused to think it over. "What about a sponge bath?"

"Not as effective, but after Brian's bath I can use that as a means to keep him cool along with giving him children's acetaminophen."

Made sense to Cici. . .and she was rather impressed. Some fathers might call an ambulance or perhaps their mother, but Luke seemed confident in handling the situation. He'd likely taken care of plenty of fevers.

"Okay, well, what can I do next?"

"Would you mind going downstairs and getting the children's acetamino-phen from the medicine shelf? It's on the very top shelf in one of the kitchen cupboards—same cupboard as the drinking glasses."

"Sure."

Cici left the bathroom and closed the door behind her. Then, just as Luke predicted, Brian let out an ear-piercing shriek. Cici's heart broke. A lukewarm bath could feel like torture when a body felt as hot as a charcoal grill. But she reminded herself that the alternative was the fever continuing to rage and Brian possibly suffering a convulsion—or worse.

She found the medicine and made her way back upstairs. The screaming had stopped and only Brian's soft whines and whimpers came from behind the bathroom door.

Minutes passed, and finally Luke appeared with his son wrapped in a towel.

"Hi, Miss Ciara." Even as sick as he was, the little guy managed a weak smile for her benefit.

She was touched to the heart by his sweet gesture.

Once Brian was clad in clean, lightweight pajamas, Cici handed the medicine to Luke and he administered it. Then they went into the living room downstairs where Luke settled the little guy on the couch before turning on the TV.

"Can I sit next to you?" Cici asked.

Brian nodded. "And my dad can sit here." He patted the cushion to his left.

Cici made herself comfortable. "Does anything hurt? Your throat or your ears?"

The boy shook his head. "I feel all better now." He scratched his tummy and then the back of his neck.

Luke sat down and released a long, weary sigh.

"Long day, huh, Superman?" Cici couldn't resist the urge to tease him.

"You can say that again." He sent her a dubious glance. "Something tells me I'll get no sympathy from you."

"Au contraire." She continued to smile. "I sympathize. I worked in children's day care, remember?" She grew serious. "That's why I barged in again tonight. I thought I could be of some help."

Luke stretched. "You did barge in again, didn't you?"

Cici grinned at the comeback. *"Touché."*

He chuckled. "Oh, and speaking of. . .your use of the French language reminds me of the e-mail William sent. I read it this morning. He and Jen are fine and having a great time touring Paris."

"I'm so jealous."

"Daddy, itch my back." A frown pinched Brian's features while he wiggled to alleviate the discomfort.

Luke gave him an accommodating scratch and glanced at the TV before looking back at Cici. "Are you jealous because you didn't get an e-mail or because you're not in Paris?"

"Both." Cici smiled, knowing she didn't begrudge either William or Jen an ounce of happiness. She only wished she were done with her master's degree, had a great-paying job, and could enjoy a trip abroad. "I'll get over it."

"Daddy, now I'm itchy all over."

Cici stared at the little boy beside her and noticed the pink spots that had seemingly appeared out of nowhere.

"Uh-oh." Cici peered at Luke, wide-eyed.

He inspected Brian's face, arms, and back before expelling an audible sigh as he met her gaze. "A couple of days ago, I thought these were bug bites, but, um..." He cleared his throat. "I hope you've had the chicken pox. Looks just like 'em, from what I remember when a friend's kids came down with the virus."

She nodded. "I had the chicken pox as a kid." She tipped her head. "And you?"

"Yeah, I'm pretty sure I did, too." He turned his attention back to Brian. "I had planned to call the doctor in the morning anyway."

"If I'm not mistaken, the county will send over a visiting nurse so you won't have to bring Brian into the office and contaminate others."

"I think you're right."

She nodded. "And I think your future is going to hold giving Brian plenty of oatmeal baths and applying calamine lotion, although I'm sure the nurse will instruct you how to treat chicken pox."

Luke groaned and flopped back against the couch cushions.

"Daddy, is chicken pox those round things you put in the oven and when they're all done we turn 'em upside down on a plate and eat 'em?"

"What?" Luke frowned, obviously trying to interpret. Then his eyes lit up with understanding. "You're talking about chicken pot pies and, no, chicken pox is different." He chuckled. "Come on. I'll show you what chicken pox looks like in the bathroom mirror."

Luke stood and took Brian into the downstairs powder room, and Cici decided she'd leave. She had left the back door unlocked since she hadn't planned on going any farther than the patio.

"I'll see you later, Luke," she called as she made her way through the kitchen. As usual, the room was in disarray. Dirty dishes filled the sink, and unwashed pots and pans stood on the stove. One seemed to have been used to cook scrambled eggs and the other to heat canned corn.

Was that dinner tonight? After eating cold pizza for breakfast and who-knows-what for lunch, those kids had scrambled eggs and canned corn for dinner?

Cici wrinkled her nose. Those were hardly the meals she'd serve her children. Seconds later, she recalled hearing of worse meals dads made for their kids. She'd read reports in which some fathers never even bothered to feed their children so they either starved or learned to steal.

She paused, surveyed the mess, and debated whether to stay and help clean up.

"Don't even think about it."

Pivoting, she smiled at Luke. "You're a mind reader now?"

He laughed. "Yeah, well, you know...us superheroes..."

Cici rolled her eyes.

"Seriously, it'll take me fifteen minutes to clean this place up. But I appreciate your willingness to help."

"Sure. Anytime." She strode toward the back door.

"And, Ciara?"

Once again, she stopped and turned to face him.

"Thanks for lending me a hand tonight with Brian."

"No problem."

She met his gaze and saw his earnest expression. What's more, she felt the fascinating kinetics between them again.

"Call me Cici. My friends do."

"I think Ciara suits you."

She laughed. "I don't know about that. My mom named me after her favorite perfume." With a smile still on her face, she regarded him, noting the intensity in his brown eyes. She felt both embarrassed and flattered by his remark.

"If you don't mind, I'd prefer to call you Ciara. It's a beautiful name." Luke's voice was but a whisper. "You're beautiful, too."

She'd never had anyone say that to her before. "What a sweet thing to say, Luke." The attraction she felt toward him escalated. "I admire sensitivity in a man."

A hint of a smile tugged at his mouth.

She moved toward him with slow, deliberate steps, wondering what it would feel like to linger in his arms and kiss him. Instincts told her that he'd like to find out, too.

But just as she reached him with the intention of slipping her arms around his neck and urging his lips to hers, Brian padded down the vinyl floor of the hall.

"Daddy, are Devin and Aaron gonna get chicken pies, too?"

"Um. . ." Luke blinked and turned to his son.

The magic of the moment vanished.

"I think they probably will," he answered. He cleared his throat as if clearing his mind, also.

Likewise, reality rattled Cici to her core. She couldn't believe what she'd been thinking.

She took two steps backward. "I'll be leaving now. . ."

Luke looked at her with an expression of remorse. Was he sorry she didn't kiss him? Or was he sorry she'd attempted?

With a parting smile, Cici left and trotted next door. She felt overwhelmed and awed by what just took place. Entering her kitchen, she closed the door to the patio and leaned against it. Her professor's warning not to get personally involved rang in her ears. Again she wondered at those fleeting seconds of what had to be sheer insanity.

Just then a shadow moved across the walls between the kitchen and living room. Cici's heart began to hammer when she realized she was about to face an intruder. But before she could react, Chase Tibbits stepped into view. His bulky frame filled the archway.

"Hey," he said in a booming voice, "you should never leave your doors wide open. Never know who might get in."

Chapter 6

"Get out, Chase!"

He stepped closer, and Cici sensed he'd been drinking. He smelled as rancid as spilled beer on a barstool.

"Hey, now don't get your dander up. I rang the bell before I walked in."

Cici narrowed her gaze and put her hands on her hips, hoping she appeared formidable. In truth, she'd never felt more vulnerable in her life.

"Quit glaring at me like that."

"Get out!"

"Look, I was just being neighborly." He swaggered slightly. "I got worried. I thought maybe you were laying dead somewhere in here so I came around back to check on you. Door wasn't locked."

"Chase, if you don't leave, I'm calling the police." Fear caused her voice to tremble, but she didn't think he noticed. "Now, get out!"

The threat of the cops didn't seem to faze him. "Tori said you're working on some report about kids and dads. I got a boy, almost eight years old, and you can study me and him all you want."

Cici tamped down her panic. The man stood over six feet and probably weighed more than two fifty. There was no way she could fight him and win. "I want you to leave, Chase."

He seemed to ignore her. "My ex-wife spoils the kid rotten, but whenever he's with me he doesn't get away with a single thing."

"Seriously. Get out before I call the cops." She snatched Jen's cordless phone off the kitchen counter.

"All right, all right. I'm leaving." He turned around and, without further comment or complaint, let himself out the front entrance.

Relieved, Cici rushed into the living room and locked the door behind him. As she turned the dead bolt, the back doorbell rang and she heard Luke calling her name. No doubt he'd heard the commotion.

"Coming." She hurried to the back door.

"Everything all right?" Luke's voice came through the aluminum screen door. "I don't mean to be nosy, but I heard raised voices, and—"

"Everything's fine." Setting down the phone, she hugged herself, feeling more troubled by Chase's intrusion than she cared to admit. How rude of him to just walk in and lurk around! She wondered if he'd stolen anything.

"You sure you're okay?"

She heard the concern in Luke's tone and gulped down the sudden knot in her throat before bobbing her head in reply. Next she opened her mouth to tell Luke what had happened, but it occurred to her that he was one of two men who had evoked intense emotions in her tonight. Cici prided herself on her even temperament, her levelheadedness.

"Ciara, what in the world is going on?"

"Good question." She forced a smile and felt her composure returning. "Seriously, I'm fine. I just had a bit of a scare. Chase Tibbits was here. He got in because I left the back door unlocked while I was over at your place, helping with Brian."

"Chase? Inside your place? You're not serious!" Before she could stop him, he opened the screen door and stepped into the kitchen. "Is he still here?"

"He's gone," she said as Luke marched into the living room, looking around. "I'm really all right. It was kind of you to come over, though."

"Chase really came in—and stayed here—knowing you weren't home?" Luke stopped in front of her and stood with his arms akimbo. "I think we should inform the police."

Cici picked up on the word "we." It warmed her heart to think he was willing to adopt her problem. Nevertheless, she shook her head in reply. "Maybe he was only here for two or three minutes before I walked in. Let's just forget it." She kept her eyes averted, fearing her emotions might overtake her common sense again and she'd land in Luke's arms one way or another. "I think Chase was drinking tonight. I'm almost certain he didn't mean to alarm me, even though he did."

"Okay, we won't call the cops. It's your decision. But you can always change your mind and file a complaint tomorrow."

"I know. Thanks."

She finally lifted her gaze, noticing—not for the first time—the strong set to Luke's whiskered jaw. Her gaze traveled up his face, and she recognized a light of interest shining in his cocoa brown eyes.

Before her senses reeled for the second time, she moved away. How odd and disconcerting that she should feel attracted to a guy like Luke. Only a month ago she would have laughed at the mere suggestion. A software designer? A Christian? No way. She'd prefer a more intellectual, academic type—if and when that time came.

"You'd better get back home. Brian might need you."

"He's sound asleep." He pulled a monitor from his pocket and held it up.

"Well, just the same. . ." Couldn't he see she was grappling with her emotions? "I, um, should really get back to work on my thesis."

He inclined his head. "But before I go, let me leave my phone number. . .just in case."

She found a slip of paper and a pen. He scribbled down the information. "Thanks."

"I'm serious. Call if you need me."

Cici was touched by his offer, which somehow only heightened her tumultuous feelings. "Good night, Luke."

"Good night."

She watched him leave and, after he was gone, she closed the door and turned the lock. Suddenly she could breathe again.

Crazy night.

She had to regroup. Get her thoughts back in line. Using a relaxation technique she'd learned in a yoga class years ago, Cici tried to free her mind and rid her body of its tension. Her thoughts came around to her best friend, and a grin tugged at her mouth; Jen could have warned her that there were two dangerous men in the neighborhood: an unpredictable lout and a Christian superhero with three rambunctious but adorable sons.

❧

Almost two weeks later, Luke found himself awake at dawn. In the rare moments of quiet, his thoughts wandered to a certain redhead next door. She'd been an invaluable help to him in recent days since the boys got sick. All three had come down with the chicken pox almost simultaneously. Turns out a neighbor kid had the virus and passed it along. Church friends and family members offered their assistance, too, but Luke found it was Ciara he looked forward to seeing every day.

But I shouldn't. She's not a believer.

His heart and conscience battled.

But she's helping me with the kids, and I'm totally in control of my emotions. Sure, I've wanted to kiss her. I'll admit it. Except I haven't. And Ciara has been nothing but polite.

Luke shifted. His body teetered on the edge of the bed as his sons, one by one, had climbed in with him sometime during the night. Unable to sleep, he stood and pulled on some clothes before tiptoeing from his room. He made his way downstairs to the kitchen, yawning as he scooped freshly ground coffee into a filter. He put it into the coffeemaker and, once the java was brewing, he strode to the window and peered outside. A golden hue illuminated the horizon, promising another gorgeous summer day. Maybe he'd allow the boys some outdoor playtime, although the nurse who'd visited warned him that, like with any virus, the kids needed to rest. However, they were feeling pent up and somewhat stir-crazy—and so was Luke.

Lord, this is the day You have made. I will rejoice and be glad in it—even though I've got three kids with chicken pox and a business to run.

Once more, he thought of Ciara's visits in past days. She played with the boys, read to them—when they could sit still long enough to listen to a story—and she gave Luke a break so he could get a little work done in his home office. Neighbors, friends, and family members came and went, offering their assistance, too, and bringing over meals. At times, Luke's front entrance seemed like a revolving door. But those folks, as thoughtful and kindhearted as they were, seemed more like company paying visits. When Ciara came by, he didn't too much care if the dishes were in the sink or the laundry basket sat in the middle of the living room. She'd seen the mess before and hadn't taken offense. A certain comfort level had been established between them, and yet a certain level of caution had developed, too. It was as if they were both battling the inevitable and, in Luke's case, the forbidden.

Lord, the last thing I need in my life is a woman who doesn't share my faith. It was heartache enough for me when Alissa abandoned her beliefs for what she thought was a good time with her friends. . .and maybe even another man.

The timer on the coffeemaker sounded and Luke shook himself. He turned from the window and walked to the cupboard where he pulled a mug from the shelf and filled it with the strong-smelling, steamy brew. Coffee in hand, he retrieved the morning newspaper from the front step. The breeze that met him smelled sweet and fresh, like dew on an Iowa cornfield, and Luke filled his lungs with early morning air.

Stepping outside, he left the front door ajar in case the kids woke up, then he lowered himself onto the cement stoop. The neighborhood was quiet except for the occasional car or pickup truck that passed on the otherwise deserted street, so Luke decided to continue his heart-to-heart chat with the Lord.

There are a lot of good qualities about Ciara. She's a very giving person. She likes to help people and she knows I'm grateful for the times she's dropped in and lent me a hand. The kids like her. . .

Someone honked and Luke startled. He recognized Tori Evenrod and waved as she zoomed off in her yellow convertible. He had to grin at the woman's pluck and flamboyance.

Ciara's got a lot of gumption, too. She's goal-oriented and determined. What's more, she seems like a loyal person.

God's still, small voice seemed to reply: *"Do not be yoked together with unbelievers. . .what fellowship can light have with darkness?"*

Reality check.

Luke drew in a deep breath just as he heard a door open and close next door. He glanced over in time to see Ciara step onto the front walk.

"G'morning."

She turned with a start, and her hand fluttered to the base of her throat.

Luke grimaced. "Didn't mean to scare you. Sorry."

She relaxed visibly. "Guess I spook easily ever since *you know who* paid me that surprise visit a couple of weeks ago."

Luke nodded. He knew she referred to the night she found Chase roaming around inside Jen's condo.

A moment passed, and he couldn't help noticing how her outfit accentuated the fact that she had curves in all the right places. A stretchy, sleeveless, multicolored, striped tank over snug-fitting faded jeans. He then saw the brown leather sandals on her feet with her polished pink toenails peeping out the front. Lifting his gaze, he pushed out an embarrassed little smile and tried not to admit he liked what he saw. Instead he took a gulp of his coffee and watched as she hiked the strap of her pink and black leather computer bag higher onto her freckled shoulder. Her blue eyes shifted from his face to the cup in his hands and Luke remembered his manners.

"Would you like some coffee? I've got plenty."

"No, thanks. I need to be on my way."

He inclined his head. "Well, have a good one."

"I'll try, but I have an appointment with my professor, and she's not going to be pleased that I'll be late handing in my thesis."

Luke sent her a sympathetic wince.

"But then I'm meeting some friends for lunch, so I have that to look forward to."

"Sounds like fun." He took another swallow of coffee.

"Yeah, should be. Have a good day, yourself."

"Thanks. I will."

Ciara smiled and strode to her car.

Luke watched her go and wondered how to proceed. On one hand he wanted to be a good testimony of God's love and goodness. He also relished the times when Ciara came over and helped with the kids. On the other, he couldn't deny his attraction to her. Could he continue operating in the middle of the road, so to speak? Riding the fence? Wrestling with temptation—and winning?

He reminded himself that with God all things are possible.

After raking a hand through his hair, he relaxed and finished his coffee. Pushing to his feet, he went back inside to open his Bible and see what God had to say to him this morning.

Chapter 7

"Are you losing your focus?"

"I—I don't know," Cici stammered, watching Professor Agnes Carter-Hill fold her hands while she sat behind the steel-gray desk. Shelves packed with books lined the entire wall behind her. Some of the titles in her vast collection included *Spock Rocks!*, *Village Parenting*, *Woman and Child*, *Females In The Mother/Father Roles*, and *A Happy Home Without Dads*. Cici had read a number of Aggie's precious volumes and, because of her own upbringing, she could relate to them on several different levels; however, of late, Luke Weldon had somehow proved each study and theory to be little more than ridiculous fabrications.

"You know," Aggie said, drawing Cici from her musings, "there's a good chance our work will be used in the State Supreme Court as evidence to support new rulings. I've documented case upon case in both my master's thesis and my doctorate dissertation, and I've taught you to do the same." A proud smile split her face and dozens of soft wrinkles appeared around her eyes and mouth. Cici was always reminded of the binding of a well-loved book whenever Aggie looked pleased, laughed, or smiled. "Do you realize that we could have a hand in changing the face of the American family as we know it?" Leaning back in her leather desk chair, Aggie raised her arms in victory. "What a boon for women everywhere in this country!"

Cici smiled, thinking her mother would be so proud. Ever since Cici was in junior high school, Mom had been forced to be both mother and father in her life. It had been difficult economically, but Mom did the best she could. Today she and Cici were successful women, despite having no men in their lives. Aggie was right: They didn't need men. But this wasn't just about single women; it was about children's welfare and what was best for them. As for those Weldon boys, Cici admitted they certainly needed their daddy, and Luke was great with them. True, she had first assumed he was a Peter Pan example for his children, but now she thought it was a beautiful thing, watching him and his young sons interact. Luke was kind yet firm, playful, but maintained proper boundaries.

Cici stifled a sigh. And whenever Luke looked at her with those penetrating coffee-colored eyes of his, her legs felt like linguini.

"You're exhausted. I can tell." Aggie sat forward. "Okay, listen, I'll grant you an extension. Your thesis must be in my office by September first. But that's it. No more extensions."

Cici stood and nodded. "You got it." She forced a smile as a skeptical feeling oozed through her. She'd had every intention of finishing her thesis by August but now even the September extension didn't sound like enough time. Her thoughts were so jangled. "Thanks for understanding, Aggie, and I'll try not to disappoint."

The professor nodded, sending the reading glasses perched atop her head tumbling onto the desk. "I know you won't." She smoothed back her short straight, dark hair. "I've mentored you to the best of my academic and personal abilities, and I expect a masterpiece."

Again, Cici pushed out a smile as her confidence dwindled all the more.

Leaving her professor's office, Cici made her way down the empty corridor. The soles of her sandals clapped against the polished marble floor and echoed around her. Not many people were on campus in early July. The six-week long summer session had just ended, and now practically everyone was gearing up and making plans for the Fourth of July holiday. Since the holiday fell on a Friday, most were making a long weekend of it.

Everyone but Cici. She was determined to hole up in Jen's office and work through the holiday weekend. No parties. No movies. No phone calls. No e-mails. And especially no distractions from her handsome neighbor next door.

Except Cici had a hunch that avoiding Luke and his kids might teeter on the impossible. The boys were just getting over the chicken pox, and Luke had his hands full. Cici knew he appreciated the help she gave him—and she enjoyed it. The only trouble was, Luke had messed up her thinking. They'd never debated any political or spiritual issues. They never discussed controversial matters. He kept his word and respected her beliefs, but he lived out his own and everything he did brought back snippets of conversations Cici'd had in the past with Jen and William. In essence, Luke was proving that everything they told her was true, and Cici was both curious and confused by this unexpected turn of events. What's more, her thesis statement had become skewed in a way that seemed irreparable; however, she didn't dare tell Aggie. The woman was a diehard feminist, and Cici had believed she was heading in the same direction until she met Luke. Now, suddenly, her entire world seemed to have been knocked off its axis.

Cici exited the building and walked across the sparsely populated lot on the university campus and climbed into her car. Key in the ignition, she started the engine and drove the short distance to the restaurant where she'd planned to meet her two college roommates, Bridget and Tanya, for lunch. She parked, entered the establishment, and found the two blonds sitting at a table near the bar area. The young women saw her approaching and stood.

"Hi!" Cici hugged first Tanya and then Bridget. "What's new with you two?"

"Nothing much." Bridget lowered herself back into her wooden chair. "Same ol' thing."

Cici looked at Tanya. "What about you?"

"Oh. . ." Tanya's expression fell. "I broke up with Ryan."

"Sorry to hear that, although it was a long time coming. Wasn't it?"

"Yes, but I really believed Ryan was the guy for me." Tears filled Tanya's hazel eyes.

"Is reconciliation a possibility?"

"Not now, not while he's got a drinking problem." Bridget answered for Tanya, studying her brokenhearted friend as she blinked away her tears. "Tanya realized, and rightly so, that Ryan needs some help before he can be in a healthy relationship."

"It's a good thing I found out before I did something stupid like marry the guy." Tanya's gaze dropped to the cola in front of her. "So much for earning my *M-R-S* degree this year."

Cici grinned at her flaxen-haired friend. "At least you've still got your sense of humor."

Tanya lifted her chin and looked across the table at her. "I'm serious. I want to get married and be a wife and a mommy."

Cici coveted a mommy role in the future, too, but she shook her head at the wifely part of the statement. "You should want to build a successful career for yourself. Don't give everything up for a man."

"Careers can come and go, Ceece, but I was always taught that love never fails. And if you were perfectly honest, you'd admit that you'd ditch that women's lib stuff if the right guy came along."

"I'll admit to no such thing." Cici gave each friend an exasperated glance. "Building your lives around men will only lead to the same anguish that Tanya is experiencing now. However, if a woman is educated and continues to learn and grow as an individual, she will always have a safety net in which to fall if the opportunity for marriage doesn't present itself—or if her husband dumps her for another woman like my dad left my mother."

"I'm all about those safety nets." Tanya sipped her cola.

The server came and took their lunch orders then fetched Cici an iced tea.

"So, speaking of men, how's your love life?" Bridget donned an impish grin. "Boring as ever?"

"I'm on a sabbatical and writing my master's thesis. I'm not supposed to have a love life right now."

Her roommates looked at each other. "Boring as ever," they said in unison.

"That's what you think." The words spewed out before Cici could swallow them down.

"You met someone?" Bridget leaned forward, wearing an interested expression.

"Sort of. He just lives next door to Jen and. . .he's single with three little boys." She muttered the latter while placing the napkin in her lap, wishing she'd never said a word.

"How'd you meet him?"

"Who is he?"

"Handsome? Good job?"

"Jen's neighbor? Unbelievable!" Bridget sat back in awe. "What's his name?"

"Whoa!" Cici held up her hands as if to shield herself from the questions they hurled at her. "Like I said, he's Jen's neighbor, and he knows her and William." She paused, hoping the association would set in. When two pairs of eyes just stared back at her, she added what should have been obvious. "He's a Christian. He doesn't drink, smoke, party, or swear. He pretty much works at his home-based business, takes care of his kids, and goes to church."

"Can I have his phone number?" A dreamy smile curled Bridget's full lips. "I'd love to date a guy who's just plain ol' nice, you know?"

"Yeah, I know. I recently broke up with a drunk who had violent tendencies." Tanya glanced at Bridget before looking back at Cici. "Does this neighbor guy of yours have a friend?"

Sitting back in her chair, Cici felt stunned. "What? The party girls would rather date a Christian than one of their 'cool dude' acquaintances? I don't believe it."

"I'm burned out." With the admission Tanya's expression fell.

Bridget agreed. "I guess we learned the hard way that it's better to leave the party early than to stay and ruin your entire life."

"Jen's a great example of that," Tanya pointed out. "She straightened up her life, finished school, met a nice guy, and now she's getting married in October. I'm so happy for her."

Cici was more than amazed by what she was hearing. This certainly didn't sound like the same Tanya and Bridget she'd been rooming with. In fact, her two party-hearty roomies were the reason she'd moved into Jen's place. She knew she'd never find a moment's peace with all their friends coming and going. In the past, Cici hadn't cared since she wasn't home a lot. But in order to write a thesis, one needed solitude and an ambiance that promoted intellect. . .

Which, she realized, didn't exactly describe her present situation, either—not with those noisy superheroes next door.

"Hey, what do you hear from Jen, anyway?" Tanya sat forward, looking eager. "How's her trip going? Must be so romantic to tour Europe with the man you love."

"I want to hear more about Jen's next-door neighbor." A teasing grin played across Bridget's pink lips.

The food arrived and the easy banter continued. Cici hadn't planned to talk about Luke, but her friends managed to pry information out of her anyway.

"So, you see, the entire situation is so confusing, not to mention distracting."

Cici picked at her seafood salad and finally popped a piece of tomato into her mouth. "I set out to prove my thesis using Luke as a prime example of an inconsequential father figure, but he seems to be proving me wrong and it's messing up my head."

"Is this the first time you've been in love?" Tanya asked between bites of her BLT sandwich.

"In love?" Cici brought her chin back. "I'm not in love. I'm just...attracted to him in a curious sort of way because he's so opposite of me and everything I've worked so hard to become."

"Hold it. You met a man who can make you pull your head out of your books and you're not in love?" Bridget chuckled. "You deceive yourself, Miss Academia."

Cici narrowed her gaze. "Very funny."

Bridget and Tanya both wore amused little smirks.

"How does he feel about you?"

Cici replied with a quick shrug. "My guess is he's interested in me, too, although he doesn't give in to his emotions. I don't know if he's just extremely polite or if I'm misreading his body language."

"Maybe he thinks it's a sin if he kisses you." Tanya pointed at her with a long French fry. "I knew a guy in high school like that."

"But we're adults." Cici didn't think that was the case at all. "Besides, I saw Jen kiss William, so it can't be that great of a sin."

"Listen, I went to a religious private high school." Bridget's voice held an authoritative note. "Intimacy before marriage is a huge no-no. It's in the Bible and everything, except don't ask me where because I never paid attention in our religion classes."

"Figures," Tanya quipped.

Cici forked another bite of her salad into her mouth and mulled over the last bit of their conversation. "I never imagined I'd be attracted to a Christian man, even though Jen's my best friend."

"But you and Jen have been friends for years," Bridget pointed out. "Would you be close to her at this point in your life if you just met Jen today, knowing she's got religion and you don't?"

The question gave Cici pause.

"To tell you the truth, I'm envious of Jen," Tanya said. "I'd rather date a Christian man than an alcoholic any day. I feel like I'm emerging from a nightmare because of everything I went through with Ryan."

Bridget reached over and clasped Tanya's hand. "You'll get over it. You did the right thing in breaking off your relationship with him."

Cici saw tears form in her friend's eyes and her heart ached. Then, suddenly the image of Chase Tibbits, intoxicated and wandering around Jen's living room uninvited, flashed through Cici's mind. His drunken presence had scared the wits out of her, and Cici was forced to agree with Tanya: She'd rather date a Christian than a problem drinker, too.

"Well, in my humble opinion, the game of love boils down to nothing more than chemistry between two people. It's all about the chemistry." Bridget took a drink of her cola. "It's either there or it's not."

Cici's insides turned warm and fluttery. She had felt that indescribable existential force between herself and Luke more times than she cared to count—every time she saw him, in fact.

"Look," she said, wondering whom she hoped to convince, her friends or herself, "whatever I'm feeling for Luke will pass soon enough. I've got a new deadline for my thesis, and I've got to concentrate on finishing it."

"Good luck." Tanya smiled. "Your heart might just overrule your common sense."

The reply rang loudly in Cici's head, like church bells on Sunday morning.
Or was it really some sort of knell?

Chapter 8

A brilliant sunset blazed on the horizon as Cici climbed out of her car. She'd spent hours talking with her friends and catching up on their lives before going to the library where she wrote several pages of her thesis. Her resolve returned once she concluded that she could present a more objective point of view and still prove her theory. According to her research, Luke's fathering skills were an exception and not the norm. Besides, he had the support of his church, which was more assistance than many single mothers received.

Cici ambled up the walkway and unlocked the condo door. She entered and deposited her laptop on the living room table, determined to immediately start working on her thesis again. But as she settled into the sofa and booted up her computer, she heard wails coming from next door. She couldn't help but wonder what was going on. Was Aaron in trouble again? Or one of the boys ill and miserable?

In spite of herself, she made her way to the Weldons' to see if she could help. Surprisingly, she found Luke on his patio, barbecuing on the outdoor grill.

"Hi, Ciara." He barely looked up from the wieners he was cooking.

"I can hear one of the kids crying, so I thought I'd come over to see if I might lend a helping hand."

"Thanks, but I can manage."

Cici thought the muttered reply sounded a bit short. "Bad day?"

"The worst."

She pressed her lips together to keep from smiling, not at the fact that Luke had a tough time today, but how quickly he admitted to it. That said a lot in her estimation.

She eyed the smoking grill. "Whacha burning?"

"Supper."

On tiptoes she peeked over his shoulder. "I don't think those hot dogs can get much blacker."

"The boys like 'em well done."

"That's good." She lifted the white plastic plate from off the grill's wooden rack. "I'd say they're as well done as they'll get."

She held the plate in his direction and, using the pair of tongs in his hand, he removed the charred wieners from the open flames.

"Why don't you take a break, Luke? I'll feed the boys."

He raked his fingers through his walnut brown hair and looked off in the distance for several moments before bringing his gaze back to her. "This'll be great for your thesis, won't it? The helpless dad who can't even get his kids fed because of all the chaos in his home?"

"What?" His question surprised her.

Luke had the good grace to look contrite. "I'm sorry. My remark was harsh. But you know what I mean. My present situation is a perfect example of why you think a single dad can't raise his kids."

"Well, to be honest, I'd normally agree with you, but considering the fact that your sons have had the chicken pox and you're obviously exhausted, let's just forget it. This is off the record. Just one neighbor helping another."

Luke half shrugged, half nodded.

Cici grinned. He resembled one of his little guys just now. "Cheer up, okay? If it's any consolation, even single moms have bad days."

"I'm sure they do."

"They do. Trust me. My mom had plenty of them. So relax for a while. I'm happy to help out." She walked into his kitchen and Luke didn't try to stop her.

Devin and Brian sat at the table, looking forlorn. Their faces were covered with scabby red dots.

"Hi, superheroes." Cici smiled.

Their countenances brightened just a little.

"Where's Aaron?"

"He was bad," Devin informed her. "So he's upstairs."

That explained the crying she'd heard minutes ago.

Moving farther into the kitchen, Cici spied an empty can on the counter and the baked beans in a saucepan on the stove. She presumed the syrupy legumes were part of the supper plan, too. The boys confirmed it and then instructed her as to how they liked their hot dogs prepared—lots of ketchup, no mustard. Once they were eating, Cici fetched Aaron. He was in the bedroom he shared with his brothers, lying on the upper bunk, sobbing. A few soft words, however, and his tears dissipated. By the time she'd led him down to the kitchen, his mood had lifted and a "cowboy dinner" appealed to him.

As she sat at the round kitchen table, watching the children eating, Cici had to grin at the term "cowboy dinner." She supposed superheroes could deign to eat wieners and baked beans.

She glanced toward the screen door and caught a glimpse of Luke reclining in one of the lawn chairs on the patio, his face tilted toward the late afternoon sun. He appeared completely exhausted, and she wished she could do more to help him out.

She gazed back at the boys, and an idea began to form. She stood. "I'll be right back, guys. Okay?"

Their heads bobbed in unison and Cici noticed the sugary syrup and ketchup collecting around their lips as they chewed.

She smiled at the sight of the boys enjoying their food and walked outside. Reaching Luke, she touched him on the shoulder. He jumped to attention.

"I didn't mean to startle you."

"No problem. I must have dozed off." He rubbed one eye and then the other. "Sorry 'bout that."

"No need to be sorry." Cici's heart went out to her bedraggled neighbor. "Listen, I'd like to take the boys out for ice cream. May I?"

"Uh…" Luke hedged.

"It'll give you time to regroup, and I promise to keep the kids away from other people so they don't share their chicken pox."

He smiled. "I'd love the break, and they're probably not contagious anymore; their spots have scabbed over." He raked his fingers through his hair, appearing pensive for a good fifteen seconds. "They only look frightening, but they've all had temperaments to match."

"I imagine they're tired of being cooped up."

Luke bobbed his head in agreement. "I figured by the Fourth of July they'll feel—*and look*—like themselves again and we can enjoy the holiday."

"That's only two days away." Cici wondered what sort of plans Luke had made. Part of her wished he'd ask her to join him and the boys, but her thesis awaited. "So what do you say? Can I take the kids out for ice cream tonight?"

"They're a handful."

"I think I can manage."

"Okay. . .yeah, sure."

In spite of his amiable smile, Cici thought his attitude was somewhat brusque. She'd noticed it before, too. Still, she knew Luke trusted her, otherwise he wouldn't allow her to take the boys for ice cream. However, she couldn't quite understand his aloofness.

Or was it that he didn't want her to go?

Cici dashed the notion. Luke was just tired, that's all.

She reentered the kitchen and, after the boys finished eating, she told them her plans to take them for ice cream. She laughed when they clambered off their chairs and jumped up and down, cheering all the while.

Luke held out his keys. "I think it'd be easier if you take my minivan. The twins' car seats and Devin's booster seat are secured in there, and I'd hate to have to transfer them."

Cici reached out and slowly accepted the proffered keys. She hadn't thought about car seats.

Embarrassment filled her. Here she was supposed to be an expert on children! "Thanks."

"Well, it's the least I can do." He spoke loudly in order to be heard above his children's excited voices.

"Can we go now?"

"I want cookie dough ice cream."

"When are we leaving?"

"Right away." Cici surveyed the upturned faces and eager brown eyes staring at her. "I just need to grab my purse and lock up next door."

"Hurry, okay?"

"Devin, remember your manners." Luke's tone held a parental warning. He turned to Cici. "We'll meet you by the garage in front."

"Sounds good."

Once again, she sensed the terseness behind the words he spoke. As she made her way back into Jen's condo, she decided Luke was certainly in one cranky mood this evening.

🕮

Feeling like he needed some adult companionship, Luke phoned a couple of his buddies and asked them to stop by. Within twenty minutes both Jesse and Trevor were sitting in his living room, lending sympathetic ears.

"There's no way I can avoid her. She's renting Jen Hargrove's condo next door. And today I had a really bad day with the boys until she showed up like a godsend, fed the kids, and took them out for ice cream. She enjoys helping me out and the kids adore her." Luke hesitated before admitting the rest. "I'm beginning to adore her, too."

"Hmm, I see the dilemma." Jesse nodded while a concerned frown pulled at his thick, blond brows. "She's not a believer, but the attraction's there."

"Why don't you just come out and tell her about your faith, your feelings for her," Trevor said, "and explain that it's impossible for you to give in to your emotions and please God, too?"

Luke considered his friend's suggestion, thinking that "Blunt" had to be the guy's middle name. "I don't want to turn her off of Christianity."

"William and Jen evidently haven't turned her off and they're pretty straightforward." Trevor lifted a can of cola to his mouth and took a swig.

"I suppose that's true enough."

"That's one way to handle it." Jesse sat forward on the sofa. "But I wasn't a Christian until I met Mandy. We worked in an office together and when I finally asked her out to dinner, she accepted the invite. I knew she was different than other women I'd gone out with, and she talked about her faith in God. But she never once snubbed me or said she couldn't date me. I grew more and more curious about her and when I realized I was in love with her, I decided to tag along to church because I knew it was important to her. Wasn't long before God got a hold of my heart, and I made the decision to become a Christian, too."

"So you're telling me to trust God and let my relationship with Ciara develop?" Luke pondered the idea. It appealed to him, of course—although he'd never been an advocate of "dating evangelism." Then again, Alissa had claimed to be a believer, and her life had ended after she'd left a bar with another man.

"If you've got enough character to let the relationship progress without compromising your faith, then..." Jesse shrugged. "I don't see a problem with taking prayerful steps forward. But I do think Trevor's right: You have to be honest with her about your faith."

"I agree with that part, but I don't think you should move ahead in this relationship one more inch." Trevor shook his head. "You're playing with fire. Unbelieving women in this day and age have no scruples, no shame."

"That's quite the generalization there, Trev." Luke reclined at the end of the couch. "I think there are a lot of non-Christian women with high moral standards."

"Well, maybe." A wave of chagrin washed over his features. "But my point is that this sort of thing is exactly how good Christian men end up falling into sin."

"Anyone can fall into sin at any time," Jesse argued the point. "When a believer isn't walking in the Spirit, he's walking in the flesh and that's when he's in the danger zone."

Luke remained silent, weighing both sides of the debate.

"Dude, there's got to be half a dozen godly single women at church who'd welcome your attention." Trevor gazed at him with a mix of confusion and conviction in his expression. "Why don't you pray about God's leading with one of those women?"

"That would make sense, wouldn't it?" Luke had asked himself that question at least one hundred times over the last few weeks.

Seconds later, all conversation ceased as two of his three boys burst in through the front door. Except for the ice cream stains on their shirts, they looked none the worse for wear, and they each wore a sunny smile.

"We're home, Daddy!" Aaron came to a halt at Luke's knees.

"I see that." He pulled his son into his arms and gently roughhoused with him. They hadn't had any kind of makeup time since Aaron's discipline this afternoon.

The boy giggled when Luke tickled him.

"Did you have fun?"

"Yes." Aaron laughed so hard his knees buckled and he landed in a heap across Luke's feet.

Luke decided to target Devin now, since he stood by, grinning.

"Were you good mannered?" Luke grabbed him and tickled him.

"Ye–he–he–es," he tried to reply while laughing.

"That's my boy." Luke kissed his cheek and followed up with a playful swat on the backside.

"Let's do tickle torture." Devin's expression said he was all about that game.

Aaron popped up off the floor. "Yeah!"

"No. We have company and—" Luke glanced around. "Where's Miss Ciara?"

"She's coming." Aaron attempted to instigate the mass tickle session, but Luke caught his little arms and crisscrossed them around his chest, locking him in place with his knees.

"Now I got you, you little monkey."

Jesse lazed back on the sofa. "Man, I'm feeling right at home."

Trevor chuckled.

Finally Ciara strolled in, holding Brian's hand. Luke realized the little guy had been crying.

Luke whispered a word of warning to Aaron before setting him free. Then he stood. "Problems?" He looked from Brian to Ciara.

But before she could answer, Brian filled him in. "I fell down, Daddy." He pulled up the hem of his shorts and pointed at his knee.

His brothers stooped to get a closer look at the scrape.

Aaron appeared concerned when he turned to Luke. "It's bleeding!"

"I couldn't grab him in time; he tripped on the curb." Ciara wore a pained expression.

"Don't worry about it. Kids fall all the time." He looked at Devin. "Want to get the plastic bandages for me? And bring the green spray, too." Glancing at all the adults, he interpreted as Devin took off to do Luke's bidding. "The boys call the antiseptic the 'green spray.'"

Brian pouted, and Ciara swung him up into her arms. Luke hid a smirk, thinking his son was playing the sympathy card, big time.

"It's okay, honey, you'll be all right." Her voice sounded soft, soothing—motherly.

"It's a skinned knee." Jesse grinned. "He'll survive. Trust me. Mandy and I are at the Urgent Care Center a couple times a week, it seems, with our brood. Oh, and by the way. . ." He stood and extended his right hand to Ciara. "I'm Jesse Satlock. I believe I met you at Jen's when she had that jewelry party last year. I dropped my wife off and poked my head in the door to say hello but didn't stay."

"Yes, I thought you looked somewhat familiar." Ciara gave him a polite smile and freed one hand, shaking his politely. "Nice to see you again."

"I'm Trevor Morris." He, too, took Ciara's hand, gave it a friendly shake, adding a nod of greeting.

"Good to meet you."

She glanced at Luke, but before he could react, Devin returned with the bandages and antiseptic spray. Luke cleaned up Brian's knee while Ciara held him.

"What a production, Luke. Good grief."

"Oh, don't be such an insensitive lout." The bit of sarcasm earned him good-natured snickers from his friends. Ciara, on the other hand, didn't look amused. Luke was quick to apologize. "Inside joke. Came from a men's retreat we all attended years ago. Don't mind our strange sense of humor."

"Mmm."

She arched a brow in mild reprimand, and Luke thought she reacted much the way both Mandy Satlock and Grace Morris would if they were here with their husbands.

Jesse must have noticed the same thing. "Say, Ciara, what are you doing on the Fourth? Mandy and I are having a few friends over for a barbecue. You ought to come. It'll be fun, but we don't have to invite Luke and his bad jokes, but, um. . ." He glanced at the three boys. "You guys are welcome."

"Yeah! Party! Party!" Aaron pumped his arms up and down, and even Brian came to life.

Trevor snorted a laugh.

"Where does he get this stuff?" Luke couldn't imagine. "He's five years old!" He quelled Aaron's reveling by placing a hand on the boy's shoulder.

"So what do you think, Ciara?" Jesse leaned forward. "Think you'll come to the barbecue—even if Luke does show up?"

She set Brian on the carpeted floor. "Thanks, but no. I have to finish my master's thesis. That's the whole reason I'm renting Jen's condo next door. For some solitude. I got an extension today, but I still might not make the deadline."

"Master's thesis, huh?" Trevor seemed impressed.

"Ciara is writing about how 'ineffectual' fathers are, and she's using me as a prime example."

"Nice." Jesse hung his head back and hooted. "Are you serious?" He looked from Luke to Ciara and back to Luke again.

"Easy, now, I'm doing my best to prove her wrong."

Ciara shifted, looking a tad uncomfortable. "Luke, you make my theory sound so petty. I'm really presenting the case on an extremely high intellectual level."

"So you're saying we're too dumb to understand it?" Trevor smirked.

Devin pulled out his blue plastic case filled with small cars, and the boys began playing with them on the coffee table.

"On the contrary; I have no idea what your intelligence level is, so why would I comment on it?" She eyed Trevor in a way that made him back off.

Luke felt like things were turning ugly fast. "Look, this is all my fault." He glanced at Trevor, then Jesse. "I like to tease Ciara about her viewpoints, and she dishes it right back at me." He turned to her. "I wasn't insulting you or trying to get my buddies here to gang up on you over your thesis."

"No harm done. In fact, I enjoy batting ideas around."

"I like batting, too," Devin said, popping into the conversation. "And pitching. I got my own mitt."

Luke smiled at his eldest son's interpretation of the topic and tousled his hair.

Aaron and Brian shouted out their love of baseball, too.

"The Weldons are a competitive bunch," Jesse commented with a grin.

"That we are." Luke turned to Ciara again. "And I'm still determined to prove your theory wrong."

She softened, right before his eyes. "Well, you've succeeded. . .sort of."

He raised his brows, amazed at the partial admission.

A hint of a grin curved her pretty pink mouth. "It's true that I am using you as an example of a single father, struggling through day-to-day issues, but I've decided on more of an objective slant. Not all fathers are 'ineffectual.'"

"Oh, yeah?" Luke felt rather pleased.

"Pat yourself on the back, Luke. You're a good dad."

Luke was touched by the compliment. Meant a lot coming from her. What's more, both Trevor and Jesse appeared impressed by Ciara's kind admission. "Thanks."

But a second later, Aaron decided to slug Devin, who gave his younger brother a return shove.

"Da–ad!"

"Knock it off, you two." Luke decided the good Lord sure knew how to keep him humble.

Trevor and Jesse both donned empathetic grins.

"I want you three to go upstairs, wash up, brush your teeth, and change into your pajamas. *Now.*"

The boys did as he asked but stomped their hardest and loudest as they made their way to their bedroom.

Trevor stood. "I'd best be leaving. I need to help Grace get our kids to bed."

"Me, too." Jesse's remark came out like a weary sigh. He pushed to his feet and tossed a challenging glance at Trevor. "Bet it takes Mandy and me three times as long to get our six children tucked in for the night as it takes you and Grace."

"I'm sure it does." Trevor grinned.

Luke didn't add that it sometimes took him half the night to settle his rambunctious boys.

"Six kids?" Ciara seemed to have parked on that particular piece of Jesse's remark.

"Yes, indeed." A proud smile curved his full lips. "Four girls and two boys."

She turned to Trevor. "And how many children do you and your wife have?"

"Just two. But they're blessings enough for Grace and me." He ran a hand over his balding head. "They're both ten going on twenty-one, and I'm lucky I have any hair left at all." He chuckled.

Luke grinned and saw his buddies out the door. He noticed Ciara hung back, and he felt both delighted and dismayed.

He closed the front door after thanking both Trevor and Jesse for stopping by and then turned to face the reason he'd asked his friends over in the first place.

Chapter 9

W ant some help putting the boys to bed?"

Luke shook his head. "No, I can manage. Thanks anyway."

Still attired in the striped tank top and jeans from this morning, Ciara took a step toward him. A small frown pleated her brows. "I'm beginning to think I've offended you. Have I?"

Again, he shook his head. "What gave you that idea?"

"You did." Her attempt at a smile wavered. "This afternoon you were brusque with me, but I attributed it to your being stressed from taking care of sick kids. Who wouldn't be? But now I get the feeling it's more than that. I mean, I sense some remoteness on your part."

She was a perceptive woman. No doubt about it.

Luke set his hands on his hips and glanced up the stairs, thinking it sounded like the boys weren't getting into trouble—yet. When he looked back at Ciara, he wondered how he could explain why their different beliefs made it impossible for him to get too close to her.

"Did my feministic viewpoints offend you? I realize I can come on strong that way, but I really do like you, Luke, and as much as I hate to admit it, you're living proof that a father is very beneficial to a family unit."

"Beneficial? Try *necessary*."

Ciara brought her chin back at his curt reply. "In your case, definitely necessary."

Luke swallowed the desire to share his beliefs. He hadn't intended to argue with her. "Listen, I didn't mean to bark at you. But I wish you'd see that a father is a key figure and role model for his children, Ciara. That's the way God designed families, with a mother *and a father*." He stressed the last three words.

"You're talking about old-fashioned ideals, Luke. But families come in all shapes and sizes: single parents, step-parents and blended families, foster families—you get the idea. But I can tell you that, from my research and experience, your parenting skills, as a single dad, are an anomaly."

"I appreciate the compliment, but—"

"Most single dads are like Chase Tibbits."

"Chase? What's he got to do with anything?"

She slipped her hands into the front pockets of her jeans. Luke thought he saw a hint of guilt in her expression. "The boys will probably tell you that we saw him and Jeremy at the ice cream parlor."

"Oh?"

"Chase insisted on sitting at the same picnic table outside with us, even after I warned him that your kids were recovering from the chicken pox. He wasn't concerned about his son catching it. But I was leery of him after the incident a couple of weeks ago. Seeing as your kids were with me, I didn't protest." Ciara pursed her lips, and she looked livid. "Almost immediately, Chase started belittling Jeremy and it made me so mad. The kid's only about a year older than Devin." Pulling her hands from her pockets, she raised them, fingers splayed in frustration. "I sat there fuming and feeling so sorry for that child while Chase picked at him for everything from not wiping ice cream off his mouth to not catching the baseball at the park. When it was time to go, I pulled Chase aside and gave him a piece of my mind." Remorse crept over her delicate features. "But I didn't realize that your kids overheard. They were supposed to be climbing into the van."

Luke rubbed the backs of his fingers alongside his jaw. "Were you using bad language or something? I'm not quite sure I understand the whole problem."

She shifted. "I called Chase a jerk, but that's as bad as I got. Chase, on the other hand, used some, um, colorful verbiage with me until I reminded him that I didn't call the cops after I caught him prowling inside Jen's condo. That finally shut him up."

"Mmm. . ." Luke thought it over. "Well, my sons know using colorful verbiage calls for disciplinary measures."

"Luke, I feel just awful about them overhearing my disagreement with Chase. But I felt that I had to stick up for Jeremy." Ciara strode toward him. "My heart kept breaking and my ire kept mounting every time the man opened his mouth and picked on his son." She wagged her head remorsefully. "You trusted me when you allowed me to take your kids out tonight, Luke, and I guess I feel I let you down."

"You didn't."

"Okay, good." She tipped her head back. "So what's with the weird distance I'm sensing from you lately? I wouldn't have taken it personally, except that you seemed more like yourself when your friends were here. Once they left, I felt like a wall went up or something."

"It's difficult to explain."

She looked like she'd just taken a blow on the chin. "So I'm not imagining it."

"No, you're not imagining it." In spite of his gentle tone, a wounded expression clouded her face. "Please don't feel hurt. But just like you have your principles, I have to stay true to my beliefs, my faith."

"That's fair." Her words belied the bewilderment in her eyes.

But before Luke could explain further, a plaster-crumbling crash sounded from above. He tensed. Aaron was parachuting again.

"Scuse me, Ciara. We'll have to finish this discussion later."

"Sure."

Luke took off for the steps.

❧

Cici returned to Jen's condo, trying to shake off her feelings of rejection. She and Luke were opposite in every way; how had she ever developed feelings for him?

Maybe they weren't real feelings at all. Perhaps it had been mere attraction and nothing more from the start. Cici had studied cases in which women entered into all sorts of commitments based on fluttery feelings that soon faded like denim.

Women such as Bridget and Tanya. Cici began to fume. How dare they accuse her of being "in love"! What a laugh. What did they know about love anyhow?

Cici showered and, afterward, pulled on a pair of loose-fitting, silky-soft turquoise capris and a matching sleeveless tank. She felt refreshed and less remorseful. After all, there was no reason that she and Luke couldn't at least be friends.

Picking up her computer, she ambled downstairs and into the living room where she booted up the laptop and then turned on the television for a little background noise. She retrieved a cold bottle of flavored water from the fridge and then got comfy on the sofa.

She'd written only a few paragraphs when the doorbell rang.

Standing, she assumed it was Luke, since he'd said they'd finish their conversation later and no one else she knew would stop over at ten o'clock at night. So she was stunned to find Chase Tibbits standing on the front stoop.

"What are you doing here?" She noticed the grocery store bouquet in his hand.

"I came to apologize."

"Oh?" Cici didn't think he seemed intoxicated.

He held out the flowers. "You were right. I was a jerk tonight and I feel bad about the way I treated Jeremy. My dad did that same thing to me, and I resented him most of my life."

She accepted the blooms, albeit with a good measure of hesitancy. "Where's Jeremy?"

"Sleeping. A neighbor's with him."

Cici was glad to hear the child wasn't alone, but she still didn't know what to make of Chase and his floral peace offering.

"I also want you to know that I'm sorry about coming in uninvited a couple of weeks ago. Guess I thought you'd like my company." His gaze roved over her in a way that made Cici feel like running upstairs and cocooning herself in Jen's thick terrycloth bathrobe.

In that moment he didn't seem like any less of a jerk than he had earlier this evening.

"I think you need to leave." She handed back the bouquet, but Chase wasn't quick enough, and the flowers landed at his feet.

"Hey, now hold on." With one meaty hand, he blocked her attempt to close the door. "I don't mean any harm, here. I came to apologize. . .for Jeremy's sake."

At the mention of his son's name, Cici refrained from slamming the door in his face. "What do you mean?"

"You're good with kids. That's obvious. I think you could be a positive influence in Jeremy's life. Maybe help me undo all the damage I've done."

"How would I do that?"

"I don't know." Chase lifted his brawny shoulders. "Maybe like the same way you're helping out Luke next door here. Me and him—well, we're sort of in the same boat, being single dads. It's tough, and I've got Jeremy for the next two weeks by myself."

Cici didn't feel an ounce of pity for him, but her heart bled for Jeremy. "You need a babysitter, is that what you're telling me?"

"No, no, no." Chase shook his head. "I need a friend. That's all. Someone who likes kids and can steer me down the right path as a dad."

Might be an act, although Cici thought he appeared genuine. Maybe he was—this time.

She watched as he bent to scoop up the bouquet of flowers. He held them out to her again. "For starters, you could come by on the Fourth. I'm having a little cookout in the backyard. Nothing fancy. Burgers on the grill and a case of beer. But you don't have to come if you're busy." Chase ducked his head, looking like a little boy.

Cici couldn't find it within herself to be completely heartless. After all, everyone made mistakes and here Chase was, standing at the doorway, admitting his transgressions and apologizing for them.

For the second time, she accepted the flowers. "Thanks—and maybe I'll stop by."

A grin split his face. "Well, hey, then I'm glad I stopped by."

Cici gave him a parting smile before slowly closing the door.

❧

Luke stood at his front screen door. He hadn't meant to eavesdrop, but when he'd heard Chase's booming voice through the open living room window, he thought it might mean trouble for Ciara. He hadn't heard the entire conversation; however, he'd gotten enough of an earful to realize that Chase was doing exactly what

Luke had determined never to do: use children to bait a woman. By the sound of it, Ciara fell for the tactic—or had she just been polite in order to get Chase off her doorstep?

Setting his hands on his hips, Luke mulled over his discussion this evening with Ciara. He'd been surprised to discover she'd left while he'd tucked the boys into bed. He had presumed the two of them would continue talking once the kids were settled and he came back downstairs.

Lord, I didn't mean to hurt her. . .and now she's considering Chase Tibbits's invitation for the Fourth of July? After he acted like such a creep? So what if he apologized!

Luke had to admit it: He felt jealous. He didn't know what to make of his feelings, although he did know one thing for sure. He wasn't about to step aside while Ciara spent the upcoming holiday at Chase's place.

He climbed the steps and checked on his sons. Taking in their peaceful expressions, he smiled. They were sound asleep. Crossing the room, he switched on the monitoring system, which he habitually did when he planned to be either outside or in the basement for more than just a few minutes. In his office, he pocketed the small counterpart from which he would be able to hear if his kids awoke.

Then he headed over to Ciara's. God willing, she'd come back to his place where they could finish their earlier conversation, and maybe he could convince her to spend the Fourth with him at Jesse and Mandy's house.

🙂

Cici had just reread the last paragraph she'd written on her thesis when the back doorbell sounded. This time she was sure it had to be Luke. Setting aside her laptop, she rose from the sofa and strode through the kitchen. She opened the back door and there he stood.

"Come on in."

He pulled open the screen door and stepped into the kitchen. Cici saw his gaze take in her pajama-like attire, but unlike Chase's lusty stare, Luke's held a light of appreciation, and it made her think maybe he harbored feelings for her after all.

"So what brings you over?" She folded her arms.

"Well, um, I was hoping we could finish talking." Luke rubbed his jaw in a way that Cici had come to know meant he felt uneasy or dismayed.

"Sure. I've got some time." She abandoned all hopes of writing more tonight but determined to start in on her thesis bright and early in the morning. "Why don't we sit down in the living room?"

"I had hoped you'd come over to my place. I don't like to leave the kids for too long, even when they're sleeping. I know from experience that once you and I get talking it's easy to lose track of time."

"True." Cici couldn't completely restrain her smile. The fact they'd been able o converse on a comfortable level had to mean they were friends.

He stared at something on the counter, and Cici followed his gaze to where he plastic-wrapped flowers lay. She'd forgotten all about putting them into water.

She turned back to Luke. "You'll never guess who those are from."

"Chase Tibbits."

A sense of surprise filled her being.

Luke must have seen it on her expression. "I overheard some of your conversation with him tonight. I honestly didn't mean to eavesdrop, but when I heard his voice I got concerned, especially after what you said happened at the ice cream parlor."

Cici was touched that Luke cared. "Nice of you to look out for me, but you honestly don't have to bother. You've got enough in your own home to manage. Besides, I'm a big girl. I can take care of myself."

"I know you're a capable woman, and I never meant to imply otherwise. It's just that I think Chase was feeding you a line, and I hope you're not swallowing it."

"Of course I'm not." She suddenly felt stupid for even briefly believing Chase was sincere. "I'm just concerned for Jeremy."

Luke took a step toward her. "You've got a heart for kids and Chase can see it. Maybe part of what he said is true—he'd like some help raising his boy. Every parent needs guidance and assistance from time to time. But I'm of the opinion that Chase has dubious intentions."

Cici tipped her head and regarded him. If she didn't know better, she'd think he was jealous. But that was absurd—wasn't it?

"I never meant to hurt your feelings, either." Luke's voice sounded soft, gentle. "I can tell I did, but if you could give me a chance to explain further—"

"Oh, it's no use, battling theories. Let's just agree to disagree and be friends."

"Ciara. . ." He glanced at the ceiling and chuckled incredulously. "That'll never work for me." He looked back at her and then stepped forward and placed his hands on her upper arms. She felt the warmth of his palms on her skin. His mouth moved as though he struggled with the words he wanted to say next. But the glint in his eyes said it all.

She knew in that instant that Luke's feelings mirrored her own.

Cici's arms intuitively encircled his waist. She stood on tiptoes, touching her lips to his. It took a second for him to respond, but when he did, Cici was unprepared for the rush of emotions that flooded her. The whole world suddenly went away. All that mattered was this very moment in which she and Luke fit each other like the final brush strokes that completed some beautiful yet dramatic work of art.

"No more, Ciara." In one abrupt move, he pushed her away.

"What's wrong?"

He let out a sigh and his breath touched her cheek like a feather.

"I've never been kissed like that." She couldn't seem to help blurting out th remark, although it earned her a little grin from Luke. "It felt so right; why di we stop?"

"Because things that shouldn't be happening are—and they're happening too fast between us. What just occurred only proves it."

"Too fast?" She stared up into his face, trying to understand.

"I've been fighting my feelings for you since we met."

"So that's it—the reason for your intermittent standoffishness?"

He turned, leaned against the counter, and folded his arms. "I'm sorry Ciara."

"Why are you sorry?" She stepped in front of him. "And why are you battling your emotions?"

"Because. . ." He swallowed hard as he touched one of her curly tendrils, stil damp from her shower. "When I fall in love again, I want to be sure I'm follow ing God's plan as well as my feelings, but God's plan has to come first."

"Because you were hurt before?" Cici recalled what he'd told her about hi wife, Alissa, how she'd likely been cheating on him. She nodded. "I certainly understand, Luke. I've been hurt, too, back when my dad walked out on Mom and me. The summer before I entered college I actually saw a therapist who helped me learn to overcome my issues of abandonment—and I'm still learning."

Luke opened his mouth to say something but swallowed the words instead He dropped his arm to his side and looked across the kitchen. It seemed he wa fighting more than just his emotions. She sensed there was more he longed to say but didn't know how to express it.

"Do you not want to see me anymore? Is that what you're telling me? Should we put some distance between us?"

His gaze flew back to her. "No." He shook his head as if clearing the fog in it. "Oh, I don't know. . ."

"I realize our philosophies on life are sort of at odds, but. . ." The last o her sentence stuck in her throat as she recollected something Jen once said Something about how happy she was to meet William and fall in love with good Christian man.

A Christian.

She wasn't one.

"I know what the problem is. It's your religion, isn't it?"

"Well, it's more than religion. It's my relationship with Christ—and, yeah that's it exactly."

"Why didn't you say so?"

"I—I didn't know how to explain it in a way you'd understand. I mean, I didn't want to make my beliefs sound cultish or offensive to you. Faith in Christ is the most awesome thing ever." Luke's entire countenance lit up. "Talk about moving mountains and parting seas—it's all that and more."

Cici didn't know what to say, how to respond.

"But, concerning you and me, I'm trying to act on biblical principle, and you never told me where you stand on Christianity. You said you've got your own religion and asked me not to preach to you because William had already."

Cici couldn't deny it. "Point well taken, Luke. You're right. We never did discuss the subject of God—and it's one that's obviously very important to you."

"It is."

She thought it over, speaking what came to mind. "Spirituality is a very positive force in Jen's life, and it's something I admire in you, too. William, on the other hand, is a little too dogmatic for my tastes, but otherwise he's a likable guy."

Luke's features softened. "Are you open to, um, *researching* what Jen, William, and I believe?" A hint of a grin tugged at the corners of his mouth.

"Maybe." Cici felt hesitant and yet she didn't know why. She'd studied various world religions in college. She was hardly mindless and gullible. She'd draw her own conclusions. "Make that a definite maybe."

Luke smiled. "I'll accept the definite part of that oxymoronic reply."

In spite of herself, Cici laughed. But she didn't argue.

"How about starting off your research by coming to the Satlocks' with the boys and me to celebrate Independence Day?"

Cici felt torn between being totally responsible and having some semblance of a life. "I planned to spend most of the day writing my thesis."

"We're not leaving until about two o'clock. Gives you all morning to work on your paper."

If certain superheroes aren't bouncing off the walls and parachuting off bunk beds.

"Think picnic, fireworks. C'mon, you don't want to sit inside at the computer the whole day."

She sure didn't. Truth be told, she'd much rather spend time with him—and the reality of that inner admission shocked her.

"Ciara?"

He was waiting for an answer. "Oh, all right. You convinced me." She smiled, thinking Bridget and Tanya would be so proud. "Sure, I'll come along. It sounds like fun."

Luke strode to the door and then turned, as if on second thought, and asked, "As for you and me: How about a *definite maybe* on that, as well?"

"You got it." She didn't have to think twice.

Chapter 10

Cici highlighted a page and a half before pressing the DELETE key on her computer. Hours of work disappeared from the screen.

She sat back in the leather desk chair and blew out a frustrated breath. She'd been doing her best to concentrate on writing her thesis, but the memory of kissing Luke last night lingered in her mind and made it impossible to think about the inconsequentiality of the male race.

A mere kiss and suddenly she'd rather spend the Fourth of July with Luke than write her thesis. What would Aggie think if she discovered this turn of events? Her professor would be aghast, appalled, and utterly disappointed in Cici's decisions of late. However, she couldn't base her life choices on whether Aggie would approve of them. Cici knew she had her own life to live—and what passed through her when she kissed Luke was unlike anything she'd ever experienced before. Perhaps the culmination of emotions she felt were some sort of sign that he was the one, and yet Cici's practical side said they were miles apart on some very fundamental issues.

Like religion.

Checking her e-mail, Cici hoped she'd hear from Jen. She'd sent off a list of questions about Christianity. In previous messages she'd mentioned Luke and finally admitted things were heating up between the two of them. But in this morning's e-mail, Cici made it clear she wasn't about to convert just because of her growing feelings for Luke; however, she felt strongly that she owed it to the both of them to at least investigate what he believed in and why.

But Jen hadn't responded yet.

Pushing the chair away from the desk, Cici stood and stretched. Then she wandered around her friend's office and paused in front of the bookcase. The volumes were neatly aligned and Cici scanned the titles. Her gaze stopped at a collection of C. S. Lewis's writings. She was, of course, familiar with the author and had read bits and pieces of his work, although she'd never been a fan of his *The Chronicles of Narnia*.

She grinned, thinking Luke probably enjoyed the series.

Cici pulled a book from the shelf and flipped it open to a random page. There she read: "A man can no more diminish God's glory by refusing to worship Him than a lunatic can put out the sun by scribbling the word *darkness* on the walls of his cell."

She blinked and read the words again, admitting the quote took her aback. In essence, Lewis claimed that God's glory wasn't lessened by those who didn't believe in Him, unlike politicians, popular movie stars, or renowned college professors who needed a large base of support in order to shine.

Interesting.

Cici took the book downstairs and pulled a cold bottle of flavored water from the fridge. Next she sat down at the kitchen table and began to read more from the published compilation. Before she knew it, hours had passed. She was amazed at how much time had gotten away from her as she stared at the kitchen clock; however, it was actually the sound of children's laughter outside that caused her to pull her nose out of the book. She stood and walked to the door, peering through the multipaned glass window. Luke's little superheroes were playing on their wooden play structure along with Jeremy Tibbits. All four boys wore bathing trunks.

Cici's gaze jumped back to Jeremy. What was he doing in the backyard? Did Chase know his son's whereabouts?

She stepped outside and sat down on the cement stoop by the back door that led to the patio. She was met by hot, thick air and a smoldering lick of sunshine. Having been in the air-conditioned condo all day, she hadn't realized how oppressive the heat and humidity felt outdoors.

"Okay, who wants to get wet?" Luke appeared from behind the fence and strode across the yard with the garden hose in one hand and a colorful plastic object in the other.

The boys whooped and cheered in answer to his question.

Cici watched as Luke screwed on the yellow, red, blue, and green attachment to the end of the hose before placing it on the grass. He walked back to the house and turned on the water. In no time streams jetted out the sides and top of the attachment and the kids began running to and fro, squealing and laughing. The happy sound made Cici smile.

"Taking a break?" Luke had spotted her.

"Sort of." She hoped she didn't look as guilty as she felt. She hadn't gotten any further along in her writing today.

Luke disappeared and returned a minute later with two folding lawn chairs. He set them up in the shade of a mature maple tree. "Come sit in the shade, or before long you'll look like a lobster."

Cici couldn't refuse his offer, although it had little to do with the possibility of sunburn.

"How's the writing going?"

She expelled a weary sigh as she lowered herself into the lawn chair. "Not so great. I got sidetracked today and ended up reading C. S. Lewis for hours."

"Narnia?"

Cici noted his enthused expression and laughed. "One of your favorites, I presume?"

He nodded.

"I knew it." Her smile lingered. "Typical superhero material. But, alas, I was reading excerpts from some of Lewis's more serious work."

"What do you think of it?"

"It's food for thought. I mean, the author had quite the intellectual take on God and Christianity, and yet the principles he wrote about are quite simplistic."

"Nothing about Christianity is difficult." Luke's gaze bore into hers. "Maybe, in some ironic way, that's what makes it so hard for some people to accept."

"Are you insinuating that I'm in the category as 'some people'?" She was only half teasing.

"No, not at all." A light of sincerity shone in his dark eyes. "I'm just stating an observation." He raised a brow. "Are you trying to pick a fight?"

She could tell he was teasing. "Me? Pick a fight?"

Luke chuckled. "I'll bet you were captain of the debate team in college, eh?"

"No, and for your information, I wasn't even on the debate team."

"Their loss."

Cici turned and rapped him on the upper arm.

He continued to grin, his gaze fixed on the boys who laughed and ran through the spriggles and sprays of the water toy.

"How did Jeremy get over here?"

"I thought you'd never ask." Luke looked her way. "I woke up thinking about last night—about how you said Chase had publicly belittled Jeremy and then came over to your place to apologize. I know it's hard to be a single dad, and I figured I could give the guy the benefit of the doubt. So, to show my support, the boys and I walked up the block to his condo and asked if Jeremy could come over and play. Chase agreed and Jeremy's been having a great time. Good for my kids, too, since they don't fight so much with each other when Jeremy's around to impress."

"Good for you, Luke." Cici was impressed that he'd selected to take the high road. But she couldn't help feeling a little wounded that he woke up thinking about Chase and Jeremy and not her—them.

"Well, I do have to admit that my intentions were twofold."

"Oh?"

"Yep. I figured I bring the research to you and save you the headache of keeping company with Chase." Luke glanced at his wristwatch. "He'll be here to pick up Jeremy in an hour or so. Feel free to interview him."

Cici suppressed the urge to laugh out loud. "Why, Luke Weldon, you act as though you're jealous or something."

He rubbed the back of his neck and then squared his shoulders. "It might seem that way." His voice held a note of amusement. "But I'm just trying to help you out."

"Sure you are." Cici smiled and shook her head. She wasn't irked by the fact that he'd manipulated the situation. Quite the opposite; she felt touched by his concern. On the other hand, she needed to let him know a couple of things about herself. "Luke, just for the record, I'm an independent woman, and I don't need to be guarded like a little girl. What's more, I'm loyal to my friends and those I love."

"That's good to know." He stared at the kids. "The loyal part, anyway."

She sensed he made a reference to his deceased wife.

"Well, I appreciate your sharing those qualities about yourself, although I'm already aware of your independence, and I think I've sensed all along that you're trustworthy. But I didn't invite Jeremy over here because of my own insecurities."

"Didn't you?"

Luke had the good grace to consider the question.

"Chase Tibbits is not my type, Luke. I'm not sure I'd even consider him friend material."

"But you're a bleeding heart, Ciara, especially when it comes to kids."

"And you think that because you and I met by way of my research and my love for children that I'll be tempted to fall into Chase's arms for the same reason?" Cici shook her head. "Have a little more faith in me. I'm not naive."

Luke didn't reply, but Cici could tell she'd hit a nerve. She hadn't meant to hurt him in any way and yet the truth needed to be said so it could be dealt with out in the open.

She watched his expression and knew by the way the muscle flexed in his jaw that he was deliberating over her remark. She often wondered why he hadn't remarried. She'd met several single women from his church when they'd dropped off meals during the time the boys were sick. They were attractive. What's more, they seemed intelligent and pleasant enough. Cici just assumed Luke never connected with those women on any particular level, and that much might hold true. Although now she wondered if there wasn't more to it. Perhaps his insecurity over the way in which he'd lost Alissa was the real motive for avoiding becoming romantically involved again—

Until now.

Cici reached over and set her hand on his. He captured it in his palm. "I've been hurt, too, Luke. Remember how I admitted to having a general distrust of men on the night of the Condo Club's get-together?"

A little grin tugged at his mouth. "I remember."

"You said you had a general distrust of women and blew my mind. I never expected we'd have a common thread."

He gave in to a smile and finally looked over at her. "I'm not so proud that I can't admit my faults. Maybe a small sense of insecurity prompted me to invite Jeremy over to play with my boys. But I have a soft spot for kids, too, and you can't be so independent that you refuse to allow anyone to look out for you. That's a man's role. Protector."

"A man's role?" Cici groaned and yanked her hand from his. "Them's fightin' words, Luke. I suppose you think a woman's role is to be barefoot and pregnant."

"Well, not *all* the time." A twinkle lit his dark eyes.

His quip took some of the wind out of her sails but did nothing to deflate her indignation. "I think I feel like writing more on my thesis now." She stood. "Thank you for getting me stirred up again. It's just what I needed."

She ignored his smirk and marched across the yard toward the back door. But then, as she reached the stoop, she felt a blast of freezing cold water hit her shoulders and back. She shrieked and spun around to see Luke wielding the water toy like a bazooka.

The kids gasped and giggled.

He sprayed her again and she looked down at her now drenched pink and white striped seersucker capris and raspberry tank top.

"Thought maybe you needed to *chill out*, Ciara."

She replied with an indignant *yipe*.

He laughed, took aim, and fired again. This time she dodged the water.

She kicked off her flip-flops. "You're in big trouble, mister." She glared at him, although she had to admit the cold water felt rather good.

"Now get *us* wet, Daddy!" Aaron hollered, gesturing at his brothers and Jeremy.

"You're already wet."

"Get us some more." The boy wiggled his backside, taunting his father.

Of course, Luke couldn't resist, and Cici felt a wave of relief that his attention had been diverted. But as he chased the kids around with the hose, a mischievous idea of her own took shape. "Hey, superheroes, let's *get your dad*."

Luke sent a shower her way, but her suggestion hadn't fallen on deaf ears.

"Yeah, let's get him!" Devin said as if hailing the troops. "Let's protect Miss Ciara from the water monster!"

"Ha! I rest my case." Luke glanced her way. "Devin just proved my point. The desire to protect damsels in distress is an instinctive thing with us guys."

Those were the last words he spoke before being tackled by four knights in dripping swim trunks.

Cici took hold of the hose and made sure Luke got a face full of water. She laughed, but then her eyes met his and she saw his determined glint. She suddenly knew it was nothing short of war between them.

Luke stood, shrugged off the kids, and charged her. Thinking of nothing but escape, Cici dropped the hose and ran. All at once, Luke caught her around the waist, clasping a firm hand around her left wrist.

"Ah-ha, now you're my prisoner." His voice, close to her ear, sent shivers down her arms in spite of the summer heat.

"The water monster has Miss Ciara!" Brian rushed toward them. "We gotta save her."

"Do you see what I mean?" Luke held out his hand and forestalled his son's head-butt. All the while his arm remained locked around Cici.

"You trained them that way."

"No, I encouraged what God already built into them."

"Whatever." Cici decided she wasn't in any position to argue.

He sidestepped the other three rescuers and actually lifted Cici off the grass as he inched his way toward the hose. She twisted and squirmed, fighting the inevitable: She was about to get the soaking of her life.

She wiggled and squirmed, trying to break free. "Don't even think about it, Luke."

"Think?" He laughed. "It's plotted and planned."

She gave out a little scream as the tip of the water toy touched her nape, sending a chilling cascade down her back.

"Don't worry, I'll watch the hair."

She elbowed him and, from the way he exhaled, she knew the jab was on target, but he still didn't release her. Instead he took turns spraying her and the boys who were still determined to save the day.

Then suddenly the flow of water stopped. The children fell silent, their little faces masked with confusion. Luke loosened his hold on Cici and, seconds later, all eyes came to rest on Chase Tibbits. He stood by the lawn chairs, cinching the hose in one meaty hand.

"What in the devil is going on here?"

Chapter 11

Cici turned her head toward Luke and spoke out of the side of her mouth so only he would hear. "Nice going, *Water Monster*."

He released her and she stumbled forward. She wiped the water from her eyes and ran a hand through her soaking wet hair. With a glance down at her drenched attire, she decided there was no way to look even remotely dignified, although she gave it her best shot.

"We're playing with the kids," Luke told Chase, who seemed to be waiting for an explanation. "Want to join us?"

"Maybe." He gaze roved over Cici in a way that made her cringe.

"If you'll excuse me, I really need to change into some dry clothes."

She hurried to the condo, ignoring Chase's tawdry remark and subsequent laughter. When she entered the kitchen, she couldn't help but turn the lock on her back door.

She stared at it, marveling at how little she trusted Chase and how comfortable she was around Luke. Imagine playing right along with the kids! Cici hadn't had so much fun since she was a little girl—before Dad took off. But if Aggie had seen her, she'd have been mortified. Intellects didn't frolic in the grass and get captured by water monsters. As for Luke, he made one very irresistible foe.

Cici smiled. She had to admit, however, that she hated the way he'd so easily overpowered her. She'd done her best to break out of his hold without success. She was hardly a weakling. Who would have guessed Luke possessed such strength?

Next she imagined fighting off Chase—not in a fun water fight, but in real life. There was no way she'd win. Even so, she refused to agree that Luke was right and women, particularly her, needed a man to protect or look out for them. Cici wasn't some poor, defenseless creature.

She squared her shoulders and realized she'd made a puddle on Jen's tiled floor. Tiptoeing to the sink, she grabbed a dish towel and tossed it over the tiny pool of water. Next, she ran upstairs to the bathroom and stripped off her wet clothes. She dried herself off, wrapped the towel around her body, and headed to the bedroom where she pulled on loose-fitting white cotton shorts and an oversized yellow and white Hawaiian shirt. It was her favorite lounge-around-and-do-homework outfit, but her hope was that its frumpiness would repel Chase's attention—if she went back outside, that is. She really needed to work on her thesis instead.

Laughter wafted up from the backyard. Crossing the room, she peered out the window. The boys had resumed their play beneath the spray of the water toy. Several feet away, Luke and Chase were sitting in the lawn chairs, talking. Things seemed amicable enough.

Stepping back, Cici had to resist the temptation to go back outside. She'd left her flip-flops on the stoop. But that wasn't a good enough reason to put off writing her thesis—again. Besides, three's a crowd. Luke and Chase seemed to be having a friendly conversation. No sense in her butting in.

Her decision made, she brushed out her tangled wet hair. Minutes later, she ambled into Jen's office and sat down in front of the computer. She reread the last several pages of her thesis, and just as ideas began to flow and her fingertips touched the keyboard, the back doorbell rang.

Cici groaned out loud and wondered whether to answer it. But as she weighed her options, someone pressed on the bell again. Was it Luke? Chase? One of the kids? Cici decided she just had to go see.

Down the steps, into the kitchen, and a moment later, she pulled open the back door to find Luke standing there. Dried grass had matted on the shoulder of his navy blue T-shirt. Remnants of their water fight.

She swallowed a grin and opened the door. "Hi."

"Hi. I'm going to light up the fire pit in about an hour. It's got a grate on it, and I told the kids they could roast hot dogs. Want to join us?"

She regarded him with mock incredulity. "Do you mean to tell me you're feeding your children hot dogs two days in a row?"

"Hold on." He held up his palms. "Before you give me the Worst Father of the Year Award, you should know that I made the boys and myself a vegetable quiche for lunch."

"You made a quiche?" Cici folded her arms.

"Spinach and cheese." He feigned an air of sophistication. "Only one of my many specialties."

Skeptical, she narrowed her gaze.

"Okay, okay, if you must know my secret recipe, I use an all-purpose baking mix, eggs, milk, mix it together, pour it over a bag of chopped, fresh spinach, add a few handfuls of shredded cheddar cheese, and throw it in the oven. It's actually very simple but tastes great."

"You're hardly a contestant for the Worst Father of the Year Award." Cici gave him a look of admonishment. "I'm really quite impressed, Luke."

"Impressed enough to dine by firelight tonight?"

"Well. . ." She surveyed the backyard. No sign of Chase.

Luke seemed to discern her thoughts. "He left; took Jeremy home."

Relief engulfed her.

He chuckled. "Coast is clear. C'mon out."

Cici felt a sting of remorse. "I'd like to, Luke, but I really have to finish my thesis."

"But you've got to eat, right? Have a dog and some pop and then work on your thesis later."

Cici hesitated to decline a second time. She'd like nothing better than to roast hot dogs with Luke and his boys.

"Say yes." He grinned and took a backward step off the stoop. "The kids are changing their clothes and then they're going to wind down for a while. After that, I'll light the fire pit-slash-grill."

"Oh, all right. *Yes.*" Maybe she'd get an hour's worth of work done in the meantime.

His smile widened. "See you in a while."

"Okay." In truth, she was looking forward to it.

❧

Luke watched his kids search for earthworms, each with his own flashlight in hand. Dusk had turned to nightfall and, against his better judgment, he kept tossing kindling into the portable fire pit to keep it aglow. The boys should have been in bed thirty minutes ago, but he just didn't want this evening to end. He thought he could sit beside Ciara like this 'til dawn. No teasing. No baiting and bantering. Just some of the best camaraderie Luke had known in a long while.

He glanced over and admired the graceful, easy way she sat in the lawn chair, barefoot, one leg crossed over the other. She seemed both amused and enthralled by his sons' antics, and she proved she wasn't afraid of brown, slippery, squirming things. She only reacted when Brian accidentally dropped his precious find on her thigh, and even then it wasn't a full-fledged scream.

As if sensing his gaze, she looked at him. They stared at each other for a long moment and then Ciara reached over and caressed his stubbly jaw. He caught her hand, embarrassed that his appearance wasn't the best. He'd been on the go since waking up and couldn't even remember if he'd shaved this morning.

"You're a pretty terrific guy, Luke, with incredible kids."

"Thanks." The compliment went all the way to his heart.

She worked her fingers between his. They felt both capable and delicate. "I have a confession. As silly as our water fight was this afternoon, it was more fun than I've had in about a decade." Beneath the light of the moon, he saw her smile. "I was in junior high when my dad left home and somehow my childhood went with him, so it was fun to *play* this afternoon."

"Well, you know what they say: Work hard, play hard."

"Whoever 'they' are." She laughed.

Luke grinned. "Seriously, I play far too often. I probably ought to be more focused on designing software. But my boys are only little once, and I've found that playing with them is a great way to supervise. I can also teach them social

nteraction skills." Just then, Aaron clobbered Devin. He winced, and his eldest
on's cry of hurt and anger seemed to fill the night. "Interaction skills like: Don't
whack your brother over the head when you want the garden trowel."

"What?"

"Scuse me." Luke jumped to his feet and dashed across the yard, but he
couldn't reach Devin before he socked his younger brother in retaliation. Aaron
responded with fists a-flying.

"All right, break it up."

"Dad, Aaron won't give me the shovel."

"I had it first."

"Is that true, Devin?" Luke was growing weary of the fighting between
these two.

"Yeah, but it's my turn." Devin pleaded his case. "You said everyone gets a turn
digging and it was my turn, so I tried to take the shovel and Aaron hit me."

"You know better than to just take something, Devin. You should have called
me instead of trying to wrestle it away from Aaron."

"But, Dad, Aaron knew it was my turn and he kept singing, 'You can't have
the shovel. You can't have the shovel.'"

Luke turned to the habitual instigator. "Aaron?"

The boy just shrugged as though he didn't care if he were punished. . .
again.

Luke looked up at the star-speckled sky and asked the Lord for wisdom.
Aaron had been a veritable challenge in the last weeks, more than usual. Luke
had tired of disciplining the boy hour after hour.

"Okay, listen, you were both wrong for hitting each other. Must be that
you're overtired and can't think straight. Time for bed."

Devin moaned and complained. Aaron threw down the trowel and stomped
toward the back door.

"Daddy, do I have to go to bed?" Brian stepped to Luke's side. "I didn't do
anything wrong."

"No, you didn't, and I really appreciate your good behavior." He hugged his
little guy around the shoulders. "But it's bedtime for you, too. Tomorrow's the
Fourth of July, and we've got a busy day planned."

"Hooray! The Fourth of July!" Brian skipped to the back door.

"Ciara?" Luke spun around on his heel. "I have to tend to my boys, but I'll
be out later to make sure that fire went out."

"Want some help?"

"No, I can manage. Thanks anyway."

"Dad, it's not fair." Devin's complaining recaptured Luke's attention. "Aaron
started it."

"Lots of things in life aren't fair, son. Inside. *Pronto.*"

❧

Cici watched Luke round up his sons. Once they were inside, she settled into the lawn chair and closed her eyes. Off in the distance, she heard the sound of fireworks—a sound that would likely continue for the next several days—but all she could think about was how nice it had felt to sit beside Luke, her hand in his.

She allowed herself to dream just a little before thoughts of her thesis crashed into her mind. How did she ever expect to earn her master's if she didn't go inside, exercise some willpower, and write? Except, the wind had shifted and now a warm, gentle breeze made for comfortable backyard sitting. The sounds of a nearby bottle rocket and the smell of grass combined with the faint scent of wood smoke from the fire pit made summer come alive all around her. Suddenly Cici hated the thought of missing it. Besides, Iowa winters came too quickly and lasted far too long. And Luke said he'd come back out after the kids were settled. The latter, Cici decided, was worth waiting for, in and of itself.

Choosing to spend time with a man over writing her master's thesis? Aggie would be horror-struck by her lack of self-discipline in the face of such a powerful distraction. Cici herself was continually amazed. So how had this happened? How had she allowed it to occur? She'd set out to prove that men were inept and unnecessary when it came to raising children. It took a woman's nurturing, guidance, dedication, and love to produce healthy, happy kids and ultimately, well-adjusted adults. To her chagrin, Luke had proved her wrong on several counts.

However, she still believed he wasn't an average, typical father.

Cici heard a screen door open. She looked toward Luke's condo, thinking he was coming back into the yard and was surprised to see Aaron skulk out onto the stoop. He wore lightweight pajamas and shot a glance in Cici's direction. When she didn't respond, he inched forward, onto the grass. Slowly, the boy made his way to where the garden trowel lay. He picked it up, and Cici knew without a doubt that Luke had no idea Aaron had gone AWOL.

"Does your daddy know you're out here?" she finally had to ask.

Aaron shrugged his shoulders as though the fact was of little importance to him. He stared at the trowel.

"Nice shovel. Bet you found lots of worms, huh?"

The boy didn't reply specifically to her question. Instead he came toward her. "This used to be my mommy's shovel."

Cici was somewhat taken aback. "Your mommy's?" She didn't think he'd remember such a thing. He'd been an infant when his mother died. "How do you know?"

"Cuz." He paused. "I saw a picture of my mommy planting flowers and stuff, so this was hers." He held up the trowel.

"Oh. . ." Cici realized interesting dynamics were unfolding. Had Aaron fought for the garden shovel, believing it was his mother's? Perhaps he had a deep-down longing to own a piece of his mother's memory—or maybe he longed to have a mom like other children his age. "I'll bet your mom planted beautiful flowers."

"She did." Aaron was at the side of Cici's lawn chair in a flash. "And I saw pictures of my mommy and us when we got born."

"Those must be special pictures for you." Without giving it a second thought, Cici hoisted the little boy up into her lap, dirt-caked hand trowel and all.

"Aunt Moira showed me. She's got a big, big book of pictures of my mommy." Aaron sat back and dropped his head against Cici's shoulder. He inspected the shovel with both hands. "Did you know my mommy?"

"No, I never did."

"You didn't?"

"No." Cici grinned, wondering if children's worlds were so small that they figured all adults knew each other.

"She died in a car crash. Aunt Moira said so and Daddy told me."

"Your daddy told me that, too. It's one sad shame, that's for sure."

"But she's in heaven with God."

Was she? Didn't seem to Cici that Luke's wife behaved very Christian-like, especially on the night she died. Of course, she'd never in a million years voice her skepticism. Who was she to judge? And if it made a little boy happy to believe his mommy was in heaven, then so be it.

"Miss Ciara?"

"Yes?"

Aaron laid the back of his head against her shoulder again. "Will you tell me a story?"

She smiled. "Sure."

"Tell me about a boy named Aaron and his mommy who planted flowers."

"Hmm. . ." Cici felt pained that the little guy obviously missed the mother he never knew. She wrapped her arms around him and gave the story some thought. "Okay, once upon a time there was a little boy named Aaron. He was a superhero who loved to dig for worms."

"Yeah."

Cici's smile grew. "One day he was digging and. . ." She groped for some religious thread to weave into the tale. Then she remembered the picture, hanging above Jen's headboard—the one with the warring angels. "And an angel came out of the sky."

Aaron twisted around to look at her. "Like Michael, the archangel?"

"Um. . .is Michael a good guy?"

"Uh-huh."

"Okay, sure, then the angel was like him."

"Cool." Aaron resumed his comfy position, his head feeling like a bowling ball now as it collided with her clavicle.

She winced but continued with her story, making it up as she went along. "So the angel came and told Aaron, the superhero, that his mommy was in heaven and that he shouldn't be sad. The angel said lots of people would come into Aaron's life and make him happy, like friends and grandmas and grandpas and aunts—and a good daddy who loved him." Cici didn't want to leave Luke out of the picture.

"What else did the angel say?"

"That—that every time Aaron planted a flower, seeds of happiness would be planted in his heart. And just when Aaron would need them most, laughter and love would spring up, just like tulips appear after the winter goes away."

Aaron turned so his forehead rested by Cici's chin. He yawned and didn't say more. She took his silence to mean that he was satisfied with her impromptu fairy tale. With a grin, she placed a kiss on top of his head. Within moments, the muscles in his small body went slack and his breathing deepened.

He'd fallen asleep.

Just then the yard light went on and the back door opened. Luke stepped out of the house. He spotted Cici with Aaron in her arms and marched toward them.

"Please don't be angry, Luke," she said quietly. She held out her hand when he reached the lawn chair. "He's asleep now. I think he just needed a little TLC."

"I think he needs a good *s-p-a-n-k-i-n-g.*"

"Oh, Luke. . ." Cici grinned, hearing the facetious note in his voice.

"Seriously, this kid gave me quite a scare when I realized he wasn't in his bed and I couldn't find him anywhere."

"My fault. I should have brought him inside, but he asked for a story so I told him one." Cici slipped the trowel out of Aaron's grip and handed it to Luke. "He told me the garden tool belonged to his mother. I think he misses her."

"He never knew Alissa. Not really."

Cici disagreed, at least in part. "He knew a mother's love for the first year or so of his young life and. . .well, maybe he knows it's missing."

The conversation roused Aaron. He sat up and Luke lifted his son into his arms.

"Tell Miss Ciara good night."

"Night." It was the groggiest of replies as the little boy put his arms around his daddy's neck. Then he lay his head on Luke's shoulder.

Luke inclined his head toward the cast-iron fireplace. "Did it finally die out?"

"The fire?" She nodded. "Uh-huh."

She stood and when she looked into Luke's face, she read anguish in his expression. Alissa's thoughtlessness had been, undoubtedly, painful to deal with, but to think his son had been wounded in the fallout was probably excruciating for

Luke. She empathized and cared, so it seemed only natural to try to comfort him.

She stepped in closer and touched her lips to his.

Just as last night, a dizzying sense of destiny fell over her, as though she and Luke were meant to spend the rest of their lives together. The *whiz*, *pop*, *bang* of a nearby firecracker seemed like confirmation.

The kiss lasted mere seconds, but Cici could tell Luke's emotions mirrored her own. He just fought his back because of his beliefs.

His beliefs—how could they be together forever if something so basic stood between them?

"I need to get Aaron to bed." His voice sounded soft and somewhat remorseful.

"Of course."

With slow strides, they both crossed the yard.

Luke seemed to regain his bearings first. "Thanks for your help with Aaron. I'll see you tomorrow. We'll leave for the barbecue about two in the afternoon."

"I'll be ready."

They parted at the fence, although Cici wished Luke would ask her over. But he didn't. Instead he called a "good night" before entering his condo.

Chapter 12

L uke could tell something was bugging Ciara from the second she stepped out the door wearing a red and white tank top and white slacks that stopped just below the knee. Her brown-red curly hair was twisted up of her neck in an attractive, sort of disheveled way, but a troubled frown dimpled her right brow.

"Everything okay?" Luke tossed a duffel bag containing extra clothes for the boys into the back of the van. Then he lifted the cooler packed with ice and can of soda pop and slid it, too, into the cargo area. "You seem upset."

"Jen called this morning."

Luke froze, fearing the worst.

Ciara must have read his thoughts. "No, no, she and William and all the others are fine. They're enjoying the trip."

Luke felt his shoulders sag with relief.

"It's just that Jen suggested I read a term paper she wrote for a religion class She uploaded it from her computer to mine. I printed it and read it, and well I found it deeply disturbing."

"Disturbing?" Luke glanced at his boys, climbing on the play structure in the backyard, and decided they were preoccupied and safe for the time being "In what way?"

"The title of the paper is: 'The Infallible Word of God.'"

Luke nodded. Nothing seemed amiss to him thus far. "And?"

"Well, after suggesting I read her work, Jen told me that I need to believe that truth about the Bible if I'm ever to be able to understand Christianity. Ciara hitched her purse strap higher onto her shoulder and then slipped her hands into the side pockets of her slacks. "Jen's paper was hard-hitting, although she presented both sides, one from a Christian's viewpoint and the other as an unbeliever who thought the Bible was merely a nice book filled with moral stories and inspirational sayings." A blush crept into her cheeks. "I think she was quoting me."

Luke chuckled.

"But here's where I have difficulty with Christianity: I can't believe that a person who doesn't believe in Jesus Christ will be separated from Him for eternity, but that's what the Bible teaches."

"Yes, but—" Luke paused and prayed for both wisdom and boldness. *Lord let me explain things to Ciara in a way she'll understand.* "The Bible also teaches that God is a patient, loving, merciful God who doesn't want one single person to perish. His desire is that everyone comes to that unique and intimate place of repentance, belief, and salvation, just the way it's written in the Book of Romans."

"The Bible."

"Right."

"So what it says in there goes?"

"That's what I believe. Yes."

"There's no gray area? Just black and white? Heaven or hell?"

He nodded.

"That's mind control, Luke." Ciara placed her hands on her hips. "When someone or something dictates a belief system as the right and only way, it's cultish and tyrannical."

He had to chuckle because at one time he had thought the same thing. "Ciara, try to look at it in this way: Our city here in Iowa has laws against stealing and murdering. If you break the law, you're going to jail. No two ways about it. Is that tyranny? Of course not. Now this country of ours has a constitution. Do we live under tyranny because we're governed by all these. . .*rules*? No. Constitutional law is in place so that Americans can live in freedom here in the United States. It's the same with God's Word."

She blinked in reply.

Luke hid a grin as he shut the hatch of the van. He dusted off his palms on his jeans, and then brought his fingers to his mouth and whistled a signal to the boys that they were packed and ready to go.

He looked at Ciara. "Still want to come to the barbecue today?" He hoped she hadn't changed her mind but couldn't help teasing her just the same. "We're a scary bunch, us Christians." He arched a brow, feigning a menacing expression and accent. "We might take possession of your mind and spirit, and you will become one of us."

Ciara whopped him on the shoulder with her purse.

He laughed.

The boys reached the van, breathless from their dash across the yard, and Luke assisted them inside. While they buckled up, he turned back to Ciara. "I'm sorry for making light of something as serious as your eternal destiny. It's just that before I became a Christian, I had the exact same opinions about Christians being cultish and all the rest of it. That's why I laughed. I hope you'll forgive me."

"I'll do more than that." She strode toward him. "I'll spend the day with you and your Christian friends and torture you all with my incessant questions."

"Bring 'em on." Luke opened the front passenger door of the van, smiling as Ciara climbed in.

The Fourth of July partygoers consisted of Jesse and Mandy Satlock and their kids; Mandy's mother was in attendance, too, as well as Trevor and Grace Morris and their two children. Trevor's brother, Shane, had tagged along. He was recently divorced and, to Cici's dismay, Trevor tried playing matchmaker several times throughout the day. But she wasn't interested in the guy, although he seemed nice enough. All she had to do was glance across the patio and see Luke to know he was the one who had captured her heart. And when his dark gaze melded to hers, she could tell he felt the same way.

Trevor must have taken note of the way they shared fond looks and little smiles, and he made a habit of distracting Luke, sitting between him and Cici, and interrupting any conversation that sprang up between them. He made it clear he didn't like Cici getting too friendly with Luke; perhaps he didn't approve of her because she wasn't *one of them*. Maybe the matchmaking was his way of testing her morals.

Thankfully, Grace Morris made up for her husband's behavior. She had a keen sense of humor and sarcastic wit that had Cici laughing hard on numerous occasions.

And then there were the children. Cici observed that the Satlocks' and Morrises' kids, like Luke's boys, were well behaved for the most part. She especially enjoyed watching the fathers interact with their sons as they played a hilarious game of baseball.

When nightfall came, everyone piled into their vehicles and drove into Des Moines to watch the fireworks. During the spectacular display, Cici's new buddy, Aaron, insisted on sitting beside her, later crawling into her lap.

By the time they'd returned to the Satlocks', repacked Luke's van, gathered his boys, and headed for home, it was well past midnight and the little superheroes fell asleep in their car seats almost before Luke reached the first major intersection.

"Have fun today?"

"Definitely." Cici regarded Luke's profile, illuminated by the intermittent glow of the streetlamps they passed. "Except for the fact that your friend Trevor took a disliking to me, I'd say today was one of my more memorable July Fourth holidays."

"Don't mind Trevor. I plan to talk to him. He was totally obnoxious today."

"I got the distinct feeling that he doesn't think I'm good enough for you, Luke. Although, apparently, I'm good enough for his brother."

Luke didn't reply, but Cici noticed the jovial atmosphere had vanished.

"Anything wrong?"

"No. I'm just miffed at Trevor." He seemed to shake it off soon enough. "But aside from his embarrassing attempt to control the situation between you and me, you had fun?"

"Uh-huh. I had a great time. I really like Mandy. In fact, she invited me to a luncheon at your church next week and I said I'd attend."

"Seriously? You're going to the VBS Ladies' Luncheon? Our church's VBS—vacation Bible school—is next week."

"Yes, so I've been told, and, yes again, I am referring to that very ladies' luncheon."

"Awesome."

Cici settled back, thinking over her decision. "I figured, why not? Mandy said a dynamic local speaker has agreed to give a brief motivational talk, and the menu sounded delicious. I plan to ask my roommates, Bridget and Tanya, to come with me."

"Super."

Cici heard the enthused lilt in his voice and gave in to the urge to tease him. "But I don't want to hear any mind control wisecracks out of you."

"What about wisecracks about inconsequential dads?"

"They're off-limits, too." She folded her arms. It mildly galled her to wave the white flag of surrender, even at half-mast; however, Luke, Jesse, and even Trevor seemed polar opposites from the fathers she presented as examples in her thesis.

"I guess I have to admit that I may have been wrong in my generalizations and assumptions about fathers *and* Christianity, but I've done my research and I know inconsequential fathers abound in this world. There's also been brutality committed in the name of the Lord since the beginning of time."

"True and true."

Cici turned off the last of her defenses.

"On the flip side, there are responsible dads out there and missionaries who proclaim the Good News who have suffered their fair share of brutality." Luke paused. "But I think God calls us to a balance, and it's a very delicate balance. A step one way leads to fanaticism and one step in the other direction leads to compromise."

"So what's the gauge?"

"The Bible, of course, and its promise that if Christians walk in the Spirit we won't fulfill the lust of the flesh, like the love of power, money, misdirected passions, and so on."

"Must be hard, walking such a tightrope."

"It's impossible, but that's where God's grace comes into play." There was a smile in Luke's voice. "He's the one who gives us the strength and wisdom to walk that tightrope."

"So when Christians fall, it's God's fault because He let them fall?"

"Sometimes it seems that way. As a dad, I watched in agony as my sons toddled around and fell while learning to walk, but I often took a hands-off approach. It wasn't that I didn't protect my sons; it's just that I know taking a knock or two is part of life—part of existing. Likewise, God, our heavenly Father, knows He has to allow us a few bumps and bruises so we learn and grow."

"Makes sense." A second later, Cici realized the irony of her reply. She cupped the sides of her face. "I can't believe I just said that!"

To her chagrin, Luke laughed the rest of the way home.

Chapter 13

Look, I'm sorry, man." Sunday morning, between services, Trevor shifted self-consciously in the crowded hallway of the church. He plunged his hands into the pockets of his brown trousers. "But I'm your friend, and friends look out for each other."

"I appreciate that, but you embarrassed me and you hurt Ciara's feelings and then, adding insult to injury, you tried to throw her together with your brother."

Trevor shrugged. "So? Neither is a believer."

"But we are, and, as Christians, we're supposed to be above all that sneaky, manipulative business."

Trevor conceded with a slight nod. "I apologize, although I think you're in too deep, Luke. You're getting too emotionally involved with this woman. Is she here at church today?" He glanced up and down the bustling hall. "No."

The comment didn't faze Luke in the least.

"You called me and Jesse over to your house less than a week ago because you felt like your resolve was slipping. Well, buddy, I think it's slipped. You should have seen yourself on the Fourth. You couldn't take your eyes off her, like you're under some kind of spell."

"That's ridiculous."

"And she couldn't take her eyes off of you, either."

"Yeah?" A surge of encouragement caused Luke to grin.

"It was embarrassing—and wipe that smile off your face. You're headed for trouble, dude. If you don't believe me, ask Jesse."

"I have already. Just this morning." Both Jesse and Mandy had a different take on the situation. Part of their more positive reasoning stemmed from the fact that Ciara agreed to attend the VBS Ladies' Luncheon this week and she'd asked a lot of questions. Obviously, she was open to hearing biblical truth. But, as Mandy stated, there were critical days ahead for Ciara. She stood on the brink of a decision that would impact her eternity. The situation called for an enormous amount of prayer.

"Might be wise to put some distance between you and Ciara."

Luke shook his head. He wasn't about to turn tail and run now. "I can handle it. I'm capable of keeping my emotions in check."

"Couldn't keep your eyes in check on the Fourth of July, and if your eyes offend thee, pluck 'em out."

Luke recognized the words of Christ and would have taken them to heart, but Trevor had used them out of context. "For your information, my eyes did not offend me. I liked what I saw." Luke grinned. "Listen, all joking aside, I'm attracted to Ciara. I admit it. I like her a lot—maybe I even more than just like her. But I'm also aware that God has some miracles to do before I can pursue a serious relationship with her. She knows it, too. That fact alone has created a distance between Ciara and me."

Trevor didn't look convinced. "You deceive yourself, brother."

"I'll be all right. As long as I have a buddy like you who keeps me in his prayers and challenges me, I'll be just fine." Luke gave him a good-natured slap on the back. "I'm okay, you're okay. Okay?"

The jest wasn't totally lost on Trevor. "Yeah, okay."

The sun began sinking into the western sky, and Cici sat on the front steps and watched its descent. The air hung thick and damp around her. Dark clouds moved in from the southwest, hastening the day's end, and off in the distance she heard the ominous rumble of thunder. Cici found the buildup to be rather exciting; she loved a good thunderstorm and Iowa certainly got its fair share. The only thing missing was Luke's arm around her shoulders, and she imagined how cherished she'd feel if he were here and together they watched the storm roll in.

Tossing a glance next door, she wished Luke would come outside. She hadn't seen him or the boys all day. She'd opted to spend most of the day at her favorite coffeehouse and work on her thesis. The usual bustling crowd was reduced to only a handful of customers because of the holiday weekend—and that worked in Cici's favor. Quiet for the most part, although she'd overheard snippets of intellectual conversations that reminded her of her determination and resolve to earn her master's.

That is until two middle-aged women, whom Cici recognized from the university, walked in. The pair sat at the table next to hers, and Cici couldn't help overhearing them. Within minutes, she found herself questioning everything she'd learned to believe, not because of what the women said, per se, but the way in which they said it.

The two talked only about hard-hitting topics as they shared the Sunday newspaper and sipped lattes. They praised a prominent female politician and insulted and denounced the men who made the news. Cici picked up on the bite in their voices and thought it seemed to rob them of their credibility. She hoped she'd never sounded so angry, so downright gauche, while expressing her views.

If she had, how had Luke put up with her this last month? Maybe she owed him an apology. Had she inadvertently insulted his gender while defending hers? A woman's worth had been taken for granted in this world long enough. She wanted to shout the equality message from mountaintops, but she hadn't meant t as a personal attack on Luke, and she certainly didn't consider herself anti-male, of all things.

Suddenly Cici recalled how complete and utterly feminine she'd felt when Luke held her in his arms. Sitting forward on the front step, she allowed herself to revel in the memory and even fantasize just a little about how it might feel to be a bride, wearing an ivory satin and lace gown as Luke waited for her at the end of the long, white-carpeted aisle.

"Hey! Looks like we're gonna get some rain!"

The daydream vanished at the sound of Chase's booming voice. Before she could forestall him, he'd traipsed up the walkway and plunked down beside her.

She scooted over. "Mosquitoes are getting kind of bad. I'm thinking of going inside."

"Sure. We can do that." He pushed to his feet.

"Um, well. . .Chase, I'm afraid you misunderstood." She stood also. "That wasn't an invitation."

"Oh."

"I don't mean to be rude, but I'm just taking a little break from writing my thesis, and—"

"Right. Your paper. Well, don't forget my offer to be one of your research subjects."

"Thanks. I might take you up on it." She smiled and glanced around. "Where's Jeremy?"

Chase guffawed. "He's the reason I came over here—to pick him up and take him home. Jeremy's been playing with those Weldon kids all afternoon."

"How fun for him."

"And great for me. Tomorrow he's going to the Bible school with Luke's kids at their church. All week long I'll have my mornings to myself, which means. . ." He leaned forward in a conspiratorial way. "I can party and I don't have to worry about taking care of a kid while I'm hung over."

Cici was so appalled she couldn't think of a single intelligent reply.

"Then the following week my parents are coming to visit."

"So you have Jeremy for a two-week stint in all?"

"Yep." Chase swatted at a mosquito. "That's the trouble with divorces. Visitation eats up one weekend a month and sucks up two entire weeks during the summer—prime time for us contractors. But the ex and her lawyer got their way, so now I've got to pay for it."

Cici regained her bearings. "Why not try enjoying your time with your son? I wish my dad would have made time for me."

"Your folks divorced when you were a kid?"

She nodded.

"Too bad."

"It is what it is." She dismissed the matter, not wanting to discuss the particulars with Chase. She had a hunch he wouldn't understand anyway.

Just then four little boys burst out of the condo next door. They laughed and began running after each other in the front yard. Moments later, Luke appeared on the walk, wearing faded jeans and a light blue T-shirt.

"Thought I heard your voice out here, Chase." His gaze moved to Cici. He smiled. "Hi, Ciara."

"Hi, Luke." She stuffed her hands in her jeans pockets, feeling like a starry-eyed girl. She couldn't imagine what got into her whenever Luke made an appearance.

"Hey, since we're all here, why don't we hang out together tonight?" Chase looked delighted that he'd conjured up such a brilliant idea. "I'll bring over a six-pack, and maybe Cici here can impress us with her womanly skills by cooking up something for dinner."

"My *womanly skills?*" Cici turned to Chase and arched a brow.

Luke let out a long, slow whistle. "Buddy, you just said the *way* wrong thing."

"What?" He raised his shoulders in a helpless manner. "What'd I say?"

"Ciara's a feminist. You know, women's rights and all that." He sent a smirk her way. "Wouldn't be caught dead doing all that domestic stuff—like cooking."

"Not true." She pursed her lips in annoyance. "For your information, Luke, I can cook—and very well, I might add."

"I'll keep that in mind."

She grinned at the comeback and lowered her gaze. At any other time, she'd enjoy setting Chase straight about "womanly skills" extending beyond the home and into the workplace where women were equally as competent as men. Instead, recipes filled her head as she imagined preparing a delicious meal for Luke and his little superheroes.

Cici gave herself a mental shake and decided Aggie would be horrified by her rationale—or lack thereof.

"We can order a pizza." Chase's tone had lost some of its robustness.

"Actually, I'm bathing my boys and tucking them in early tonight." Luke set his hands on his hips. "Morning's going to come awfully fast. I have to pick up some other kids for VBS, as well as Jeremy, so I'll be ringing your doorbell before eight o'clock."

"Oh, right." Chase glanced at the boys darting around the front lawn. "I suppose I should get Jeremy to bed early, too."

Cici stifled a sigh of relief and considered asking Luke if he wanted some help with the kids. She soon thought better of it, suspecting Chase would impose on the offer. Besides, it'd be rude if she extended the offer to Luke in Chase's presence. "I need to get back to work on my thesis." She gave both men a parting glance and grin, but her gaze lingered on Luke several moments longer than necessary. She couldn't seem to help it. "Good night."

She entered the condo, feeling the sting of remorse. She would have enjoyed spending time with Luke and reading stories to the boys—and in all surprise and wonder, she realized that the whole homemaker role wasn't unappealing to her at all. She always imagined herself with children, but now she could see herself as a wife—Luke's wife.

She closed the front door and leaned against it. "What in the world is happening to me?"

※

Lightning flashed and thunder cracked, shaking the very floor on which Luke and the boys had camped out for the night. When the storm approached, the boys had gotten scared and wouldn't settle down, even after Luke tried tucking them into his own bed. So he'd decided on a "cowboy campout," and arranged their sleeping bags in a circle. The kids took to the idea and, at long last, had fallen asleep.

Another blitz of lightning and the power went out. The television, on which Luke had been tracking the intense storm, flicked off. Thunder exploded as lightning illuminated the living room.

"Daddy!"

Luke set his arm on Brian's arm. "It's okay, son. I'm right next to you."

A second later, Brian was sleeping soundly again.

"Daddy?" This time it was Aaron.

"Yeah?"

"I'm wondering if Miss Ciara is okay."

Luke couldn't help but grin. Ciara had won Aaron's heart, too. "I'm sure she's fine," he whispered.

"What if she's scared?"

Luke pondered the question and guessed at her actions. "She knows we live next door. If she's scared, she'll come over and knock on the door."

"Yeah, and she can camp out with us."

Luke swallowed a laugh. That'd be real cute. However, he didn't bother explaining the impropriety of the suggestion because he knew Aaron made it in all innocence. "Aaron, it's really nice of you to think about Miss Ciara. I'm proud of you."

In reply, his little boy rolled over and set his head on Luke's shoulder.

"Now, go back to sleep."

"Okay, Daddy."

"Daddy?" Now Devin.

"Yes?"

"I think we should check on Miss Ciara."

"I'm sure she's just fine, but we could pray for her and let Jesus take care of her."

The guys liked that idea and settled back into their sleeping bags.

Eyes closed, Luke began in earnest. "Dear Lord, we come to You tonight asking for Your hand of protection over Miss Ciara and us. You calm the winds and the seas. This puny thunderstorm is nothing for You to take care of."

"Cuz Jesus is a Mighty Superhero!"

"Shhh. . ." Luke sensed Aaron was getting wound up. Amazingly enough, Brian didn't awaken. "We're talking to God now." Luke kept his voice low and calm.

Aaron quieted.

"Lord, You said 'peace be still' so we know we don't have to be afraid of storms or anything, for that matter." The situation with Ciara scampered across his mind. "You've got it covered, Lord. We love You and we thank You for taking care of us—and the people who matter most to us. We also thank You for keeping us safe. In Jesus' name. . ."

The boys ended the prayer along with him.

"Amen."

Chapter 14

H i, superheroes." Cici waved to the kids as she tossed out a bag of garbage late Monday afternoon. To her surprise, they came running over.

"Did you hear the big storm last night?" Devin's brown eyes were wide with curiosity.

"I heard a little thunder, but I fell asleep and slept as hard as a rock."

"Then our prayers worked!" A broad smile spread across Aaron's face.

"Your prayers?"

"We prayed God would make you not be ascared of the storm."

"That's sweet." She gave all three boys a little hug. "Well, I wasn't scared."

"I didn't pray," Brian admitted, accepting the hug anyway, "cuz I was sleeping hard as rocks, too."

Cici laughed and lowered herself onto the back step. She hadn't even turned on her laptop today but instead dusted, vacuumed, and cleaned Jen's condo. The epitome of procrastination.

"So how was your vacation Bible school this morning?"

"Fine."

"Good."

Brian stood by and bobbed his head in agreement with his brothers.

"Did Jeremy like it, too?"

Devin shook his head. "He got a stomachache, and I had to walk him to the office and they called his dad to pick him up."

"What a shame. I hope he feels better soon."

"His dad didn't come, though," Devin explained, "so our dad took him home."

"Hmm. . ." Cici's opinion of Chase dropped another notch as she remembered how eager he'd seemed last evening to turn over the care of his son to Luke and the church's VBS program every morning this week.

"Our dad stays at church, cuz he runs all the computer stuff for the skit and for the pastor's talk."

Aaron and Brian affirmed Devin's statement with more nods, and Cici took in the proud expressions on all three boys' faces.

"Yo, guys! Where are you?" Luke's voice wafted over the wooden fence. There was an unmistakable urgency in his tone.

They turned to run along home and almost collided with him at the edge of the patio.

"We were talking to Miss Ciara." Aaron hung his head back to peer up at his father.

"So I see." Luke tousled his son's hair and smiled a greeting at her. "That's fine." He surveyed all three boys. "You've got another hour to play before supper and then it's showers and an early bedtime."

"But, Da–ad. . ."

Luke forestalled Devin's complaint with a stern look. Then all three raced through the yard to the play structure.

He watched them go, letting out a sigh that sounded both weary and relieved. "I always freak when it gets too quiet in the backyard."

"Can't imagine why." Cici laughed. She thought about how Aaron liked to parachute off the top bunk.

"Have we been too loud this afternoon?" He crossed the patio and sat down beside her. "I had Jesse and Mandy's two boys for a while, and the kids got kind of rowdy."

"Didn't hear a thing. Of course, I had the vacuum running off and on for the past couple of hours."

He turned toward her, feigning an expression of shock. "Cleaning? How domestic of you."

"Very funny."

Luke chuckled. "How's the thesis coming?"

"Don't ask." She set her elbows on her knees and rested her chin in her hands.

"That good, huh?"

Cici groaned. "I haven't even turned on my laptop today—not even to check e-mail."

"Writer's block?"

"I don't know. . ." Cici could hardly blame Luke for her inability to finish her thesis; however, it was he who'd crept into her thoughts throughout the day.

Silence hung between them.

"Are you still planning to attend the ladies' luncheon tomorrow?"

"Uh-huh." She nodded and turned toward him. "And Bridget and Tanya are coming with me. Should be fun."

A grin crept across his mouth and features so even his eyes seemed like they were smiling.

"Are you going to be home tomorrow afternoon? I'd love for you to meet my friends."

"Yeah, I should be around."

"Good." Cici felt pleased. She knew Bridget and Tanya would enjoy meeting Luke.

They talked for a little longer about friends in general, Luke's business, and again about Cici's thesis.

"Maybe you need a new direction."

"I've already strayed off the narrow path my professor laid down for me to follow."

"Well, here's hoping the guest speaker at tomorrow's luncheon gives you some ideas. I overheard some people talking about her today. Seems Beth Orana gives quite the motivational talk. A few guys were saying they planned to sneak in to hear her, although if Mandy's at the door they won't get by her." Luke chuckled as he glanced at his wristwatch. "Well, it's getting to be that time. I should feed my kids."

Cici stood just as he did. "What are you making for supper?"

"Not sure yet."

"Would you allow me to throw something together for you and the boys? We could eat dinner together."

"Are you trying to impress me with your culinary skills or procrastinate on writing your thesis?" He dipped his head so that his face was close to hers.

"Maybe a little of both."

Again, he laughed. "Okay, sure. If you want to make supper for us, I'm all for it. We eat just about anything."

"That makes it easy. Give me about an hour or so, all right?"

"Sure."

Smiling, Cici entered the condo and ran upstairs where she booted up her laptop computer. She logged on to a popular recipe site and found a famous chef's recipe for a "Cowboy Chicken Casserole" that didn't look too difficult to prepare. What's more, she was certain that Luke and the boys would love it— pepper jack and cheddar cheese, vegetables, and cut up boneless chicken breasts in a seasoned sauce all folded over tortilla chips and baked in the oven.

Perfect.

After printing the recipe, she hustled back downstairs and took a quick inventory. Then she listed the ingredients she still needed and hurried off to the grocery store.

❧

Luke prayed over their dinner and then dug in. His mouth had been watering for the last fifteen minutes, ever since Ciara arrived with the casserole. It smelled delicious and—

"Mmm. . .tastes great." He didn't think she'd mind that his mouth was full when he uttered the compliment.

His sons bobbed their heads but ate in silence. A sure sign they'd been starving.

"I'm glad you like it. I wasn't sure if it'd be too spicy."

Luke chewed and swallowed. "No, we like spicy stuff. The boys love salsa and chips during a good baseball game on TV."

"We like the Royals, but my grandma and grandpa cheer for the Twins." Devin scrunched his face up.

Luke chuckled and interpreted for Ciara. "That's Kansas City Royals and Minnesota Twins."

"Got it." She took a tiny bite of casserole, chewed, and then swallowed. "Which set of grandparents live in Minnesota?"

"My folks."

"And the other grandparents are here in Iowa?"

Luke nodded. "They live in Des Moines."

Ciara seemed to digest the information, and he could practically guess the questions swirling around in that pretty head of hers.

"Alissa and I met at a Christian camp in Minnesota one summer. We were both camp counselors. Things progressed, we got engaged, and since she wanted to stay in Iowa, I found a job with a software firm here in Des Moines. We got married, rented an apartment in Des Moines, but eventually bought a house—in the subdivision where Jesse and Mandy live. But after the accident I sold the place and bought this one. I wanted something small and easy to maintain. Too hard chasing toddlers around a four-bedroom, three-bathroom home with a living room, dining room, and gigantic kitchen—which wasn't used an awful lot, I might add."

"My mommy was a good cooker, right, Daddy?"

He noticed the hopeful glimmer in Aaron's eyes and wondered about it. Maybe Ciara had been right about him missing his mom. "Right. A good cooker." Luke didn't add that she only heated formula and jars of baby food to perfection. Alissa's actual cooking hadn't been the best. They had often gone out to eat after they were married, and when Devin came along, she gave up preparing meals altogether. Luke had usually been the one to throw together a dinner when he arrived home from work, and they'd eat when the boys were asleep for the night.

When the twins were almost two years old, Luke began dining alone most nights while Alissa went out with her girlfriends. After her death, he wondered why he hadn't stopped her, hadn't insisted she stay home with him and their sons. But even his cajoling had sparked arguments, and Luke had wanted Alissa to be happy. So when she complained about being cooped up with the kids and insisted she deserved to go out with friends, he'd shut his mouth and tamped down his disappointment. It hurt that she hadn't valued his companionship. Still, he had trusted her. . . .

"And that's when you began your own business. Is that correct, Luke?"

"What?" Puzzled, he glanced at Ciara.

"After you moved into your condo?"

"Oh, right." He nodded, recalling that he'd told her how God had brought he self-employment opportunity his way. "Such a blessing."

As if sensing his troubling thoughts and disturbing memories, Ciara set her delicate hand on his forearm. Her touch somehow had a healing effect on him.

"I'm glad you enjoyed the casserole. Would you like a second helping?" She ent him a sweet smile. "There's plenty left."

Luke glanced at his empty plate and then grinned. "Don't mind if I do."

❧

While Luke washed dishes, Cici read to the boys and tucked them into bed, giving each a kiss on the forehead.

"You'd make a good mom." Devin sounded drowsy as he turned over in his bed, which was up against the wall adjacent to the twins' bunk beds.

"I'd like to be a mom someday." *I wouldn't mind being a certain software designer's bride, either.*

"We could use a mom around here to make cookies and stuff." Aaron yawned.

Cici laughed at the remark. Then she glanced at Brian who stared back at her with his soft, thoughtful brown eyes.

"Yep, you'd be a good mommy."

The comments earned each boy another good night kiss on top of the head before Cici turned out the light and made her way back downstairs.

"You have the sweetest kids."

Luke was nearly finished loading the dishwasher. "Thanks."

"They went to sleep without a single complaint."

"They're exhausted."

Cici caught sight of the casserole dish, still coated with cheesy sauce and bits of chicken. She reached out and inched it toward the front of the stovetop. "I'll take this back to Jen's and soak it overnight."

"You sure?"

"Uh-huh." She smiled, noting Luke's expression of relief. "Positive."

An awkward moment passed.

"Dinner was terrific. Thanks."

"My pleasure." She ran her finger along the edge of the range. "Would you like to watch a movie together tonight?"

Luke hesitated.

"We don't have to." Cici ignored the swell of disappointment. "It was just a suggestion. I should work on my thesis anyway."

He caught her elbow as she lifted the casserole dish and turned to leave. "Wait, don't go. I'd like nothing better than if you stayed awhile longer. It's just that—"

"I know; we agreed to take things slowly."

"No, you don't understand. It's not that. . . ."

Cici set down the casserole dish and regarded him. "What is it then?"

Luke scratched his jaw. "Game's on TV."

"Game?"

"Royals. They play late tonight because they're in California." Luke headed for the living room. "Do you like baseball?"

"I never gave it much thought."

"Come on." He dropped himself onto the couch and patted the cushion beside him. "Have a seat." Next, remote in hand, he turned on the television.

Deciding that soaking Jen's casserole dish could wait until she got home, Cici straggled in and sat down beside him. He slipped his arm around her shoulders as he pointed the remote at the screen.

"This is sort of an important game. Royals are having a bad year, but a win tonight could turn things around."

Cici cozied up to him and decided that maybe, just maybe, she could learn to love this sport.

Chapter 15

Cici left for home shortly after the game ended. In spite of having a limited knowledge of sports, she'd enjoyed watching the game with Luke. She could easily envision herself getting hooked on baseball and football—just so she could share that part of his life.

And what part of her life would Luke share? The debates over women's issues at the coffeehouse?

"Good night, Ciara." He'd kept an eye on her until she reached the back door of Jen's condo. Cici had insisted it wasn't necessary, but Luke, being the superhero he was, had been determined to see her home safe.

"G'night, Luke."

Glancing at the clear, starry sky, Cici realized there wasn't room for Luke in the academic cocoon she'd built around herself. In that instant, she also became aware of how alone she really was in the universe. Like the stars in the heavens, she'd become a solitaire among solitaires. Sure, she had friends, acquaintances, and colleagues; however, until now, she'd never known what it felt like to be inextricably intertwined in another person's life.

Upstairs, she booted up her computer, intending to work on her thesis, but thoughts of Luke wouldn't leave her mind. About a half hour later, she decided she was too fatigued to write, so she changed clothes, called it a day, and crawled into bed.

🐝

The next morning, the melodious tone on her cell phone woke her up.

"Ceece, you all ready for the luncheon? Bridget and I are leaving now to come and pick you up."

"What?" With the phone to her ear, Cici glanced at the clock, realizing she'd slept most of the morning away. "Oh, wow."

"Must be working really hard on your thesis, huh? You lost track of time?"

"I wish that were the case." Cici tossed off the bedcovers. "To be honest, I just woke up."

"You? Were you working into the wee hours of the morning?"

"No, I was watching a baseball game on TV with Luke and I was home before midnight." She sighed. "I haven't worked on my thesis in two whole days."

Silence.

"Tanya?"

"I'm in shock, okay?"

"Get over it and come pick me up." Cici laughed. "I'm hopping into the shower right now."

She ended the call and, although she said she'd "hop," she more or less dragged herself into the bathroom.

But thirty minutes later, she'd managed to come to life and had slipped into a pair of lightweight beige capris and a flattering rust-colored cotton blouse. She piled her thick, curly hair on top of her head, and she'd even gotten in a few sips of coffee before Bridget and Tanya rang the front doorbell.

The ladies stepped in while Cici slipped into her sandals and collected her purse.

"Okay, I'm ready."

They chattered like magpies on the way to the church and found their way to the multipurpose room in which the luncheon was being held. Mandy Satlock met them soon after the three entered through the doorway.

Cici made the introductions.

"I think I met you both a while back at Jen's jewelry party." An easy smile played across Mandy's full lips.

Recognition shone in both Bridget and Tanya's expressions.

"Follow me. I'd like you to meet some more of my friends." Mandy led them through the large, noisy room, stopping every so often to make introductions. Then, after about a half hour of the informal meet and greet, an announcement was made that lunch would be served.

Cici sat at the same round table with Mandy, Bridget, and Tanya. She was more than impressed by the smoked salmon and feta cheese wrap and tossed green salad. Simple, yet elegant.

When they'd finished eating, the keynote speaker took the floor. Cici guessed the woman was about forty-something. "I'm Beth Orana," she began, before listing her impressive résumé. "Did you know that godly women are meek? Are you meek?"

Cici sat back in her chair and almost groaned aloud. Bridget and Tanya glanced at each other, and then at her. Incredulous, Cici arched her brow but decided to give the woman a chance.

Beth grinned. "I suppose I should explain to you what most Bible experts interpret the word 'meek' to mean in conjunction with a woman's conduct. The world as we know it has perverted the word. I'm sure every woman in this audience cringed to think of herself as some sort of weakling or doormat. But that's not what I mean by meek."

Cici folded her arms, listening.

"Meek, in essence, means to possess a controlled strength. Like Deborah, a judge. Her story is written in the Bible; when a soldier asked her to come with him and lead the way into battle, she accepted the challenge. I mean, picture it: Charlton Heston as Ben-Hur, driving his chariot into battle, but only after *asking a woman* to lead the charge. Can you imagine?"

Many in the audience laughed at the visual and even Cici had to smile. She'd seen the movie on television, after all, and who hadn't read the classic novel?

"Well, the situation was similar when a soldier named Barak approached Deborah and said he'd go into battle but only if she went along with him. Barak stated that if she didn't go, he wouldn't either.

"Deborah agreed to it, lending him the courage he needed. But she wasn't a shrew or loud and overbearing. Deborah had a decided meekness about her, yet she was authoritative and possessed great leadership skills. But the victory wasn't Barak's. Or even Deborah's. It really belonged to a woman named Jael. She was the one who actually defeated the enemy."

Cici felt a bit amazed. The Bible recounted stories of women who were stronger and braver than men? Did that mean today's Christian women didn't have to swallow their ambition in order to please God?

She glanced around the room and noted the variety in the types of women in the audience. She was surprised to discover that she felt quite comfortable in their midst.

Beth continued talking about Deborah as well as other women in the Bible, noting their strength and courage was made possible only by God's grace.

Then she segued into the salvation message. "God's grace is available to anyone who asks. The apostle Paul wrote in his letter to the Ephesians that it's by grace we're saved through faith. What's faith? It's an exercise of your own free will. It's believing that what God says in His Word is true. It's with the heart that one believes and with the mouth that one confesses to salvation. The Bible says in Romans chapter ten that 'everyone who calls on the name of the Lord will be saved.'"

Cici had heard the Romans verse plenty of times before from Jen and William—and Luke, too. But somehow the passage never connected with her—until now.

Then suddenly everything she'd heard came to light.

"Ladies, forgive me if I sound preachy," Beth said, "but I must share the Good News with you. We hear so much bad news these days. That's why it's good to know, or be reminded, that Jesus Christ died for *you*—because He didn't want to spend an eternity without *you*. He loves *you* so much that He willingly went to the Cross when in fact He's God and could have summoned a host of angels to destroy His accusers."

Tears filled Beth's eyes, and Cici realized they were tears of awe and joy—like the tears brimming in her own eyes. "The very One who breathed the universe into existence deemed you important enough to come to earth and rescue you from an eternity of darkness and misery. Now, that is good news, isn't it?"

Light laughter flittered around the room.

By the time Beth finished her oration, Cici knew what she heard was Truth. She needed no more convincing; she'd seen Christianity played out in the lives of three very special individuals.

God, I believe. You're the real. . .Superhero.

Beth's gaze roamed the room and she smiled. "If you'd like to accept the free gift of salvation that God extends to everyone, it's very easy. You just take it—and tell Him. You can do so now, by praying along with me." Beth bowed her head and Cici did the same.

"Jesus, I admit that I'm a sinner who deserves the worst of punishments, but I believe that You died and rose again to save me. Please forgive my sins and come into my heart and live forever. In Your precious name I ask this. Amen."

When Cici looked up, another woman stood alongside Beth. She closed the session by inviting everyone to come back and visit again.

Applause broke out and everyone stood.

"So, what did you think?" Mandy stepped toward Cici so she'd be heard above the din.

"I think Beth's talk today was exactly what I needed to hear. . ." Cici paused before adding, "to believe."

"You?"

Cici nodded. "I asked Jesus to save me."

An expression of immense happiness spread across Mandy's features before she hugged Cici. "I'm rejoicing with the angels right now." She pulled back. "Come with me. I'd like you to meet a few more of the ladies here, and you really ought to say a personal hello to Beth."

Cici followed Mandy and spoke with several different women, including their speaker. After about forty-five minutes of chatting, she, Bridget, and Tanya made their exit.

"So what'd you think, Cici?" Tanya slid behind the wheel.

"Beth Orana's quite a good speaker and a nice person. She's sincere and I believed everything she had to say about Christianity." Cici pulled on her seat belt. "I've concluded it's the real deal."

"Seems like it." Bridget's voice drifted up from the backseat.

"I know it's the real deal. All I had to do was think about Jen during the luncheon and my decision was made." Tanya laughed. "I've never felt so encouraged in all my life. Christianity is exactly what I needed to start living again after the mess I went through with Ryan."

"Jen will be ecstatic. Two out of her three roomies got converted today." A smile tugged at Cici's mouth when she thought about telling her best friend. And Luke—she could hardly wait to inform him of her pivotal decision. He'd be ecstatic, also.

"Maybe a third roomie'll get converted, too." Tanya glanced in her rearview mirror.

"I'm still thinking it over," Bridget said from the backseat. "I'm not sure. . ."

Cici could relate.

"I attended religious schools growing up, and I'm not sure I want to go back to having all that religion in my life."

"Luke told me it's not religion so much as it's a relationship with God."

"Same difference as far as I'm concerned."

Cici pushed out a smile. "Well, you'll figure it out." It was one of those things a person had to struggle through on their own. Cici knew that now.

Tanya let Cici off at the curb. "Let's do lunch soon."

"Don't you want to come in for a while? Maybe Luke's home. I'd like to introduce you."

"Another time." Bridget suddenly appeared to be in a crabby mood. "I've got some things to do back at the apartment."

Cici didn't pursue the matter even though Tanya seemed disappointed. She got out of the car and waved to her friends and then stood and watched the car drive away.

Once inside the condo, she heard sounds of laughter and peeked out the back window. She smiled at the sight of Luke sitting in the yard, his computer on his lap, while the kids splashed nearby in a wide, white plastic swimming pool.

She stepped out of the condo and he glanced her way. "Hi, Ciara. How'd the luncheon go?"

"Good." She trudged through the grass. "Excellent speaker. Marvelous meal." When she reached the shady part of the lawn where he sat, she held out her arms. "So, do I look any different?"

His gaze flicked over her and a little frown marred his brow. "Not sure what you mean. New hairdo or something?"

"No, you goof. I'm *one of you* now." She laughed, referencing his Fourth of July jest in which he equated believers to aliens from outer space.

He raised his eyebrows.

"It took me only minutes today to realize what Jen had been trying to tell me for the last couple of years." The smile lingered on her face. "Luke, I'm a Christian."

❧

Too easy. Couldn't be true. But as Luke and Ciara conversed for the next hour, he sensed something truly different about her.

She pulled up a lawn chair. "What's cool is I didn't have to change myself in order to be Christian. Somehow I assumed I had to dress and behave a certain way in order to be accepted—like at the university." She shook her head. "I can simply look at a person and tell if he or she is a serious student. I can see it in their faces, by the clothes they wear."

Luke just listened, keeping one eye trained on his boys.

"I think acceptance is what every person is searching for in one form or another. Love and acceptance."

"Which is what God offers us."

"Exactly—except, I didn't realize that until today." Puzzlement wafted across her freckled, feminine features. "It's so easy. Why did it seem so difficult before?"

Luke chuckled. "I know exactly where you're at. I was there, too." He pulled up a program on his laptop and handed the computer to her. "Take a look at this online Bible program. It's free and it's awesome. You can type in questions and get answers directly from God's Word. You can even search by topic."

"That's awesome."

Just then Aaron and Brian began quarreling. Devin attempted to break it up but only made things worse. Luke stood and walked to the pool to settle the matter before someone drowned.

"Daddy, it's my turn to play with the water worm." Brian pouted and pointed to the Styrofoam floatation toy.

Luke noticed his son's lips were tinged with blue and the boy shivered, not entirely out of agitation.

Dipping his hand in the water, Luke decided the pool's temperature was still rather cold. He'd filled it with the garden hose earlier, but the frigid water had felt rather good in the heat of the day. Now, however, the sun had moved to another part of the yard.

"I think you guys have had enough swimming for today."

They protested in unison.

Luke relented. "Okay, take one last dunk while I fetch some towels." He glanced at Ciara. "Would you mind keeping an eye on them?"

"Of course not."

He jogged to the house and let himself inside. He had to pause and praise the Lord for the miracle that occurred in Ciara's heart today. It went beyond his fondest hopes, his wildest imaginings.

Taking the stairs two at a time, he reached the linen closet in the hallway between two of the three bedrooms. But just as he grabbed an armful of clean towels, Ciara's shriek split the quiet summer afternoon.

Luke raced back to the first floor, but as he reached the kitchen, curiosity replaced his alarm. His kids were belly laughing. As he looked out the back door, he saw the reason why.

There in the middle of the pool sat Ciara, fully clothed and pushing the water out of her eyes.

"What in the world's going on out here?" He crossed the patio, chuckling because his sons were still cracking up over whatever it was that had happened.

Aaron could hardly speak, he laughed so hard. "Miss Ciara. . .sh–she splashed us."

"Yeah, big time," Devin chortled.

"Oh?" Luke arched a brow.

"Water's a little chilly, Luke."

"Yeah, I could have told you that." He swallowed another chuckle.

"But it feels sorta good." She lazed back in the pool, purposely knocking Devin off balance.

He hollered in fun and fell over, like a dramatic little clown.

The twins were in stitches.

Ciara laughed along with them. "Good babysitter that I am, I figured if you can't beat 'em, join 'em."

Chapter 16

The night air hung thick around Cici and Luke as they sat side by side on his cement patio, the cushion from the chaise lounge beneath them. Their backs were up against the cement stoop as they watched the flames dance in the fire pit. Luke had draped his arm around Cici's shoulder. She felt the warmth of his palm on her skin as he slowly, methodically rubbed her arm. Snuggling beside him, she thought it all seemed so perfect. In fact this whole evening had been perfect, from eating a pizza supper with Luke and his boys to watching a DVD with them and, finally, tucking the little superheroes into bed.

And now, being here, like this, with him. . .

"Luke?"

"Hmm?"

"I think I'm falling in love with you." She leaned her forehead against his jaw.

"I feel the same way, but it scares me a little."

She brought her head back. "What do you mean?"

"I dream about you, Ciara. I think about you all day long. You consume my thoughts. Sometimes I wonder if that's healthy."

"Oh, Luke. . ." She turned and placed her hand on the side of his face before bringing her lips to his. As always, a feeling that they belonged together filled her being.

Luke gathered her in his arms. The kiss deepened.

"Hello?"

A woman's voice, and its amused tone, shattered the intimacy of the moment.

"So sorry to interrupt." Another female's voice.

Cici squinted past the fire pit and into the night. "Bridget? Tanya?"

They stepped out of the shadows, giggling like teenagers.

"Ceece, we're sorry to barge in on you like this." Tanya spoke up first. "We just decided to grab some dinner at that comedy club in Des Moines, and we wondered if you'd like to come along."

"But we can tell you're sort of busy." Bridget laughed again. Her earlier dark mood had obviously blown over.

Cici glanced at Luke. "Meet my roommates."

He scrambled to his feet. "Hi."

Cici could tell he was embarrassed.

"Can I get you something to drink? A can of soda? Bottle of water?"

"Don't invite them to stay." Cici meant the remark in fun. "They just might."

"I'll take anything diet."

"Me, too."

"See?" Cici raised her hands in a helpless gesture. "What did I tell you?"

Luke headed for the kitchen, chuckling.

She turned back to her friends. "Nice going."

"We'll leave if you really want us to." Bridget sounded sincere. She brushed her blond hair back, made a ponytail, and then let it fall again, a practice she often did when she felt uncomfortable. "And I'm sorry for snapping."

"Not a problem and no, don't go. Luke and I agreed to take things slow between us and, um, I guess we were moving awfully fast there."

"I'm shocked. Talk about role reversal." Tanya dragged a lawn chair closer to where Cici still sat on the cushion. "It's usually you walking in on one of us."

"Yes, except I lived there."

Bridget, too, found a chair. "We tried to call, Ceece, but you didn't answer your cell."

"You were obviously *preoccupied*."

Cici puffed out an exasperated breath. "Oh, stop teasing me. And please don't tease Luke. He's a sweetheart of a guy."

Luke returned with two plastic cups and handed them to Bridget and Tanya. "Diet cola on the rocks."

They murmured their thanks, and he reclaimed his seat beside Cici.

"So how long have you lived next door to Jen?"

"Ever since she moved in."

Cici liked his easy tone. She felt certain her friends would find him charming and personable.

They chatted just minutes longer before a booming voice split the night. "Hey's this where the party's at?"

Chase sauntered into the yard, Jeremy in tow, and Cici wondered why the little boy wasn't in bed, sleeping.

"Mind if I join you?"

Luke, ever the polite host, stood and found another lawn chair for Chase. Meanwhile, Cici scooted over and offered the end of the cushion to Jeremy. He plunked himself down.

"Where's Devin and Aaron and Brian?"

"They're in bed for the night." *And you should be, too,* she wanted to say, although it wasn't her place.

"Bridget, Tanya, I'd like you to meet another resident of Blossomwood Estates, Chase Tibbits."

"How do, ladies."

Cici watched her roommates greet him in all politeness.

Another conversation ensued, Bridget and Tanya each taking a turn to tell both Chase and Luke a little about themselves. Cici listened on and then, to her surprise, Jeremy curled up and put his head in her lap. He was sleeping in minutes.

Cici glanced at Luke. He'd brought his legs up so that he leaned on his knees. He caught her gaze and then spied Jeremy.

She inched closer to him. "Could he sleep on your couch? Maybe he'd be more comfortable."

Luke considered the idea.

Chase must have overheard her. "Is that kid sleeping?"

Cici cringed at his gruffness.

"Listen, if it's okay with you, Jeremy can bunk with my boys tonight. I'll put a sleeping bag down on the floor."

"Well, I guess. . ."

"He's coming to Bible school with us again tomorrow morning."

"Yeah, okay. He can stay. Clothes should be clean. He had to change after dinner because he spilled milk all over himself at dinner. Clumsy kid."

"He's not clumsy, Chase. All children spill."

"Adults spill, too," Bridget pointed out.

Luke roused the boy, who nodded to the question about "camping out" with Devin, Brian, and Aaron. Then he gathered the child in his arms and stood. Cici pushed to her feet and followed Luke into the house, intending to lend a hand.

But Luke proved himself sufficient. He lent Jeremy a pair of Devin's pajamas and collected and folded up the youngster's jeans and T-shirt for tomorrow.

Jeremy yawned and crawled into the sleeping bag and put his head on the stuffed animal pillow.

Luke tousled his hair. "Everything's fine, buddy. Sleep well."

"Okay."

Cici backed up as Luke tiptoed from the room. His children didn't even stir.

"I feel sorry for that little boy. I think Chase is mean to him."

Luke reached out and caressed her cheek. "He'll be all right."

Somehow his touch made Cici believe him.

Placing a hand at the small of her back, Luke guided her to the steps. "VBS really tuckers kids out, what with all the games and activities. Parents like Chase sometimes don't realize that fact."

"Single dads like Chase aren't in tune with their children's feelings."

They walked back downstairs.

"You're generalizing again. I mean, you don't know that's the case with Chase and his kid."

She paused before they reached the kitchen. "Well, I'd like to find out. If

I'm right, Chase is the perfect example to prove my thesis—at least in part. I've agreed to be objective and I haven't forgotten that."

"I'd say now's a perfect time for researching your theory, all very discreetly, of course."

Cici smiled. "Of course, although Bridget and Tanya will know what I'm up to right away."

Luke didn't reply and, as they made their way out into the backyard, Cici wondered why.

🐝🪶

Fiddling with a twig, Luke tensed as Ciara tossed another question at Chase. He didn't mind her research per se. In fact he admired the way she'd been up front about her motives. No sneaky reporting. But what bothered Luke as he listened to Ciara question Chase was that she sounded so *interested* in the guy.

It bugged him, even though Luke reminded himself that she'd just admitted to falling in love with him. Likewise, when he looked into Ciara's eyes, he thought he glimpsed forever. When he kissed her, he'd felt almost complete again for the first time since Alissa's death.

Maybe that's why he felt so vulnerable, too; Ciara held that proverbial key to his heart. Could he trust her with it?

She worked her hand around his elbow now as the last of the embers dwindled in the fire pit. Her touch bolstered his confidence; however, he couldn't seem to completely shake his insecure feelings.

"Wow, it's almost ten o'clock." Tanya stood. "If we want to make that late show at the comedy club, we'd better hustle."

"Oh, right." Bridget stood also. "Want to come with us, Chase? We're driving into Des Moines to have a few drinks and some laughs."

"Yeah, sure, I'm all about drinks and laughs with pretty ladies." He stood and stretched. "Don't have to worry about my kid, thanks to Luke."

"Sure. Anytime." Luke pitched him a cordial grin.

"What about you, Cici?" Chase squared his shoulders. "Coming with us? You can ask me more questions about how I raise my kid."

"No, thanks."

Luke turned to her. "Don't stay behind on my account. I plan to go inside and call it a night. I'm beat." He held his breath, wondering if she'd go and praying she'd stay.

"No, I have to write my thesis. I haven't worked on it in days." She looked at her roommates. "Hear me, girls? I said *days*."

They both feigned heart attacks and Luke chuckled. How could he possibly think he had anything to worry about where Ciara was concerned?

Even so, he felt like an actor with opening night jitters. After all, this scene was all too familiar to him. The friends. The going out. The "drinks," the "laughs"—and the tragic ending.

Chase grew impatient. "Hey, if we're going, let's get a move on."

"Yep, time to go." Ciara shooed them out of the yard like pigeons. "Thanks for stopping. Next time call first."

"Next time keep your cell phone with you," one of her roomies retorted.

Their laughter echoed between the condos.

Ciara returned, still smiling. "See what fruitcakes I live with and why I begged Jen to let me stay at her place this summer?"

Luke stood and regarded her with an appreciative gaze. He thought she was beautiful, graceful, delicate, even in faded blue jeans and a white sleeveless shirt with her curly hair springing out from its ponytail. He suspected Ciara was one of those women who could wear a potato sack and still look lovely, and if Luke knew it, other men had to see it, also. Like Chase Tibbits.

"Weren't you tempted to go out with them? You need some fun in your life, too."

"I had fun today, acting silly with your kids." She laughed and tossed her head toward the swimming pool that still stood in the middle of the yard. "And the luncheon today was enjoyable. I've had a great day."

Luke folded his arms and leaned against the side of the fence. "So you don't go out with your roommates?"

"I have on occasion." She began folding lawn chairs. "But Bridget and Tanya seem to have more energy than I do, not to mention they're both a little on the nocturnal side. Me, on the other hand, I'm up at the crack of dawn."

"Yeah, me too." Luke felt suddenly at a loss for words. He didn't want to part company, but it was getting late.

"I suppose in lieu of the fact we're both early risers we should say good night, huh?"

"I suppose."

She tipped her head. "Everything all right? You don't seem yourself."

"I think maybe I'm overtired. VBS exhausts us parents as well as the kids." It was the honest truth.

"Ah. . ." Beneath the radiant, white beam from the neighbor's yard light, he saw her smile. "Understandable." She stepped forward and slipped her arms around his waist. Luke touched her hair and traced his finger alongside her upturned face. "I can tell you're exhausted."

He felt her breath on his chin. "Yeah. . ." She pressed her lips to his in a quick kiss that left him longing for more.

"Then I shall say, as they do in Italy, *arrivederci*."

"Doesn't that mean good-bye?" Why did that pluck such a sad cord in Luke's heart?

"You're right." Ciara scrunched up her features, deep in thought. "I helped

Jen learn some Italian for her trip—what's the word for good night?"

"Buona notte."

"That's it." Smiling, she took a step backward. "Buona notte, Luke."

He watched her walk around the fence. "G'night, Ciara."

Chapter 17

The writer's block lifted and suddenly Cici's fingers danced across her computer's keyboard.

Some single fathers consider it a burden or a nuisance to care for their children. They equate parenting to paying child support: It's a necessary evil. These inconsequential fathers become victims of their own selfishness. Cici thought about Chase Tibbits and how he seemed so eager to allow Jeremy to attend VBS and spend the night at Luke's place so he could shirk his responsibility and party. After speaking with him last night, Cici understood the man would rather let a congregation of a church and a neighbor take over caring for his son so he wasn't inconvenienced. *This anti-nurturing mentality and its subsequent actions burden society and create within the child feelings of rejection.*

She sat back and reread the paragraph. She smiled, thinking Aggie would be so proud. As for Chase, any trace of respect she might have had for him had vanished last night. And Luke? She smiled, deciding that he was an exemplary role model. Not a perfect dad, of course, but he loved his boys.

Other single fathers build their lives around their children—

The doorbell rang and Cici glanced at her wristwatch. Just after high noon. As she made her way to the front entrance, she half expected to see Luke standing just beyond the screen door.

Instead she found Chase Tibbits.

"Hey, I need your help."

"Oh?" She took in his disheveled appearance, unshaven jaw, mussed hair, swollen red eyes, and the same clothes he wore last night. "Hung over? Need aspirin or something?"

He ignored her cynicism. "Jeremy's missing."

"What?" Cici stepped out of the condo. "How can he be missing? He's with Luke's kids."

Chase shook his head. "One of Luke's kids is missing, too."

Cici's hand flew to her mouth, but she couldn't conceal her gasp of alarm.

"Luke just called to tell me. He and everyone else at church are searching for the boys right now."

"Which one of Luke's sons is it—just so I know who I'm about to go looking for?"

"I don't know. He said the kid's name—one of the younger ones."

"Aaron?"

"I think that's him."

Cici figured so, the mischievous little superhero. Her insides twisted with worry.

"I called Roberta Rawlings. She vowed to scour the entire complex just in case the kids happened to walk this far from the church."

"What time did they go missing?"

"No one's exactly sure. Bible school ended at eleven thirty. The boys were supposedly on the playground with other kids. I'm told there was adult supervision. But Luke said when he went to pick them up and bring them home, one of his boys and Jeremy were missing."

Cici lifted her gaze to the summer sky. "Please don't let anything happen to them." Her prayer was but a whisper.

Chase caught her wrist. "Come on."

She tossed reason to the wind, leaving her computer turned on, her purse and cell phone behind, and the condo unlocked. Nothing seemed to matter except finding Jeremy and Aaron unharmed.

Cici climbed up into Chase's pickup. "Where do you think Jeremy would go?"

"This isn't Jeremy's fault." He fired up the engine.

"I never said it was anyone's fault."

"I trusted Luke with my kid, and he or some other adults should have been watching him. I'm thinking about suing."

"Think about finding your son first." Cici pulled the seat belt across her chest. "And bear with me. I'm trying to guess two little boys' thoughts. I know Aaron's got an adventurous streak. Does Jeremy?"

"Maybe. . .I mean, he is a boy. All boys are adventurous, I guess."

"That helps a lot, Chase."

He obviously caught her sarcasm and cleared his throat. "Jeremy's a good kid. He knows if he gets out of line he'll have me to deal with."

Cici fixed her gaze on Chase's meaty hands as they tightened around the steering wheel. She recalled how intimidated, even frightened, Chase had made her feel in the past, and she wondered if he ever abused Jeremy. Then she recalled the verbal mistreatment that she'd witnessed last week at the ice cream parlor.

"Do you think Jeremy would try to run away? Maybe Aaron felt compelled to help him."

"Stop blaming this on Jeremy." He pounded the wheel. "I'm worried sick about my kid. Can't you see that?"

"Truthfully? I see an angry, selfish man right now." Cici couldn't believe her own audacity. Now was not the time to pick a fight with Chase Tibbits. One wrong swerve, and he could kill them both. Even so, she had to speak the truth as she saw it.

Much to her amazement, Chase seemed humbled by the remark. "You think I'm a bad father. Well, maybe I am. Kids don't come with directions, like m power tools. Can't ask a buddy to show you how it works, and you can't take back to the store if you don't like it after you try it out."

Cici listened, her heart breaking for Jeremy. It seemed Chase was saying h didn't love his son.

Or was he merely admitting that he didn't know *how* to love his son?

Several moments went by in silence before Chase seemed to give himself mental shake. "What am I thinking?" He turned the truck around.

"Where are we going?"

"I just realized that maybe we should stay at my place in case Jeremy show up or someone tries to call me with his whereabouts."

Seemed like a good idea.

"I guess I didn't have my wits about me. All I could think of was that I ha to find my kid."

"Ditto." Cici had to admit her thought pattern hadn't been the most strate gic, either. But the urgency of the situation still caused the adrenaline to shoc through her veins and hasten her actions.

She decided to call Luke right away and find out where she should b searching or what else she might do to help.

They reached Chase's condo and he parked. Getting out of his pickup, she fol lowed him inside. The place looked like an antiquated bachelor pad, as if Chase ninety-year-old great-uncle had died and left him his furniture. Messes lay every where, from used paper plates and plastic cups on the coffee table to clothes strew about the living room and a laundry basket at the foot of the stairs.

"Can I use your phone?"

"On the desk, over there."

Cici strode across the beige carpeting and moved a pile of unopened mail t get to the cordless device. Lifting the receiver, she thought it smelled like ranci beer.

"Hey, what do you know; Luke's here."

She dropped the phone and rushed to the doorway. She looked aroun Chase to see Luke open the sliding van door. Four boys jumped out—includin, Aaron and Jeremy.

Elation bubbled up inside her, and she pushed past Chase to get outsid She jogged across the lawn and gathered Jeremy in one arm and Aaron in th other. "Thank God you guys are all right!" After hugging them close, she pulle back. "Where have you been?" She looked at Aaron.

His brown eyes stared back at her in all innocence. "He wanted his mom I had to help him find her."

Cici pressed her lips together and gazed at Jeremy.

364

"I want to go home." He pouted. "I don't want to stay with my dad anymore. I want my mom."

"Well, you still shouldn't have run off like that—either one of you."

Hearing Luke's voice, she flicked her gaze at him. He stood by, hands on his hips, watching the scene unfold. His usually soft, soulful eyes looked like polished mahogany. But what had she expected? Luke had just been through quite a scare. No doubt he was upset and stifling his emotions until later when he could express them.

Chase stepped up beside her and began to berate his son. "What's up with taking off like that? Don't you have a brain in your head?"

"Must you be such a brute?" She instinctively hugged Jeremy to her. "Instead of yelling at him, why don't you tell your son how much the thought of losing him forever scared you?" Taking the boy by the shoulders, she made him face his dad. "Tell him how proud you are of him, Chase, because he can hang by his knees and do all sorts of really cool things. Tell him he's special. Tell him you want him to be part of your life. . .tell him that you—you love him."

Chase swallowed hard before he hunkered down. He stared at his boy. Seconds later, he enveloped his son in a bear-like hug. The sight caused tears to well in Cici's eyes.

She turned her attention to Aaron and put an arm around his shoulder. "You scared me to pieces."

He leaned against her hip, as if in silent apology.

"Scared us, too," Devin said.

Brian bobbed his head in agreement.

The kids closed in for a group hug, and it was then that Cici wished Luke's sons were hers, also. She wished Luke was her husband, and they were one big, happy family.

Could that really happen to her? Love? A family?

"I know you scared your dad to pieces, too." Again, she glanced at Luke. Stepping toward him, she touched his arm. "You okay?"

"I'll be fine."

She thought he averted his gaze. But why?

"I'd better get these boys home." He lifted Aaron out of her arms and set him inside the van. Devin and Brian scrambled in after him.

"Can I help you feed the kids lunch? In fact, I'll watch the boys this afternoon and give you a break."

"I can manage." Luke closed the sliding door. "Besides, Chase needs you more than I do."

"What?" Cici didn't think she heard him correctly. She turned to see Chase carry his son into the condo before looking back at Luke. "What's that supposed to mean?"

Without a word, he climbed behind the wheel, closed the door, and drove up the block. Cici could do nothing but watch him go.

🙚🙘

Luke heard the faint knock at the back door but ignored it. He knew Ciara wanted to talk, but he just didn't feel like discussing anything with her at the moment. He'd experienced a wide gamut of emotions today and he didn't think he could handle much more. He'd been terrified when Aaron and Jeremy were reported missing. Then with a sickening dread, he'd phoned Chase with the news. Minutes later, once Devin and Brian were situated in the van, he'd tried to reach Ciara but was disappointed she didn't answer her cell. When he spied the two boys in a nearby subdivision, Luke had never known such elation. Jeremy had gotten homesick and thought he knew the way to his mother's house, but he was afraid to walk there alone, so Aaron volunteered to escort him—taking his superhero role too seriously.

Luke spent the afternoon talking to his sons about the dangers of wandering off. He explained, grilled and drilled them, and all three crossed their hearts and promised to always tell him or another trusted adult where they were going.

He rejoiced that the outcome was a good one. Still, he was haunted by the interest Ciara had shown in Chase last night. Then the sight of her today, with Chase, leaving the condo with him. . .

Luke felt physically ill each time the memory played back. Why had he ever entertained the notion that he'd be enough for her, that she'd be satisfied with his less-than-exciting way of life?

And then the effect she had on his bawdy neighbor. Amazing, really. She'd reached him in a significant way today. When Chase finally embraced his son, her eyes filled with joy.

Except Luke hadn't put it there—Chase did.

An overwhelming swell of gloom lodged in his chest. But he figured it was better to come to grips with the truth now and sever his relationship with Ciara than to relive the nightmare that had resulted from Alissa's wanderlust.

Another light *tap, tap-tap* sounded at the door, but just as before, he refused to answer it.

Chapter 18

What a big baby!

Cici wasn't sure if she was more irritated or hurt that Luke had been dodging her for a week. But she finally gave up trying to corner him to explain herself. She'd deduced that Luke had jumped to inaccurate conclusions about her and Chase and now his insecurity had overtaken his common sense. But if he wouldn't listen, how could she set him straight?

A few more days passed, and Cici tried to consume herself with her thesis; however, on a Friday afternoon, after a frustrating appointment with her professor, she arrived back at Jen's condo to find Luke in his driveway. He'd loaded suitcases, sleeping bags, and pillows into his van.

He froze when he saw her coming up the walk.

"Looks like you're going somewhere."

"I decided to spend a month in Minnesota, visiting my folks." He turned and resumed packing. "Need to get away."

"From me? But I've been trying to let you have your space." When he didn't reply, an indescribable sorrow sank into her heart. Her hopes to discuss the situation with Luke before Jen returned home vanished. "Oh, fine, Luke. Have it your way. I thought you'd be a decent enough guy to flat-out tell me your feelings had changed—or at the very least, *say good-bye.*"

She fought the familiar angst of abandonment. Her father hadn't bothered to say good-bye, either. One day he just up and left.

"Luke?"

He closed the hatch with a forceful shove. "I've got to get the kids in the van and hit the road. We've got a long drive ahead of us."

Disappointment and confusion assailed her. But what more could she say—that she'd been right about him and every other man on the planet?

She swung around and saw Tori Evenrod and Michayla Martinelli across the street. They looked her way and waved, and Cici suspected her voice had carried a little too far, and now her relationship with Luke and its heart-crunching demise would soon be the talk of Blossomwood Estates.

Great. Just great. She returned the wave and pushed out a friendly smile as if nothing were wrong. Nothing at all.

❦

The month of August progressed miserably for Luke—and it had nothing to do with the humid weather and the mosquitoes or the fact that he came down with a bout of the flu and lost an important client. He felt like both Job and Jonah combined, what with his trials and running from God. He was only too grateful that his parents picked up the slack.

"Why don't you just move back home here where you belong?" His mother, plump with short dark hair, moved about the kitchen as she prepared dinner. She peeked out the window to where the boys played in the yard. "The boys love it here, they can run free, and I could take care of all of you. I'd feed you, make sure you had clean clothes. You'd have more time to concentrate on your work. I mean, what's in Iowa anyway?"

"Not a baseball or football team, that's for sure," Dad groused from behind a section of the newspaper.

"Alissa's family's there. They help me out when they can. My church is there. My friends. . ."

Ciara.

"They can all come visit. Lord knows there's plenty of room in this old farmhouse. And if they don't want to stay in the house, we'll set up the camper."

Somehow Luke couldn't envision his rather persnickety in-laws in either a farmhouse with no central air conditioning or a pop-top camper.

His father must have guessed his thoughts. "There's always the hotel in town for those who don't want to *rough it.*"

Luke had to chuckle.

Dad rustled the pages of the newspaper before setting it in a heap on the table. "So what's really eating you?"

"Besides the bugs?"

"Yeah. Besides the bugs." His father regarded him over his bifocals. His keen, walnut brown eyes pierced Luke in a way that made him want to confess.

"Okay, okay. . .there's this woman—"

"I knew it!" Mom hurried across the room and sat down beside Luke. "I knew it was a woman. Didn't I say that, Daniel?"

"Yeah, you might have mentioned something along those lines." Dad ran a hand over his graying short hair.

"So who is she, what's she like. . .and why are you acting so lovesick?"

"Mom." Luke bristled. Despite his best efforts and accomplishments in life, his mother still treated him like he was in high school. Little wonder he didn't want to move back to Minnesota. "In all due respect, will you just cool it?"

She sat back in her chair and pressed her lips together.

Luke rubbed his jaw. On one hand he was thankful his mother loved him. Some guys only wished their mothers cared about them. Still, Luke had to draw the line with her from time to time. He was just glad she had grandchildren to absorb that overexuberant motherliness left over from raising him and his brothers.

With a sigh of resignation, Luke began telling his folks about Ciara, how they met, how she came to know Christ and believe, and how they fell in love.

And, yes, he did love her.

"The kids adored her. Aaron even started talking about having a mom. . ."

"Oh, Luke." His mother's fingers fluttered to the base of her neck.

"But everything seems so impossible between Ciara and me now. I want to think it's for the best, but somehow I can't accept it."

Mom set a hand on his forearm. "Why not give her a call?"

Luke gave her an incredulous look. "She'll hang up on me. I mean, I'd hang up on me if I was her."

"Then send her an e-mail," Dad suggested. "You're a computer guy. Send her one of those fancy Internet cards."

"Or a text message on her cell phone."

"And say what? I'm insecure because of what happened with Alissa so I acted out by behaving like an insensitive jerk?"

"That'd be a start." Mom smiled, leaned over, and kissed his cheek. "That'd be a very good start."

🐝

"The pictures and DVD from your trip are amazing." Cici sat forward and took a sip of her hot, spicy tea. It was hard to believe the summer had flown by and Jen and William were back in Iowa. The Labor Day weekend was just days away.

"I'll never forget it." Sitting cross-legged on the carpet, Jen flicked strands of her silky, golden-brown hair off one slender shoulder. "And sharing all those new experiences with the man I love"—she sent William an adoring look—"made everything all the more special."

Cici glanced over in time to see him reply to Jen with an affectionate wink. She shifted on the sofa, feeling like the fifth wheel on a wagon. "I suppose I should get going." She stood. "I have a meeting with Aggie tomorrow, except I don't know why. She already disapproved of my thesis and said she won't recommend me to my committee of professors."

"I read the draft of your thesis that you e-mailed me earlier in the week." William pushed to his feet. "I'm still impressed. You laid out examples of bad and good parenting, cited why single fathers are disadvantaged from a societal viewpoint, and then ended on a hopeful note. You allowed readers to form their own assumptions. Excellent."

"I wish you were my professor." Still, Cici felt satisfied with her achievement, and the fact that William complimented her work took some of the sting out of Aggie's discouraging assessment. In a word, Aggie *hated* it. The trouble had all begun when Cici changed the title of her thesis back in early July, and things with Aggie went downhill from there.

"Well, at least you stayed true to what you believe." Jen sprang up from where she'd been sitting on the floor. "I'm proud of you."

"Thanks, except it's doubtful I'll earn my master's now."

"What a shame." Stepping forward, she slung one long, slim arm around Cici's shoulders. "I know you worked so hard. But you took the high road and didn't compromise on what you know is true. That takes courage."

Cici shrugged her reply. "I don't know how brave I am, but at least I was offered a job with the county's department of education. It's not the one I had my eye on, but it'll pay the bills."

"Congratulations!" Jen gave her a little hug.

"See, God came through for you in spite of that professor." William smiled.

"The job is answered prayer, that's for sure."

Jen released a happy sigh. "And to think you're not just my best friend in the whole world now, you're my sister, adopted into the family of Christ. I don't think I've ever been so happy as when I learned you became a Christian, aside from the day William proposed to me, of course."

"Of course." Seeing the joy on Jen's face made Cici smile, too, although she continued to grapple with various biblical truths. Like, what if God decided He didn't want her in His family? Would He dump her like her dad and Luke had? No reply. No explanation. Just here one day and gone the next?

"Cici, as long as we're on the subject of your conversion..." William stepped forward. "Part of being a Christian is learning and growing by hearing God's Word. So, I'd like to invite you to come to church with us on Sunday."

"No way." Cici shook her head for emphasis.

"Oh, Cici." Jen looked disappointed. "We're a friendly congregation. You can sit with William and me."

"I've been to your church. I like your pastor and all the people. I especially enjoyed meeting Jesse and Mandy Satlock this summer. It's just that...I don't want to run into Luke." She shrugged off Jen's arm and lifted her mug of tea from the coffee table. "The only reason I came over here tonight is because he's still gone."

"So you only became a Christian because of Luke?" William stood with his arms akimbo.

"No, I didn't. And for your information, I plan to attend Sunday service at a small church near the university. Tanya expressed interest in attending with me. For myself, I knew it was the right place because it was like God spoke to only me when I glimpsed a wood engraving on the altar. It read: *I will never leave you nor forsake you.*"

"And He never will, either." Earnestness narrowed Jen's gaze.

Cici smiled. "Well, I'm willing to give Him a chance. As for Luke...what can I say?"

"The two of you need to talk." William seemed determined.

"I've tried talking to Luke numerous times. He either gives me curt answers r doesn't reply at all. Then he left without even saying good-bye. He knows I've struggled with abandonment issues in the past. He wanted to hurt me on purpose." She headed for the kitchen, intending to dump her unfinished tea in the sink. Her heart ached just thinking about Luke. Despite his hateful actions, she missed him and his precious children.

"I know Luke. He wouldn't hurt you on purpose." William's deep voice wafted in from the living room. "Sounds to me like he was being selfish and only thought about himself and his own feelings."

Both he and Jen came to stand in the kitchen archway.

"Luke got jealous and for no good reason." Cici turned from the sink. "Although, I understand in part. There is history behind Luke's feelings of insecurity because of how his wife died. I'm willing to work through it with him. But he's shut me out of his life and that. . ." She swallowed hard. "Hurts so much."

Her friends grew thoughtful for several long moments.

"I wonder what Luke will say when he finds out Chase and Bridget are dating." Jen had to smile.

A grin pulled at William's mouth. "Maybe that'll quell Luke's jealousy once and for all."

"I doubt it." Cici folded her arms. "I think Luke needs something more along the lines of counseling."

"He knows the Almighty Counselor."

"Maybe Luke's shunning Him, too." Cici rolled her eyes.

Jen shook her head, looking amazed. "Chase and Bridget? Who would have thought it? They suit each other, you know? Rough around the edges, but big softies inside."

"If you want to know the truth, they're both getting on my nerves *big time*." Cici couldn't help venting. "They're together all the time." She flung up her hands in frustration. "Oh, maybe I'm the one who's jealous now. I wish Luke and I were a couple."

"At least you can admit it," William said.

Cici shrugged.

Jen stepped closer to her, compassion etched into her every feature. "I'm sorry you're hurting. You're my friend and I love you."

Cici's eyes filled.

"As for Chase and Bridget, if they bother you, you can move in with me for a while."

"What? You and William are more the lovebirds than Chase and Bridget." Cici laughed in spite of herself. "Seriously, thanks, Jen, I appreciate the offer, but no—especially with Luke living next door."

"But you know you're going to have to face him, hopefully sooner rather than later."

Cici tipped her head, curious.

Jen's eyes widened. "I'm getting married in a month."

"I know. I'm happy and excited for you."

"You don't understand." Jen blinked. "Both you and Luke are standing up in the wedding!"

Chapter 19

Luke dropped the boys off at school. Devin started first grade this year, and the twins began half-day kindergarten. They weren't babies anymore. Pretty soon they'd be driving.

He winced. The thought gave his heart a jump start. It also served as a reminder that he didn't want to journey through life alone, but he almost believed he was incapable of trusting another woman with his love.

Pulling into the driveway, Luke parked the van and got out. As he made his way toward the front door, he spotted Jen who, judging by her professional attire, was leaving for work. They'd only briefly chatted since he arrived home yesterday—Labor Day.

He waved.

She waved back. "Say a prayer for Cici. She starts her new job today."

Luke almost missed a step at the mention of Ciara's nickname, but he grinned politely nonetheless.

Jen didn't say anything more as she climbed into her sand-colored coupe. Her tone had been so nonchalant that Luke wondered how much, if anything, she knew about the situation between him and Ciara.

Say a little prayer...

Luke had been speaking with the Lord, but he hadn't felt a particular leading, although his senses seemed to petrify each time he considered contacting Ciara.

She starts a new job today.

He unlocked the front door and let himself inside. More than a month had gone by since he'd last seen or spoken to her. Had she finished her thesis?

I've got no right to ask.

Luke walked upstairs to his home office. He shook off his thoughts of Ciara and did his best to focus on a new program he'd recently sold to a local company. Around lunchtime he heard the mail arrive and went to get it. The house seemed far too quiet, what with Devin in school all day and the twins at the Satlocks' for the afternoon. He was grateful that Mandy offered to help him out three days a week. Even so, the silence would take some getting used to.

He ambled out to the mailbox at the curb and sifted through the envelopes as he made his way back to the house. Glimpsing Ciara's name and her apartment's address, he halted in mid stride. A second later, he tore into the large, square envelope, too curious to even wait until he was inside.

Dear Luke. . .Seeing as we're both in Jen and William's wedding party, I'd like to formally ask you to agree to look beyond ourselves and focus on celebrating our friends' special day. I ask this so neither one of us will feel awkward and uncomfortable. . .

Luke blew out a breath and continued his trek inside. He'd forgotten all about it, not the wedding or agreeing to be one of William's groomsmen, but the fact that he and Ciara would be together in some capacity for the occasion.

Collapsing into the sofa, he regarded the colorful blank card in which she'd scribed her proposed "agreement." He felt both foolish and wrung out emotionally, but the least she deserved was an apology and a promise that he'd be cordial and friendly at the wedding next month.

As for himself, he recognized now as the time to call his pastor and seek out godly counsel. Life was just too short to live in misery.

🐞

Cici parked her car and walked through the lot to her apartment. Only the first week of September and already it felt like fall. Low humidity, temperatures in the upper seventies. It almost seemed like summer had never existed. July she associated with falling in love with Luke and August with nursing her heartbreak. Both months were best forgotten—so that took care of the majority of her summer.

But at least she enjoyed her new job.

Taking the stairs to her second-story unit, Cici decided she couldn't wait to kick off her shoes. After being barefoot or in flip-flops for the last few months, leather pumps with a three-inch heel for nine hours a day took some adjustment.

"Look what came for you today!"

Cici had barely gotten into the apartment when Bridget made the announcement. Surrounded by textbooks on the couch, her blond roommate nodded toward the coffee table and the beautiful bouquet of pink and purple orchids with curly willows added for decoration.

Cici set down her purse and work bag. "For me?"

"Yep. But I couldn't even snoop to find out who sent them because the card attached is in a sealed envelope. But I'll bet the flowers are from Luke. Either him or your cranky professor. Maybe she's sorry she trashed your thesis."

"Are you kidding? Aggie doesn't apologize to *anyone*. But, you know what? I'm okay with it." Cici tore into the envelope. "I'm all about pleasing God, not her."

"Way to go."

Cici read the type-printed card. *The words "I'm sorry" didn't seem like enough. Can you ever forgive me?*

"And? Who's the arrangement from?"

"Luke." Cici was tempted to take his flowers and toss them out the window.

He'd wounded her deeply, but he was sorry—and she believed he meant the apology. What's more, he had contacted her in a positive way. She no longer had to dread seeing him at Jen and William's wedding.

Now it was time to do her part, please God, as she'd just touted, and forgive Luke.

🐝

Cici's footsteps echoed in the nearly empty church parking lot. For the past month she'd felt confident about the rehearsal dinner tonight and about facing Luke. Now, however, with the moment at hand, she felt anxious flutters filling her midsection.

She entered the building and made her way to the sanctuary, but as the sole of her brown patent-leather dress shoe touched the carpeting, she heard the soft, sure timbre of Luke's voice, followed by his carefree chuckle.

She spun around on her heel—

And almost collided with Jen.

"Cici! I'm glad you're here. We're about to start. I'm trying to round up everyone."

She smiled, noticing her best friend's harried expression. "Can I help?"

"Nope. Just have a seat up front." She paused. "Oh, and I love the outfit. Can I borrow it sometime?"

"Only if you dry-clean it before giving it back." Cici grinned and some of her tension ebbed. The joke was that the russet silk dress belonged to Jen.

Continuing up the aisle, Cici slipped into the second pew from the front in the large, oval-shaped auditorium. She spotted Luke out the corner of her eye. In honor of tonight's semiformal affair, he wore a dark suit and a lavender dress shirt. He clowned around beside William, pretending to hang himself with his necktie.

She swallowed a laugh and lowered her gaze. One of the things she loved about Luke was his sense of humor. . .

"Can I have everyone's attention?"

Cici set her small handbag aside and trained her eyes on the pastor, but despite her best efforts to keep focused, she saw Luke in her peripheral vision as he sat one pew up, to her far right.

The pastor, stout with a graying goatee, continued with his instructions. They were going to practice walking down the aisle. Grandparents, parents, and then Jen's sister, the maid of honor, would step out first on the arm of the best man, William's brother. Mandy and Jesse were slated to go next, followed by Grace and Trevor Morris.

Finally it would be Cici and Luke's turn. It came as no surprise to her, after Jen listed the attendants; however, she never fathomed her legs would be so unsteady as she made her way to the back of the church.

After hellos to Mandy and Grace, she lined up beside Luke in the spacious foyer.

"Hi."

"Hi." She tried to act natural, calm, cool. He certainly seemed his jovial self as he bantered with his buddies. It seemed to take forever for the couples to make their way to the altar, but at long last they neared the entryway.

"Would you like a breath mint?"

Cici gasped. "Do I need one?" She stared at the tiny plastic container in his hand.

"No." He paled in what seemed like a mix of chagrin and horror. "I only meant to be polite, break the ice—I mean, not that there's ice, really. . ."

Cici raised her brows. A heartbeat later, she guessed his nervousness matched her own.

"I, um. . .well, what I meant is ice as in icebreaker. . ."

While he sputtered on, she helped herself to a mint, just in case. "Thanks." She popped it into her mouth.

"Sure." Luke pocketed the peppermints before offering his arm.

She threaded her hand around his elbow. Then it was step, pause, step, pause, step. . .

"Now, remember, ladies, you'll be carrying bouquets in one hand." The pastor's wife spoke the reminder into the microphone in order to be heard above all the milling around.

"Thank you for the flowers, by the way." Cici threw out an icebreaker of her own. "I enjoyed them."

Step. Pause.

"You're welcome. I wasn't sure what it meant when I didn't hear from you."

Step. Pause.

"But," he added, "William said you were willing to forgive and forget."

Step, pause.

"He's right and I did."

In reply, Luke pressed her hand between his arm and rib cage. A subtle gesture—a token of friendship?

Step. Pause. Step.

They reached the platform and parted, Cici to the left. Luke to the right. She turned in time to watch Jen and William head for the altar. Cici's best friend glowed with happiness.

All went well for the next several minutes until Cici made the mistake of glancing across the platform at Luke. Her gaze melded to his warm brown eyes as he returned her stare. In that instant, Cici knew her feelings for Luke hadn't changed a mite.

"Cici? Would you mind handling that for the bride? Cici!"

"What?" She snapped back to reality, noticing the pastor and his wife, Jen and William, and the entire wedding party were waiting for an answer. Embarrassment crashed over her. She wasn't even sure who'd spoken. "Um. . . could someone repeat that question?"

※

Rows of white linen-covered tables filled the paneled banquet room. Sitting at one of the four center tables, Luke finished the last of his apple pie, a marvelous dessert after a delicious meal of grilled rib-eye steak, homemade hash brown potatoes, and an autumn medley of stir-fried squash. Luke set aside his plate, feeling like he might burst.

Sitting back, he let his gaze wander around the dimly lit room. Strains of classical music played in the background while everywhere people mingled, some at tables and others standing in clusters. Luke searched for Ciara but didn't see her anywhere. Last he'd glimpsed her, she was sitting somewhere behind him, near the front of the room.

He slid his chair back and stood.

"Where are you going?" Mandy looked up from across the table.

Beside her, Jesse's gaze lit on him, as he sipped from his coffee cup.

"I think I'll mosey on into the lobby and walk off some of my dinner."

"Well, you might want to mosey out to the patio." Mandy threw a thumb in the direction of the bank of sliding glass doors leading outside. "I saw a certain redhead in a flattering sienna-colored dress head that way a few minutes ago."

"Thanks for the tip." Luke grinned. And thanks to Ciara's blunder at the rehearsal, he, along with everyone present, knew she had feelings for him. Her distraction had become the rolling joke all evening, but to her credit, she took it in stride, with her slim shoulders squared and her delicate chin held high. Luke had pitied her, having been the object of his friends' good-natured wisecracks in the past, but Ciara's brief preoccupation with him as they'd stood near the altar this afternoon was all the encouragement Luke needed to seek her out now. There was so much he longed to say to her.

With deliberate strides, he made his way across the banquet room and through the floor-to-ceiling glass doors. Outside, he found himself on a wood-plank, wraparound porch that overlooked the now dark golf course—deserted except for Ciara. Luke spied her slim, shadowy figure meandering along a cement walkway, her arms folded.

He seized the moment, making quick business about descending the steps around the corner and reaching her on the walk.

She heard him coming up behind her, stopped, and turned.

"Want some company?"

"Okay, sure."

Luke tried to cover his breathlessness from the sprint.

"How have you been? How's life?"

She laughed. "I'm fine and I like my new job. It's not the one I wanted, but it'll do."

"I read your thesis."

"You did?" She turned and regarded him beneath the moonlit sky.

"I inquired about it, and William forwarded the copy you sent him."

"What did you think?"

"Thought it was a commendable piece. Any single mother who reads it will feel empowered, but not at the expense of single dads. I was especially impressed by the way you handled 'Example B'—the guy who resembled Chase Tibbits. You described his parenting skills as 'loathsome' and yet you ended on a high note, explaining that even the most insensitive of men can learn to nurture their children. Great job."

"Thank you."

They walked on at a slow, unhurried pace, and seconds of silence ticked by.

"So, how are you?"

Luke didn't think he could describe what all he'd been through in a mere reply, so he settled for, "I'm okay."

"How are the boys?"

"Great." Luke told her about their experiences at school and Devin joining a soccer team.

"I miss them," she said wistfully.

"They miss you, too. Aaron talks about you all the time. For some reason he still thinks you live next door. I've explained time and time again that you were only staying there until Miss Jen got back from her trip, but. . ." Luke rolled his shoulders with uncertainty. "Maybe it's a form of denial—like the kind his old man's been plagued with for the last three-plus years."

"What?"

Luke halted and Ciara did the same.

"I've been seeing a Christian counselor. He's a friend of one of my pastors. Godly man as well as a down-to-earth guy. Counsels me from God's Word and not from his own opinions and experiences. He reminds me of my grandfather, wise and to the point." Luke paused in momentary thought. "I didn't realize how much baggage I'd been carrying around since Alissa died. But the counselor helped me see that I never had time to grieve or come to grips with the issues surrounding her death because I had three young children who needed me. Then I met you and those emotions that were stuffed away, ignored, and denied resurfaced. But I'm dealing with them."

"Oh, Luke." Ciara turned her head, glancing across the darkness that veiled the golf course before looking back at him. "I was never interested in Chase. Not ever."

"I know."

"That day Jeremy and Aaron went missing—"

Luke pressed his fingertips to her lips. "I know." He cupped her face in his hands and gently pulled her to him. "And I'm so sorry I hurt you. There are no words to express my regret." A single tear fell onto his thumb. "Don't cry."

He enveloped her in his arms and kissed her. He'd only dreamed of this moment a million times, prayed it'd come true.

"I love you, Ciara." He placed a kiss on her temple. "If you'll give me another chance, I promise I'll never hurt you or leave you—you'd be stuck with me for better or worse."

She sniffed. "I love you, too, Luke." Her voice sounded soft but thick with emotion. "I'd like nothing better than to be stuck with you." She lifted her lips to his.

He kissed her again.

Chapter 20

"You're a gorgeous bride with a perfect wedding day."

Cici swung her gaze from the full-length mirror and to her best friend. Only seven short months ago, Jen had been the one wearing white satin and lace.

Now it was Cici's turn. Today she would become Mrs. Luke Weldon. And to Cici's delight, her mother was ecstatic about becoming a grandmother.

"I'm so happy."

"With good cause." Jen, the matron of honor, adjusted Cici's veil. "I had doubts about an outdoor wedding, but the weather's perfect. It feels like summer but it's only the end of May."

"A gift from God—you don't know how hard I prayed that He'd keep the rain away."

"Your prayers were answered, but now. . .it's time to go. William sent word saying *your sons* are racing around the yard in their tuxedoes, getting hot, sweaty and giving their grandparents a run for their money—including your mom."

Cici wagged her head. "That's my superheroes for you."

"You sure you know what you're getting into?"

"Positive." Cici had never felt more certain of anything in her life. Being Luke's wife and his sons' mother was everything she'd ever wanted and more.

"Oh, and I should warn you: Aggie came."

"You're kidding, right?" Cici brought her chin back in surprise. She'd sent her professor an invitation but received no reply.

"Apparently, she brought a date."

"A *date*?"

"Yes, and he's a very distinguished-looking gentleman."

"Shut *up*," Cici said facetiously and Jen laughed.

"She seems quite smitten with the man. Perhaps her hard-line feminist views are softening. Maybe she'll even reconsider your thesis."

"Perhaps," Cici agreed. "But for now, God, Luke, and the boys are enough to fill up my whole life."

Jen smiled. "So, are you ready?"

"Ready."

She and Jen hugged each other, and Cici felt so blessed to have such a good friend.

Together they left the tiny fieldstone cottage, which served as the women's dressing room. Outside, sunshine spilled through budding treetops. Cici caught Devin by the collar as he made a dash past her.

"Settle down now," she whispered, brushing blades of grass off the shoulder of his black tux. "The wedding's about to start."

"Finally."

Cici smiled at his impatience and, after a kiss on the cheek, she sent him to the front of the queue.

One of Luke's cousins manned a keyboard and started playing the wedding march. The procession began, men in black tuxes and women in flowing, sea green tea-length gowns.

At last Cici walked the grassy aisle, her gaze fixed on no one but Luke. Then, standing beneath a canopy of silk gardenias, she held his hands while he recited his vows. She'd never felt more loved and cherished, and she knew each word came from his heart.

". . .to have and to hold, from this day forward, as long as we both shall live."

Luke gazed deeply into her eyes and gave her fingers a meaningful squeeze.

Then it was Cici's turn. As the pastor led her, she promised to "love, honor, and cherish."

When the vows were finished, Jen read from 1 Corinthians 13: " 'Love is patient, love is kind. It does not envy, it does not boast, it is not proud. It is not rude, it is not self-seeking, it is not easily angered, it keeps no record of wrongs. Love does not delight in evil but rejoices with the truth. It always protects, always trusts, always hopes, always perseveres. Love never fails.'"

Cici knew it was true.

"I now pronounce you man and wife. Luke," the pastor said, "you may kiss your bride."

Cici smiled—until she glimpsed the mischievous spark in Luke's brown eyes. "Be nice." She warned him without moving her lips.

"Always."

Luke drew her into his arms and then dipped her backward before pressing his lips to hers.

Their guests applauded.

"Show-off."

Luke chuckled and their sons jumped up and down, laughing.

"Do that again, Daddy." Aaron clapped his hands.

"I'll do that lots of times today."

Cici considered herself fairly warned.

Arm in arm, they walked past friends and family members who tossed bird-seed at them in celebration of their union. They made their way toward the white canvas tent. Beneath its billows, the bridal party formed a line so they could greet everyone who entered the makeshift reception area for food, wedding cake, and punch.

"I love you, Ciara," Luke whispered close to her ear.

She smiled. He told her that at least twenty-five times a day. "I love you, too, but those words can't come close to expressing how I feel right now." She pressed herself close to him. "I guess I'll just have to spend the rest of our lives showing you how much I love you."

"I'll look forward to it." He kissed her again.

"All right, that's quite enough." Aggie appeared, wearing an ivory blouse and peach-colored slacks.

"I'm glad you came." Cici's eyes filled as she hugged her once-beloved professor.

Aggie only halfheartedly returned the gesture, but she'd never been one to display outward affection.

"I wish you every happiness in the world." She gave Luke an appraising glance. "You, too."

"Thank you." He inclined his head in a single, gracious move.

Aggie introduced her gentleman friend and they moved on.

Next Tori Evenrod congratulated them, followed by the lovely Michayla Martinelli.

Michayla kissed both of Cici's cheeks in a European-like fashion. "Lovely wedding, and Roberta has outdone herself once more with the amazing spread of food."

Cici agreed and, not for the first time, felt grateful for Roberta Rawlings' organizational skills.

Bridget, Chase, and Tanya stepped in front of them, congratulating both her and Luke.

"Say, who's the guy on the piano keyboard?" Tanya aimed her gaze at the man across the decorated yard.

"That's my cousin."

"Married?"

A grin crept across Luke's face. "Actually, no he's not."

"Is he a believer?"

Luke inclined his head. "He is."

"Cool." She turned and headed for the nice-looking pianist before Cici even got a hug.

Cici laughed and had to admit her former roommates would probably get their "M-r-s" degrees before Cici earned her master's. But that was fine, because she'd found joy to last a lifetime with Luke—

And three little superheroes who had once lived next door.

A Letter to Our Readers

Dear Readers:

In order that we might better contribute to your reading enjoyment, we would appreciate you taking a few minutes to respond to the following questions. When completed, please return to the following: Fiction Editor, Barbour Publishing, Inc., P.O. Box 719, Uhrichsville, OH 44683.

1. Did you enjoy reading *Heartland Heroes* by Andrea Boeshaar?
   ❑ Very much. I would like to see more books like this.
   ❑ Moderately—I would have enjoyed it more if _____
   _____
   _____

2. What influenced your decision to purchase this book?
   (Check those that apply.)
   ❑ Cover   ❑ Back cover copy   ❑ Title   ❑ Price
   ❑ Friends   ❑ Publicity   ❑ Other

3. Which story was your favorite?
   ❑ *Prescription for Love*   ❑ *The Superheroes Next Door*
   ❑ *Courting Disaster*

4. Please check your age range:
   ❑ Under 18   ❑ 18–24   ❑ 25–34
   ❑ 35–45   ❑ 46–55   ❑ Over 55

5. How many hours per week do you read? _____

Name_____

Occupation_____

Address_____

City_____ State_____ Zip_____

E-mail_____

HEARTSONG
PRESENTS

If you love Christian romance...

$10.⁹⁹

You'll love Heartsong Presents' inspiring and faith-filled romances by today's very best Christian authors. . .Wanda E. Brunstetter, Mary Connealy, Susan Page Davis, Cathy Marie Hake, and Joyce Livingston, to mention a few!

When you join Heartsong Presents, you'll enjoy four brand-new, mass-market, 176-page books—two contemporary and two historical—that will build you up in your faith when you discover God's role in every relationship you read about!

Mass Market, 176 Pages

Imagine. . .four new romances every four weeks—with men and women like you who long to meet the one God has chosen as the love of their lives—all for the low price of $10.99 postpaid.

To join, simply visit www.heartsongpresents.com or complete the coupon below and mail it to the address provided.

✄- -

YES! Sign me up for Heart♥ng!

NEW MEMBERSHIPS WILL BE SHIPPED IMMEDIATELY!
Send no money now. We'll bill you only $10.99 postpaid with your first shipment of four books. Or for faster action, call 1-740-922-7280.

NAME _____

ADDRESS _____

CITY _____ STATE _____ ZIP _____

**MAIL TO: HEARTSONG PRESENTS, P.O. Box 721, Uhrichsville, Ohio 44683
or sign up at WWW.HEARTSONGPRESENTS.COM**